LIVING
IN
HOPE

BY

SUE ALLAN

domtom publishing ltd

ISBN 978-1-906070-14-4

First published 2011 by domtom publishing ltd

Printed and bound in the UK by
DPS Partnership Ltd
www.dpsltd.net

This book is based upon the true life stories of three women from the same family.

My family.

I wish to dedicate this book to my dear Aunt Doris and her mother, Edith May.

For Freddie and Doris.

Introduction.

When I was a much younger woman, I used to dream a recurring dream. It was a dream that came immediately after the birth of each of my four precious sons. It was a dream so disturbing that, after having roused me from the depths of exhausted sleep, it had me utterly convinced that it was real.

After all these years, I now know that it was not my dream at all. It was someone else's living nightmare.

Sue Allan

Mary's Story

Mary's Story.

Mary Hendren was born in Ballinderry, near Glenavy village in County Antrim in Northern Ireland around 1793.

Chapter One.

I loved John Witherup and I always had; ever since we were childer and he used to run, raggedy-arsed, with my brothers at play back in Antrim. For sure, weren't we Hendrens and Witherups very great with each other[1], what with them being some friends of ours[2] through my grandfather's family.

Ah, but didn't those boys always fancy themselves as soldiers? Even as tiny muddy-faced runts in the fields following on behind our da's planting potatoes, their minds would be off and away with great imaginings that they were warriors, marching out to war.

When they could, my brothers and John would break away from their chores and sneak off out along The Prog to parade about. Or else they would be running off across the fields to The Crew Stone, where famous battles were fought in the long past and where the Kings of Ulster were once crowned. There, the boys would lob rotten spuds, all the while pretending that they were gunners pounding some unseen enemy to smithereens with

---

[1]   Great with each other -very friendly, close.
[2]   Some friends of ours -relatives.

their cannons. Or else they would be riflemen, armed with weapons fashioned out of bits of dirty old stick and such that they had found lying about the ditches. And then didn't the Witherup lads get a clout around the lugs for it later, when they were found out! For their da didn't hold with soldiers at all. Yet even he couldn't put a stop to their imaginings.

They were only wee boys, after all, when the Rebellion had come about and the redcoats were all about us hunting down United Irishmen after they had been defeated in battle, only some ten miles away from our house. What did mere childer understand of the hanging of some of these very same men at nearby Crumlin? Or the ins and outs of it all that had some of our neighbours and kinfolk so vexed at the time. The boys were simply hankering after the glamorous uniforms and the excitement surrounding all of the soldiers' comings and goings. So, stuck in the back end of nowhere as they were, with nothing more than the dreary goings on of farmers to inspire them, it was only natural enough that most wee lads dreamed about being soldiers too. But with John Witherup, even then, it ran altogether far deeper in him than just a passing boyhood fancy.

The only time that I could ever recall John taking a bit of notice of me back then was when he shooed me away as I tried to tag along behind him and my bothers.

'Will you not get back home, Mary Hendren, to yer mammy and yer dolly?' he shouted out tersely. 'Dhere is no part in this game for a wee crowl like yourself to be playing!'

John may have blooded his shins and elbows that day from playing at soldiers but he also badly grazed my heart. Utterly dejected, I had turned about on my bare feet and headed off back home in tears while the boys marched on triumphantly away in search of the *enemy*.

No, even as the years passed by and we both grew up, John ne'er seemed to mind me at all: not even as I began to mature towards womanhood - a process that he would not be around to see me complete. For at the age of just fifteen, John took himself off one day without a word to anyone. He was gone and, as far I knew, he was gone forever.

John had never seen eye to eye with his da who I can recall was a gullion[3] of a crature. To him John was ever the *'wee get'* [4] in line to feel the toe of his boot or to be the recipient of the gift of a well aimed thump for even the mildest error of his ways. John, being quiet and with more of his dead mother's temperament than that of his fiery da, could never do a thing right by his father's reckoning.

With the patience of a saint, John was always taking the blame for this or that, whether it was down to him or not. But never was John's younger brother, James, found to be out of his father's favour. 'Twas as if the sun shone out from that lad's crack, as far as John's da would have it. Even though the entire parish knew that it was James who was the troublemaker. And wasn't James just the reckless one when it came to codding about? All that John had ever done his life long was to cover up for his brother.

Then, all of a piece, John's patience must have eventually snapped entirely. For suddenly one day he was gone away to England to play the big game for real. The story goes that after John had walked out of his homestead and up the loanin towards the Lisburn road, he happened to pass his simple cousin digging in a field. They had exchanged warm greetings – as they always did.

'And where would you be going?' the cousin had asked, as he screwed up his face.

'Lisburn,' John replied.

---

3   Mean wretch.
4   A contemptuous name for a child; a bastard.

'Is dhat so? But dhere is an awful crowd of men coming by here to Lisburn dhese days. Why's dhat dhen John?'

'The British Army is recruiting in Lisburn just now. And I am going to join dhem!' John replied triumphantly.

'So you really are off to enlist dhen?' the cousin pressed.

With a gleam in his eyes, John answered him resoundingly with 'yes', and then for good measure, he showed the cousin the scant bundle of belongings tucked in at his side.

'I am fifteen-years-old now,' John had continued, 'and with a mind of me own so I have. No-one can stop me now! Not even me da!'

'Aw, sure enough', his cousin replied, roused by the younger lad's enthusiasm, 'but aren't I fed up with shovelling shat and aiting mud too? And just living in hope dhat something better will come along? I am t'irty-two and still single. And without a penny to my name. Surely dhere must be more dhan dhis to life for a man?'

With that, John's cousin suddenly threw down his spade in the dirt and cried, 'I'm comin' wid yer!'

And so he did, taking with him nothing more than the dirty rags he had hanging off his scrawny back.

John's poor cousin came home again just a few years later. He had caught a wretched fever in Europe that ruined his lungs completely, so it did. Still, he got his discharge papers and came home to Antrim with what was, by English standards, a miserly pension from the Army for his troubles. But in Ireland it was just enough for the cousin to get a start to wedded life and raising a family – which was more than he could have hoped for by staying at home. But of John Witherup? There came no news at all. The cousin had ended up serving in the infantry, and he had not seen John again either...

Chapter Two

By rights, as far as John Witherup was concerned, that should have been that for me and an end to the matter. He was gone away and in all likelihood would never be coming home again. And yet I could not get him out of my head, no mater how I tried.

During those difficult years that followed for me, I could never bring myself to look at another lad. No matter how hard the brave young bucks tried to woo me, polite requests like, 'Will you not be taking a walk with me along the lane after church, Mary?" I would flatly turn down, as I would also invitations to the harvest dance or other such rare delights that might break the monotony of Glenavy Parish life. So, in the end, the long and the short of it was that the young men eventually stopped asking me altogether.

'She's a hard nut to crack that one,' I would hear one of them blethering behind my back. 'Hardly worth the bothering when there are so many others here abouts ready to take up the opening.' For *'here abouts'* hadn't I heard the minister ranting that chastity had never yet been regarded as the mother of all virtues?

I didn't care a jot for that, or for them. And nor for the withered shawlies[5] nattering on to old Miss Quigley, who was firmly married to the Glenavy Post Office, about how, at the age of seventeen and never been a-courting, hadn't I just the right attitude entirely for becoming an old maid?

With sixty-eight houses and a population of three-hundred-and-nine souls, Glenavy village was the centre of our simple universe then – because it had everything. For apart from the Post Office, Glenavy could boast of a brand new cotton mill and no less

---

5   Old women wearing shawls.

than five grocers, three tailors, two blacksmiths, two shoe makers, a turner, a mason, and its own doctor. And most importantly of all, there were two fine public houses and an inn.

Amid the buzz of all this prosperity, the nearby parish church, however, was looking as if it was fit to collapse at any moment. And although the just and the good of the parish voiced high hopes that somehow it would be built up again before it did collapse, unsurprisingly, no one was in much hurry to stump up the money.

But for all this great crowd of businesses, the village had become a far quieter place of late, mainly because the twice yearly fairs had been banned for the past two years. Evidently, when they still ran, there had been too much fighting and rioting in their wake. For sure, there were certainly far fewer black eyes to be seen about! So at that time nothing much seemed to happen in Glenavy, apart from the odd marrying and the odd burying, and all the birthings in between, and on top of a great deal of gentle shopping.

So it came about one glorious summer day—as it seemed the world and his wife were out busily white-washing their cottages—that I dandered into Glenavy village with a veritable glut of fine brown eggs in my basket and a good round of my Ma's best cheese, with the high hopes of bartering them all for some tea.

I had come to the bridge and had been thinking to myself how gaudy-looking the lichen was— being set against the fine grey of the stonework and spoiling the look of it entirely. Daydreaming, I thought that if only I were the Queen of the world, how I would have all the old shawlies in the parish rounded up and forced to pick it all off with of their fingernails!

Then *it* happened. As I walked on not a dozen steps or more, I suddenly felt a dreadful stabbing pain in my right foot. So, stopping sharply, I put down my basket, stepped out of my boot and proceeded to shake out the wretched stone that had somehow got lodged in it. It was then, just as I happened to look up towards Ferris' inn, a sight met my eyes that shook me to my toes. What did I see but the fine figure of a soldier stepping out through the door. As he did, he half turned towards me for a moment. It was a moment long enough for his soft brown eyes to catch a firm hold of mine.

Oh what a gawping eejit I felt! There was I, with barely a thread of decent ribbon left upon my shabby straw bonnet, and standing with my toe peeping out from the hole in my stocking, and with my boot dangling from my hand, as I heard the soldier call out, 'Mary? 'Mary—is dhat you?'

At first I hardly recognised John. For one, he looked so broad across the shoulders. And his face! Oh, his face had changed completely – from that of a good-looking boy into that of an even handsomer man. He looked older, too – older and altogether so *different* in demeanour from my brothers and his brothers, who had stayed behind in Antrim. It wasn't just the uniform, though he certainly looked the part in that, so he did! No, it was his face that looked to have a whole new story etched upon it by the years that he had been away.

'My, my John!' I said struggling to get my boot back on. 'But don't you look brave in your nice blue coat and red collar and cuffs.' I tried to remain cool, though my face felt as though it had suddenly been set on fire.

'Aye', he replied proudly, showing me his insignia. 'Royal Horse Artillery so I am – Seventh Battalion.'

'Well, what a surprise it is to see you. And dhere was I with no idea dhat you were home at all.'

'I'm not yet,' he laughed wryly. 'I've not even been back to dhe homestead yet.'

8

'Is dhe war with Bony over dhen?' I asked naively, because I truly did not know. News of great events often reached Glenavy with all the speed of a lame donkey.

'No, not at all!' he exclaimed. 'And I shall be back to it soon enough, no doubt, just as soon as I am all healed up.'

'So wounded, is it dhen that you are?'

John nodded, and I got to feeling that he did not want to be drawn further upon the nature of his injury. But I was relieved, for I had hardly the stomach to contemplate the guts of the chicken that was waiting back home on the kitchen table for me to prepare, let alone some gaping wound on the body of a grown man.

'I only stopped here for a totty of Dutch courage,' John explained still smiling, 'before I go on to see dhe ould fella.'

Oh, how I then knocked that beautiful grin from off his face?

'Dhe ould fella? Oh John!' I said despondently. 'Dhen you'll not know?'

'I'll not know what, Mary?'

I felt awful at having to break this sad news to him.

'It's your da, John. Your da is dead...'

The unexpectedness of it all clearly shook him.

'Dead? When?' were all the cracked words that he could muster?

'It was dhe year before last. Aw, but didn't we lose two' three men to dhe fever dhat spring,' I sighed.

John shook his head and I could see the regret filling his eyes.

'Dhat's altogether too sad,' he said. 'I was hoping to square a few t'ings away widh him at long last. I never once t'ought dhat he wouldn't be here...'

I watched as a tear slowly trickled down his handsome cheek, and then quickly followed by another. I so wanted to reach out and kiss them away. But before I could do so, John quickly raised his hand to staunch them himself.

'And my brothers?' he asked.

'James and Robert? Oh dhey took over the running of dhe place well enough after your da...'

Oh dear, I seemed to be saying all the wrong things. Bad enough that the poor man had to come back to hear such news... and there was I making it worse with my big mouth, yapping on before my brain had worked out the tactful thing to say.

John fell silent for a moment or two, but then went on.

'And Isabella? Is she married yet?' He asked with love suddenly glinting in his eye. I knew only too well how much he adored dhat girl.

'No, Izzy is not married,' I replied. 'Dhough it's not for dhe lack of my brother trying to persuade her into church!'

'Your brother Thomas and my sister? I don't believe it!' John threw back his head in an almighty laugh. 'She was always hissing at him like a cat.'

'And maybe she still does, John, but not near so often as she is seen out canoodling widh him down the lanes on a Sunday afternoon.'

'Well well...' John laughed again. 'Who would have dhought? My Izzy and your Thomas!'

It was good to see him break into laugher again, for it so much better suited his heaven-carved face.

But then, after this happier discourse, I found my mind stumbling to find anything else half intelligent to say for myself. And with John not seeming eager to come to my aid with even a smidgen more conversation himself, we dried up speaking altogether. And so, reluctantly, I thought it perhaps best that I made some excuse to go.

'Well... I best be getting along,' I said picking up my basket and hoping all the while that John would speak up and beg me to stay a while. But he did not.

'Yes. And I had best be making my way to the ould place now,' he said quickly. 'Especially now dhat I have no more need of wet courage. Good day to you Mary. It was grand to see you again, so it was!'

With that John turned, and with his head held high and his shoulders back, he strode smartly off towards the Witherup farm, leaving me standing there feeling like a complete fool for not making more of the opportunity God had just given me. He'd been away for four years, and twenty-three days, and that was the best I could do.

Chapter Three

It was on the Saturday, just as I was about to cross the threshold of our house after seeing the chicken coop door was shut for the night, when my mother stopped me dead in my tracks before I could clear the doorstep.

'You can't be coming in looking like dhat. Tidy your hair girl,' she whispered urgently. 'Fayther has a visitor in the parlour!'

'Who in the divil would be calling on my fayther dhis late?' I said to myself. Thinking that it could only be the church minister or such, I did as Ma said before going on into the house. And when I did, what did I see but John Witherup sitting as snug as a bug on our best chair and being generously watered with my da's best whisky.

'Ah! Mary,' Da says with a grin. 'We have a visitor.'

'Sure I can see dhat, Fayther,' I replied feeling the blood rushing to my cheeks. 'Good evening to you, John,' I said, glancing towards him with what I hoped was not the smile of an eejit on my face.

'Good evening yourself, Mary', he replied calmly.

'Will not have a totty more,' Da grinned broadly, bringing the bottle up to John's drained cup.'

'Ah, just a wee smell dhen,' said John, as my father poured him out a great slop.

Against my expectations, my da poured no whisky for himself. Instead, he put his cup down and stowed the bottle back in its place up on the mantle, before making to leave us.

'I expect the two of yous will be having a lot to talk about,' Da said, with a broad smile and a divilish wink of his eye, 'so I will be off now to check on my cows.'

'We will?' said I, not knowing what on earth he was getting at.

Da closed the parlour door behind him and, for a moment or two, I didn't quite know what to do with myself. I looked at John and again found myself feeling like a blethering fool in his company.

'Come, Mary,' he said, holding out his outstretched hand. 'Come and sit widh me. I've got something to tell you.'

I did as he asked, but all the while I was thinking to myself, what on earth could John Witherup have to say to me, of all people? But no sooner was I seated than he got right to the crux of the matter with the longest sentence I have ever heard pass through his lips.

'Dhe Army is my life, Mary, and it's a hard life being a soldier's wife, and I don't suppose for one minute dhat you would be wanting to take up dhat sort of a life with me, for even if you did, you could never really be more dhan a *mistress* to me, not while I am married to the Army, so what do you say?' And then he gulped for breath.

I stood dazed and bewildered – like I had just been caught in an artillery barrage. I could not believe my ears! Had I really understood what I thought John had just said?

'John Witherup! I eventually blurted. 'Are you after proposing marriage to me?'

'Why yes', he said, looking all perplexed. 'Of course I am! But I'll understand completely if you turn me down.'

'Turn you down? Dhere's me without even a moment to myself to take in the asking and you have me turning you down already?'

'Well?' he continued quite indignantly. 'Are you refusing?'

'No! I never said dhat,' I snapped defensively. 'It's just dhe shock of it all.'

'Dhe shock of it all?' said he. 'Surely you must have known, Mary, how I have felt about you all dhese years?'

'Shock did I say? I declare it's more like stunned dhat I am! I had not an idea at all!'

'Well, you know *now* the way it is. Dhat's why I've come home - to ask you to marry me while you still have the chance.'

While I still had the chance? Oh, the cheek of the man!

'And what made you t'ink I'd be free?' I replied coolly.

'Well, dhat would be my captain.'

'Your captain?'

'Yes, Mary. He wrote to the squire here asking after you. To check up, see, to make certain dhat you weren't a prostitute or such before he gave me permission to wed.'

'A prostitute!' The word nearly stuck in my craw on the way out, for the very thought of it offended me deeply.

'No Mary! Of course I know you are no such person,' he blurted out only half apologetically. 'But you have to understand dhat when a woman marries a soldier widh the Army's blessing, dhen she officially belongs to dhe Army too. And dhey don't want to be taking on any ol' bit of baggage you know!'

I felt outraged. Outraged that some distant and faceless stranger I had never set eyes upon would ask the squire, who I'd never seen either, to report upon *my* suitability to marry a man who had never before said much more than 'boo' to me.

'Well dhat's grand!' I protested. 'You'd talk about dhis with strangers before you would say one word of it to me!'

Then it was John's turn to look like the eejit, and I don't think he knew which way to go with it at all. But then he suddenly pulled himself together to come back at me.

'Well, dhat's dhe way it is widh dhe Army. For a soldier to marry widhout consent is a punishable offence, so it is. And widhout permission, Mary, dhen I would never have got leave in dhe first place to come and ask you. And permission is not always granted, you know, except to dhose who deserve it!'

'And so what *exactly* did the squire tell your captain dhat persuaded him dhat I was good enough for your precious Army?' I demanded through clenched teeth.

'Dhat you were of a spotless character, Mary!' he beamed. 'In fact, he said your reputation as a veritable paragon of chastity amongst a population of mostly wanton young women was widely known and to be admired!'

To that, I really did not know what to say, but felt another blush flash across my cheeks, suddenly as hot as they felt when I opened our oven door on bread baking day.

'Besides,' John continued, 'we have your father's blessing... so... is dhat a 'yes' dhen, Mary? Only if it is, dhen we need to get dhe banns read tomorrow morning.'

'Tomorrow morning? Where's the rush? Can't a woman even have time to t'ink!' I exclaimed, but feeling as though I had just been in three rounds of a bare-knuckle fight, with my senses being knocked this way and that, so that I felt altogether dizzy.

'Sure she can,' he said as cool as you like. 'But not if she wants to be wed before I have to leave again in a fortnight.'

I did so desperately want him, though. Of that I was completely certain. Even if it had been sprung on me like a trap on an unsuspecting rabbit. And even if, as John had warned, I was likely to find myself playing second fiddle to his beloved Army. I could see myself being strong and, like any brazen-faced mistress, willing to wait patiently until my man's other 'wife' tired of him and eventually agreed to let him go. Yes. Anything. I knew that I would do anything to be with John at last!

So it was on Monday the sixth of August, eighteen-hundred-and-ten, that I became Mistress John Witherup – a gunner's wife in name and his mistress by nature. We married at Ballinderry in the plain, white-washed *Middle Church* of my youth that suited well our simple taste in worship. Even though it was meant to be a day of work, every pew in the place was full. And weren't folk even spilling out into the aisle, as John and I made our vows? But nobody was more surprised by the match than I was!

Later, back at Da's, the barn was near shaken down to dust by the mad frenzy of dancing that went on until well into the long sultry night. Then, many a sore-footed soul, worn out by jigging to the three best fiddlers in all of Antrim, and by far the worse for whisky, lay amongst the hay in the barn to sleep it all off. Ma and Da had gladly given over their own bed in the house to John and me for our wedding night, while they bunked down with our impromptu guests for the night.

When John and I retired, we discovered that my brothers had pulled all kinds of shenanigans with the bed sheets. So, with mixed feelings of shyness and humour, we had to remake our bed completely. And then, as soon as we eventually blew out the candles, my brothers started rattling the doors of the house and tapping on the windows, until my Ma came out and hooked them off to the barn.

Then, as I lay in John's arms at last, expecting him to make me a woman, he turned his head to me and said softly, 'We can't be after doing anyt'ing *intimate* just now, Mary my love. We dare not risk catching you widh a child before dhe Ballot.'

'Dhe Ballot?' I asked, in voice louder than it should have been. 'And what ballot is dhis?'

'Like I said, Mary, I am almost fit for active duty again and bound to be sent overseas soon.'

'Yes,' I said, 'and you said dhat I could go with you.'

'Ah! But it's not quite as simple as dhat, my love. When dhe regiment goes abroad, only a few women are allowed to go widh it. And a woman widh no childer stands a far better chance of being chosen to go. So you see, it is for dhe best, Mary, if we wait a while for... well you know what.'

With that he gave me a quick peck on the cheek and rolled over, facing the wall. I found myself at a loss for words. I wanted John to say something more, but he remained silent, though his breathing slowly grew heavier... as he fell sound asleep, leaving me in wonder and puzzlement about it all.

If I had any more disappointments, there was but one; that we were to be almost immediately off and away to England before I could see my brother Thomas married to John's sister, Isabella, in the November.

Chapter Four

England was so big! Much bigger than I had imagined it would be. And so crowded! As we passed in and out of villages and towns there seemed to be hoards of people everywhere. And the further south we got the more crowded it seemed to be. As for London? Well, I never did see anything like it! There were so many houses, all crammed together, and with streets overflowing with horses and carts and such, and with folk going in all directions and at such a pace as would stop your heart.

Then, after more than twenty days on the road, and some eight miles below London, we finally reached Woolwich. The town lies upon the banks of the River Thames, having been very much improved of late, mainly due to the yards and works raised up there for the service of the Royal Navy and Ordinance. For here the Thames is about a salty mile or more across at high water, and the tide runs very strong. With this stretch of the mighty river being free from shoals and sands, and boasting a depth of seven or eight fathoms, it is the ideal place for even the Navy's largest ships – most of the largest ships in living memory – to ride in safety, and even when the water is low. As a result, it seems that these docks claim some great favour and seniority above all others, especially bearing in mind their great importance to the country in times of war, such as then.

The dock-yard itself, and the buildings belonging to it, are wrapped about with a great high wall and, as John informed me, are abundantly filled with all sorts of stores and naval provisions. There is also a large rope-walk, some four-hundred yards long, where huge cables are made for our mighty men o' wars.

Perched above the river on a fair hump of ground, the Anglican Church of St Mary Magdalene stands proudly to attention, dressed in its red coat of bricks. As John pointed

18

it out, he explained that beneath its plain red-tiled roof, it was large enough inside to easily fit over fifteen-hundred people. What with him being brought up in the Church of Ireland, he had often attended services there while garrisoned in the town before. It was the outside of the church that struck a cold shiver in my soul. In its neat burial ground I noted the ranks of departed Artillery men – waiting silently beneath the earth for Christ's revelry to trumpet them forth once more.

Now in one respect, on first seeing the civilian town itself, I found myself thinking that wasn't it just a wee little bit like a big Glenavy? A sprawling, straggling affair of a place all spread out along one road, which in this case stretched out for over a mile or more. But I soon found the similarity waning. For unlike back home, off this one street were dozens of smaller ones, mostly crammed full with an irregular jumble of hundreds of houses. Most of these were old and very small, though elsewhere in the town there were plenty of grand house to be seen too.

Unlike Glenavy, which could boast five grocers, here in Woolwich there seemed to be dozens. And there were other shops of all sorts and sizes selling all manner of goods, some of the likes of which I had never seen in my life before. Believe it or not, there was even a shop that sold nothing but ribbons, buttons and lace – imagine that! John explained that folk came from all over Kent to Woolwich to buy things that they could not get at home – and sometimes not even in London! As for the crowds, well, it was utter Bedlam! We had arrived on a Friday which was Market Day and so in consequence had a terrible time of it making any headway along the main thoroughfare.

'Dhere is nothing better for trade at home dhan a war overseas!' John laughed.

'Is dhat so?' said I.

'T'ink of it, Mary. Dhe Army is a great consumer of goods, so it is. Not just of food, horses, and armaments. It puts work the way of every tradesman you can t'ink of. And Woolwich is a fine example of dhat!'

I could see that he was right; there were tradesmen of every description at each turn of the eye.

John and I struggled on through the town for a good while, taking in the sights before heading off southwards. We went as far as the high London Road, near to the *Shooter's Hill*, then on towards Woolwich Common and The Royal Artillery barracks, where John then promptly reported back for duty. And what a shock the revelation was for me to learn that I too, as a woman *on the strength*, had to report in, and what that would entail exactly.

The Royal Artillery had moved to the common from the old Arsenal buildings and into custom-built barracks some thirty years before. These looked really grand from the outside, but then proved more than disappointing to me once we got inside. I found our accommodation to be damp, cramped, and no matter how hard we women scrubbed it back, a stubborn black mould ate up the whitewash and persisted in creeping out from the corners of the ill ventilated rooms.

Now as a recognised wife of the regiment, I was entitled to live in at these barracks with my husband, but I never expected to be living so closely alongside other wives, their soldier husbands, childer, and single soldiers too – all thrown in together in one big dormitory. There was not a scrap of privacy to be had, and this was even noticed by me, someone used to being crammed into a tiny cottage – with all my brothers and sisters, and a cousin or two often thrown in for good measure. And despite the great rigmarole made in vetting *my* fitness to marry John, there was many a regimental wife I met who was not a fit or descent human being, and certainly not for me to be living with cheek by jowl. I even came to know of one woman who was flogged for having soundly beaten her own soldier husband!

Although some of the men had married without permission and had wives in lodgings away in the town, I soon came to understand completely why John had been so adamant not to marry without the Army's blessing. As well as being allowed to live with John in the barracks, as a *'wife on the strength'* I was also entitled to draw a half-ration of Army food – although even that didn't come completely free of charge. John was already obliged to pay for a part of his rations, and I was expected to earn mine by washing and sewing and such for the rest of the regiment.

Those *unrecognised* wives and soldier's women, who were kept outside the barracks, fared far less well than we who were. For one, these women were not entitled to any food rations at all, and so had to work to support themselves and any childer in any manner that came along. Just as wives on the strength were entitled to rations, so were their legitimate childer, who were also recognised by the Army. Each recognised child was entitled to draw between one quarter and one third of the ration of that of their soldier father, and many got schooling too. But the offspring of soldier's unrecognised spouses got nothing at all; they might as well not have existed.

At the time, many of the soldiers in John's particular barrack room were just like him; wounded but not quite recovered enough to go back into battle, and not wounded severely enough to expect to be pensioned off.

'Show him your embroidery!' John was once asked by an old soldier passing through the barracks with a new recruit in tow. 'Show him what a sabre can do, Private!'

The first time that this happened in my company I was quite shocked, for I had not even seen my husband's torso naked before. John was more than willing to oblige, so off came his shirt – to reveal a huge spiralling cut stretching from his right thigh and up and across to then end under his left breast. It was completely healed over, but still an angry dark purple colour set against his pale underbelly, and with the imprint of some quite shockingly uneven stitches still eminently visible.

'Beautiful, isn't it?' John laughed.

'Beautiful? For sure dhe man who did dhis was not so handy with a needle!' I exclaimed in horror.

'Handy enough dhough to sew me up quickly and see to it dhat I didn't get an infection.'

'Sure,' I agreed, 'but even our poor country doctor in Glenavy would be ashamed of stitches like dhat!'

'It wasn't a doctor,' John laughed. 'Dhe doctor was too drunk at the time to stand, let alone thread a needle! No, it was our darling Sergeant. Like a mammy to us he was – God bless his soul!'

I realised then that it was indeed beautiful. It was beautiful because John was still alive to tell the tale.

John and the Seventh, I knew, had been fighting in Europe, but he rarely spoke about it, at least not in front me and the other women. But later, in the long nights of far off years still to come he would. And then he would speak of the bloody carnage to which he had been a party to and had barely survived.

I soon found out that life in the Army was ruled by endless routines and regulations, which brought home to me the hard-hitting realisation that I was no longer to be my own woman – or even John's come to that. The men, and us wives with them, would be rudely woken a good two hours before sunrise, by a great long drum roll emanating from the foot of the barracks stairs. At this the unmarried soldiers would leap out in pairs from their double berths while we '*marrieds*' took a wee piece longer. Moments after getting up, we would *all* be expected to quickly remove the bed slats from the middle of the bed to the foot end, thus, I suppose, removing the temptation for any idling upon them during the day. After that, we had to fold and tidy the bedding and then lay it out upon the head end, as dictated by strict regulations. This bedding consisted of a straw-stuffed bolster and pailliasse[6], and a pair of sheets that were so rough that you might be forgiven for thinking that they were woven from string. These were then topped off with two wool blankets and a knotted bed rug, with each piece stamped boldly with 'GR' - just to be sure of the damned ownership of the thing. Sure, only the likes of King George could afford to own so many blankets and yet loathe to lose a single raggedy one of them!

After this, our men would make ready for the day by washing vigorously, paying particular attention to their hands faces, necks, ears and fingernails, which they knew would be thoroughly inspected. Hair was combed and neatly parted too; all this carried out in a gloomy half-light using only as much of our precious ration of candle as we dared.

Then some lucky person would have to slop out the night bucket. If the weather the night before had been fair, then those men finding themselves in need would usually have stepped outside to relieve themselves instead against the outside walls. And sure enough wasn't the smell of those walls at times as ripe as a cowshed in July! After a freezing cold night though, the bucket would invariably be full, and somebody had to dispose of it.

---

[6]   A thin mattress filled usually with straw or sawdust.

Meanwhile, usually another wife and I would take up our besoms and help sweep up the mud and dirt walked in on boots. At the same time we would get rid of, as best we could, the vile gobs of spent chewing tobacco from off the barrack room floor. While we did that, the orderlies for the day would be busy raking out the ashes from the previous night's fire and cleaning the hearth, making it look spick and span.

What with it then lightening up outside, morning parade was called. The drummers, by now joined by buglers, would then sound out the 'Troop' and our men would line up in their fatigues. And woe betide any man found missing from the file, unless of course he was away on guard duty; for he would be noted immediately and put on report. While the men's inspection was going on outside, the officer of the day would come inside the barracks to check that all was in order and to make certain that nobody – not a man, woman or child – was still abed!

After morning inspection, and with the weather permitting, the bedding would then be taken out to the barrack yard and aired. The paillasses were also taken out and beaten soundly, to see off any insects that might be planning on setting up home in them. Bed bugs were a real problem in the barracks.

Then came time for breakfast, after which the drums would send our lads scurrying off to their assigned work duties and leaving us women to get on with ours. For those men who were not on work, mess or guard duty, there was always the seemingly endless cleaning of kit to be done. However, once that was out of the way, the rest of the morning could then prove to be a of time relative ease with plenty of opportunity for chatting and even playing cards or other games. And of course, everywhere you looked there would be off duty men leaning out of the windows to puff away on clay pipes – for isn't smoking the scourge of almost every soldier that I have known?

An hour or so before noon, the 'Troop' would sound again; this time for full dress parade. And then, after arms and accoutrements had been fully inspected, our men were dismissed.

At midday the guards would be changed; relieving those men who had been on sentry duty for the previous twenty-four hours. How John hated guard duty! Especially because it entailed a two-hours-on-two-hours-off shift throughout, this meant that it was almost impossible for a man to get any sleep between shifts. Meanwhile, even when not actively on guard, they were none the less obliged to remain inside the Guard House, fully clothed and armed and in a state of 'readiness' should anything untoward occur.

After dinner, the bedding would be brought back inside from the yard, unless of course it had rained beforehand, which would have led to real scramble by those who could to fetch it in. This would then be arranged once more, just as it had been for morning inspection, but it was still not allowed to be sat upon.

Only at day's end and with the night drawing on did the barracks truly come to life. Then the tables would be unceremoniously shoved back against the walls to make way for jigging and singing and such. And of course drinking. For it was no offence in the Army to drink, though it certainly was to be found drunk!

At night we 'marrieds' were allowed to screen off a wee corner for ourselves by hanging up some blankets so that we might at least undress and lie together away from prying eyes. But even then I found the night times at first almost impossible to bear – what with the noise of babies and childer crying, mingled with the moans and groans of women and men at lust, and the giggles of loose women, smuggled in by the singletons, as they were passed between the berths to pleasure those men.

Twice a week the soldiers were thoroughly drilled, and on a Sunday the entire regiment was inspected and drilled, and with those off duty expected to attend church.

Our life together at Woolwich went on until, as we knew it must, the time came for John and the others to prepare to be posted back overseas. And with that I knew that soon the awful process of the Ballot would eventually have to take place.

'If you can't come with me, dhen dhe Army will arrange for your passage back home to Antrim,' John explained to me. 'At least dhen I will be able to go into battle picturing you dhere, and knowing dhat you were living a respectable life in safe hands.'

John had then grasped my hands in his and gently drawn them up to his lips, where he tenderly kissed them.

'But I promise you dhis, Mary my love,' he continued softly, 'I swear on my mammy's eyes dhat while I am away, I will remain faithful to you. No matter what wicked temptations might come my way.'

'What about dhe wives who are not chosen', I asked him.

'Mostly dhey will go away back home to dheir families who will help widh dheir upkeep. Or if dhey have none, dhen their own Parish is obliged to support dhem on dhe Poor Rate.'

Indeed, I thought this the height of callousness on the Army's part.

John also explained that there was no procedure set in place whereby a soldier could be enabled to send back his pay to support his own wife and family. And I was shocked to learn that if I were chosen to go away with John and he was subsequently killed in action, that very day the Army would stop his pay and even my food rations. As a result, battlefield wives who suddenly found themselves widowed in foreign lands were routinely left to fend for themselves – sometimes only the Lord knows how. So for the sake of desperate necessity, such a woman might find herself being quickly taken up by another man from the same regiment, just to stop her from starving. Thus sometimes a woman might find herself passing through the hands of a succession of soldier husbands - passed on from one man to another, perhaps seeming to be like a woman of easy virtue, until either her luck or her looks ran out. John had explained all this to me in graphic detail before the Ballot – but even the grimmest of prospects could not stay either my hand or my heart from wanting to enter into it.

At the crack of October, John learned of his new posting. To our utter surprise he was not being sent back to the Peninsular as we had expected. Instead his battalion was to be deployed to one of the Sugar Islands – Barbados – almost half-way across the world.

The orders posting our men to this area also stipulated that no childer were to be taken whatsoever. This meant that any wife wishing to enter the Ballot must be prepared to give up her childer into the care of relatives, or else to abandon them altogether at the Royal Military Asylum.

It was a cruel ultimatum to put upon the women. I cannot even now bring myself to relate the heartbreak that it caused for so many of the wives, women with whom by then I had lived for almost two months and bonded with as if they were own kin. Remembering such miserable partings, as I witnessed at Woolwich, still brings me straight to tears, even now after so many years have passed. It all created the kind of bitter pain that never heals. And yet this order was not one given out of callousness on the Army's part. Strangely enough, it was intended to be an act of kindness. For it transpired that for a number of years, doctors upon some of those Caribbean islands had been reporting recurrent outbreaks of a wretched disease that particularly afflicted young childer – regardless of their lineage or station in life. This disease would manifest innocuously enough, presenting itself as no more than a mild malady. But then this would always rapidly escalate into a shocking fever, bringing about terrible sweats and unstoppable shaking. Almost without exception, within two weeks of its onset, this wicked sickness then killed its young victim. There was no known cure.

At John's insistence, he and I had still yet to consummate our marriage. And so I was one of the dwindled number of women to be entered into the Ballot – and then to find myself among the chosen few to accompany the men to the Sugar Islands.

Chapter Five

At first I hated the sea. No sooner had we left the calmer waters of the English Channel to make break for the open Atlantic than the ship began to heave, with my queasy stomach quickly following suit. And then, for days, I cowered below deck with a bucket clasped tightly between my knees, being as sick as a dog. There I sat, trying so very hard not to look at the draw-string bag slung from a hook opposite my bunk, as it swung back and forth with the motion of the ship. If I as much as glanced at it, I would wretch all more. I could not eat. I was unable to even keep water down, let alone anything else. And the only words that I could to get out of my mouth were a cross between a cuss and a prayer;

'Sweet Jesus let me die!'

And die I might well have done, had it not been for John searching out a kindly marine to take pity on me. This man gave me salt biscuits to nibble on, which I did like a wee sick mouse. Then he gently cajoled me away from my bucket and up to the bracing sea air on the open deck. There, he told me to try fixing my eyes upon the distant horizon for as long as I could bear. I did as he bade and gradually, to my greatest relief, I quickly began to feel better. As my eyes became accustomed to watching the rise and fall of the sea, I felt my stomach ease into the rhythm of the constant pitching of the ship beneath my feet. Soon I found my sea legs, and from that point onwards I fell in love with the sea and would go up on the deck for as long and as often as I could.

The Atlantic Ocean is an awesome expanse that seems to just roll off into infinity. Often, as I looked on, she would shift and change through perhaps as many as a dozen different colours in a day. And the roar of her! I never had heard the likes of it all before.

The sea has a voice of its own: a mighty voice like the word of God howling out across the world.

As for the ship we were upon, I had no such love for *His Majesty's Ship Enmity* at all. It was a hulk of a thing; a tired old frigate plucked out of the fleet and turned into a transport ship. She bristled with guns though, and looked like a regular man of war. The food aboard was rank, and the journey monotonous almost beyond endurance, save for those stolen moments in the company of the sea and the thoughts tumbling inside my head while my eyes wandered off into the horizon, being ever hopeful of sighting land.

We reached Barbados on the second day of February, eighteen-hundred-and-eleven. I fair marvelled at the beauty of the place – with its dazzling blue skies, mirrored by the even bluer sea below, and the endless stretch of palm fringed beaches.

But alas, no sooner were we settled on land than John was informed that he was being sent on detachment to another island, called St Vincent. I was distressed at the prospect of having to leave such a lovely place so soon, and to endure yet another cramped sea voyage. But my spirits lifted when I heard that this time it would be a short journey.

When I first saw the island of St Vincent, my heart leapt with excitement. From the deck of our troop ship the land looked like Paradise; a lush, verdant mound rising from a perfectly beautiful blue sea, crowned by a majestic mountain called *La Soufrière*. Perched upon a promontory, above where we anchored, Fort Charlotte stood resplendent as a dazzling white sentinel keeping watch over the bay and the picturesque town of Kingstown below – with its many whitewashed houses gleaming like clustered pearls in the brilliant sunshine.

However, I had foolishly forgotten my ma's long held favourite words of wisdom; that first impressions can be divilishly deceiving. For once ashore, I soon realised that the reality of this place was a far cry from the heavenly prospect I had surmised. Encountered up close, the buildings I had first admired from a kindly distance had turned very shabby. They now looked more like the rows of worn-down, tobacco and rum-stained teeth that I encountered from the smiles of so many local faces.

Indeed, Kingstown, despite its regal name and somewhat grandiose aspirations, was but a filthy and smelly meddle-muddle of a place. And the climate turned out to be not nearly as pleasant as that of Barbados, where the Trade Winds freshened the air. The heat and humidity of Kingston was at times so great that you could imagine yourself being melted away, like butter in a pan. Sometimes I feared drowning in my own perspiration. Didn't this climate also have the unhappy knack of tarnishing metal before your eyes, and making good leather and clothes mouldy overnight? And wasn't there also a plague of wee flying beasties to eat a person alive? And as for the storms! This island often takes a good battering from such ferocious tempests that they call them hereabouts 'hurricanes'. So much so, that barely three years before John and I landed, almost every building on the island had been flattened.

John and I reported with the others to the barracks at Fort Charlotte – a great hulking warren of a place armed with thirty-four pieces of artillery. At some six-hundred feet above the sea, it had a commanding view across Kingstown, the bay, and the chain of tiny islands beyond called the Grenadines. The barracks could accommodate some six hundred men, and although the entire fort had only been constructed some five years before, they were like a shabby oven inside and wanting in even the basic comforts that we had taken for granted back in Woolwich. I found being there almost unbearable.

But thankfully, within a few days John's new sergeant found me better accommodation, when he found me a position with a Lieutenant's wife down in Kingstown, where my husband could visit me whenever his duties would allow.

It is said that the very first inhabitants of this island were of the same race as some indigenous – or so-called '*Indian*' – people of America, and who are here and now called '*red or yellow Caribs*'. Then, some hundred-and-forty years or more before John and I arrived, there was a Dutch ship which was wrecked close by – compelling many of its so-called '*cargo*' of African slaves to swim to the shore. Those slaves that had survived settled on the island and intermarried with the indigenous Caribs, resulting in their 'free' offspring becoming known as '*Black Caribs*'.

Then, although St Vincent had been claimed in the name of the Crown of England, the Caribs allowed the French to settle upon the island. These settlers in turn then brought African slaves to work upon their plantations. And then, after almost half a century of turbulence, during which there were periodical wars and disputes with the Caribs – the island passed back and forth into the control of French and British forces. Eventually, in seventeen-eighty-three, St Vincent became British sovereign territory permanently.

The island is tiny, being only some eighteen miles in length and about eleven or so across, and much of the land is unyielding and dense forest, still untouched by human hand. Where the land is cleared, it is smothered by profitable plantations of tobacco, cotton, indigo and sugar cane. When John and I were on St Vincent, these were tended by countless numbers of African slaves, who were pressed hard to work in a most unnatural way upon the numerous estates.

By this time, I was missing Ireland terribly, and especially my ma and da and the rest of our family. John often consoled me and told me how sorry he was for having taken me away, but I didn't blame him at all for my homesickness. It had been *my* choice; I had known full well what I had been letting myself in for when I decided to marry a soldier. No, I did not feel sorry for myself, but I certainly did for those slaves. What choice had these poor souls had? They had been wrenched away from their loved ones and cram packed into ships under conditions you would not suffer cattle to endure, and then transported to the other side of the world. There, they were condemned to a lifetime of unpaid and brutal servitude. How, I wondered, could men profaning to be Christians do this to fellow human beings? How could anyone justify buying and selling other people's lives for profit? I could never comprehend this. I still can't.

Growing up in Ireland, I thought that my parents had raised me well enough to hold my own in any place in this life. So when I first went across to England, in my 'greenness', I thought that I would be treated in the same way I had back home. But I soon found that I was sorely mistaken.

When I walked out and about in Woolwich, gentleman would hold open doors for me, shopkeepers would enquire, 'May I help you?' But didn't such courtesy change the instant I opened my lips to speak! Then, it would be as if vermin were tripping out from my mouth instead of words. Doors would slam in my face and instead of, 'May I help you?' I would be met with a brisk 'Yes?' while the assistant's eyes glued upon me as if I were a tinker about to steal a gold watch.

In consequence, I quickly learnt not to talk unless I had to, and when I did so, to keep my tone as quiet as and as *English* as I possibly could, so that I might escape the worst of any English prejudice directed towards me. If *they* could do that to me, what chance did these poor brown folk on St Vincent have? Fortunately for me, I did not have to wear my 'Irishness' upon my skin for all to see.

With me being the *'Irish type'* of British, in England wasn't that surely a station or two below that of my *English* British counterpart? And then, to my utter surprise, I found that my lowly status as such was suddenly enhanced once I set foot upon this accursed island. For on St Vincent, even the lowly Irish wife of an Irish British soldier in His Majesty's Army was considered to be of far better standing than that of many native Vincentians. For, even worse than it was in England, society on St Vincent was complicated further by so many extra strata – which varied greatly – largely determined by the race or descent of your ma and da, and of course, how deep a shade of brown your skin was.

I came to realise that if a person was white, regardless of nationality, they were almost always considered *'superior'* in social standing to any St Vincent resident of either Carib or mixed descent. Of course some exception was made if a non-white person happened to be particularly wealthy. Then they could be received into British society on the island with what was presented as some good grace – well, on the surface, at least to their faces!

The terms *'Black'*, *'Yellow'* or *'Red' Carib* were easy enough for me to understand, but when these folk then intermarried with others, their offspring's place on this wretched island's disgusting 'pecking order' became almost impossible to comprehend. Even so, there was always a determined effort to cobble together racial and social differences – including the lineage of each resident – to determine a person's 'rank' in society as a whole.

And so, the child of a black parent and a white parent was given the name 'Mulatto', while the child of a Mulatto parent and a white parent were termed 'Quadroon'. And then the child of a Quadroon and a white parent was determined to be a 'Mustee', and the offspring of a Mustee and a white parent was a 'Mustafini'. Meanwhile, the Cabres had parents who were both Mulatto, and a 'Sambo' would be the child of a Mulatto and a Negro. And yet, for all this ridiculous and fine classification, didn't I find more natural born ladies and gentlemen among these local-born Vincentian folk than among all the so-called English gentry I have ever met?

As a result of this absurd racial pecking order, coupled with the existing lack of English female company and the restrictions that the recent Ballots had placed upon the new intake of Army wives, Susanna, the Lieutenant's wife began to treat me not as a servant – and that was all I expected to be – but in many respects as her paid companion. And so, as I went about my sewing repairs for this new 'mistress, I did not find myself confined to some dreary back room. But instead, my place was in the parlour, sitting with Susanna upon the best chairs and drinking tea in between listening to her gossip about the town's going-ons. For sure, she was kind to me in her own way, but I never truly had any deep liking for her as a person, especially because she could be so terribly patronising – and all without even realising it!

Susanna was a stick of a woman with a great expanse of forehead, which begged a terrible favour of her lank and thin hair to try to cover it over. Her eyes were dark and beady like those of a crow, and sure wasn't she also a forthright and opinionated crature! I took her age to be of maybe six-and-twenty-years, and though she was without any childer, she sometimes spoke of young babies with an intimate knowledge and a glint of regret in her eyes. This made me, for fear of opening up old sadness, hesitate to ask if ever she had some of her own. Instead, I would just listen at those times without offering any specific remarks or observations of my own.

But despite her shortcomings, I suppose I do have to thank this woman for one thing at least; she liked to get out and about on the island as much as possible – but never liked to go alone. So, instead of sitting darning or being likewise fastened to some dreary work, I would often find myself heading off with her on some sort of excursion or another. I must admit that these were often both pleasurable and edifying.

Susanna's one abiding passion seemed to be for sketching, with flowers and landscapes being her favourite subjects. For flowers, we often spent the day together at the Botanical Gardens, just a short step from the centre of Kingstown, where there were plants from all over the world. Here the air was full of birdsong as we walked beneath the huge fronds of tropical palms and other trees, and admired the beautiful under-planting of an array of the most heavenly blooms imaginable. It was here that I recall being mesmerised by the sight of my very first humming bird. It was the most fascinating of cratures to watch, as it bibbed and bobbed its great, long, slender beak deep into the throats of spectacular flowers in search of sustenance. It was all of a-hover on tiny wings that appeared to flap backwards at an awesome rate.

The obliging garden guide, who accompanied our every step on our frequent visits, would periodically pluck leaves from the various plants, encouraging Susanna and me to squeeze them between our fingers to release their pungent smells and thus delight our noses with the exotic scents of cinnamon, nutmeg, bay, and camphor, to name but a few.

There were also many beautiful flowers growing wild all over the island, with Hibiscus and Bougainvillea being my own particular favourites. Mistress Susannah made it her business to sketch as many of the native plants as she found possible. She used a great leather-bound note book that she always took out and about with her. It was sometimes funny, though, to see her reaction after asking locals what such-and-such a plant was called – because they were often found to be named in the bluntest of descriptions. 'Foul-Foot-Grass' and 'Bend-But-Never-Break' were well enough for Susanna to jot down, but when it came to the likes of '*Jump-Up-And-Kiss-Me*', '*Bastard Fiddlewood*' and '*Piss-A-Bed-Cashie*', sure didn't she blush! Meanwhile, it had me straining at my sides trying not to burst out into laugher.

We would sometimes leave Kingstown altogether, and then hike up along the Leeward Coast to the tropical rainforest, where the trees were filled with brightly coloured chattering birds called parrots. With the island being so small and compact, it was possible to take off on excursions of all sorts that would never last more than a day away – although we never went anywhere without a small armed escort. Occasionally this included Susanna's husband, who would, when he thought of it, second my John as an escort so that we might also enjoy such outings together.

The most memorable of these trips had been up the windward side of the island. Leaving Kingstown, we had soon come to the Mesopotamia Valley, where I had found myself wondering what Da would have made the terraces cut into the steep valley sides and planted up with all manner of exotic fruit and vegetables, sugar cane, and groves of breadfruit – the staple of slaves. Here and there we had passed by tiny homesteads perched on high with an equally tiny plantings of crops, which I surmised might just be enough to support the occupants – providing their appetites were poor. At other times our eyes were met with the mansion-like homes of wealthy planters and, almost hidden away out of shame, the shambling slave huts.

37

From the valley we travelled eastwards, past beautiful rivers, and then onwards towards the coast. Here the road skirted magnificent beaches, where lively Atlantic waves crashed to their rest in the gentle embrace of the golden sand. For a brief moment, I lifted my gaze up and out across the great expanse of blue ocean, trying hard in my mind's eye to picture Ballinderry, so far beyond, and wondering if I would ever see my ma and da again.

On and on we travelled, up along the coast road, until we eventually came to Georgetown, in the northern quarter of the island. There we stayed overnight.

Early next morning, we had headed off north from the town along the Rabacca Dry River, before following the foot track to make the three-and-a-half-mile ascent of the mountainous *La Soufrière*.

La Soufrière means '*sulphur pit*', for that is exactly what it was is – a great crater more than half a mile in diameter with a depth that I thought must extend down into hell itself. The sides of the crater were very steep, and covered with all manner of exotic flowers and aromatic plants, the sweet scents of which I had never smelt before or ever encountered the like of since. Amongst the plants of this most beautiful of spots, birds sang out from every quarter with a melody that could shame the heavenly choir itself. Many of these birds, I was told, were quite unknown anywhere else on God's earth.

In the middle of this crater was a strange cone-shaped little hill decorated with a fringe of shrubs and vines, and riddled with a series of fine cracks from out of which a white smoke seeped, sometimes with a lick or two of blue flame. At the base of this hill were two small lakes; one strongly tainted with sulphur while the water of the other was perfectly clear and sweet to drink.

I remember standing, looking down upon the serene beauty and solitude of this wondrous place, with my hand held fast in John's, and thinking to myself that it was like a dream of Eden, or perhaps a glimpse into Heaven to come.

'*La Soufrière* erupted about a hundred years ago, you know?' the Lieutenant told John in a very matter of fact way. 'Can you imagine that? One huge bang and then a great red river of boiling hot lava pouring forth from out of this very mound? Played havoc, I expect, with the natives.'

'Is dhat so, Sir,' John had replied cheerily. 'And what is to stop it doing dhat again, Sir?'

'Oh, I wouldn't worry myself, Private Witherup,' the Lieutenant had said dismissively. 'The likelihood of that ever happening again in our lifetimes is very remote indeed, I am told.'

'Is dhat a fact, Sir?' John beamed mischievously. 'Dhen dhat's a blessed relief, Sir!'

A red river of molten lava flowing out from this beautiful place? I could not imagine it all, so I couldn't.

When we were clear from ear shot, John quietly took me aside so as not to offend his superior. Then he whispered, 'Like a smouldering furnace widh its fires banked up is what I've heard it is!'

'But the Lieutenant talked about it so coolly, John,' I whispered back. 'Surely it couldn't have been dhat much of a calamity back then?'

'Ah, Mary,' John reasoned, 'sure, but doesn't dhe greatest clap of t'under become but a rumble to dhose in dhe distance? All dhe great events of history get muffled by time, so dhey do!' Then he laughed and told me not to worry about it. And so I did not.

Chapter Six

It was towards the back end of March, eighteen-hundred-and-twelve, when I was roughly awoken in the small hours of the morning. The house was all of a jiggle and rattling so terribly that, as I tumbled out from my bed, I could feel the earth shuddering beneath my feet. But then, just as mysteriously, by the time I had gathered my wits together and run out of my room, the shaking had stopped. My immediate thought was that this might have been the aftershock of an explosion up at the fort, and knowing that my John was on duty just yards from the black powder store, I felt sick.

I stepped out into the street to find countless others there – all looking as bewildered as my da's daft sheep. No one seemed to know what had just happened, and as I looked up towards Fort Charlotte I could see the sudden flicker of lamps being lit and then hurried movement, wavering too and fro. But there was no tell-tale plume of smoke or any other sign of fire or the possible explosion that I had dreaded. So I thanked God that John was probably safe up there.

Mistress Susanna had followed me outside. Altogether she looked quite the sight, with her hair all contorted and tied up in rags and with a bed sheet wrapped about her shoulders like a large modesty shawl covering up her nightwear. The Lieutenant's wife strained her chicken neck skyward, as she surveyed the chimneys and the rooftop to see if all was still sound. Shortly after, and with no reports of any damage from amongst our neighbours, Susanna curtly ordered me and her black maid servants, Abigail and Ebony, back inside the house and away to our beds, as if we were naughty childer.

'Tremors' is what Susanna called them.

'They're well known phenomena in this part of the world,' she assured me. 'There is no need to worry over them.'

But I did not feel in the least bit reassured. I wanted to be with my John. I wanted to hear him say that there was no cause for alarm before I would believe it myself. Besides, there was more than just me to worry about.

John remained on duty up at the fort during the days that followed: days when the ground often shook as it had before. Indeed, many of those living on the western slopes of *La Soufrière* had seriously considered leaving their plantations altogether.

However, as these 'trifling disturbances', as Susanna had dismissively termed them, caused little or no damage, those on the Georgetown side of the island likewise paid them little heed and continued with their lives as usual. In fact, as the days of mild tremblings passed on into weeks, the islanders gradually accepted the slight movements beneath their feet – which we felt from time to time – as normal. They came only briefly and went away again swiftly.

All the same, the commander of Fort Charlotte had sent a party of soldiers up to the rim of the crater of *La Soufrière* to investigate. They had strict orders to report any change in its condition immediately. And so it was that during the last week of April news was conveyed, with the utmost urgency, to the Fort that the water in the crater's lake had become very discoloured and started bubbling – as it would in a simmering cauldron.

***

'Mary! Mary! Wake up!'

And so I did wake up, with a terrible start, to find my John standing over me in the half-light.

'John? What on earth are you doing here?' I exclaimed.

'I've come to get, you,' he replied quickly. 'Gather up your t'ings. I am taking you up to the Fort.'

'Dhe Fort? Why?'

'Orders from Captain Cleeves. All dhe British are to be evacuated from dhe town. It's La Soufrière... They think she's going to blow...'

'Blow?'

I threw on my dress and my boots, grabbed the few things I possessed, and bundled them up in a blanket. As I did so, I still could not comprehend what was happening.

Susanna was already dressed and in the hallway as John and I left my room. She was surrounded by her native servants who were jabbering in their mother tongue, and were clearly deeply distressed. Susanna shouted at them to arrest their attention. She ordered Abigail and Ebony to lock themselves in the house as soon as we were gone, adding that the two were on no account to let anyone else into the house. And then she warned that if the girls did not protect her and the Lieutenant's belongings, she would see to it that her husband would have them soundly beaten on his return.

'The town is filling up with all sorts of riff-raff,' Susanna sighed with a huff of exasperation, 'and I cannot be certain about trusting *these* two not to let them in!'

'Ma'am!' John interjected urgently 'we must leave *now*! Dhere is an armed escort waiting at dhe door to see you away to safety at once!'

Sure enough, through the open door I could see that the streets were crowded with people just brought in from the country. Many were carrying bundles of most treasured possessions, and in the glow of many torches I noticed that everyone had the look of

42

trepidation about them. It was then that I suddenly noticed the strange odour in the air, as it suddenly wafted into the house and began to catch at the back of my throat. It was the unmistakable stench of sulphur.

John took my bundle and led me outside and into the street, shielding me as best he could from the panicking crowd quickly closing about us from all sides. As we pushed our way forward, John called out to some soldiers a little ahead of us, and told them to help to clear a way through for us as I was beginning to be severely jostled.

'Susannah!' I cried out. 'I can't see Susannah!' She was nowhere in sight.

John told me not to worry about the Lieutenant's wife. Instead, he urged me to just concentrate on myself and on keeping my footing. If I fell, he warned, I might get crushed underfoot by the frightened crowds.

It was heavy going – making our way up Battery Hill and onwards towards Fort Charlotte. As we passed the cemetery, I could see more hoards scrabbling over the burial mounds and heading towards us. And then, as I glanced back down the hill, I could see countless others trying to force their way up behind us; also intent on trying to seek shelter at the Fort. Most, however, were forcibly turned back by a cordon of armed soldiers, who had their bayonets fixed and ready. We and the few other white people among the throng were allowed to trickle through the scarlet line and on along the final few hundred yards of road.

After our group, quickly followed by the last platoon of soldiers, passed through the Fort's gates, the drawbridge was raised. This invoked desperate and angry remonstrations from the swelling numbers of mainly Carib people still trapped outside.

'Can't we help dhem?' I cried.

'Dhere's no room for dhem,' John explained. 'Dhe fort is fit to burst as it is.'

I could see that he was right. There was barely any room left at all.

No sooner had we arrived at Fort Charlotte, than reports were received of a great eruption of steam that had arisen from the crater of *La Soufrière*. It continued to gush and hiss intermittently, hour upon hour, until these seemingly minor eruptions suddenly rushed into one great, tumultuous, ear-splitting roar – sending a torrent of boiling mud cascading down the valley, mainly following the course of a dry river bed, until it eventually reached the shoreline and poured into the sea in a roaring billow of steam.

And then we reaped the harvest of our weeks of complacency. The most dreadful explosion reverberated through the air – like the mother of all thunder claps. The earth shook and rocked, as if the most enormous invisible giants in great hob-nailed boots were stomping across the island.

From the safety of the Fort we watched as a great, ominous, black column of smoke, spiked with flashes of lightening, rose like the Divil's own beacon from inside *La Soufrière*. As if in judgement of mankind's wickedness, the volcano had spewed the vomit of hell across the island. The acrid stench of sulphur, coupled with the terrible trembling in the earth, had me feeling convinced that we were all about to die. Even now as I write, I believe that the fear of it all will surely haunt me until the day I truly do draw my last breath.

And yet *we* were the lucky people. We who were perched high in the solid safety of Fort Charlotte. There, we took turns to peer through a spy glass, to watch a huge, vividly-coloured fiery cloud advance swiftly towards Georgetown, barely five-and-a-half-miles from the centre of the eruption. My worried thoughts turned to the kindly Scottish family that lived in a house near that town. They had put John and me up when we had visited the crater with Susannah and her husband. How I prayed that God might keep them safe.

44

We at the Fort, numbering by now a thousand or more, watched this dreadful spectacle unfold, knowing that for each one of us safe within those walls there were countless others now caught in the deadly havoc of the eruption. It was sheer awfulness to think about all those poor people. No doubt they were huddled beneath whatever pitiful shelter they had found, as the scarlet deluge of molten rock showered them with death and carnage. It made me feel sick to the pit of my stomach, made all the worse by a sense of guilt – knowing we were safe while there was nothing on earth that we could do for the others.

Then, during a barrage of deafening detonations, there came a blizzard of grey ash, which began to fall across the island like dirty snow. From the walls of the Fort we could see the ash falling upon the decks of ships that were fleeing out of Kingston Bay. We heard later that ash even floated on the surface of the sea, like some kind of hellish manna.

'That'll be them away, then!' John's sergeant sneered looking down upon the fast disappearing vessels. 'The great and the good – away like rats!'

Shocked by his comments, I looked about me and suddenly realised that I could not see *any* high ranking officer or their wives or families amongst us. They were gone. They were all being spirited away on the very ships we were watching disappear into the distance.

After the wind direction changed, the air soon became harder to breathe. So we were forced to retreat inside the barracks as the sky darkened and the sun all but disappeared from sight. There we remained for most of the next three days and nights, until the eruptions became less frequent and less devastating, weakened into rattling convulsions, and eventually died with a few twitches and rumbles.

Over the days and weeks that followed, the true extent of all the death and destruction that *La Soufrière* had inflicted upon the island become clear. As Kingstown became swamped by a huge tide of terrified people pouring in from the plantations of the north, so it became awash with the mind-numbing accounts of horror that they brought with them. Many thoroughly traumatised people, some suffering from the most dreadful burns, spoke of a terrible blast – like a fiery hurricane – that had overturned trees and blown out glass windows in its path, followed by a hailstorm – of countless tons of red-hot rocks. Houses had been set aflame like kindling, as had anything else that could burn. *La Soufrière* belched out choking ash and searing hot pumice – which settled as a grey shroud over the island's now dead vegetation. Scalding hot water that had turned into steam had then mixed with ash to form a hot sticky mud. This, after it had settled on various surfaces, proved impossible to remove.

Where falls of ash had accumulated the deepest, it remained hot for days afterwards. And when surface water then seeped into these hottest layers, it often caused an explosion that threw up a column of steam. This would spread panic among already deeply traumatised people haunted by the fear that another eruption was imminent.

Many of those who were injured bore terrible burns from hot debris that had fallen on them, but most of the deaths had not been caused by burning or by fires. Instead, they had been brought about in the most horrible way when victims had inhaled hot dust or gasses. However, countless other lives had been saved when quick-thinking people took shelter in cellars and in underground store-rooms. Indeed, though all the deaths were terrible, the overall loss of life was far less than one might have reasonably expected. Yet my thoughts turned towards those slaves I had once seen working in the fields on the slopes of *La Soufrière*. How many of those people, I wondered, had died after their masters had fled for safety? We would never know, for I later came to understand that slaves' lives were never regarded as precious as those of freemen, and that in many cases loss of slaves had been accounted for in the same tally as that of livestock and other chattels, and not in the tally of *human* lives that had been lost.

The loss of the crops was disastrous and, beyond the Fort with its vast store rooms, food supplies were therefore in danger of running out quickly. But thankfully our island's ships returned laden with relief from Barbados and the other islands.

But as if it had not been bad enough that we should have found ourselves victims of this most dire calamity of nature, another disaster was about to strike us British. This time it was to be dealt by the hand of man. For just as we were reeling in the wake of *La Soufrière*, the young American republic declared war on Britain, in a cowardly move to seize our lands in Canada.

The war with America would scatter John's battalion and the Royal Artillery to many places across the West Indies and even on into Canada and other regions of North America. Not for naught, I discovered, was the Royal Artillery's motto 'ubique' – 'everywhere'.

However, John and I were fated, it seemed, to remain on St Vincent. And then in August, less than five months after *La Soufrière* erupted, I was delivered of my first child. We named him Thomas, and despite the wretched heat and sickness we suffered in that place, and against all of the odds stacked against him, our little son thrived while other babies born there did not.

Chapter Seven

While John and I remained in St Vincent, we heard with growing dismay news filtering back from England. Eighteen-sixteen is a year that shall always be remembered for its widespread *strangeness*, and not only for its strangeness but also for the great feeling of foreboding that came to envelope almost every beating heart in the north of our world.

From pulpits the length and breath of the northern hemisphere, preachers beseeched those packed into their churches to prepare for Armageddon; for we were surely facing the end of the world and God's retribution for our miserable part in the great slaughter of so many innocents during the recent bloody years of war.

That summer John and I heard news from soldiers freshly come from Canada of how a terrible and most devastating unexpected frost came out of nowhere to kill off nearly all the precious young crops so newly sprung from the earth. As if this had not been disaster enough, June was then shaken by the almost unbelievable advent of snowstorms, which brought over a foot of snow falling in parts. As a result, it had devastated those few crops that had not succumbed to the frosts in May, and also claimed many lives amongst the poor.

Unsettling as that news was, we who were stationed on St Vincent were devoid of any thought at all that anything like the same calamity could also be happening half way across the world back home. And the added shock of it all was that it was so.

That year there came no summer at all in Great Britain. Instead of sun, the British Isles were to suffer almost incessant rain and chill until September, when came the shocking sight of sheet ice upon the River Thames.

I had never before considered myself to have been living a life of plenty. I had at times known hunger back in Ireland, when the crop had not come in as good as hoped for, which resulted in food running thin before the spring had come. Yet never a time like that which came upon our friends and families back home: a time when nature turned hostile towards poor people and stripped their larders bare. And all we could do was to look on, helpless to aid them in their destitution.

Quickly the dark spectre of starvation and famine loomed over a Europe already broken in the wake of several previous years of poor harvests, and still in want after the terrible effects of the war with Napoleon. And at home, many of our brave soldiers were newly returned from fighting the enemy, only to suddenly face the very real prospect of starvation. So grave was the situation that horse oats and even quantities of animal feed were being seized by starving people in a desperate bid to feed themselves.

Meanwhile, John's fellow artillery men still based at Woolwich faced the grim possibility of being ordered to fire upon such people, who formed mobs that regularly run amok as they tried to loot warehouses of their scanty hoard of precious grain. These mobs included tens of thousands of now unwanted ex-soldiers who had returned to a country with neither the will nor means to support them.

At least in the barracks at St Vincent, my child and I were assured our ration of daily bread at a time when thousands of other poor mothers back home struggled in absolute desperation to feed their broods. Yet even our bread on St Vincent was not the soft white *Tommy* [7]bread of old, which had been so beloved of the soldiers at barracks.

---

7   "Soft Tommy, or white Tommy; bread is so called by sailors, to distinguish it from biscuit."
Definition taken from The 1811 Dictionary of the Vulgar Tongue, originally by Francis Grose.

Our bread now contained more locally grown grains since there was no wheat to be had from either home or from Canada, where we learned that loaves made of ground acorns, sawdust and goodness only knows what else had become the staple of most people.

Even after a year had passed, the weather did not settle back into its previous conditions, though a gradual improvement over time held the promise of an eventual return to normality. But even when this came, the country did not seem able to crawl out of the slump as it had after poorer times before. With the war over, a great deal of trade had simply died overnight, and the still steady stream of soldiers returning to England added to the country's misery of hungry mouths. As a result, many a weary soldier returned to the prospects of finding neither a home nor gainful employment.

This was the England that John and I returned to after departing from St Vincent on March the twenty-seventh, eighteen-hundred-and-eighteen, after more than seven years long years of duty there.

On his return, John was transferred to the First Battalion as a gunner and driver. And then, instead of moving back into barracks with our wee son, we decided to rent a home of our own. We moved into a small house in Red Lion Street, not far from the Woolwich Common. All in all it was a squalid hovel of a place, with window frames so rotten that you could wriggle your finger into the flaking wood and pick your way almost through to the other side with no effort at all. And although we shared that house with three other Royal Artillery families, at least we had our own room to keep to and a good deal more privacy than we had ever had together before.

Although John drew rations for both Thomas and me, they really were not enough for me to feed us all properly. So I, being the mother, often went without to make them last. If John had known that, as I dished out our meals, I was favouring him and our boy, he would have been angry and forced, I am certain, some of his portion upon me. But I knew full well from the other wives how divilish the Army could be at the best of times at keeping a close watch on their men. For if the Sergeant had then as much as suspected that John had been sharing *his* ration with me, he had the power to stop Thomas' and my rations altogether and then force John back into barracks. And then we would not be reunited as a family until the Army saw fit. Meanwhile, Thomas and I could find ourselves turned out onto the streets with nothing at all.

During the day time I busied myself by taking in sewing and such to help eek out John's meagre pay. By that time Thomas had grown into a fine boy and was attending the Army school. In the evenings, it was wonderful to see Thomas sitting at the table together with John, trying to teach his father to read.

John was so very proud of Thomas.

'Dhat's the wonder of an Army education!' he would exclaim proudly. 'Wid him reading and writing so fine dhe world is bound to be dhat boy's oyster. All he needs to do is reach in and snatch out a pearl!'

John often looked to the future, a future beyond the Army. John built his dreams around our son. They were dreams of how – with the part of his father's inheritance owed to John by his brothers back in Antrim, coupled with the pension that he would one day receive upon his discharge – he and Thomas might buy a little farm back in the old country.

'John Witherup & Son – yeoman farmers'. Now doesn't dhat have a ring about it, Mary?' he would jape.

Altogether, we three settled quickly back into Woolwich and a stable family life; even more so as I was shortly expecting to give birth to another child. Now that John had his son, I felt able to wish for that one treasure my heart yearned for, a daughter for myself. I would share the days with her, and together we would do all the things that I had enjoyed at own my mother's side. However, the child delivered was another son.

We had him baptised at the church of St Mary Magdalene and named James, in remembrance of John's late father. He was such a sweet little thing, with a shock of red curls, but he was sickly from birth. After just ten short weeks of struggling to live, he died. He was buried in the graveyard at the church, and on the day of his funeral he was laid to rest along with five other babies, all under the age of one year old.

It was shortly after this tragedy that John chose to give up the Anglican way of worship and to attend instead the modest Scots Church in Green's End, which was favoured now by so many of his friends at the Royal Artillery. It was a move that apparently would not go unnoticed.

In the September of the following year, I was delivered of another child: this time a healthy baby girl. Mary Ann was duly baptised at the Scots Church, much to the pleasure of its minister, Mister Jonathan Blythe. Ah, but wasn't our joy altogether complete? I had a daughter, who John also adored, and our son, Thomas, who so loved of his tiny new sister that he would sit for hours gently dandling her on his knee and singing softly to her. Money and food was often short, but love was never wanting in our hearts.

Those winters we spent in Woolwich after our return to England were some of the hardest that I had yet known. The snow and the cold, which felt like it had blown in all the way from Russia, came on a really icy wind, which seemed to cut right through to the bone if you stood about outside long enough.

However, on bright and still winter days, when I was wrapped up well, I liked to walk out by the river – something I never did come late spring or summer. For the smell of the Thames was rank when heated by the sun, and it had all manner of unmentionable things bobbing about in it at high tide – or else left washed up upon its banks or amid a filthy scum at low water. And the bodies? There were so many poor drownded people!

'Are the folk in London such a clumsy crowd,' I remember asking John before we had been posted to the West Indies, 'dhat dhey so easily pitch into dhe river and drown?'

I can recall John giving me 'that look'. That look of his when he thinks I have spoken before thinking something through. That look and a queer little silence, as if he was giving me time for my brain to catch up with my mouth and for me to fathom the answer myself before he felt compelled to give it to me. And so it occurred to me that what I had just said could not be so, and then got to considering that some of those poor cratures might have been helped along in drowning. Or maybe worse than that, some of them may have jumped into the water of their own accord to deliberately put an end to their lives. It was always hard when watching the watermen hauling a body out of the Thames – especially those of childer: for wasn't it altogether that more awful to witness the end of wee lives that had been washed away before they had barely begun?

The winter of eighteen-twenty-two came upon us quick and hard. By December twenty-third it was so cold that there was ice to be seen floating upon the River Thames. I was pregnant again and remember spending that bitter Christmas Eve huddling up in bed alone, because John had drawn guard duty for that night and well on into most of the following day.

53

I got up on Christmas morning and made ready to go to church with the childer, but it was so slippery outside that I had turned back before even reaching the end of our Street for fear of falling on the cobbles. So the childer and I returned to our tiny cold room where I lit the fire and settled to boil up the nice big beef bone I had got from the butcher the day before. As I began to cook it with dried peas, carrots and potatoes, I was determined to welcome my husband home that night with a tasty and hearty Christmas meal.

Thomas eagerly helped me to peel the potatoes, and then, when he had finished, went off towards the common in search of more wood while I cooked and did my chores. By the time Mary-Ann woke up, her brother had returned with two fine faggots of sticks tucked under his arms. He placed them by the fireside and then sat on the bed and played with his little sister, taking up the wooden doll that John had whittled for her and making it dance a merry jig, while Mary-Ann lay snug and warm beneath the shabby old moth-eaten Army blankets.

By two in the afternoon, the sky had clouded over and turned that strange shimmering pewter colour, as it always does just before letting forth buckets of snow. And so it fell, softly at first, like goose feathers drifting gently down through the still cold air to settle finely upon the window ledge outside. But then it came faster and thicker, with flurries of snowflakes swirling in the air in all directions. Soon it had covered the cobbled street beyond our window and the rooftops of the mean terrace of houses on the opposite side of the road.

'When is Da coming home?' Thomas asked expectantly.

'Not until tonight,' I replied. 'He is on guard duty and so I do not expect him until late.'

'I'm fierce hungry Ma!' he groaned.

With that I helped him, Mary-Ann and myself to a cupful of the stock from the cooking pot. Then I pulled the ill-fitting wooden window shutters across the cracked panes of glass in a brave effort at attempting to keep in some warmth. After this, I moved the cooking pot to the edge of the hearth where it would not spoil, and then damped down our one last remaining large log and put it on the fire to burn down slowly. Then I joined Thomas and Mary-Ann under the covers of the bed for a much needed sleep.

It was pitch dark when I woke with a start. I had just heard the street door opening and then felt the house shudder slightly as the door was quickly slammed shut again. Then came familiar footsteps upon the bare boards of the hallway towards our room. The door suddenly burst open and in walked John. Wet snow from his shoulders rolled down the surface of his wool great coat and his ears and nose were as scarlet as rose hips. But instead of his nice warm hat being on his head, it was clutched firmly to his chest with one hand while from the other a bucket full of coal swung at his side.

'Goodness me, John!' I exclaimed. 'You look fair foundered[8]! Haven't you dhe good sense to be wearing your hat on such an awful night as dhis? And where did you get dhe coal?'

With that he walked across to the table and put his hat down on it. Then, quick as a wink, he lifts it up again to reveal great bundle wrapped in muslin.

'What is it?' I asked

John smiled wryly as he opened up the cloth to reveal a great pink lump of fancy roast ham with a golden crust all studded with cloves. And sitting with it, if you please, was whole plum pudding.

---

8   Frozen.

'Dhat? Dhat's from the officers' Mess!' he laughed.

'No! You didn't t'ieve it did you, John?'

'No, I did not, Mary!' he insisted. 'More like '*liberated*' so it was! And widh dhem officers all being as drunk as lords from toasting dhe Duke of Wellington in his weight in brandy, I t'ought dhey wouldn't be missing dhe going of it.'

The four of us feasted like kings that Christmas night. It was the best Christmas I can ever recall, with John, and the childer and me all snug and warm and the unborn child within me kicking about with all the force of a buck rabbit.

Then, at the height of a snowstorm, our second daughter, Eliza Jane, was born that following January. It was about this time that John was really beginning to complain about his bone ache. He had always had it, but only mildly before he was posted to the West Indies, where it gave him not a bit of grief all the time we were in St Vincent. But since we had returned to England, it had fair begun to plague him. And as he tried to rise from his chair at night, to ready himself for bed, we realised that his legs and arms were growing steadily stiffer.

'My but aren't I dhe ould fellow all of a sudden,' John joked, trying to make light of it all. But I saw through his attempt to play down the severity of it all. I could see that he was worried about it getting worse, which would lead to him failing his next Army medical. For if that should happen, John would face being discharged as unfit for duty. I could tell that he was rapidly growing beside himself with worry about such a terrible prospect.

But then, the following year, didn't the most tragic thing occur in our lives to make that prospect pale into insignificance?

Chapter Eight

I never did see a man so soft about the eyes as I had the day it all happened. I knew my John as a seasoned soldier, a man trained to kill, a man well used to death. And yet, as he sat in the dappled light by the window with our little daughter, Eliza Jane, lying weakly in the crook of his arm, I never did see a more gentle or a more sorry man.

'Nothin' bad is going to happen to dhis wee lassie,' he said, with tears glinting in his eyes. 'I promise you, Mary my dear, by the breat' in my body, I'm promisin' you dhat she *will* be alright!'

As I looked steadily into his deep-set brown eyes I so desperately wanted to believe him. Yet, clearly visible on the dark blue sleeve of his uniform, was a smear of rich Kentish earth from the place where he had buried our beloved son, Thomas, earlier that morning. So how could that man stand there promising me anything?

I cannot find words to tell you how awful the death of our son was. From the moment of their quickening, when I could feel them stirring in my womb for the first time, I yearned to hold each of my unseen childer in my arms, even then longing to protect them from the world. And yet no matter how hard I tried, I knew that I could not protect them from everything. Losing a wee baby is hard enough, I can tell you, but to lose a lusty boy of eleven is just almost beyond bearing. For the endearing ways of a child are not yet fully formed in an infant, and it is those little ways that make the parting with an older child all the more sorrowful to deal with.

My lost baby was not like any other baby in the world, and yet I found that in time their little face merged in my memory into those of every other babe that I encountered thereafter. My time together with my lost baby had been so very brief and so maybe that softened my sense of loss a little, because I soon came not to remember my own child's features as clearly as my heart had hoped I would. But my lovely boy? Our Thomas was standing on the threshold of manhood and John and I had come to know him so well over so many happy years. I shall never, ever forget a single expression that passed over Thomas' face or the lilt of his voice as he called out my name. Or his laughter, and his tears. Or the snatches of conversations shared with him – that often came suddenly flooding back into my memory in the waking hours of a restless night. Or that certain look that he might have given when I had scolded him in the past for some minor misdemeanour. Or the glint of delight in his winsome blue eyes over some moment of joy we had shared.

But it is not only the loss of the child that cuts deepest into the core of a parent's heart. It is also the sudden death of all of the hopes and dreams that you had for that lost child that adds to the overwhelming grief. And for a father, like John, it was especially hard when that lost lad was also his da's best friend.

There were a lot of childer who fell ill that July; all down with a wretched outbreak of sickness, no doubt made worse by the long hot spell of weather we had just had. The heat strengthened the all-invading great stink of that cesspool of a River Thames as it flowed through Woolwich and carried all sorts of filth and disease from the city.

Mary-Ann had already had a nasty dose of it but had recovered well enough after just a few days. But not Thomas. He had fallen ill at about the same time, but instead of shaking it off as his little sister had, it just dragged him down and down over four days. We watched his life fading away and there was nothing we could do to save him. Ah, the Army surgeon turned out to the house for sure, but said that the infirmary was full with many more of the same and that it was just as well for Thomas to be nursed at home as there was nothing more that he could do for the lad there that I was not already doing.

'Time will tell,' was all the doctor would say. 'Either the boy will rally... or he will not. There is nothing left to do but to bide our time and pray.'

Within hours of the doctor coming, our Thomas slipped quietly away.

John and I weren't paupers but with a young family to support on a private's pay, we couldn't afford anything more than a simple burial for our son. Comrades of John's purloined an old rifle box from the armoury and we laid Thomas to rest in that, wrapped up snugly in new army blanket, courtesy of the kindly quartermaster. John's friends helped him to carry our son's body to the churchyard of St Mary Magdalene and to lay him in the grave that his own father had dug at first light.

John was already out of his mind with grief and barely able to speak for it, when along comes the Anglican priest, Reverend Fraser to perform the burial rites. Fraser was as ever the most miserable crature ever put on this earth. I never did see an ounce of God-given joy in the Reverend's bones, not even at the best times. When we still used to attend his church services, I didn't see him smile or hear him speak a kind word even as he baptised wee babies!

He paused by the graveside and opening up his small black book, hastily mumbled but a mouthful of words from it. Then Fraser hurriedly made the sign of the cross, snapped his book closed, and then turned to walk off again back towards the church.

'Wait Reverend! Wait a minute! John called after him with tears streaming down his deathly ashen face. 'Dhat can't be right, can it?' he said. 'Surely dhat can't be a fit service for my lad!'

The wretched preacher then turned slow and deliberately upon his heel to look

John straight in the eye with a stare so hard that it could have nailed up a coffin lid. Then he replied, as blunt as blunt could be, 'I am done here, soldier, and that is an end of it! I am a busy man with my *own* parishioner's funerals to attend to. Besides', he sneered, 'you should have considered more carefully when you chose to leave my ministry for that of Mister Blythe.'

John was by now so incensed that he screamed, 'Done is it, dhen?'

And with that, my husband had to be restrained by his fellow gunners from grabbing Reverend Fraser and maybe doing him some great harm.

After John and the others had finished filling Thomas' grave, John stormed off to who knows where, for he did not come home to me again for two or more hours afterwards.

Not long after John returned, his Sergeant came to the house and said that the Captain had received an altogether serious complaint from Reverend Fraser regarding the earlier '*incident*'. John explained the circumstance of the ruckus and the Sergeant listened intensely.

Then the Sergeant shook his head and tutted. 'You cannot go about, Private Witherup, haranguing an Anglican priest like that and expect to go unpunished. No matter how much he deserves it!' he said, with a look as sombre as a hanging judge. 'Take a care John. The Army's cutting back and would it not take much of an excuse for them to find a good reason for your discharge...'

After Thomas' death, the joy in John's heart was stilled for a long while, as was the ready whistle of a tune upon his lips silenced. 'Twas as if there was a great invisible hole rent in him, large enough to drive a horse and gun carriage through it. And I was so deep down in my own grief that I could not climb out of it to reach John and help him. For some unknown reason I blamed myself for my son's death. What had I done wrong that he became so ill? What did I do differently in the way that I nursed him from the way I nursed my daughters who recovered? Was it truly my fault that I let him slip away from us?

The gaping hole left in our crowded house was more than John could bear. He suddenly spent long periods of time away from us and stayed at the barracks instead, or else slumped in the tavern at the end of Red Lion Street and away from my bed. I never cried so many lonely tears at night as I did during the weeks after Thomas died. And for a time, I feared that our happy marriage would not survive this dreadful loss either.

But little by little, as time silently marched on, we began to heal a little. And so John eventually returned to me and his two wee daughters and tried hard to pick up the remnants of our family life. And isn't it often the curious way – that has one soul departing this world in order to make way for another coming in?

On the fourteenth day of June, eighteen-twenty-five, and with me in my thirty-fourth year, John and I were blessed with a healthy boy child. We named him Thomas in memory of his dear brother, departed but eleven months before. And for the first time in a long time, I noticed a spring return to John's step and a lightness in his manner that had been gone away from him for far too long now. It was as if this new young Thomas was taking up some of the emptiness that his older brother had left in his father's heart.

Chapter Nine

John was a career soldier, and I had known that from the first night of our marriage. Not lightly had he taken up the King's shilling; that very same shilling he still had in his possession as his 'lucky piece'. Tucked safely away in his inside pocket, John carried it with him wherever he went in the course of battle. But even the best of luck finds itself run out at some point. John's ran out in June, eighteen-twenty-six, when he was discharged from the Royal Artillery on account of 'chronic arthritis'. He was given his final marching orders, which meant he and I were disposed of by the Army the very next day.

Now isn't His Majesty's Army a most wondrous thing at accounting for the Government's money? For sure, I wouldn't be surprised if they knew every one of their men's worth down to the nearest farthing – for they certainly knew ours! On the back of John's discharge paper was the carefully calculated sum of *Marching Money*. This was an amount of money that the Army is obliged to provide to pay for the return of a discharged soldier back to whence he had first enlisted. In John's case that was Lisburn.

The distance for us to travel back to that town had been worked out by the Army to be exactly 'two-hundred-and-eighty-six-and-one-half miles' from Woolwich. For that, John was to receive the generous travelling payment of eight pennies a day and an additional sum of six shillings, with a further lump sum of some five pounds and seven shillings and sixpence by way of a family allowance 'for a wife and three children'. Generous indeed, if it were not for the wee fact that the Army had also reckoned that the journey back to Ireland would take John, me and the childer only twenty-nine days to complete. That meant that as a family we were expected to walk at least ten miles a day–

come rain or shine- in order to live within that eight pence a day without breaking into the precious lump sum.

By that time Mary-Ann was six years old, Eliza three, and young Thomas was too young to walk at all. A blind man at night could see that it was going to be nigh impossible for us to achieve that distance every day, what with carrying the childer along with all of our possessions! We already knew that the longer we took to complete the journey, the less money we would have to keep ourselves fed along the way, and to start our new life once we had got back to Antrim. Considering all the hardship and suffering that John and I had put up with in the service of His Majesty's Army, I felt that they were out to cheat us of what was hard earned – now that John had outlived his usefulness to king and country. I could have happily spat in His Majesty's eye, so I could!

John had toyed with the idea of buying a donkey, but then he had been warned by the Quarter Master that it might prove unwise. He had heard from other soldiers returning to Ireland who had done exactly that... only to be told as they were embarking ship that the beast could not be taken on board. Then the local horse dealers, primed by the ship's captain, would circle like vultures – offering to relieve the soldiers of their burdensome beast for only a fraction of the price that had been paid for it. And so wise to this, John instead purchased a small handcart to take his soldier's trunk into which we crammed the few possessions that we had. And so off it was that we went from Woolwich.

The England through which we travelled on our return to Ireland was not at all the country I remembered from our coming some sixteen years before. There wasn't a town or village we passed through that hadn't been fouled by poverty. There were beggars scrounging on almost every street corner, and we noted that many of them were grey-haired and pitiful former soldiers. Lacking in both limbs and dignity, and clothed in little more than tattered rags, they pleaded with passers by for what ever pittance they could get to keep themselves alive.

At the start of our journey, John could not bear to walk past these men without giving them something, and so gave a penny to the first few beggars he saw. He soon stopped doing so when he realised that there were just so many of them – and we had little enough for ourselves.

'You can't give away anymore,' I had to scold John gently. 'Or dhere shan't be enough to feed dhe childer.'

'I know, Mary,' he sighed, 'but these were my brodhers on dhe battlefield. Would you just take a look at dhem now?'

He knew he could not afford to give anymore, and yet he found it unbearably hard to look the other way and pass on by – as so many other folk were doing.

But it was just as well that John got his discharge when he had. I do not think that we would ever have managed that same journey come the winter time. At least with it being summer, the hours of daylight were at their longest, which meant that we were able to stop long before dusk to set up a makeshift camp for ourselves outside a town or village. Then John could gather up some wood, light a fire for a brew of tea and some hot food, and then settle the little ones for the night. By saving money that might have paid for a roof above our heads each night meant that at least we had enough to buy good victuals.

Even so, there were days when it rained nails and the road turned to mud and coaxing Mary-Ann and Eliza Jane into walking at all became a real trial. Then we would have to hole up for a while, until the weather eased enough for us to press on towards Ireland. And so it was that we eventually reached the *Witherup* farm in Ballypitmave in the first week of August.

I would like to say that it was a warm welcome that John received from his brother James – but it was nothing like it! James had married and made it quite clear that his family was already dreadfully in want, and so he could do without the extra *burden* of having to take in his brother.

'Burden?' John was furious. 'Burden is it dhat I am?' he roared at his younger brother. 'Dhat's grand coming from you... widh your arse sitting on *my* birthright!'

So after more thundering and raging between the brothers, John shamed James into agreeing to let us stay on *temporarily* at the farm.

To be fair to James, we soon realised that, indeed, there was terrible want throughout Antrim. Hundreds of loyal discharged soldiers, just like John, had already straggled back to their former homes looking to take up the lives they had once left behind in order to serve in the British Army. There were some fifty-one returnees in Glenavy Parish and eighty-three in Ballinderry. Most were returning to the land and mainly to the small tenanted farms still in the hands of other family members. Some of these men had been away for more than twenty years and, like John, they had not come back *alone*. Most of them had wives and childer in tow, and for a small farmstead to accommodate just one man coming back to it was asking an awful lot for the land to support. And so expecting it to provide for an extra four, five, six or even more extra mouths to feed was proving near impossible.

Like mainland England, Ireland had suffered near starvation after the failings of the summer that never was and its aftermath. And even more hardship followed after the loss of trade generated by the war with France. For example, the mill in Glenavy, which was only newly founded a few years before, was floundering because there was no further demand from the Army for its products, since many soldiers had since been disbanded.

Apart from these hardships, Glenavy just wasn't the same place that it had been before I had gone away. I felt that much of the very spirit of the place had been sucked out of it, what with so many of the folk that I had known back then having since passed away. There was a new church, though. The old one, in which all the Witherup brothers had been baptised, was now no more, having become so dilapidated that just two years after I had left, it had to be pulled down. There had been too many changes for my liking. So many that it no longer felt like the home I had missed and dreamed of over the years.

We stayed for but a short while and very uneasily with James and his family. The Witherup's cramped little house was busting at the seams, and so after just a few days, we went to stay with my brothers at my late parents' old farm. There we were given a welcome even warmer than that given to the prodigal son of the Bible, though the farm itself was not so hospitable. The soil had grown tired with so much giving.

There had been changes at Ballinderry too. The ancient church, where John and I had been married, had been abandoned in favour of a new one, but at least the old building was still standing. I had a great affection for that place, for it held many of my fondest memories. In all my years of growing up in Ireland, my parents and we Hendren brood had dutifully tramped down the lane to it every Sunday morning, as surely as my brothers would get into all sorts of mischief. Like the time when my da had nodded off during the sermon and they suddenly banged their boots so loudly against the door of our box pew that Da had near jumped up out of his skin! There he was, suddenly wide awake and sat bolt upright like a newly hammered in fence post, only to immediately be met by the glare of the minister's glass eye – pinning him down like a criminal.

My brother Thomas, and his wife, Isabella, had a brood of childer of their own by then. John, their oldest, was a strapping fine lad. I watched my own John's face when my brother introduced him. I knew from my man's expression and that far off look that suddenly glinted in his eyes that he was sharing my thoughts – about our dear, dead Thomas, and how much this young John looked like him. And I could wager, just as I was, he was thinking the same thing: if only... At least three times I heard my husband miscall his nephew by Thomas' name. Tactfully, young John said nothing of it.

Our oldest niece, Isabella, was a truly lovely child, and also uncannily close to how I remember her mother looking at about that same age. Her younger sister, Margaret, was her father Thomas' daughter, without a doubt. She was a Hendren through and through, and favouring so many of the fine features of our late mother, as did their youngest son, who was also named Thomas.

Though John had his pension coming in to help out the family finances, it was still a struggle for our extended family to support itself, and even more so when the following spring came and I gave birth to another son, James. Despite the fact that the land was straining to produce enough of a crop to feed us all, bless them, Thomas and Isabel would not hear a word of our leaving. John searched about for a piece of land of his own to rent, but vacant land in the parish was as rare as hens' teeth. My brother's family continued to grow, as did ours, and yet somehow we managed to struggle on together.

Then, in the June of eighteen-twenty-nine, the last of my childer was born. But my baby daughter, Isabella, lived only just long enough to be hurriedly baptised. We buried her in the old churchyard.

On top of our sorrow, we also had to wrestle with crushing worry. We simply could not bring in enough food to feed the mouths that remained. And so John and I realised that, for the survival of us all, we must somehow move on. But to where? And how?

Not long afterwards, John came home one night from the public house in the village brim full of talk about emigrating. He had been talking with Stafford Wilson, who, like John, had been discharged from the Royal Artillery. With him had been John Grant, Michael Carroll, Will Mclean, and a few other Ballinderry ex-soldiers, all talking away about the very same thing for most of that evening.

The conversation had centred mainly upon how the Army was now offering free land in Canada to old soldiers in return for agreeing to have their pensions commuted.

'Imagine dhat, Mary!' he enthused, with his breath reeking of whisky. 'Free land! We could have our own farm instead of rotting away in dhis muddy puddle.'

And so John became one of the many old soldiers who agreed to have their pensions commuted – in return for free passage across the ocean for them and their families, and a grant of free land from the Crown.

Chapter Ten

We arrived in Quebec towards the end of August in eighteen-thirty-two. From Quebec we travelled to York, where John was to report. I found York to be a fine looking place indeed, and full of promise. There were grand buildings and bustling streets which soon got me to thinking that maybe this was not as backward a country as idle chit-chat on the voyage across the Atlantic had led me to believe.

From York, we as a family no longer had to maintain ourselves out of our own pocket. Instead, we were amply provisioned by the Government agent for our journey of some seventy miles back along the river to a place called Cobourg, and then on from there to the town of Peterborough. But my brother, not being an ex-soldier like John, had to buy his own stores and secure to his own passage, which meant that John and I ended up going on ahead of him by a good few weeks.

On September the eleventh, there were many others in line ahead of us at the office in Peterborough, all signing up to buy land with the government Emigration Officer – Mister Rubidge. When it came to John's turn, he stepped up smartly and handed in his discharge papers. Rubidge was a sharp man with a blunt tongue. He had been a pioneer settler in Otonabee Township some thirteen or fourteen years prior to our arrival and so was more than well acquainted with the prospect that lay in front of us.

'Irish?' he grunted. 'Farmed before, have you?'

'Yes, sir' John replied confidently. 'Born and bred to it. Dhat is before dhe Army, sir.'

'Hmm!' Rubidge reached across his desk and drew a great ledger towards him and opened it up to reveal a large sheet of printed tickets. But instead of tearing one off, Rubidge instead handed John one of several that were loose.

'Here,' he said, 'this is the location docket for your allotment of land. One-hundred acres on the fifth concession. Lot seventeen. The south half.' Then he added with what I took to be a knowing look upon his face, 'Good luck, soldier,' as if we were going to need it.

Again, we were provided by the authorities with a reasonable amount of provisions. These were mainly flour, pork and potatoes, to tide us over for the first month or so of our settling on the land. We were also told clearly and firmly by Rubidge, and in no uncertain terms, that after they were used up, we were on own until the next allotted supply was sent out to us. And then, come the spring, this aid would cease and we would have to fend for ourselves entirely.

Rubidge then appointed an ageing Yankee teamster, named Old Joe, with a wagon and a span of horses[9] to guide us to our property. We were assured that once there hired help had been arranged to erect a small house for us.

So it was with a light heart and an even lighter head, filled with pretty visions of our new homestead that I happily endured the most dreadful twenty or so miles of journeying that I had ever experienced to reach the township of Dummer. The roads were so bad that, to my mind, it would have been impossible even for the divil himself to think of way to make them worse! It made me laugh out loud to think of the number of times that I had heard some English people referring to Ireland as being a 'backward place'. At least back home in Antrim we had properly made roads!

---

9   A pair of horses abreast.

We rode on the wagon loaded with our possessions, constantly all of a jiggle as we encountered innumerable ruts, holes, fallen trees, and rocks, along with bone-shaking sections of watery road that had been in filled in with logs which Old Joe gave the gentle name of *corduroy*. I found it so unbearably uncomfortable, and soon I was sore from head to toe, although the childer didn't seem bothered at all. I supposed that was because their young bones were more adaptable and their bodies still supple.

As we jerked, bounced and thumped on, I tried to soften the blows by picturing in my head all of the little settlements that I had previously seen dotted along the shore of the St Lawrence, as we had made our way to and from York. They were neat little houses surrounded by neat little gardens and proudly tended fields. And so sure wasn't I then thinking that we were heading to something very much of the same?

The farther we got from Peterborough, the more I started to notice such rudimentary-looking buildings that at first I took mistook them to be barns for livestock. That was the notion I had until, to my utter horror, Old Joe explained that these 'barns' were called 'shanties' and were what passed, here in the backwoods, as houses. When I heard those words, I was straight away filled with despair. My rosy dreams wilted and my hopes lay trampled upon. I felt utterly betrayed by my naïve expectations – and once again by the Army.

Old Joe must have sensed my growing unhappiness, because he quickly jumped up in praise of the advantages of these rude buildings.

'They may not look so purty on the outside,' he enthused, 'but inside, come winter, you'll be as snug as bugs!'

My mournful gaze then fell upon the dark and sinister woods looming over us on both sides of the road. We were slowly and painfully making our way through a vast, never-ending, impenetrable tangle of trees. I then listened with growing anxiety as Old Joe explained that this was how our land at Dummer would be.

'It's not so bad as it looks,' Old Joe added, trying to jolly me up. 'You just need to know how to tame it!'

He explained to John that to make proper progress in clearing a patch fit to farm, first the 'under bush' would have to be cut down as close to the ground as possible and then heaped into enormous piles for burning.

'Here in Canada,' Old Joe said,' *'under bush'* describes anything that you can get the span of your arms around.'

I smiled a little as I thought to myself how the word *'under bush'* would not be applying to our driver then.

'That just leaves the large trees,' Old Joe continued. 'Once them is down and the side branches are all trimmed away neat like, then them is the ones used to build a shanty with.'

He also explained how the great, long, straight trunks are cut into lengths for the side walls and then either dragged by oxen, or of if there are none to be had, man-handled on rollers made of logs, onto the building site ready for positioning.

Shanties roofs are made out of Basswood trees, which are first cut to length and then split and hollowed out with an axe. These hollowed out logs are then laid out in much the same way as pantile roofs are laid back in the old country, overlapped to throw rain water off the roof and away from the house.

'Your shanty should be built upon a high point where the ground slopes away, so you don't get flooded out,' Old Joe warned John. 'And make yourself a real good clearing all about yer, too, coz there is always the threat of fire in the bush. And the slightest breeze can quickly fan a spark into a fiery inferno.'

John then remarked to Old Joe how he had purchased some tools in York and found the axes here in Canada to be an altogether more dangerous-looking article than those to be had back at home.

'That they are,' he laughed, 'and not for the hands of the faint-hearted or wimin!'

In consequence, it transpired that accidents with axes seemed to happen more frequently here, and were all the more nasty for the people unlucky enough to have to suffer them.

Just then, as the land gave way to the gentle roll of low hills, I caught sight of a very odd hut indeed. It had a strange sort of open basket-work affair of poles at the top, from which a fine rise of reddish smoke was escaping. Indeed, it was this smoke that had first caught my attention. Old Joe must have noticed me craning my neck to look as we passed it by.

'Cah! That'll be Injuns,' Old Joe shrugged in a casual manner.

'Indians?' said I. Will dhere be Indians in Dummer too, Joe?

'Of course there'll be Injuns!' Old Joe threw back his head in a hearty roar that almost cost him his hat. 'There are Injuns all over!'

Indians. I had heard stories about how cruel Indians had been in the past. And, naively, I had not realised we would be living in such close proximity to them here in the bush.

'Don't go paying them Injuns no heed, ma'am,' Joe said. 'There are good and bad in all races, but mostly these Injuns here don't do no harm to no one no more. Not like those back where I come from! You may find Injuns following game onto your land and hunting and such but there is an unwritten law amongst settlers that says that you just leave them be. They will only ever take from the land what they need to live on, and besides, their trade goods are mighty useful. And most of them here about are darn good Christians to boot!'

Christian? I hadn't expected that, and I must admit it eased my mind no end to hear Old Joe say that.

As the light was beginning to fade, the even narrower and rougher dirt track we were on by then ended abruptly.

'Well. Here we are!' Old Joe exclaimed. 'This is your lot!

'Here?' I exclaimed facing a great forest of trees.

'Yup' Old Joe replied pointing towards a rough track newly hacked out through the undergrowth. Yonder, two or three hundred yards and you will find a clearing. But if I were you I would set yerselves up here for the night.'

Old Joe jumped down and led John and me away to inspect the site while the childer stayed put with the cart. When we got to it our hearts sank- the shanty that was meant to be already erected for us was still only a sorry pile of timber set amid a small clearing chewed out from the forest. Who ever it was who had been assigned with the task of greeting and helping us, was nowhere to be seen.

'Never you mind, Mary,' John said reassuringly. "tis a fine evening and I can soon fix us up a tent back by the wagon to see us through for a few days.'

'That's the spirit!' Old Joe laughed. 'Keep that up and it will see you through.'

No sooner were we unloaded from the cart than Old Joe was driving away leaving us stranded amidst our pile of belongings.

True to his word, John quickly fashioned a makeshift tent out of two old army blankets. Meanwhile, young Thomas and his sisters had been directed to gather up some of the dead wood lying about to build a fire.

It was then that I noticed something moving from out of the corner of my eye. There was a man striding up the track towards us; a very menacing-looking fellow indeed who was wielding a great axe.

'John! John!' I whispered worriedly. 'Look!'

John turned to see what had grabbed my attention.

'Halloo!' the man shouted. 'I've a message for you.'

'What is it?' John shouted back and stopped what he was doing to walk over to meet the fellow.

'The men directed by Mister Rubidge to raise your shanty are laid up with the ague,' the stranger replied.

How my heart sank at those words.

'But,' he continued, 'if you're willing to lay on some victuals then I can see to it that a swarm of men is drummed up here to help raise your house the day after tomorrow. With oxen and tools and all! How are you with that?'

'Ay! I am happy with dhat arrangement, so I am!' John replied with hearty laugh of relief. 'And grateful widh it!'

'And *nectar*,' the fellow added. 'The *bees* will be needing some *nectar*. I'm thinking a shilling's worth should do it. I could sell you some and bring it with me?'

John laughed knowingly, and then clasped the man's hand in a great friendly shake. 'Yes. Do dhat ! John Witherup's the name, by the way, and this is my wife, Mary.'

'Payne,' the man responded with eager friendship. 'I am Levi Payne.'

75

Then Mister Payne bad us a cheery goodnight and, with that, went back along the track and disappeared into the growing shadows.

'Dhere! T'ings are not so bad after all!' John laughed.

Much of the wood the childer had gathered turned out to be green. And so as night fell and it burnt on the fire, every now and then it crackled and spat, like an ill-mannered old shrew, sending a shower of red sparks up into the velvety sky above our heads. There was a lot of fallen wood all about us, and all within just a stride or two of where we had set up our camp. Beyond that though, the trees stood tall, dark, and impenetrable, like a vengeful army standing guard over the remains of its fallen comrades lying in a heap back at the clearing made for the shanty.

'Just t'ink, Mary,' John smiled as he poked a wayward branch back into the burning pile, 'How many times have you sat foundered back in England and all for dhe want of a few measly sticks of wood to stave off dhe cold? Well, I don't t'ink you shall ever want for firewood again!'

How true those words were. For if I had been given a penny for every time that I had sat frozen to the marrow back in Woolwich, all for the want of some fuel for a good roaring fire, I would have become a wealthy woman. John's money had always been quickly spent on food, and so we often had none left for buying good wood.

John looked altogether content with himself, so he did, as he bathed in the light of that very first fire made up from the wood of his very own land. This had been his dream; to be his own master. Now it was all suddenly come real.

John and I pared a few strips off the hunk of cured pork we had in our provisions. Neither of us had either the light or the inclination to hunt amongst our jumble of belongings, heaped up upon the ground where Old Joe had dumped them, for a pan. So instead, John fixed the meat onto long tapered twigs to hold them over the fire to cook.

'It's like being in Eden,' he chuckled. 'And aren't we a fine Adam and Eve?'

It was only then that I noticed that the childer, bless them, had already fallen fast asleep under John's great Army coat. They must have been completely overtaken by exhaustion.

'They'll be fine,' John whispered. 'We can fix them up a good breakfast in the morning.'

John and I ate the hot morsels with our fingers and then began to settle ourselves down for the night. Then John suddenly got up and went off to make water, or so I thought. But then, when he came back, he was carrying another huge armful of wood for the fire.

'Surely we'll be after letting the t'ing burn out?' I said to him.

'Surely we will not!' he tutted, fussing over the fire. 'We need to keep it going all night – just in case.'

'In case of what?'

'Well, we'll not be wanting to wake up to dhe company of wolves, would we now? Or even a bear...'

'Bears? Oh no!' I exclaimed. 'No one said anyt'ing about bears!'

For sure, as if I was going to sleep a wink after John said that? And so while he was quickly away in the land of nod and snoring his head off, there was I with my heart banging away at every creaking tree I heard and at the flicker of every moon shadow.

I hadn't at all liked the prospect of sleeping out in the open in the first place. In truth, great outdoors and I could never make great bedfellows. Indeed, I think my fear of the woods goes back to the time when I was just a wee girl and would take off in play trying to catch up with John and Thomas and my brothers. One or the other of them could be relied upon to lay up in wait for me, usually behind some great tree trunk or such, until I caught up. Then they would suddenly jump out, scaring the bejabers out of me! No – I had no great liking for being in the woods then. But John? John was revelling in all of this as if he was suddenly a boy again.

So, while John slept like a baby, I lay awake for fear of the woods. Well, that's not completely true. I feared whatever crature it was that I could then hear yowling a short way off. It was a howling, screeching crature that chilled my blood with fear and made me feel lonesome. No amount of later reassurance from others living in Dummer, telling me that not a single body had ever been attacked by wild animals in those particular woods, would ever ease my future apprehension at finding myself forced to be alone in them. And while it may have been true that woodland beasts had never been known to kill a body, wee, winged beasties-like the wicked black flies and mosquitoes, certainly succeeded in all but eating me alive.

As I lay wide awake that night, above my head the stars shone brilliantly in the clear night sky. 'Eden?' I remembered thinking to myself, just before sleep finally came to claim me. 'For sure, but didn't even Eden have a wicked serpent slithering about in it?'

Chapter Eleven.

Although it was still only early September, I remember well feeling the chill creep over our paradise before the break of dawn that next morning. I had not then realised how much sooner the autumn would begin to set in here in Canada.

When I looked about me, John was missing. And so were young Thomas and James.

'Did you see your da go off?' I asked the girls, who were already wide away but still huddled together under their father's coat.

'No Ma,' Mary Ann answered as her little sister nodded in agreement.

Just then I heard a loud crack from out of sight somewhere beyond the tree line. Then with a shriek and a whoop, Thomas came running out of the shadows followed close on his heels by his brother, James, who was wielding a fine looking stick.

'Good morning, Ma!' Thomas shouted with a great beaming smile in his face. 'We've been looking at our land. It's enormous!'

Then John appeared and added, 'Aye, dhat it is! We've been following dhe blazes upon dhe tree trunks marking it out. But it went on so far dhat we had to turn back or we'd be back in Antrim, so we would!'

We lit a fire and cooked a grand breakfast which the childer bolted down like scabby dogs. Then John and I set about sorting through our belongings and getting them into some kind of order. After that, we spent a happy and care free day with the childer, exploring our new home.

Early the following morning, a whole gang of men arrived at our plot. Work began on the building of our log cabin in the woods while my daughters and I prepared as much food as we could to feed our hungry helpers, come the time for tools down. It was then that I came to most appreciate the Dutch oven that John had bought me in York. It proved a godsend for cooking all manner of things, especially the lump of salt pork we had with us and the making of bannocks for breakfast.

By the end of that first day, the walls of our shanty were up. While their fathers had been working upon this, some of the youths had helped gather together a fine collection of stones for a hearth and chimney which, by the dimming of the light, had already been swiftly mortared together.

When it was time for our workforce to down tools for the day, they made short work of the dinner of pork, potatoes and pea soup that Mary Ann, Eliza Jane and I had spent all day preparing. It was poor fare, but a meal heartily received by our exhausted *bees* who sat and buzzed over it loudly with chatter. Mouthfuls of food were interspersed with a good lungful of raucous laughter and a slug of the *nectar* as it passed from hand to hand to lubricate their voices and ease their weary bones. Canadian whiskey is a great reviver, so it is, and essential for any *bee*.

Next morning, just as Old Joe had said, our *bees* started to roof the house. It was then that I snatched a look inside the shanty. Without any openings yet for the windows chopped out, it looked awfully closed in and gloomy to me, and so I walked away again terribly disheartened. It wasn't my idea of a house at all.

However, the next time I ventured in, the window spaces had been cut to bring in some welcome light, and the sleepers were in position ready to take the floor above where a small root cellar had already been dug out. It was beginning to shape up into a house, rather than a solid dark lump of a barn.

By then the gaps between the logs, both inside and out, had already been filled in with a mortar made of clay and lime, while several men set about hewing the inside walls, with broad axes, to make them smooth.

Meanwhile, John turned his attention to glazing the windows. He discovered, much to his annoyance, that almost half the box of assorted glass panes that we had bought from the store in Peterborough had been either cracked or broken completely on that wretched journey to Dummer. It was also a complete shame that we had no good seasoned wood at hand for making windows that could be opened. But John did the best he could with what he had, saying that we could always leave the doors open for airing the place until we could fix up proper window frames, perhaps in time for the next summer. The important thing now was to have somewhere warm and snug for the bad weather which our *bees* warned would be fast approaching.

And so there it was. Our new home was soon complete and standing proud upon its little hill. Well, *complete* is not entirely true, for there was no seasoned planking to be had for either love or money for the floor and we could not make do with just the bearers now that the cellar below had been dug out. There was also no way that we could afford the extravagant luxury of sending away to nearest sawmill at Peterborough for some. Instead John hired some fellow from there in Dummer to saw some down out of green wood. This he quickly did, and although they were far from perfect, and bound to shrink or twist once we had laid them down, we did not care. They did the job and at least we would be ready to move indoors in time for the weather to turn. And we were ready too for my brother, Thomas, and his family when they eventually arrived from Peterborough a week later. At least we were able to offer them our roof above their heads until their own shanty could be raised on their plot.

As I have said, we had already noticed how early the frosts had come on in Canada; much earlier than we would have expected back home. By the middle of October they had become keener still, and yet the middle of the days were often bright and hazy and still pleasantly warm – again, not a bit like they were back home. Then November arrived, as soft and mild as an Antrim spring, only to suddenly give way about two weeks later to deeper and sharper frosts soon followed by snow.

John had planned that, from that time until spring that he would concentrate his efforts on chopping down trees and clearing and fencing as much land as possible, with my brother and his boys helping out whenever they could spare time away from clearing their own land. Three acres cleared in a year, was what John had thought reasonable to achieve, and so that is what he set out to do.

John tried not to heed the warnings of other settlers who advised him not to become too disheartened when he came to realise just how little work he would be able to do come the winter. The lack of daylight, coupled with days of extreme cold and snow, greatly limits the number of working hours. But they also said that, at the same time, John should come to bless the coming of the snows, for the roads would suddenly be transformed into highways of delight. The rough terrain would magically be smoothed out affording much easier passage for journeys undertaken by either shank's pony[10] or sleigh.

Although I had happily settled into the shanty and soon had it looking homely enough, I found the view from our two small widows somewhat depressing. Although

---

[10] By foot.

Built atop a small hillock, with only such a small space cleared about it, not much light found its way into the shanty from the oppressive woodland beyond.

In fact the outlook gave the impression that, if at but at moment's notice, the trees might take it into their minds to march forward and smother us out of existence. On the ground that was cleared, huge black stumps stood all about like great grim tombstones marking the demise of those felled trees whose bare bones we had seized to make our home. I hated the ugly things but there was nothing we could do about them straight off. John said that it would be effort wasted on 'aesthetics' which could be made far better use of by on concentrating on felling even more trees and leaving even more stumps!

'Dhe effort to take out even one would be too much time and labour,' he explained, 'while if we just leave dhem dhere, dhey will rot away in four or five years on dheir own...'

I could understand his reasoning. So instead I would just have to put up with the stumps, along with the huge inconvenience of having to turn over the unbroken soil in between them to plant up my planned kitchen garden as best as I could.

'A good crop of spuds will soon break up dhe soil!' John had laughed. 'Dhat is what we would have done back home on a virgin plot, Mary. Dhat's if we could have found one in dhe first place!'

Apart from potatoes, come spring, I already had it in my mind for the girls and me to plant my garden close to the shanty with the sort of crops that the Indian women grew hereabouts. In one patch they would set Indian corn, beans and pumpkins to grow together. This provided their families with a staple diet to supplement the hunting done by their men. The corn could be made into a sort porridge that proved good with milk, when we could get it, or ground down into meal to make our wheat flour go further.

In time, I could add to my kitchen garden wild strawberries, raspberries and currants—all of which I had been told grew wild in the area. Meanwhile John was hopeful of having several acres of valuable wheat in the ground in no time.

Not only was there our plot to clear, but with our land grant had come the compulsory duty to clear and maintain a set distance of roadway adjacent to it. It was that which would prove a dreadful burden, because clearing and maintaining the road took up invaluable time and effort which was desperately needed for growing food for our table. And John was only one man with only me and young childer to help him.

In many ways, I had already thought that my brother's new lot in this new life would be easier than ours. Thomas had the blessing of grown up sons to help with the burden. And my nephew, John, was bound to soon marry and live in a shanty on his father's land. It would mean that they could collaborate on tasks jointly for their mutual benefits, while to help us out with something required them to lose even more time and investment in labour by having to travel first to us.

While John had not to pay a penny for his Crown grant of land, my brother certainly had to for his. He therefore needed to earn enough money to then pay for that land within the set time allotted by the government. If he failed, then he risked losing both it, his life savings and the future security of his childer.

John had already lost his only income when his pension was commuted, and so we would be forced to live on credit from the store to see us through until to our first harvest the following year. Then we would repay our debts from the surplus. Well, that was the plan, anyway. But to do this, John desperately needed to clear enough land to plant crops, and so the race for *our* survival was on.

The thing with virgin plot, such as ours, was that with it being entirely covered over with huge trees it was hard to see what way the land lay underneath. When approaching Dummer for the very first time, John and I had readily noted the landscape beginning to roll which had been made evident by the rising and falling away of the road. We were not in the least deterred. For what good farmer worth his salt cannot plough on the side of a hill?

However it was not until later, once we had started felling the trees back away from the shanty that the true nature of our own plot was suddenly unearthed. Quickly we discovered that the patch John cleared for himself pitched dreadfully like a deck in a storm at sea. It ran this way and that, alternating betwixt unyielding hummocks of earth and great sodden hollows in the ground which hardly ever dried out. And the lumps of stone which we had thought at first to be a blessing for building a chimney and putting up dry stone walls soon became our curse. John had but to scrape away the surface of the earth with his spade for stone to come peeping out of the ground. At every turn there were masses of rocks and stone – some so large that John swore it would take a whole barrel of black powder to shift them!

'Don't worry Mary, my love.' John tried to reassure me. 'It can't all be as bad as dhis. Not all of it! No, not even the Divil himself could make a whole hundred acres as bad as dhat.'

I had dreaded the first really heavy snow coming, because I had heard from other women – long settled – how harsh and long the Canadian winters are. Their warnings proved true at the end of that first November when the snow came – when it fell by the cartful! But once it had been tramped down though, it did not look nearly so daunting.

We received word that my brother Thomas had had some real luck at hunting and had suddenly found himself with more meat on his hands than he could handle. He had kindly suggested that if John and I were to come to him with a small hand sledge, we could do him a great favour altogether by taking some of the game away with us.

Eagerly, our whole family set out in the brilliant sunshine, walking in our everyday footwear, for at that time we had neither snow shoes nor moccasins. John took the lead and childer and I followed on like his troop.

The girls and I happily took turns at dragging the sled behind us, with the wee boys hitching rides when their little legs gave out on them. When it came to my turn, with my head partially covered by my shawl and bent over as I tramped along, looking down I noticed how the snow below began to suddenly take on a queer, bluish haze-like appearance. And then the imprints of John's previously sharply defined footprints suddenly blurred out of focus. Yet when I quickly lifted my head to look up, my vision changed back to being clear and sharp again.

In what seemed no time all, and hardly feeling the cold, we soon turned out of our lane and onto the Fourth Line, heading towards my brother's homestead. Here and there we passed by trees with branches creaking under blankets of white diamond dust. These sometimes shifted to send showers of fine powdery snow spilling down through the still air like fairy blizzards.

I remember thinking then about how walking that line in the snow was not a bit like walking through Woolwich during the harsh winters that I had experienced there. We had snow a plenty back then, but I had never experienced the thrill of walking upon such a perfect fall as we were that day. Back in England, by the time I had turned out of our miserable house and set out upon those Kentish streets, the snow would already be ugly –

blackened by the tramp of hundreds of other feet. But for sure, wasn't that the case with so many things in England: over used and destroyed by the masses?

As we approached Thomas' lot, we were speeded on by the sight of a tall column of smoke spiralling slowly upwards into the sapphire clear sky. The happy thought of a cosy seat by a warm fireside with hot tea was brewing in my mind.

Isabella had thrown open the door with a great welcome before we had even reached the stoop, and then her youngest childer spilled out from it in all directions with outstretched arms waiting to welcome their little cousins with a hug. It was a typical Hendren welcome!

No sooner were we all across the threshold than John and Thomas were on their way out of the door and heading off to the barn. No doubt my brother wanted to show off his spoils! Isabella and I did not mind in the least: the childer were already playing, which left us with the rare opportunity to sit and catch up with each other's gossip.

Looking about and from what Isabella had already said, Thomas and young John were going great guns about settling their place. With pangs of guilt about feelings I suddenly sensed stirring within my heart, I found myself getting just a wee bit jealous that John and I had so far achieved very little in comparison. It was an ungrateful thought, which I quickly regretted, considering the great generosity that my brother and his wife always showed us.

Isabella and I spoke about the upcoming Christmas. She had insisted that John and I should come to their home with our childer and that we celebrate it altogether as one big family, just as we had in Ballinderry. She even told me that Thomas was already brewing a batch of his best black beer to help it along.

Heading home, with our sledge groaning under the weight of fresh venison, I soon noticed the sky above quickly dull. The wind came up and pinched wet at our warm faces and made me shiver for the first time that day beneath my previously adequate woollen shawl. I pulled it up tighter about my head and shoulders as we pressed homeward a little more keenly than before.

Then the wind suddenly dropped off almost as quickly as it had stirred, leaving a swathe of blue sky above us, but this time now scattered with puffs of pink-tinged clouds. Then the entire firmament coloured up beautifully with swirls of crimson and bright grey all smudged in together, in the way that it only does when sunset is close to hand and there is snow in the offing. Then within minutes, the sky had turned again, this time to a ghostly white.

'I don't like the look of dhat one little bit,' John said. 'We had better hurry up.'

No sooner had he spoken than a sweep of white came down the road from beyond the darkening trees. Then the wind began to speak in growls and groans, sending wet flakes splattering hard against our warm and bare faces with all the force of a slap.

John told the childer to keep in step sharp behind him.

'Keep close,' he said, 'And I will to try to keep some of dhis chill from you.'

Thankfully, we soon turned off the line towards the familiar landmark of a gnarled, old, lightening-struck tree, now fully clothed and softened in white. We were almost home.

At our stoop, we vigorously stamped the snow from off our feet and I shook out my shawl before we burst forth, as one, into the shanty. Without even stopping to unbuckle his greatcoat, John was immediately busying himself fixing the fire.

We warmed ourselves with a brew of tea, the leaves of with we had already steeped several times before.

'Do you t'ink dhat's dhe snow set in now?' I asked my husband.

'I should t'ink so,' he replied. 'Canadian winters are famed to be hard and long, so I should t'ink dhat dhis is the shape of the weather to come until spring.' Then he paused for moment before adding wistfully, 'You know, Mary, I am t'inking now dhat I should have bought dhat pair of snow shoes from the Indians when I had the chance. Maybe I should see if I can't cobble somet'ing like dhem together for you and dhe childer before we go to Thomas and Izzy's for Christmas.'

After that, John and I went back outside to hang the meat from the sledge up high in the rafters of the barn, away from the attention of rats and mice. It would soon freeze solid of its own accord and then keep fresh for months if need be.

'Now dhere's a fine sight, is it not?' John said with a laugh. 'Who would have t'ought it? The likes of us set to dine on venison? Didn't I tell you, Mary my love, dhat we had come to Eden?'

Chapter Twelve

That first winter, we were soon to find, was not to be as other winters. The snows came and went throughout December in fits and starts of freeze and thaw – that completely wrecked the road for waking from our shanty to my brother's home for Christmas Day.

Coming up to Christmas, John had tentatively set off to try to make it up the Forth Line, only to find himself forced to turn back shortly after and arriving back home in a filthy state.

'It's muddy enough for a duck,' he said with a frown as wide as a Monday.

So that was that as far as our hopes of spending a family Christmas went. For us, there would be no Isabella's legendary goose and gravy or Thomas' heavy black beer. Instead, our meagre Witherup celebrations consisted of John wringing our scrawny cockerel's neck for the pot. I was loath to part with one of my fatter handful of hens and to lose any of the few precious eggs that they still occasionally laid.

I also well remember that New Year's Day. It was so warm outside that we were dandering about without even a coat or shawl, and so John took full advantage of this to get ahead with some of his chores. I even found myself throwing open the doors of the shanty, because at times the girls and I could not stand the heat indoors as we cooked.

This strange weather continued for several weeks, but by month's end had turned back as cold as it should have been all along, and snow once more lay deep upon the ground. Then the first day of March came. It was the coldest night and day that either John or I had ever experienced before or since. It was unimaginably cold!

John was in the habit of building up the fire during the winter evenings, and then letting it burn down slowly throughout the night by throwing on a big damp log last thing before bed. Although the fire might have burnt out by morning, it usually served to keep the edge off the cold indoors overnight, without the risk of burning the place down in our sleep.

I remember waking early that morning and hearing little James sobbing his heart out beside me in the bed. His teeth were chattering away ten to the dozen. Only then did I realise that there was hoar frost on my pillow and all across the top of the sheets and blankets. It must have been from where my and John's breath had frozen solid. I sat up and almost immediately started to quake with cold. My chest felt so tight that it hurt to breath. Quickly I reached over and roused John.

'Sweet Hades!' he exclaimed, as the cold hit him, too. 'We have to get some heat in here quickly or we'll die!'

The childer and I huddled together beneath the blankets. I rubbed the boys' arms and legs briskly to try and get their circulation going while Mary Ann and Eliza Jane rubbed each other.

Meanwhile John struggled to get the long dead fire going once more. Once he had, I got up and set about trying to fix some breakfast to warm our chilly insides. I picked up the part loaf of bread that I had left sitting out on the table the night before, only to discover that it had frozen like stone. So instead of trying to use it, I quickly set the Dutch oven to warm by the fire and hastily stirred up the makings for a batch of hot corn bread. Everything that I touched which was made of metal seemed to adhere to my fingers with the cold. It was most annoying.

John wanted to know how much snow had fallen overnight. As he started to rub the condensation away from the widow pane, he found instead that the opaqueness was due to a layer of ice that had formed on the inside of the glass.

Undeterred, he then went across to the door, only to find that he could not open it. It had frozen shut. And then, in his struggle to free it up, John all but ended up kicking the damned thing off its hinges. When he eventually had it open, John was met by so much snow piled up behind it that he had to start digging a way out through it. At least once he had, he could then get out to the barn where we still had most of our meat and supplies stored, and where my chickens were shut away against the cold.

Meanwhile, I boiled up a kettle of snow so that I could brew up some hot tea for us all. As I stood after stooping into the hearth, I clearly heard a sharp 'snap' as my head met with something unexpected. It was John's thick work shirt that I had set out to dry upon a line strung between the rafters the night before. It was now hanging there as stiff as a plank of wood!

John soon came back into the shanty, carrying an armful of logs for the fire.

'T'ank dhe Lord we have a supply of wood to hand in dhe barn!' he exclaimed. 'Because I couldn't be asked to go off searching for any of dhose trees I already logged. I doubt if I could find a frigate hidden out dhere! Dhe snow is dhat deep!

'And my chickens?' I asked worriedly.

'They're fine,' he said. 'All bunched up together in one corner trying to keep warm. But if you are wanting any pork bringing in, Mary, dhat's another matter. I should have to break open a barrel with my axe and try to hack some off. It has frozen into one solid lump!'

John then sat by the fire warming himself with little sips of my welcome brew. Then he again began bemoaning the fact that he had foolishly passed upon the opportunity to purchase those snow shoes that the squaws had offered to trade at our door in October. But winter had seemed so far off then, and John had taken to the notion that the squaws would no doubt call back again some short time later. But of course, it was our bad luck that they hadn't.

Once the fire was roaring, and my family had hot food and drink inside their bellies, we were surprisingly warm and snug in our shanty once more. We had food, warmth and a supply of tallow strips to light our way, so thank God we could afford to sit out the worst of this weather on what stores we already had. In future years, though, we would not always find ourselves so well placed.

It was towards the close of that day that something quite unexpected happened. It was extremely unsettling.

I had just got the younger childer to bed and off to sleep. John was making up his bed close to the fire so that he could keep replenishing it during the night, when suddenly the shanty door flew open to a flurry of snow blowing in and revealing two ominous-looking strangers standing at the threshold. They were Indians.

Without so much as a by your leave, the two of them came inside the shanty shutting the door firmly behind them. I looked at John and John looked at me. Then he stood up calmly and stood by the fire with his hand casually coming to rest upon the stock of his gun which was hanging on the wall above it.

'Good evening, gentlemen,' he said with a smile on his lips and a tone in his voice as relaxed as three whiskeys.

Our unexpected visitors suddenly reached into the sheaves hidden at their sides. Simultaneously, each drew out a long hunting knife which glinted menacingly in the fire light.

I sat clamped to my chair with fear. In my mind I was certain that these men were making ready to murder us, and all I could think about were my childer.

John did not so much as flinch; instead he just stood where he was, looking the strangers straight in the eye. The Indians stared back for what seemed to be an age. Then they suddenly smiled broadly and proceeded to place the knives, joined by two tomahawks and an ancient-looking rifle, at John's feet. Then the two duly took off their fur hunting mantles and planted themselves on the floor by the hearth, where they quickly removed their wet moccasins and set them before the fire to dry.

'Fetch some hot food, Mary,' John said with an even broader smile of relief. 'Dhese two gentlemen look near foundered!'

After an eventless night, at daybreak the Indians departed as suddenly as they had arrived, and without so much as a word having passed between us and them in all that time. We thought no more of our visitors until several days later when John went out of the house one morning, only to almost trip over a fine brace of ducks which had been laid upon the stoop and tied together in the Indian manner. After that, we had no more fear of these people.

It was after that first winter when I noticed that John's arthritis was really beginning to take a heavy toll upon the poor man. It had always been worse in winter anyway, but it had never been as bad as it was then, or as bad as it would become over the winters that followed. The arthritis would near cripple him and have him walking like an old man before his time.

Nights were always the worst for John. All night long he would constantly shift position, trying to ease the pain that unfailingly grew worse as soon as he laid himself down to rest. After struggling to get a little sleep of a night, there followed the painful process of trying to get up and get going again in the morning. I often watched him trying to coax his limbs into movement so that he could get about doing his chores. He was always fretting about getting on with his work.

Usually, come spring, being out of doors and in the natural warmth of the sun, John often seemed to shake off a great deal of his stiffness. However, after that first winter, come spring, his hands did not un-cripple from their winter claw-like condition as much as we had expected. Neither did his creaking knee joints ease back to how they had been even just the autumn before.

With each winter thereafter, John's mobility diminished, and his ability to do that which had come with relative ease when first we had arrived in Dummer swiftly waned. And as his ability to move lessened, so did our ability to clear our land sufficiently to make a good fist out of feeding ourselves.

***

It was at a *bee* that we first came to meet Robert Haighle. He had purchased a plot of land just a short step along the lane from ours on the third Concession, but on an altogether much better parcel of land than we had.

When the Haighles first arrived in Dummer, Robert was sick and as weak as a newborn kitten. For sure, he barely had enough strength in his body to lift a hand to help himself, let alone his wife and wee childer. So we neighbours got together to hold them a *raising bee*, so that at least they would have a roof above their heads in good time before the winter.

95

However, Robert Haighle's troubles had not ended there. For once he had recovered from his initial illness, didn't he then go and cut open his foot so badly with an axe that he was poorly for more than a month or so? Had it not been for my John helping that family out by chopping fire wood, and doing as many chores as he could afford alongside seeing to our own, then the Haighles might have been all the sorrier that winter.

And so, when Robert was fit and well enough to return the favour, he came to us and helped John out one day. But what I hadn't expected was for his wife to then arrive, unannounced, just as I had finished preparing the dinner and then to have the bare-faced cheek to invite herself and their childer to share in *our* family's meal. Then all in all, weren't we to find the Haighles a strange kind of folk indeed, even for Scots. '*Strange*' maybe isn't the right word for what the Haighles were. *Callous* perhaps? Or even '*cold-hearted*' might better suit. But whatever they were, the Haighles were not *our* sort of people. Not the sort of people that John and I would naturally want to forge a friendship with. But then, in the backwoods, one oftentimes finds oneself doing things that don't at first come naturally.

What with Robert coming forward to help us out, and then with the Haighles being such near neighbours, it made it difficult from that time on for John and me to keep ourselves to ourselves, and away from them entirely, without causing much offence all round. For here in the bush it is the unwritten custom that anyone settled on the land is expected to treat his neighbours as a friend, and woe betides anyone who is seen to shun the advance of any neighbourly friendship that is offered. That person would soon find themselves shunned by the community as a whole, which is not an enviable position to find yourselves in. And especially not in such wild place as Dummer, when the opportune assistance of neighbours can so easily come down to a matter of life or death. None the less, it was hard indeed to like the Haighles, even after the tragedies they had already lived through, and were yet to encounter as they forged new lives for themselves in Dummer.

Our passage to Canada, though tediously long and vexingly uncomfortable, had been on the whole thankfully uneventful. But not so was the Haighles' crossing.

'Sixteen days out and '*The Susan*' from Exeter struck us!' Robert exclaimed, as he and his family plundered the dishes of food that I had set out upon the table for my own family. 'Tore a hole in the bow, so it did,' he said, as he continued piling more potatoes onto his already full plate. 'You should have heard our folk screaming! I did nay think we were going to make it at all. I thought the ship was going down to the bottom of the sea for sure!'

'Aye,' Janet chimed in with a mouth full of food, which we could all see slopping around the inside of her mouth as she spoke. 'Aye, that we did – but it didn't!'

'It was nay two days after that our youngest child died,' Robert added, without the slightest hint of emotion either in his voice or on his facial expression. Nor, indeed, was there any shown on the hard, thin face of his wife.

Naturally, at first, I had thought that they were putting on a very brave show for our sake and that of the childer sitting down to eat with us. That is what I had thought, that is until Janet finished chawing on a mouthful of pork and then continued with what her husband had been saying.

'And we threw her carcass in the sea.'

Her 'carcass'? I could hardly believe that a mother could describe her own dead child in such a heartless way. Her *carcass* – as if she had been talking about some insignificant dead lamb she had disposed of, instead of the body of a precious young child. But then the horrible truth about that couple dawned for me. As I watched Robert and

Janet with their remaining hollow-eyed childer, I witnessed little that might pass for love and warmth flowing from either father or mother towards their offspring. *'Her carcass...'* I remember thinking to myself; what on earth could those words be conveying to those poor remaining little mites listening at the table? Were they wondering, perhaps, if they too were worth so little in their parents' affection that, should they die, too, then they also would warrant such tossing aside?

True, the Haighles had been tough hill farmers back in Scotland. They had been born of tough farming stock and therefore expected to be hardened to life. And yet, to me, they were hard far beyond anyone's expectation.

'My mother died too,' Janet said, stretching both arms across the table to help herself to a heap more food, without as much as a sideways glance towards her scrawny little ones whose plates were already scraped clean. 'On Grosse Isle, it was...'

I remembered Grosse Isle well enough. It was a place I was hardly going to forget in a hurry. When our ship had arrived, the health officers from ashore had been on us quicker than ticks on a dog, despite the fact that our ship hadn't experienced a single death or had a soul taken real sick during the passage over.

Then John had learned that there was a terrible outbreak of cholera ashore, and that it was believed to have been brought into the country by immigrants. As a result, no-one was to enter Canada proper until they had spent a proscribed amount of time in quarantine. And then, without so much as a 'by your leave', we then found ourselves being herded into small boats and heading for shore with barely the respect afforded to livestock, let alone human beings.

Looking back from the boats, the view down the mighty St Lawrence River, girded by a long spine of mountains, was simply enough to take your breath clean away. Grosse

Island itself had looked deceivingly beautiful: stony and rugged and sparkling in the sunshine like a polished gemstone. Dotted with wooden houses, to us weary travellers, the island appeared welcome and inviting. Yet had I had not heeded my lesson from St Vincent?

Once we were landed properly on the island, John and I were immediately shocked by the sight of hundreds of unruly and gaunt-looking passengers, and by the din that they made, which was far worse than a flock of gulls on a heap of fish guts.

It was then that we saw the sheds where those poor wretches who were suspected of being infected with cholera were confined. The similarity between those sheds and the cattle pens at the Glenavy slaughter house was not lost upon John and me... not for a moment.

'We'll not be mixing with dhem as we didn't come across with,' John whispered sternly in my ear. 'For heaven alone only knows what disease dhey might be carrying!'

I had clasped my youngest childer tight at my side as John made us hold ourselves back a bit from the rush that the other passengers suddenly made going forwards. My husband made certain that we kept ourselves to ourselves, until he spotted some other ex-soldiers, like himself, who had also been on our ship. They had been thinking likewise, and so from that point on we stayed together as one group and eventually moved ourselves to the furthest limits of the quarantine area of the island, away from the rabble. There, on Grosse Isle, we also had bided until such time as we were deemed fit and well enough to be allowed to continue upon our journey.

Janet said that her mother, Mrs McRoberts, being an old widow with nothing left to hold her in Galloway, had willingly immigrated to Canada with her daughter, so as to be of some use to her and her son-in-law.

'Aye,' Robert Haighle butted in. 'The old bird was well enough in herself. Why, she was even up and walking about right up until the day afore she died...'

Robert went on to explain that their ship, like ours, being full of immigrants, had also been forcibly landed on Grosse Isle. When they had disembarked, the examining doctor had passed them all as being fit and well, and yet even so, they too had found themselves immediately placed into compulsory quarantine. Cholera was again raging so furiously that deaths in the sheds on the island were running at more than thirty a day, while in nearby Quebec it was more than a hundred. Then, with fifteen-hundred detainees under guard upon the tiny island, food supplies were running short. What little there was in the island's store was sold at extortionate prices to its captive customers. And making matters worse, the soldiers had orders to turn every one out from the sheds and into the fresh air during the daytime – no matter how cold or how hot the weather. This meant that these weary and hungry people were left to mercy of the elements, as too were their worldly possessions. This luggage, when left unprotected, was often stolen by thieving opportunists. When old Mrs McRoberts died, the doctor had said it had been due to the effects of being exposed to the elements... and from no other cause.

'Thrown into a great pit, she was, with dozens of others,' Janet explained. 'Pitiful sight, so it was, to see so many survive the journey across only to end up in there.'

The Haighles' seven-year-old daughter had then caught cholera, but against the grimmest expectations she had recovered. Then, on eventually reaching Dummer, all of the family had caught the measles, with Robert having been the most badly affected.

Yet despite this shaky beginning, the Haighles looked set to do very nicely in the future. Only a short way along from our plot, the Haighles parcel of land was far better in every aspect and was quicker to clear and to return the favour with a crop. Less than six months after their arrival, the family already owned a cow, and with Janet earning five shillings a month for milking the cows of others, the Haighles were soon much better off with their fifty acres than we were with our one-hundred, which even after three years of relentless toil, John had hardly broken into. And yet I counted myself far luckier than they were, for I had John and my childer and my brother's family close by, and with them all the love a body could wish for. And, with my loving husband at my side, what was there to bring me fear?

Chapter Thirteen

Those first few years had proved very hard on John and me indeed. For, after the glorious collaboration that raised our shanty, came the stark reality of being left completely reliant upon our own resources to tackle the sudden burden of our innumerable day-to-day tasks. Everyone else newly planted into Dummer was more or less in the same position – struggling to maintain at the very least a subsistent standard of living. Our neighbours and our kin, all stretched almost to breaking point with their own tasks, rarely had time to help out anyone else with theirs – unless of course there was a *real* emergency. When someone else was found to be in serious need, then others could be relied upon to drop their work tools and rally around those in dire need as much as possible. That, then, is the backwoods' way.

Being faced with such a harsh nature as was to be had in these backwoods at Dummer brings about a strange coming together of folk as is rarely to be encountered back in the old country. Here we are cast about with neighbours of great diversity of character and custom – Scots, English, Yankees, and of course us Irish. And then there were those born here, who naturally regard anyone other as incomers, and yet without jealousy. And there are folk of much diversity in Christian faith, too: for I had never experienced before the coming together of Anglicans, Presbyterian, Methodists and the such, under one roof to share their Sabbath in worship together, and to gain succour where and as best they might. Although I must add that the Irish Catholics amongst us settlers kept themselves to themselves of a Sunday, with many choosing to go without churching altogether than to join with 'Proddies'. But John and I fondly experienced a real feeling of camaraderie amongst the settlers of the district – especially so amongst the many ex-soldiers like John.

While upon the subject of soldiers, I am not accusing the authorities of doing anything untoward in the allotting of our soldiers grants of free land, but I always found it a curious thing to see how those played out over time. For didn't it always seem to us that the officers, who in every case received as much as two or three fold the allotment of land that lowly privates like John did, nearly always went on to fare far the better through it? It seemed to me that their land always turned out to be *'luckier'*: luckier because it turned out to take far less clearing, or luckier because it had no swamp to it, or luckier in that it enjoyed a much better aspect altogether, like bordering on water or some other such unfair advantage over ours.

The likes of us near broke our backs and hearts in clearing a plot that, at the end of our labours, proved unable to support enough of a crop to barely even feed us. Of course, one might argue that there was always the value of the timber upon it, but then there was always an over sufficient 'enoughness' of timber in Dummer to make having any barely an advantage. After all, to have value, we first had to fell it and then log it and move it to where it might fetch a bit of a price. And in the meanwhile, you can't feed a body on timber.

Yet there were others that I knew who were worse off than we were. Good men, faithful old soldiers – some missing limbs or even blinded on the battlefield – all had been talked out of their pensions by the Government and into penury upon this *'gift'* of land. A person with half a brain could never expect these disabled men to be able to clear such land as this without the additional support of an income. Many of these men became so very destitute that they were later to be found starving in plain sight of visiting officials, who at first did nothing about their plight. This caused so much anger and resentment in the township and beyond that in the end numerous petitions fell upon the Government, until eventually it was shamed into supplying some relief.

With the advantage of hindsight, John and I had also come to Canada too willingly. We had both believed in the promises that the Army had bandied about – promises of a better future for us and our childer. In reality, I do not think that His Majesty and his Army cared about us at all. I believe that all the English Government wanted was the empty Canadian landscaped filled with settlers; preferably settlers with the experience to form an effective militia should the occasion arise of some future attempt of invasion by American Yankees.

Also to be considered were the great sums of money being drawn down from the Army by way of a pension to *idle* soldiers, and how that expenditure might be cut. There must have been whoops of glee along the corridors of power the sorry day that *the plan* was thought up... the plan to offload worthless lumps of land at the back end of nowhere in Canada to these unwanted soldiers, in return for their hard-earned pensions. But surely it would have served both the Government and the country better to have let our men retain their pensions, at least for as long as it took for them to start making a living from the land, instead of leaving us to our fate as it had.

I watched my John. I watched his face as he continued with his never-ending struggle to plant our crops, to chop our wood, to do the multitude of tasks that other fit folk could take in their stride, but which he no longer could do. He was a proud man who had served his country long and well. No battle could break him; not in mind, not in body, not in spirit. Yet that brutal land in Dummer was now breaking him by degrees, and I could hardly bear to watch the destruction of my man.

We had so counted our blessings on first coming to Canada, as we dared to believe that for once in our lives we were masters of our own destiny. Yet, almost from that first day in Dummer, it soon became as if everything we touched went from gold to tin. Come that first spring, we only got half of the chitted potatoes planted on time, because John was so ill with the ague. The task had then fallen instead to Mary Ann and me, while Eliza Jane minded her sick father and helped care for her brothers. It proved to be a task beyond us. Mary Ann and I had tried our best, but although the plot intended for the potatoes had been cleared, John had not yet broken all of the ground. In desperation, my daughter and I took a pick to it, but we had neither the muscle nor the stamina to do it all. And with my brother's family struggling to plant their own crops, it would have been very unfair of us to impose upon them with pleas to come to help us with ours.

John's first planting of winter wheat failed. The Indian corn came up bothered by big white pustules filled with black ooze, and everything else was cursed with what looked like rust, which covered leaves and stems and made them crisp, curl up, and then die. Everything, that is, which had survived the onslaught of attacks by mice, squirrels and wicked beasties they have here that go by the name of *racoons*.

Not one single year after that did our crops fulfil even our modest expectations. Instead, they fell foul to late springs, late frosts, rain, drought, pests, or disease. And so at the end of a season there was never enough of anything produced to both feed us and have a margin left over to sell to help pay off our debts. Life became ever more difficult as we slid further onwards down the slippery slope towards ever greater hardship. No more could we afford the luxury of tea or coffee. Instead, the girls and I turned our hands to digging up and drying out dandelion roots, which we roasted and ground to become our substitute beverage. Acorns eked out our flour and I sought out as many wild foods in season as I could, and I re-invented recipe after recipe to try to accommodate them.

I watched the pain in John's face as he swallowed his pride and eventually went to my brother to beg for help. But by then it was too late. We had slipped too far into debt with the store and were unable to pay it off at year's end without asking immediately again for credit with the very next breath. We were losing. It was the beginning of the end of our battle to hold on to our precious land.

By the end of the fourth year, we had already been forced into the position of having to let go of our Mary Ann. She went to work out as a farm servant in Douro. I was loathe to lose her help in the field and the house, but as the eldest of our childer she felt keenly that it was her duty to go away to ease our burden and to send some money home.

Then one day a couple of strangers arrived at or homestead. From the shanty window I saw John, who was already outside chopping wood, put down his axe and go to see what it was that they wanted. I stayed inside, but all the while watched the strangers with the curiosity of a cat. It was the woman that drew my attention the most.

Electa was her name. It was a name as fancy as the fine leather boots I noticed peeping out from under the hem of her skirt, as her feet rested upon the kick board of her equally fancy wagon.

'Sure,' I thought to myself, 'but haven't them Yankees always the God-given knack for appearing to be a cut above the rest of us!'

Electa stepped down and immediately made her way towards our shanty ahead of her slower and less obvious husband, who instead quietly introduced himself to John as Timothy Curtis Haskell, before then following on behind his wife like a subdued dog.

106

I had the door opened only a crack, but before I knew it, Electa was all the way through it and into the house. I was dumbstruck as she then casually removed her glove, and began to run her fingertips along the edges of the furniture and mantle looking for dust. I was mortified at the cheek of the woman and about to serve her up a piece of my mind on the sharp edge of my tongue when she suddenly turned to me and remarked as bold as brass; 'It's a clean house that you keep, Mrs Witherup. I commend you on your cleanliness.'

What could I say after that? I did not know whether to be cross with the woman or flattered.

'Your family came highly recommended to me by an acquaintance in Douro,' she continued, 'who said that of all the shanties in Dummer I should expect to find yours the most orderly kept. And I am not disappointed.' With that, Electa Haskell smiled. It was the most beautiful smile that a body could smile, even for a Yankee.

Who on earth, I had then wondered, could know what the inside of my house was like? Then it hit me. This acquaintance of Mrs Haskell's must be one of the very same folk where my Mary Ann worked.

'And that is why I have come to see you,' Electa continued. 'I would very much like to hire your daughter as a house-maid.'

'A house maid?' I replied. 'Not a farm servant?'

'No,' she said emphatically. 'I have farm labourers enough. What I am in need of is a *personal* maid for household duties only. Someone I can rely upon completely. And in return for that I am willing to pay top dollar. And I also promise to keep her respectably clothed and shod. So?' she smiled again, 'What do you say, Mrs Witherup? Would you trust your precious daughter to me?'

I called for Eliza Jane who up until then had kept herself hidden out of sight behind our curtain divider. Out she stepped and introduced herself while Electa looked her up and down as if she were buying herself a horse at market.

'She looks a real credit to you, Mrs Witherup. And I would be more than pleased to hire her for seven dollars a month, that is if she would find me agreeable enough to work for?'

If my daughter would find *her* agreeable enough? I knew from the moment that those words left Electa's mouth that Eliza Jane would be treated well. Any qualms that I might have first harboured about the woman disappeared in an instant. Besides, seven dollars a month was a powerful good offer of money indeed.

In time I would learn that Electa Haskell had been born in Vermont, in the United States of America, to a wealthy family who owned both a saw and a gristmill there. And that at the time of our first meeting, Electa's father, Timothy Johnson, was still alive and living with his daughter in Canada. He was almost ninety years of age and had fought under George Washington against the British in the War of Independence.

'I can still remember the party my parents gave in Vermont in celebration of the coming of the new century,' Electa later recalled. 'We held a dance at our home and were led in a merry jig by an old fife player from the Revolutionary Army. Then, as I recall, one of the guests fired his pistol up into our old log chimney. You should have seen the black blizzard that tumbled down and covered him from head to feet in soot. Oh how we howled with laughter!'

Exactly what circumstance had then led Electa and her family to turn their backs upon America and to settle instead in the then wild place known as Smith Creek over in Durham County? I never did find out. I can only think that perhaps they had somehow become disillusioned with their new and independent America, for them to have willingly chosen to return to live within the British fold.

Whatever the reason, in the March of eighteen-hundred-and-three, the Haskell family moved to Canada and became one of the first five white families settled in that particular place, which eventually became the Township of Hope. And that is how Eliza Jane came to live in Hope, and how our Witherup family got involved with the Haskells.

After Eliza Jane's going, we struggled on with trying to clear more land; at least enough, we hoped, to pay off our mounting debts. But with John's relentlessly advancing arthritis, this proved impossible.

However, we were not alone in our miserable fortune. Indeed, a petition had already been sent to the Government questioning the wisdom of having lured so many disabled ex soldiers out of their pensions and onto such wretched hard land that even fit and young able bodied men were finding difficult to conquer. It accused the Army of having stripped its wounded and disabled soldiers of their meagre pensions and then knowingly abandoning them to their fate in the wild woods. But too late for us came a reinstatement of partial pensions for those in the deepest distress on the land, for that year, on December thirty-first, eighteen-forty, John was forced to sell half of our grant of land to William Clysdale. Then, not long after, we lost the rest of our land, bar one small parcel on which our homestead stood, which instead we were allowed to rent back. John's dream of being a land owner was finally dead.

My bother Thomas' family plot was thriving though. Even so, after eight years of hard toil and all of the advantages he had over us, out of my brother's one-hundred acres, he and his sons had still only managed to clear thirty acres together.

Chapter Fourteen

He was crushed by a falling tree in eighteen-forty-two. It had been rotting and listing and one that he had been meaning to fell for some time. He just hadn't got around to it yet. So it killed him instead.

Robert Haighle had been barely alive by the time his eldest daughter, Margaret, had discovered him lying under the great tree trunk and run out along the road to raise the alarm. Perhaps mercifully for Robert, by the time my John, and our other close neighbours had got to him, he was stone dead. For with the dreadful injuries that Robert had received, one can only imagine the extent of the cruel agonies he suffered in his final moments.

While the men folk saw to the practicalities of retrieving Robert's shattered body from under the tree, we women prised Janet and his still screaming daughters away from his corpse. We led them back up to the house; there we plied both the childer and a shock-silenced Janet with sweet tea laced liberally with whiskey. I helped to fetch and carry things and helped care for the Haighles' two youngest daughters, four-year-old Elizabeth and little Mary, who was barely two, until Robert was buried. A week later, Janet was able to manage the family by herself. Yet in all that time, I never did see their second eldest daughter, Ellen, shed a single tear or indeed show any emotion at all.

I can not say that, in the wake of her husband's death, I saw a softer side to Janet either. Although, just for a moment or two, I thought that I had.

'I will never get over my husband's death,' she said to me one day, but then went on to qualify what had momentarily seemed to be heart-felt words with, 'for we are very lonesome for any work that needs doing about the place. And to hire in labour is such a cost!'

Life was hard for Janet Haighle, and I must admit that a lesser woman would have buckled under half the strain. She had to sell off all the pork that she had worked so hard to produce that season in order to settle up some debts incurred by her husband's death. As well as that, she had to part with her oxen. Even so, this still left her much better off than a good many others I can name who were struggling to make ends meet in Dummer – including ourselves.

Janet had two cows, two heifers, four sheep, and two pigs. And out of Robert's fifty acre plot, seven were now cleared and under cultivation. It was sad though, to see her young daughters struggling with the threshing after their father's death. So hard, that although we urgently needed our fifteen-year-old son James ourselves, I loaned him to Janet, to help her family out for time. However, I am almost certain that it will prove to be a kindness that will not go unpunished.

The year of Robert Haighle's tragic death was also the year in which our daughter Eliza Jane got married. She wed Wallace Haskell – Electa Haskell's nephew. And Eliza Jane's marriage would not be the only union between us Witherups and the Haskells. For on the tenth of February, eighteen-forty-five, our son Thomas married Wallace's sister, Wealthy. A year later, they presented us with our first grandson, named John in honour of his grandfather. And I never did see a prouder grandfather than my, dear John!

So for two of our childer at least, there would be no looking back. Both were settled in the Township of Hope and thriving upon the fertile land there. Both were welcomed with open arms and hearts into their new Yankee family, and both could hold their heads as high as any of their neighbours.

In short, with or without our initial grant of land, Thomas and Eliza Jane were now living the life that John and I had always dreamed for them. For that, John and I were eternally grateful. Although our own lot in this country has been bitterly hard at times, John's and my sufferings have paled away into insignificance amongst the happiness and pride that we now feel for these childer. Although, for me, my happiness would have been complete if only I had not held such worries for the future of our youngest son, James.

'I fear for him, I really do!' I confided in John one day.

'Why, he's a fine fit lad?' was his reply.

'Yes, but he is easily led,' I explained.

'Led? By whom?'

'Dhat Haighle girl – Ellen. She's awful bold with him, John, and I do not like her one little bit. She's not right, you know. I've known dhat since her father died. Do you know, she did not cry at all?'

'Not right for James?'

'Not right for anyone. John, dhere is something... something awful dark and festering in dhat one dhat I would not want James to be a party to when it eventually comes out!'

'Is dhat so?' John laughed. Then, still laughing, he tried to reassure me that James was nobody's fool and would surely soon take up his brother's offer to go work with him in Hope, and that like Thomas and Eliza Jane, James would no doubt end up settling down there too.

'Dhem Haskells is a big family,' John added. 'I am certain dhat dhere is a fine lass among dhem just waiting to meet our James!'

***

I was so busy feeding my hens that I did not hear my husband creep up behind me.

'Will you come for a dander widh me Mary?' John said, slipping his arms around my waist, and pulling me close to himself.

'A dander widh you, is it?' My husband's request had taken me completely by surprise. 'And where were you t'inking of taking this stroll?'

'Perhaps down to Indian River?'

'Dhat's a tidy step away for just a stroll, John?'

'I was t'inking of perhaps making a day of it. Just you and me, Mary.'

'Just you and me? Walking all dhat way to Indian River just for dhe crack of it? And what about your poor legs?'

'Never you mind my legs,' John breathed softly in my ear, as he nibbled gently on the lobe. 'My legs are fine, so dhey are. I have had a summer full of warmth on 'em, Mary, and I would like to be giving dhem all the use I can before dhe damp and cold has me stiffened up again. Besides, can't a man take his best girl away for a picnic? Tell me, when was the last time we did such a t'ing?'

'Tell me John,' I said playfully, pushing him away and continuing to throw the grain I had caught up in my apron to the chickens, 'when exactly was it dhat you last asked? Besides which I have a heap of chores around this place to do without gallivanting off with dhe likes of you, you old fool!'

'But isn't it the wonder of wonders dhat chores are always with us, Mary?' he said sidling up to me close again 'When days like this are not. Look up dhere in dhem trees. Look, dhe leaves are already beginning to turn. Come on!' he goaded. 'Come on. Take off your apron, woman, and come away widh your man for dhe day...'

And so I did.

113

At Indian River the breeze rose up in gasps. As it did, the sunlight played upon it like a shoal of dazzling, diamond fish breaking the surface. On an island set like a jewel, haggled trees stooped down their weary boughs to all but sip at the cool, clear water.

John and I walked on a ways to our favourite place to wonder at the natural pavement of great stone slabs set at impossible angles. Sometimes laughing, sometimes slipping or loosing our footing, we scrambled along it like little childer at play as it meandered in and out of the tree line. Now and then we stopped at the caves and pot holes dotted along the way to listen to the water rushing by below. This place is so mysterious and magical that it is held in great reverence by the local Indians and unfailingly spikes the curiosity of settlers like us.

Then by a stand of fire-tinted sumac, John and I came across a clutch of native women. They acknowledged us momentarily with a glance and a smile before busily continuing to gather wild foods from amongst tangle of bushes. One woman had a sleeping baby strapped fast to her back, oblivious to his mother's frantic bobbing as she stripped branches of their treasures. Meanwhile, a small, beady-eyed child who was clutching at the buckskin dress of another giggled at John as he suddenly pulled a mischievous face for her. At times like this I am minded never to forget how great is the debt that we owe these gentle people, for without those skills that they have taught us white incomers, like John and me, would not be settled in Canada now.

I do not think that until that moment I had realised just how much I was coming to love this backwoods country. Over my past years in Canada, I have come to recognise that the forest that envelopes our lives is a living entity in its own right: that these woods which at times are capable of filling me with such dread when on my own, in the company of others never fail to instil within me awe and wonder at every turn. From the teeth marks of beavers left upon the trunks of fallen trees that would have foxed a man to fell, to the scampering antics of slinky black and grey squirrels as they furiously gather up Jack cones for the winter; from the majesty of bull and cow moose with their curious calves, to the strangely gnarled trunks of ancient trees; snow hares, lynx and grey-horned owls - I have come to learn that each have their part to play within this great living entity.

I have learned that this is a place that neither summer drought nor fire can destroy, for in the wake of both, Mother Forest immediately springs forth with new growth. Nor does she succumb to the vicious Canadian winters that can freeze over a flowing river with as much as three feet of ice. Defiantly Mother Forest instead stands resplendent, clothed in her wintry white gown and crowned with a diamond-stud halo of hoar frost as patiently she bides her time until spring comes once more to redress her glorious green for the summer until, as now, she turns once more towards her stunning Autumn display of reds and golds.

Walking on, John suddenly took up my hand and then turned to me and asked, 'Do you regret coming here, Mary?'

'For a walk widh you?' I laughed.

'No, Mary,' he said with a look like a doe deer. 'Don't tease. I meant coming here to Canada?

'Regrets?' I said. 'Well for sure I have had a few regrets. I wouldn't be human if I hadn't, would I? But on the whole, John, what regrets I have had are not worth dhe bodher of lingering over.'

'Don't you sometimes get to t'inking that we should have stayed put in Antrim?'

'And what for?' I exclaimed. ''Tis as hard to be scratching out a living back there as it has been for us here. T'ink of all dhe recent letters dhat have been coming to folk around us talking about dhe blight upon dhe crops back in dhe old country? And of famine, and dhe utter hopelessness of it all? Would you have wanted dhat for our childer, John? Because I for one would not! T'ings can only get better for dhem here. Look at our Eliza Jane and Thomas and dhe fine position dhey are in.'

'But we had such high hopes for dhis land, Mary,' he continued, lowering his head like a shamed dog. 'And I have failed you all by not being able to make a proper go of it.'

'You haven't failed, John,' I said, lifting his hand to my lips and then kissing it. 'Failing is having a dream but dhen lacking the courage to go after it. You went after your dream, John.'

Then I lifted his stubbly chin and looked him straight in the eye.

'John,' I said, 'I have not once seen you idle for idleness's sake; or shirking from your responsibility towards either me or our childer. I know dhat you have always done your best for us and dhat is all dhat can be asked of any man. It's not your fault dhat you had a Herculean task set before you dhat even Hercules himself would have struggled with! T'anks to the Army blinding us widh worthless promises we did not get dhe farm dhat we had dreamed of but dhe reality is, dhat in spite of it all, we are far better off here dhan ever we would have been back in Ireland. No John, I have no regrets in following either my man or his dream.'

With that I held him in my arms for what seemed like an age. I felt so suddenly close that, for the life of me, I could not bear to let my husband go.

Meanwhile, John and I hadn't noticed the weather changing. Above us the blue sky was slowly bleaching to grey. So we hurried on to take shelter by a large tree, just in time before the heavens opened and rain hissed down upon the leafy canopy above us like a thousand angry snakes.

I let slide my shawl and carefully laid it out upon the mossy mound beneath the tree. There, John and I sat for a spell as we waited for the shower to pass by. He pulled my blue kerchief from out of his pocket and unwrapped the hunk of bread and cheese that I had hurriedly fetched from the kitchen table just before we had left home. He handed it to me and I broke it in two, passing him back a share. We devoured that scant fare as if we were feasting upon the finest banquet – and instead of quaffing wine we made merry upon the pure contentment rising within us.

Soon the rain eased into a soft pitter-patter, but we were by then in no hurry to be on our way. John turned to me and, smiling, said, ''Tis soft now, Mary, isn't it? Soft like an Antrim mist.'

'Yes', I replied, 'So it is, John.'

'Do you remember, Mary my love, how we walked to Lough Neagh after dhe banns had been read and we were about to marry? And how we stopped under a tree just like dhis one to kiss and cuddle?'

'I certainly do!' I laughed back.

'And do you remember dhat woman come by...'

'Mrs Dooley?'

'Aye, dhat's it, Old Mrs Dooley. Remember dhat stare of hers dhat she gave us?'

'Dhat I do!' I replied.'Dhe ol' bat had an evil eye on her dhat would have frightened Lucifer himself!'

John laughed as he tried to mimic the look. 'Eye, dhat she had!'

We both fell about giggling heartily like a couple naughty childer.

'Come here,' John said softly, as he gently pulled me to himself and folded me into his arms. 'Kiss me, my Mary. Kiss me, my beautiful girl!'

So I did. And then, as he pressed his mouth hard upon mine, he gently laid me down upon my back.

'Will you stop it, you old fool!' I told him, giving his wandering hand a real tap as I sat bolt upright again.

'Stop what, Mary?' he replied, with his hand creeping up and over my shoulder, as a great smile beamed across his face.

'Your fooling around, John Witherup,' I told him sharply. 'We are much too old for malarkey amongst dhe bushes!'

'No we're not,' he said, pulling me down beside him once more and planting a great, long, passionate kiss upon my lips.

I raised myself up again so that he had to break off. 'And supposing somebody happens along and catches us?' I said.

'So what if dhey do?' he said. 'What are dhey going do about it? Run off and tell our mammies? Dhere is no law against a man laying down widh his wife. Besides,' he added, as he began to kiss me again, 'dhere is no-one around...'

The rain stopped, but we did not.

I wanted to tell him then and there. I wanted to share with him that which had been weighing so heavy upon my mind of late, but it did not seem right for me to spoil his happiness. That day, I knew, would soon become a cherished memory for him; a time to look back upon with warmth and smiles when the sun had gone out of his life. How could I take that from him? How could I taint that memory with what I had to tell him? That precious day would all too soon be gone. What I had to say to him would keep. And so, instead, I let my husband take his pleasure while he could. The most important thing then was that we had each other, and so long as we had one another, then nothing could ever dampen our spirits, or take away the love that our hearts held for each other. No matter how cruel the elements were that were already closing in about us.

As we made our way homeward, more clouds came on to swiftly swallow up the last fleeting patches of blue.

'You can almost smell dhe season changing,' John said.

John was right. I could smell it; suddenly all about me I could smell the faint odour of death and decay upon the rising breeze. And I knew that I was powerless to stop it, just as I was powerless to stop the gathering clouds overhead. All I could do was to bide my time while nature took its course.

***

About the shanty, the few remaining trees are bear, yet the branches are still strung with whispering memories. Somewhere, off in the distance, excited shrieks carry in the still cold air to unhearing ears. Childer are casting boiling maple syrup upon the snow[11] to make a holiday treat of taffy.

While others spend this Christmastide steeped in joyous festivity, my John quietly keeps to the house while I, in turn, bide outside in the barn. There, in peaceful repose, I wait patiently for him to come to me. Eventually he does so.

John approaches the long cedar box that he has painfully hewn and lovingly fashioned with his own aching hands. Then, through a haze of tears he slides open the lid and in broken whispers says; 'Oh Mary, my darling... my darling girl. What am I going to do widhout you now?'

Then he reaches in and caresses my snow-white cheeks with his lips before lightly kissing my ice cold mouth.

---

[11]   The result is a sort of instant toffee treat much enjoyed by pioneer children.

Outside the ground is as hard as iron, and so I will not reach my welcome rest clothed in sacred earth until once more it yields to the spade come spring. Until then, my husband has my company still, and I have him.

I want to tell John not to grieve. I want to tell him that he has no need to touch me to feel me; just as there is no need for him to open his eyes to see me. I *am* with him; I shall always be with him. So long as I am in his heart and in his mind, I shall never be far away. And I shall never leave this place. For this land and I are now one.

End

Mary Ann's Story

Mary Ann's story.

Mary Ann Wetherup was born in the Township of Dummer, Ontario in 1850.

Chapter One

That's the trouble with the past. It is like a damned wasp that buzzes about you at a church picnic- try as you might, you just cannot shake it off. Or worse still, if you get to thinking that you have, then there it is, suddenly come back to sting you. That is how it was with me and my past. I just could not shake it free.

It came back one day when I least expected it. I had been in town shopping and minding my own business; carrying my baby Frank in my arms and with my little daughter, Lily, holding on to my skirts as she walked at my side. When all of a sudden a man stepped onto the sidewalk in front of me and blocked my way. Then, within the space of the few, short moments that followed, he snatched my life away from me...

I had first arrived in Bruce County with my family some fourteen years before. I had come there to start a brand new life. And for the first time ever I was hoping to find what true happiness really meant.

My life had not been happy in any sense of the word for a very long time: not since I was a very young girl growing up far away in Dummer Township, near Peterborough. At least back then I had my grandmother Witherup to watch over me and to keep a check on my welfare. After Grandma died, I was left to the mercy of my mother – a woman for whom the word 'mercy' meant little more than a cuss. Then in eighteen-eighty we moved to Bruce and I was suddenly 'born anew'.

We settled in quietly with my aunt's family on her small farm in Amabel. There I was suddenly free to be like any other twenty-one-year-old woman; going to the harvest dance, giggling and trying to catch the eye of a future husband. Then I met William Norton and fell head over heels in love with him, only to immediately fall foul of his mother.

Harriet Norton was of strict Wattenberg stock; hard-working, God-fearing people who were intent on their son, William, marrying into the same. Mrs Norton held a very low opinion of us 'Irish', and so she was determined to suppose me as being little more than a divil in a petticoat and a threat to her plans for her son.

'But Mary Ann was born here,' William had argued in my defence, and argued quite intensely from what he later told me. 'She was born here just as I was. So that does not make us Dutch or Irish but Canadian.'

'Those people are not like us,' his mother countered, 'and that cannot be bred out by simply being born in another country. Those Irish are notorious for their bad ways!'

'But her kin, the Esplins and the MacLean's, are well known here,' William tried to reason. 'They are good people who work hard...'

'You cannot judge this girl by her kinfolk alone...'

'But isn't that exactly what you are doing, Mother?'

'Now, William!' his father, Levi, rebuked him soundly. 'Did I bring you up to talk to your mother this way?'

'Sorry father. It's just... it's just that if mother only got to know Mary Ann, then she would grow to love her, I am certain.'

'Love? What do you know of love? You walk out with this first girl you see and suddenly you are in love! I don't trust this girl. There is something... I don't know what exactly... but there is something wrong about Mary Ann. She is just not like the other young women her age. There is something... something that sets her apart from them... Haven't you noticed how the other young women have so very little to do with her?'

'That is their doing, Mother, and not Mary Ann's. They are only jealous because she is so much prettier than they are. And they make it hard on Mary Ann to socialize with them because they all grew up here and Mary Ann is a newcomer.'

'No. It's not that,' Mrs Norton had replied. 'They see her for what she is. She is a user, William. She only wants you for your prospects. And I will not hear anymore talk of you marrying her!'

I took on board all that William had confided in me. I knew that if I were going to win out over his mother, then I would have to tread very carefully with him indeed. I needed to maintain *his* faith in me and to redouble my efforts to hold onto my tongue and not to give into the temptation to counter any future attack that his mother might make upon my character. Instead, I knew that I needed to meet any such scorn by praising Mrs Norton's virtues when speaking to William – by saying that she was a good mother to be worrying after her son's welfare, and that I was certain, given time, she would come around to seeing that I meant him no harm and instead only good.

Then, one evening in the middle of supper, Pa had dropped his lightening bolt.

'We are packing up and heading back to Hope just as soon as we are done helping your aunt in with the harvest...'

'What?' I gasped. 'But we have only just settled here...'

'Your ma isn't so well,' he explained, as he passed around the bowl of barely boiled potatoes. 'And she is pining to go to back to Hope. So...'

I said nothing. I just tried hard to swallow my food as well as I might with a stomach that was suddenly tightening up like a noose and choking the very happiness from out of me. If I was certain of one thing at that moment: it was that I had no intention of going back to living in Hope. I was beyond that now, and firmly decided that I was going to stay in Bruce and to finally live *my* life on *my* terms. I did not care that I might never see my mother again. Instead, I would now use all of my womanly guile to try to woo William into marrying me. I would also make an extra effort to get along with the other young women and go out of my way to befriend them, if it helped to win over William's mother. I would even consider letting the skittish one amongst them braid my hair, as she had once suggested, or even let her tie it up with damned ribbons if that is what it would take. I would 'join in' wherever I could, and endure their endless drivel – engaging in their mindless conversation over such frilly trivia as seemed to occupy their silly minds. And I would make absolutely certain never to talk negatively about Mrs Norton to anyone. I wanted to settle down with William so desperately that I think I would have done *anything* in my power to see that I made that happen.

'I love you so much!' I whispered breathlessly in his ear at our next clandestine meeting. 'So much so that I have cried myself to sleep at night, feeling that my heart is breaking at the very thought of us having to part...'

'Having to part?' He exclaimed with a look of horror. 'But why should we have to part, Mary Ann?'

'For one,' I said tearfully, 'on account of the way your poor mother feel towards me. I would never want to cause any heartbreak between you and her on my account. I just couldn't live with myself if I did that to you.'

'Oh, you are so kind and patient, Mary Ann! If only *she* knew you the way that I do.'

'Well, sadly that will never happen now...'

'Why?' he asked, sounding even more alarmed. 'Why do you say that, my love?'

'Because my ma is ill, and my pa wants to take my family back to Hope.'

'And you want to go with them?'

'No! Of course I don't, William. But what choice do I have?'

'We could get married, Mary Ann,' he said. 'You are of age and so am I. I don't need my parents consent to marry you if I have a mind to...'

'But your mother... She would be so very upset.

'I don't care!' William said hotly. 'I love you and I won't let you go. But what about your parents, Mary Ann? Do you think they would give us their blessing?'

'Ah, well that's an entirely different thing completely,' I reassured him. 'I talk about you all the time and they say that it pleases them no end to see me in such good company and so happy. I am more than certain that they would give us their blessing.'

'Really! I had no idea!' William's face suddenly beamed as if he had just bobbed the biggest apple in the barrel. 'That is wonderful news, Mary Ann! Yes, then we shall do it! I shall tell my parents tonight. I'll tell them just as soon as I get home. I'll do anything, Mary Ann,' William said, grasping my hands in his. 'I will do anything to keep you here, my love...'

So with doe eyes I kissed him full on the mouth, as long and lingering as any man would wish. And while I did, I gently guided his hands to my breasts as I then deliberately leaned my body in to press hard against his as a foretaste of what delights were to come. Judging from his sudden breathlessness, I knew that had the desired effect. He was hooked. And so in the December of eighteen-eighty-one, William and I were married in the Presbyterian Church at Amabel, much to the continued misgivings of Levi and Harriet Norton.

With the arrival of our first baby, Robert Arthur, the following October, thankfully Mother Norton's attitude softened completely. Little Robert was such a beautiful baby that his Grandma and Grandpa Norton soon doted on him entirely, as they also did on his little brothers and sisters who soon followed him into the world over the next dozen years or so. And my life...my life was just as I had wanted.

Then came that day and that wretched man. He stopped me in the street and, in full hearing of the townsfolk, shouted at the top of his voice; 'Well now! As I live and breathe, if it isn't the notorious Mary Ann Wetherup?'

'I'm sorry, Sir,' I replied quietly, hoping and praying that he would follow my lead and at least lower his voice, 'but I am afraid I haven't a notion of what you're talking about.'

With that, I stepped to the side and quickly tried to steer little Lily past him. But he again impeded me – by coming to stand in front of me once more and continuing his barrage of unwanted attention. The brute leaned into me and was so close by then that I could smell the rankness of his vile whiskey-sodden breath in my face.

'Come on Mary Ann?' he slurred. 'You never used to be this shy back in Hope.'

'Go away!' I said, in a voice louder than I had intended it to be. 'Go away, you are frightening my children!'

Then, frantically, and unaware of the gathering crowd of onlookers, I tried to push past him. Somehow I managed to wriggle by and stepped sharply off down the street to make my escape. To my utter horror as I did so, this fellow shouted after me at the top his voice. 'Whore! You filthy whore, Mary Ann!'

His words cut me like a knife. As I hurried on, my back seemed to be burning from the countless stares now fixed upon me. I realised with dread and a chilling certainty that *it* was not going to end there.

'You know me full well, Mary Ann!' my assailant screeched on. 'And I know you! You murderer!'

Chapter Two

On Saturday, November the first, eighteen-seventy-nine, the *Daily Guide* newspaper screamed out the headline: *'Inquest on the body of a mutilated child to be held today – A horrible theory...'*

A dead child found mutilated on Halloween – if anything was certain to get emotions running high, this was it! A baby had been found slaughtered on the Divil's own holiday – so of course the newspapers jumped on the story.

A Coroner's inquest, to see if foul play was suspected, duly opened that afternoon at Moon's School close to where the body had been found. The school house was only a short stride away from my family's old home on Grey's Farm, near Garden Hill. It was the same school house that my younger brother and sisters had erratically attended whenever Ma was in a mind to let them.

I was not present that Saturday, but I gathered from all accounts that the tiny school room had struggled to hold the enormous number of people who had braved the bitter cold in the hope of hearing about the grisly murder. Those who managed to cram inside were not disappointed. It was indeed a case of murder to be investigated, but without a suspect, and with nobody knowing who the baby was, the inquest had to be quickly adjourned until more evidence could be found. Yet enough had been said to allow the *Daily Guide* to eagerly follow up its original article with another one – this time reporting upon gruesome details of the injuries inflicted upon the young victim. It was such a sensational report that, although not going as far as to name the person suspected of committing such a terrible atrocity, the newspaper did, however, provide enough information to leave no doubt in the minds of local folk as to the identity of the culprit. And that person was me.

That is how I found myself hailed as a monster overnight, and suddenly to have become the most hated and reviled person in the district. So much so, that by the time the authorities had turned up at the hotel in Port Hope where I was working to take me, I had to be given an armed escort to bring me back to Garden Hill to face questioning. Otherwise they feared that I might be grabbed by an angry mob and lynched on the spot.

Though still bitterly cold and with snow in the air, the resumption of the inquest on the following Thursday, drew a vast number of people, not only from the local area but all across Durham County. Such had been the effect of the *Daily Guide* article that the case of the murdered baby was now the stuff of almost every conversation and fuel for unstoppable gossip and speculation. The ghoulish appetite of the public at large to know more was insatiable. So much so that after the witnesses had been admitted to the School House, an impromptu 'ballot' for the few remaining spaces inside resulted in a hoard of bystanders jostling outside in a desperate bid to get in, while guards had to be posted at the doors to prevent them from doing so.

Warmed by hot coffee, generously supplied by the school mistress from a small portable wood stove, many people who found themselves shut outside chose to stay anyway and to brave the bitter cold – just to be amongst to first to hear details of what was being said inside; chilling details which were relayed to them like a string of Chinese whispers from inside.

Long before the inquest resumed, I had already been spirited into the School House by way of a side door and secreted into what was then the school mam's private parlour. Through a flimsy diving wall, from there I was able to later hear every word that

130

was said in the makeshift courtroom next door without any but the authorities having the faintest notion that I was even present in the building.

I had been held in that room for hours already before the inquest started, and although I was extremely hungry, I had not even been offered so much as a bite to eat as evening began to draw on. Instead I had been left there, locked in and alone, with only the wondering of what was going to happen next to sate my appetite.

The Coroner, Robert Maxwell, resumed the proceedings by recalling the physician, Dr Weston Leroy Herriman, to the stand. Then he asked the doctor to relate again his findings of his autopsy on the infant. This he duly did, but with such ambiguous sounding medical terms and with such long and strange words that I doubt if many present could understand much of what he had said. That is until Coroner Maxwell then asked the doctor at his conclusion; 'And in your learned opinion, Doctor Herriman? To what do you attribute this infant's death?'

'In my opinion,' he calmly replied, 'wilful murder. This child was born alive and well and yet met with a most unnatural, painful and horrible death.'

With that, I heard the commotion on the other side of the door explode. Someone cried out and I heard a loud thud- a woman had fainted. Others in the room were apparently so visibly outraged by this revelation that Coroner Maxwell quickly ordered a short recess before the inquest could get underway again. The School House doors were flung open to the clear starlit sky so that frosty calm might begin to cool the heated clamour now flared within.

Peeking out from my room I watched people spill outside. Some huddled in a small group under the window, where I crouched to one side listening to their eagerly exchanged comments about the evidence that they had just heard. Meanwhile, the ushers were struggling to keep the jurors segregated so that they might not have their own thoughts 'contaminated' by those openly being voiced all about.

When the proceedings were resumed, Maxwell spoke in his calming manner – appealing to those present not to allow themselves to be carried away upon their emotions, but instead to keep a clear and calm demeanour so that justice might run its course in true Canadian tradition.

After this, several local women in quick succession were sworn in. One was a close neighbour, Jane Moore. She and I had never actually met, but that did not stop her from having her say. Miss Moore said: 'Lately this girl kept pretty much to the house,' and only afterwards added, 'I am not up on that line often so I had little chance of seeing her.' Then she continued in a knowing tone, 'However, I do know that she never was married. I did not know much about the family either, as they only came here last year. But I have heard enough about them. And the neighbours know enough about her. Mary Ann has a bad character...'

Her snidely brother, Reuben Moore, also testified against me saying; 'I have my own ideas about whose child it was. There was a young woman living in the neighbourhood who did not look just as a young woman should look...'

That sanctimonious Reuben Moore! How I wanted to shout out and say; 'What about my little sister, Ellen, who works out at your farm? Your brother Job is more than altogether familiar with her!'

My sister Ellen? It was then that I start thinking about how, if I found out that she had said anything about me to the Moores, I would tear her hair out. But for the time being I would keep quiet. What could they do? I knew full well that there was no evidence to prove that I had harmed that baby.

132

After Reuben Moore was dismissed, the school room burst into uproar as I was then led in. My eyes immediately fixed upon the man who was at that moment opening a pot belly stove in the corner. I could hardly bear to watch as he then threw more wood into the inferno within. It made my stomach feel queasy.

Even though I had been flanked by two strapping 'guardians', I was badly jostled as I was led to a chair where I would give my evidence.

Feelings were running hot and ugly and, although he was a professional with many years' experience of holding such inquests, Coroner Maxwell looked as though he feared that violence might break out at any moment. However, when he rose from the school teacher's desk and banged her gavel, loudly demanding 'order', to his obvious relief, and to mine, the room snapped into silence.

Meekly, I took up my position, not daring to raise my head as much as to glance about the room. Instead, I fixed my eyes upon Maxwell, whose face remained void of expression, as I laid my hand lightly upon the proffered Bible and gave my holy oath that I would tell the truth.

'Miss Wetherup...' Maxwell addressed me, 'are you aware that on the afternoon of Friday last, the body of an infant was found close to the house that your parents' occupied until recently?'

'Yes Sir, I am,' I replied. 'The constable that came to me at Port Hope told me so.'

'Miss Wetherup, I must caution you not to commit yourself, and advise you that you have the right to remain silent. However, I must ask you... are you the mother of this child?'

You could have heard a mouse whisper as I brazened it out.

'No sir,' I said emphatically. 'I am not!'

'Miss Wetherup, have you been recently delivered of *any* child?' Maxwell pressed.

'No sir, I have not!' I insisted.

'Have you any knowledge of any other female in your household having been delivered recently of a child.'

'Not that I know of, sir. No!'

Coroner Maxwell dipped his pen into the dull pewter inkwell at the front of the desk and quickly noted something down before then asking, 'Miss Wetherup, you say that you are working away at Port Hope?'

'Yes, sir,' I replied.

'Then can you tell me if you have had reason to return to your parents' house recently?'

I hardly took a breath before answering, 'Yes, Sir. I have.'

'And how long did you stay?' Maxwell asked.

'Just a few months, sir. I was fierce homesick and yearned to visit a spell with my younger sisters.'

'A few months?'

'Yes, sir. Like I said, I was really homesick.'

'And your Mother? I expect that you were really missing her too.'

I lowered my head, loathe to answer.

'And your Mother?' Maxwell repeated.

I looked up and replied, quietly, that it was common knowledge that she and I did not get along well. Though of course I came home, out of duty, to see her too.

'I understand your mother to be a woman in her late fifties, is she not?'

I nodded in agreement that this was true.

'Therefore,' the Coroner continued, 'ordinarily I would be led to assume that the child was not hers. However, Mrs Wetherup must be an extraordinarily robust woman for her age, as I note from neighbours that there has been the addition of several young children to your family in the past few years?'

I declined to comment, and a knowing murmur went up about the room.

'Where are your parents, Miss Wetherup?' Maxwell continued.

'I cannot say, sir.'

'Cannot say... or will not say?'

'I cannot say, sir, for in truth I do not know where they have gone'.

'You do not know where they have gone? Or why they left so quickly?'

'No, sir. I do not know why that was. I must have already gone back to my employer in Port Hope when they left.'

'And do you not think it odd that they should have removed themselves so swiftly without telling you first? Their daughter?'

'No sir, I do not. Paw often owes folk a lot of money that he does not have, and he has been known to flit before without warning. Maybe that is why he up and left, sir.'

'Very well,' Coroner Maxwell said. 'You may step down now.'

I was led away, back to the safety of the side room from whence I had been previously fetched. This time not a word was said and no-one tried to lunge at me as before, which I took as a good sign.

From out of sight, I listened intently as Maxwell pressed on with the inquest. He recalled Doctor Herriman to the stand. This time he was accompanied by a second physician, Dr Corbett of Port Hope. I had been seen by both men earlier in the day.

'Dr Herriman,' the Coroner continued. 'I understand that you have examined Miss Wetherup this day as to her physical condition?'

'Yes sir, I have,' he confirmed.

'And you, Dr Corbett. You have also, independently, examined this young woman today, have you not, sir?

'Yes sir, I have,' Dr Corbett replied.

'And what are your findings, Dr Herriman?'

'It is my professional opinion that Miss Wetherup has recently been delivered of a child.'

A collective gasp followed like a rush wind.

'And you, Dr Corbett. What is the outcome of your findings, sir?'

'I have to concur with my colleague,' he replied. 'This young woman shows all the physical signs of having recently given birth.'

'And there is no room for doubt upon this matter?'

'None at all,' Dr Herriman replied.

'No. None at all,' Dr Corbett agreed.

With this the inquest closed to an uproar. The school room was ordered to be cleared once more, apart from the jury who remained inside to consider their verdict.

Outside, a few of the women retired to their buggies wrapped up in furs. Others collected around the flickering of flames of a makeshift bonfire lit to ward of the chill by those determined to stay put – so that they would be present to hear the outcome of the trial. I watched them drinking hot coffee while covertly passing a bottle of whiskey between themselves, to lace it against the cold. It is just as well that they had, because the jury deliberated until well after midnight. When it had done, a unanimous verdict was brought in – that the dead baby had come to its death 'by violence at the hands of some person unknown'.

'Persons unknown', when I heard that I naively thought that I was going to walk free. Instead, immediately after, I found myself being arrested and taken from the school room under armed escort.

Despite it by then being the early hours of the morning, outside the school house an angry mob was waiting. Again they jostled my guards. I felt like a hen that had gotten into a fox-house, as they tried to get at me from all sides. I was called the most foul-mouthed names that would spoil the mouth of the most profane of sailors. One woman even got close enough to launch a great globule of spit at my face before I could be bundled inside the prison wagon and taken away to Cobourg Jail...

Chapter Three

The resulting letter from Coroner Robert Maxwell, to Mr J. Kerr - the County Attorney- turned out to be anything but impartial. On informing Kerr that the body of a newly born infant had been found on the Eighth Concession of Hope Township, Maxwell went on to state that:

'The case is a mysterious and intricate affair, indeed horrible and of such importance as is thought requires very close and very careful investigation. And requires your council and advice on behalf of society and The Crown. A family of the name of Wetherup, who resided there in a house on the eighth concession of Hope, hastily and clandestinely removed away on Monday night last, the twenty-seventh of October. It is supposed that they are gone to the Township of Dummer in the County of Peterborough, and their daughter, Mary Ann, is strongly suspected to have had this child and is its mother. She has had other illegitimate children and was in prison before for a likewise offence. She is by report an adept in this horrible business...'

With that damning letter, my fate was all but sealed.

Shortly after being arrested, I was taken to jail in Cobourg. It was inside my wretched cell there that I first encountered the *'Great Detective'* himself–John Wilson Murray.[12]

He was a tall man, and as he removed his hat, he revealed a high forehead from which his neatly trimmed, fine, brown hair was fast receding. Under his long, loose overcoat, which he had quickly unbuttoned from his under his chin and opened part way

---

[12]   A brief biography of John Wilson Murray's career can be found at the back of this book.

down, he was extremely well dressed – in a dark blue suit, high starched collar and neck tie. Beneath his finely sculptured nose, nestled an enormous walrus moustache, completely covering his lips, which twitched as Murray spoke as if it had a life of its own.

'Miss Mary Ann Wetherup?' he said with a strange mix of accents that wasn't quite American but not entirely Scot either. It was that familiar twang that I could hear in his voice, as clear as clear. He was no doubt a Scot, although I suspected like my own ma, Murray had been away from Scotland for many years by then.

'Yes sir,' I replied. 'I am.'

'My name is Murray. Detective John Wilson Murray,' he said, quite expecting that his reputation had preceded him and that I must surely have known who he was. But Detective Murray was soon to be disappointed. I had not heard of him.

Murray, it transpired, was at that period Ontario's only full-time, paid criminal detective. As such, he was deemed to be a constable of every county and district in it, and with the authority to act in any part of the province. In his own words, Murray later described his job to me as being 'to follow criminals to any place and run them down,' and yet in practice he rarely intervened in a case until his help had been specifically requested by the local authorities. In my case, it had.

I would soon discover for myself that this John Wilson Murray, was a man of few words but who, none the less, was capable of making a big noise. And, as our numerous meetings over the coming weeks would bear out, he was also mightily puffed up by his own sense of self importance.

The days dragged by into weeks as I languished in Cobourg jail. It was like hell on earth – to suddenly be cooped up like some animal in a pen at the abattoir as it awaits its grim fate. Throughout that time, Detective Murray interrogated me relentlessly. And no matter how often I told him that I did not know where my parents had gone, I am certain that he did not believe me.

'Why not tell me where they are so that we can get this over with?' he kept saying.

But I could not tell him because I truly did not know. When Pa had put me on the train back to Port Hope, he gave me no hint at all about his and Ma's planned disappearance – that is if indeed he had known himself.

I knew any trial could not take place until Ma and Pa had been found. Until they were, I would remain confined to that awful place. But even had I known for certain where Ma and Pa had gone, I would not have been in a hurry to offer any help that might find them. Best for me all round, I thought, if they were never found at all. I was bright enough to realise that if they were not found, then eventually the case against me would have to be dropped. Without a witness, I knew that the authorities could not prove that I had done *anything*.

The problem was that Detective Murray was not a man to give up lightly. So he took to visiting me daily in my cell in an effort, I guess, to step up the pressure on me. Then one day Murray appeared in my cell with an opened letter grasped in his hand.

'I intercepted this at the local post office,' he said. 'It is for you, Mary Ann.'

I hated how he called me *Mary Ann* – like he was smarming up to me deliberately, in order to get me to confide in him.

'You shouldn't go interfering with a body's private letters!' I rebuked him tersely. 'Even I know that is an offence against the law.'

'And so is withholding evidence from an officer of the law,' he countered in his strange monotone way.

Murray handed me the letter, but at the time I had not noticed him craftily keeping back the envelope, which I now assume he must have slipped inside his pocket, for I never saw him do it. I did not give the envelope a thought. I just wanted to see the letter.

'Here. You may have it,' Murray said. 'I was unable to make out a word of it in any case. The handwriting is too bad.'

I had no way of knowing if the detective was telling the truth or not. I snatched the letter out of Murray's hand and immediately set about trying to read it myself. The writing scrawled upon the scrap of paper was bad indeed, but I recognised it instantly as being Pa's. I knew it was my pa's hand, but it sounded more like its contents came directly from Ma. She could not make her own letters to create such an epistle of abuse of her own, and that was the only sort of letter she could compose. When my pa set down to write a letter of his own accord, it was far less of a scrawl and with fewer splatters of ink. This one was so unruly and blotted that it would have been a wonder if Murray had been unable to decipher its meaning, for it was giving me trouble, coupled with the fact that my own reading was not so good either. As I laboured over it I must have been inadvertently forming the silent words of its contents upon my lips, because Murray started to quiz me about it.

'Is it from your father, Mary Ann?' he asked.

'You know full well it is!' I hissed.

'I have not read it, Mary Ann. So why don't you read it to me now?'

'I can recognise my pa's writing, but I think it is from my ma... and so it has made his writing real bad, so that even I can't work it out,' I lied.

'Is he afraid of your mother?'

I found that laughable.

'Sure, aren't we all?' I replied dryly.

'Will you not tell me where she is?'

'No. I told you before, I do not know where they are.'

'Then tell me about your family, Mary Ann,' Murray pressed.

'What is there to know?' I snapped back.

'What are they like? Your ma and pa?'

I didn't see why he needed to know but I told him anyway.

'My pa is a good man, from good people,' is what I told Murray. 'My pa is as soft as a puppy, if you know how to catch him right. But my ma? There is no catching her soft side – because she does not have one!'

Ma's mother, Grandma Haighle was a hard woman, too. I remember Grandma well from when I was a little girl back in Dummer. She was a hard and tough woman – but she was fair. She never rebuked without good cause, and she never hit me like Ma did. Hard, Ma was. She was hard through and through and especially so after she'd just had a baby. You know, I cannot recall one happy time in my childhood spent with my ma. I can't bring to mind one single kiss from her, or a hug or some other touch of tenderness. Not like from Pa.

'My ma?' I said. 'She comes from queer folk and it makes her difficult at times, that is all.'

'And your siblings?' he asked.

'Sib...?' I did not know the word.

'Your brothers and sisters?'

'Oh, I got lots of brothers and sisters!'

'Tell me about them', he said.

Again I did not see the point of the question, but I answered it anyway.

'Well,' I replied, 'my brother John is the eldest. Then I came along next...'

As I began to rattle off the names of my brothers and sisters, some of my earliest memories came flooding back. Memories of me, as a very little girl, soaking a piece of rag in milk and trying to get the latest baby to suckle on it until my ma returned to the shanty. I was the one that truly mothered the little ones who came along after me. I was the one who came to them when they were hurt or crying for comfort, not her. That is until I was about eleven years old and she farmed me out, a way off in Douro.

One day, when my father was away hunting with Uncle Thomas, a man came by our shanty asking directions to a certain homestead looking to hire a servant. Ma invited him in, and before the kettle had even boiled on the stove to make the man some coffee, my mother had me all packed up and on the seat of the man's wagon ready to go away with him. I never even had the chance to kiss my pa goodbye before I was gone. Twice a year after that time I was allowed to come visit at home. I would arrive on the stoop and before I had stepped inside Ma had taken the pouch with my money in it, and then she gave me nothing but chores to do until it was time for me to go back again.

'Did they get along with your mother?'

'I suppose so.'

'But you did not get on with your mother at all well?'

'It wasn't my fault!' I jumped to my defence. 'It wasn't as if I was a difficult child, because I was not. It was just her. She was the difficult one'.

In truth, I had fallen down on my knees and blessed the day when I was farmed out away from *her* clutches.

'And Dummer?'

'What about it?' I asked.

'Tell me all about it.'

'I grew up there. And that is it. We lived in a shanty on my grandmother Haighle's land, until she sold up and moved away to Bruce County.'

'Then?'

'Then we lived on the Sixth Concession, close to my Grandpa John. He was a good man. And so, by all accounts, was my pa's mother, although I never knew her.'

'And how did your mother get on with them?'

'Ma didn't much care for Grandma Mary. And she hated Grandpa's second wife, Grandma Victoria, even more. Grandma Victoria once called after my pa, asking him not to be walking dirt into her house by forgetting to wipe his feet. Ma snapped after her not to be telling Pa what to do, because she wasn't his mother. Grandma Victoria had shouted back that if she had been, then she would have seen to it that Ma would never have been Pa's wife in the first place. After that, they stopped talking to each other altogether.'

Murray picked up his leather case that had all the while been lying unopened upon the small table in my cell. He proceeded to sift through the file of papers he had stuffed inside it until he stopped at one, which he then plucked out. Laying it on the table, he started to read aloud from it.

'Calendar of prisoners for June, eighteen-sixty-seven. Mary Ann Wetherup... committed April the twenty-seventh... guilty of concealing the birth of a child...'

I couldn't look at him. I just couldn't. And I couldn't bear to think about that time either. But Detective Murray made me do so. I don't know how he did, but I found myself telling him anyway. I could not help myself. He asked and the details of the whole terrible affair just started tumbling out of my mouth.

144

I told Murray how the first family I had worked away for was fine. The Missus was kind and treated me very well indeed. But then her husband up and died, and with her having no sons to carry on the place for her, she sold up and went to live with her married daughter in Toronto.

So I went home. But Ma soon had me farmed out again. It started out well enough with the next couple. This time the Missus was younger, but sickly and childless, and often confined to her bed. So my main dealings were with the husband. He was alright at first, but then, in time, he started to act strange around me.

'Strange?'

'He would get to deliberately bumping into me. Or his hand would *accidentally* brush up against my thigh, as we rode into town on the wagon, or as I was doing my chores about the farmyard. At first I made nothing of it, because I was young and green. I was only coming up to fifteen, sir. And I didn't know any better. Then, after a while, he started to creep up on me and then touch me in places where I knew he should not. And then I told him to stop.'

'And what did he say to that?'

'He scolded me, sir. He told me that it was only a bit of fun and that if I said anything to the Missus, he would fire me on the spot, and send me packing back to my ma, and that he would tell her what a trouble I was.'

'And you didn't want to go home to your mother?'

'No sir! I did not.'

'So what happened?'

'Well sir, I got in deeper than I should have...'

In truth I hadn't known what to do. I didn't know how to fend my employer off. Or what would happen if I tried to.

'Before I knew what was happening, he was on me and doing his business. And after he had, he would be really kind to me.'

'Kind? In what way would he be kind?'

'He would always tell me, privately, how pretty I was. Or how different I was compared with his barren and shrivelling up wife. And how much he loved me. But he also said that we couldn't let the Missus find out.'

'And did you believe him, Mary Ann, when he flattered you?'

I paused to remember. Yes, I had believed him with all my heart and soul. He made me feel special. And more than that, for the first time in my miserable life, I felt loved. It is so hard to explain that to someone who has grown up basking in the warmth of their parents' affection. To explain what it is like not to be hugged or held by your own mother, to long for such affection, but then instead to be beaten and belittled every day, going to your bed each night as a wee child wishing that you might never wake up again, just to save yourself from the pain of going though another day with her. Then, how terrible it was to grow up – to realise that your true value to your mother could only be calculated in how many dollars a month you were worth when hired out as a servant.

The Mister had held me gently in his arms. The touch of his mouth on my skin had become my reason to breathe. His fingers tousling my hair like the warm breeze of the most idyllic of summer's day, making my soul feel free and at ease. And the glint in his eyes after he'd had me became like my sunshine – shining just on me and nobody else. And I was blinded by the light of it. I had never known such feelings before, such warmth and contentment, and so I came to crave it more and more. Soon, I wanted to be with him for every opportunity we could snatch away from his wife. I would even be in their room, tidying up their bed and plumping up their pillows and imagining – no, hoping for – what it would be like taking the Missus' place and making love in it with the Mister at some not too distant day in the future. For that is what he often described to me as I lay in his arms. One day his invalid wife would die and then he would make me his wife instead.

It was time for me to answer Murray's question.

'Did I believe him? Yes, I did sir,' I replied. 'I believed every word he said. That is until *it* happened.'

Murray didn't say a word. Instead he just sat impassively jotting down words on his note pad until I paused. Then he had simply looked up at me, void of any expression, and nodded in gesture for me to carry on. So I took a deep breath, and continued.

'I started feeling really sick. Then my belly started to swell until I could feel it. I could feel a baby growing inside me...'

I remember thinking to myself, how could this detective possibly understand what that had been like for me? Murray looked like a man who had enjoyed a privileged upbringing. How could he understand what it was like to be a poor young girl being used easily by a man nearing forty? He could not imagine how frightening it was to have been pregnant and knowing that very soon everyone would know exactly what the Mister and I had been up to in the barn for all those months. And yet at the same time, I had been living in hope that somehow he would still make good all of his whispered promises to me, and that he would stand by me and the baby.

'And what was your employer's reaction?' Murray asked.

'When I told the Mister, his face just burst into bright red, like it was fit to blow! He shouted a tirade of abuse: calling me a stupid little bitch and such. Ranting on and on he was, and telling me how I had to go, and that I was never to come back to the farm again. And he threatened me, saying that if I told on him, how he would say that he had caught me in the act with one of the labourers against the wall of the cow shed, and that he would claim that I was just being spiteful in return for being dismissed.'

I didn't tell Murray about how hard I had been sobbing after I told the Mister I was having his child. I did not tell him how the Mister, forgetting himself, had raised his voice so loud that we were surprised by his wife who suddenly came upon us in the barn. I did not tell him how, when he saw his wife, he had turned quickly on his heels to tell her, as bold as bold could be, that I was pregnant by another man and that he was giving me my marching orders.

'See this, Katherine?' he ranted. 'This no-good girl has been tupped by one of the farm hands! Look here! She has a belly on her as big as a sow! So I have told her, Katherine... I have told her that she has to go immediately!'

I then told Murray how, without further ado, the Missus then snatched up my things from my room and threw them out of the house in a fit of rage. As I scrabbled about in the dirt picking them up, the Mister fetched some coins and pushed them into my hand, saying that if there was any more owing, then he would send it on to my pa.

'I wanted to tell her,' I blurted to Detective Murray, 'I wanted to tell her *exactly* what her precious husband had done to me, but I couldn't... I couldn't get the words out for choking on my own distress. And who would she have believed anyway? Me or him?'

'And so in revenge, you got rid of his child?'

'No sir! It wasn't like that at all.'

'Then tell me,' he said quietly, 'tell me what it *was* like, Mary Ann.'

So I told him. I told him how I made my way home. And how, as that night drew in, without a crumb of food on me, I was forced to make myself a bed out of leaves beneath an old tree. I didn't tell Murray, though, that I had cried myself to sleep. What was the point? He had already demonstrated that he was impervious to my tears or any show of emotion on my part, which could only strengthen my belief that he must be incapable of feeling any such emotion himself. Instead, he simply continued his endless note taking, only pausing whenever I fell silent.

'When I got home, as soon as my ma opened the door and saw me, she knew,' I told him.

'And how did she react?'

'She yelled at me, 'You filthy little whore!' Then she slapped me so hard across the face that I was lifted clean off the stoop, before falling really hard on the ground. Then I started groaning in pain, but before I could even pick myself up, Ma grabbed me by my hair and quick-marched me around to the back of the shanty and locked me away in the shed out of sight.'

I did not go into any great detail with Murray. I did not tell him about the blood I then found trickling down the inside of my legs and soaking into my petticoat. And I did not describe the sudden onset of the most dreadful pain I'd ever experienced – excruciating pain that came and went in waves and gripped my insides like a vice. I did not tell him how I cried out in vain – for my ma to come and help me. I did not tell him how terrified I was when, eventually, the tiny baby slithered out of me and just lay there among the dirty straggles of straw on the floor, where I crouched with a limp blue baby still attached to my body by its long grey cord. I didn't tell him how afraid I was, and how I was too shocked even to reach out and touch it.

Only at length did Ma come. When she glanced down at her tiny dead grandchild, she snatched it up in a rag like she was picking up dog dirt from the shanty floor.

'When the baby came, it was dead,' was all I said to the detective.

'It was born dead?' Murray's eyes stared even colder as he asked me this question; colder as if there was real doubt in his mind that I was telling him the truth.

'Yes!' I insisted, fixing on his eyes. 'It *was* dead.'

He was silent for a moment and I hoped that his questioning was at an end. I was tired. I felt drained out like a cup of cold woe and I did not know how much more I could take of it. But relentlessly Murray continued.

'Tell me what happened then?' he asked.

'Then Ma came to the barn, by and by,' I replied, 'and ordered me out and off into the under brush. There she had me on all fours, digging like a dog between the tangle of tree roots, trying to make a hole big enough to bury the baby in. Then, when I had buried it, she told me to get into the house and to clean myself up before Pa got home.'

'And what did your pa do?'

'He did not know a thing about what happened. Ma told him that I came home with a fever and that was why I was in bed. And I dared not contradict her.'

'And so how was it that the authorities were alerted?'

'It was *him*. The Mister. He turned up at our shanty a few days later. I could hear him from my bed as he stood on our stoop and told my parents how he and I had an affair. And that he had confessed all to his wife.'

But again, I didn't tell Murray everything... like how those words made my heart begin to skip and how I had thought, for a few mad moments, that the Mister had come for *me*. But he had not.

'He had told his wife about the baby, and then she said that she wanted to bring up the child as her own.' I continued.

'What baby?' my pa asked 'My Mary has no baby.'

Then I told Murray how the Mister demanded to see me for himself. And how, when he saw with his own eyes that my belly was empty, he demanded to know where the baby was. So when he got no answer he stormed off to Peterborough to inform the authorities.'

'Then what happened?'

'They brought in a dog – a dog that can sniff out dead things. And they found the baby and I was arrested. They could not prove either way whether my baby was dead or alive when it was buried, but they charged me anyway with concealing the birth. And so I went to jail for a year...'

I took my punishment. It made me hard. And from that time on I was determined never to let my ma bully me again.

My parents had already moved out from Dummer and gone to live in Hope. And as soon as I was out of jail, I immediately went to work out as far away from Dummer and from my parents as I could get.'

'And where was that?'

'Port Hope. I remember Pa and the Reynolds at Dummer talking about some kin of theirs who lived in that town. They are Irish, like Pa. I found Mr Reynolds at his hotel and dropped into the conversation how I am great friends with his Dummer relatives, before I got round to asking him if he had any work for me.'

'And did he?'

'Yes. It turned out to be a big hotel that old man John Reynolds had built for himself, and so he took me on as a servant.'

I stopped talking for a moment, as I gathered more of my thoughts. I hadn't had that man Reynolds in my mind for a long while, and I was not altogether happy about thinking about him again. Besides, what had it to do with anything? I had worked like a slave for old man Reynolds, I truly had. For five years I had cleaned and scrubbed the rooms and made up all the beds on my own. I helped to wash the dirty linen and pick up after the guests. It was a busy place, mostly full of young men– sailors, railway men, and stone cutters – with lots of comings and goings.

'And...' Murray seemed impatient.

'I'm tired sir,' I told him. 'Can't we stop?'

'No,' he said. 'Answer my question.'

I was also getting angry by that time. And hungry. And my head was hurting from his endless questioning. So I let him have it...

'There were so many single men and so many opportunities, sir,' I told Murray bluntly, 'so *naturally* I helped myself to a few.

I watched Murray closely as I spoke. He blushed. I swear the man blushed! There was I, thinking that he was 'unshockable', and yet he had grown extremely uneasy as he listened to me talking frankly about sex. Then, for me, that was like a red rag to a bull; seeing beads of sweat suddenly rolling down his self righteous forehead and on to his white starched noose of a collar, making him look very uncomfortable about his neck. I had just spotted a chink in his armour! So I did not set the break upon my words.

'The truth is I liked the men, sir,' I said very matter-of-factly. 'I liked the feel of them between my legs and all the pretty things they would say to me as they huffed and puffed away at their business. And I liked *that* feeling, sir. That feeling I got inside – like some awful itch was suddenly being scratched. I enjoyed the fornication, sir, and I enjoyed it whenever I could get it. It was like a craving that got satisfied. It was the only thing that made me feel alive!'

Before that day I had supposed the Detective to be a lot of things, but a prude was not one of them. Then again, he wasn't a Scot like my ma's kin. Murray was a breed apart. He was a *Catholic* Scot; full of angst as to whether or not his soul would end up in purgatory. 'That's the difference between us and them,' I had once heard a Protestant Scotsman say, 'they have a riotous Saturday night, like sewing their wild seeds, then next morning, while we are minding our sore heads, they are down on their knees begging their priest for forgiveness and praying that the crop don't come in. They haven't a notion of how to live like men like us!'

Detective Murray took a long drink of water from the glass set upon the table and then gestured with his hand for me to continue, as if his words were stuck in his craw. But I took my own sweet time before I did so.

The long and the short of it was that I had inevitably fallen pregnant again. Undeterred by this mishap though, I had quickly set my cap at John Reynolds's son, William, instead. William was a couple of years older than I was and worked as a conductor on the railways. He already had an eye for me and so I let him think that I had quite a shine for him, too.

Old man Reynolds was passed sixty by then, and always on about how it was high time that he sold up and moved out of Port Hope. Reynolds kept talking about how the family should move somewhere 'smarter' to start up another hotel. And then, recently, he had even started talking about how William could have the running of that new hotel once his pa had retired from the business.

It was not difficult for me to then lure William into sneaking about and meeting with me in unoccupied rooms so that he could have the run of my body. And as he did, I would lie under him daydreaming – about him and me being married and running that grand new hotel somewhere ourselves.

Of course it never happened. When William told his father that *he* had made me pregnant, old man Reynolds had a blue fit. He put his foot down, and I was sent away with a flea in my ear while William was quickly married off to someone 'more suitable'. More suitable indeed! Old man Reynolds must have forgotten what a muddy pool he had crawled out of himself!

The last I heard, John Reynolds had sold up in Port Hope and started a new hotel in Millbrook, just as he had planned. Then he lorded it as a 'retired gentleman' while William become the hotel keeper. I heard that William and his wife had a child not long after I had given birth to my bastard. And adding insult to injury, they had seen fit to name their daughter Mary Ann.

'I got pregnant again, sir.' I eventually told Murray. 'About two years before that, my cousin, Rebecca, had an illegitimate child, too. My uncle Thomas and my aunt had taken on the child as their own and were raising it. So I got to thinking to myself about all those years that I had worked away and how every penny I had broken my back to earn had been sent back home to Ma and Pa to have the benefit of it. Well, I was older by then, and in a fix, and for once ready to stand up to Ma. So, when I went home and told my parents about the baby, I also told them that it was only right and proper that they should repay me for all my years of slavery, by helping me out with my child. They owed me that much at least, I reasoned.'

'How did they respond?' Murray didn't even lift his head from all that scribbling of notes he was doing.

'Ma stormed at me in a fury – screaming that she had already done her duty to me the day she let me grow into long dresses and showed me how to put my hair up. She said that there was hardly room enough in their cabin for them and the youngest children, let alone for a bastard brat of mine. Then she swore at me and ordered me to leave the house.'

'What did you do?'

'I refused, sir. Instead I folded my arms and firmly stood my ground saying that after all I had done for them they owed me a duty – which meant they should help me out in my time of trouble. To my relief and utter surprise, Pa agreed with me. And so my daughter, Margaret, was born... and then later, another child, my son Joseph.'

'What happened to these children?'

'I left them in my mother's care while I went back to work in Port Hope. As far as the neighbours knew they were hers; little Margaret was my sister and Joseph my younger brother'.

'Didn't you miss being with them?'

'No sir, not much. Not at first. I didn't hold on to any feelings for their fathers, so I guess I didn't hold onto much for them either,' I reasoned. 'They were a hindrance to me going back out to earn their keep, so it seemed the best thing to do all round to leave them to Ma. Later... later I did miss them, as much as I ever missed my other brothers and sisters when we were apart.'

'And what about the dead baby found close to their house near Rice Lake? Did you get pregnant again but decide this time that you had enough illegitimate children already, so you killed it?' he asked with eyes that I could see did not care a jot about anything I might be feeling. I was guilty, as far as he was concerned, and all he wanted was for the untidy ends to be neatly sewn up so that he could be on his way out of there.

'No! No, I didn't! I swear!' I screamed at him as I jumped to my feet.

Quickly, the detective stood, too. Then I encountered something that I had not thought I would. I saw real anger in Murray's face. Until that moment, the detective had been like a patient bird trying to twist a snail from out of its shell. Now, suddenly he had become like a bird that instead smashes the snail against a rock to get at what he wants from inside.

'Mary Ann,' he said sternly, 'from your own submission, you are a highly immoral young woman and an adept liar. I suggest that you give this denial up immediately and admit to the murder of your child. Let us get this trial done with! Confession is good for the soul and there is still a slim chance of saving yours. Confess now and throw yourself upon the mercy of the court and our Lord God. If you don't, you will surely go to hell!'

'I will not go to hell', I retorted. 'I do not believe in the notion of hell. My ma says that there is no God and that only fools believe that there is!'

'Then what about hanging?'

'Hanging?'

'You have told me that you do not believe in God or hell. But do you believe in suffering and death, Mary Ann? Because hanging is a most painful and horrible death.'

I fixed my eyes on his steely gaze and knew from that deathly look upon Murray's face that these were no mere empty words. But I said nothing more.

'I think that I have heard enough, Mary Ann,' he said bluntly. 'At sixteen you were found guilty of concealing the birth of another newborn child found buried near to your home. Now both Doctors Herriman and Corbett will testify that you *were* delivered of another child shortly before this dead infant was also found near one of your parents' homes. And then there is Coroner Maxwell's damning conclusion, that this latest child was born alive and subsequently dispatched by you in the most horrible manner imaginable. The evidence is overwhelming. It is enough, Mary Ann!' he said slamming his note book down upon the table. 'It is enough to convince *any* jury in the land to convict you of murder. And when they do – you *will* hang, Mary Ann. You will hang by the neck until you are dead!'

I felt as if all the air had suddenly been sucked out of the room and that I couldn't breathe. It was as if Murray had me hung now by those accusations, and all I could do was to kick out in the air in a vain effort to save myself.

So I broke down. I broke down and told him everything...

***

Murray may not have been able to decipher the letter that I had received from my pa, but he was a cunning one. He was able to work out from the postmark franked upon it that my pa had posted it from way up on the Huron Peninsular. Murray almost immediately went there, searched out my parents, and then brought them all the way back to Cobourg.

On December the fourth, my father and mother were brought before William Irvine Staunton, Police Magistrate and Justice of the Peace at Cobourg, to make sworn statements touching the events that surrounded the death of my child. In those statements given before Irvine, my parents confirmed that I had given birth at their house: that I had returned home to them on Grey's farm in the July of that year, pregnant.

My parents also stated that a day or so before I had left their home on the twenty-seventh of October, to take the train back to Port Hope, and that I had been delivered of a child – a live child. Pa also stated, categorically, that I had taken that child with me, and when last he had seen it, it was alive and well.

My heart sank when I heard that from Detective Murray; heard that my own pa had signed my freedom and future away. I could not believe that he, of all people, could have done that to me. I felt so suddenly betrayed – betrayed and alone. I broke down and cried.

So it was that I was officially charged: that I, Mary Ann Wetherup had 'feloniously, wilfully and of my own malice aforethought' killed and murdered my newborn baby. The chief witnesses for the prosecution would be my own parents...

Chapter Four

It was almost six months before my case came to trial, during the following April. For all that time I was held in the jail at Cobourg and had hardly seen anyone other than the wardresses who guarded me.

At the start, I was occasionally allowed to mix with the other women prisoners. However, I soon learned the hard way that neither my fellow inmates nor the wardresses intended to offer me any crumb of comfort during my time of custody there. They all knew who I was and why I was there. One wardress had even taken great delight in reading aloud to the other prisoners the charges that had been laid against me. She read from a crumpled newspaper cutting from the Port Hope Guide, which she had ceremoniously pulled from her uniform pocket.

'It is not often we have such an evil child-killer amongst us', she exclaimed as her captive audience hung on every grisly detail of '*the Inquest on the body of a mutilated child*'. Supposing that there could be no doubt at all that I was indeed the heartless murderer of this tiny helpless baby, they tried to deal me out their own summary punishment, which I escaped. But instead, I was afflicted with something equally cruel – solitary confinement.

For me, the most awful part of being imprisoned was not being able to see the other members of my family. My younger brother Robert, and my older brother, John, did not come to visit me as expected. No-one came, and I do not know even to this day whether that was because they were turned away at the prison gates or whether it was because they were too ashamed to come visit me. The only person who visited me, and who continued to come, was Detective Murray.

On the day before my trial, I met my Council, Mr William Jex, for the first time. He was a slight and short fellow with very handsome features and a fine English accent to match. To me, he did not look old enough to be a barrister, but when I asked, he said that he had been called to the bar almost five years before. I suppose, like me, he was far younger looking than his years.

He despaired at my untidy state.

'I want you to wash your hair tonight,' he said. 'I shall have the wardress dress it for you in the morning, in a fine bun, like our beloved Queen Victoria. And I shall see to it that you have a freshly laundered dress to wear.'

Then he began to instruct me upon how I must act in court.

'You must do exactly as I say,' he said. 'And this it is very important, Miss Wetherup, so listen carefully. Do not, under any circumstance, show the slightest emotion whatsoever when the witnesses for the prosecution are on the stand; especially when they come to talk about the child. No matter how detailed or distasteful Doctor Herriman's evidence may be, do not react to it. When he starts to speak, I suggest that you try to think about something else – anything at all – that might help your mind to distance itself from the impact of what is actually being said. Try to keep a neutral expression upon your face at all times. And on no account smile at any juncture. If the jury see you smile then they might interpret that at best as contempt for the proceedings, and at worse, as a sign of utter callousness. On the other hand, if you appear to be upset or distressed by what is being said, they might take it as a sign of remorse and guilt at the awful thing you are *alleged* to have done. Make no mistake about that at all, Miss Wetherup, your life may depend upon something as trivial as the look on your face. At all costs, I want you to remain detached and composed. Do you understand?'

I nodded that I did.

'And do not be tempted to speak out – no matter how provocative anything a witness might say may be. You will only speak tomorrow to tell the judge your name, and that your plea to the charges is one of 'not guilty'. After tomorrow, you will only speak if and when you are placed upon the stand to give your own evidence. If so, then I urge you to say only that, and *exactly* that, which you have told Detective Murray during your interviews with him. No more, and no less. But with luck, that won't be necessary. Once all the prosecution witnesses have been called, I expect that this whole bloody mess shall be over.'

I told him that I understood and that I would do as he had said. But I have to say now that Mister Jex's visit had left me with very little confidence in his ability to defend me. With those last few words, I had begun to fear that perhaps Mr Jex had no intention of defending me to the best of his ability at all, that perhaps the verdict had already been decided and that all I would be receiving the next day would be lip service to the name of justice.

Very early the next morning, I was taken from Cobourg Jail the short distance to Victoria Hall and the court. There, I was held below in a cell until all was ready for me to be led to my trial.

I was escorted through a doorway that opened onto a short flight of steps leading into the *Old Bailey Court Room*. It got its grand name from being modelled upon the great court of the same name in London, England – the mother of our own Ontario court system. It was a grand room, almost overpoweringly so to my mean mind. And I felt hugely intimidated by my surroundings.

The first thing I noticed on entering the courtroom was the coat of arms in the centre of the opposite expanse of wall. It was the Her Majesty's royal coat of arms, with a great rampant lion adorned in a crown to the left and to the right with a graceful crowned unicorn. All picked out in white, red and muted gold, the arms looked to me as if it was solid; either carved out of the plaster work, or made out of wood and stuck onto the wall. However, I learned later that it was no more than a very clever painting intended to give that effect.

Running almost the entire length of the same wall was a dais, flanked on either side by two identical doors at each end of the wall, where short flights of several steps led down on to the main platform. Set upon this, and directly in front of the coat of arms, was a grand, lone, studded leather chair, where the Judge, the Honourable George William Burton, would soon sit and preside over the proceedings that would determine my fate. Directly below the Judge's fancy perch, the Court Recorder was already busy at his station, set within a roomy panelled box, assembling an assortment of pens and papers. Either side of the Recorder, and within a pace or two's distance, stood two identical boxes to house the witnesses when they were called to give their evidence.

Running along the left side wall were two tiers of benches, where the jury was already seated in solemn repose and enclosed behind a panelled wood stand. Across the room from them, in an identical span of benches, sat many people I knew, who had no doubt been called as witness. Amongst them were an equal number of faces I did not recognise.

The warder moved me on with a sharp tap to my right shoulder. As he did so, he told me to go down the steps to the large box below. Looking straight ahead, I did as I was asked. Once there, another man, dressed in a dark suit, held open the small panelled door through which I entered the dock. I did as I was instructed, and before I could even take my lonely seat within, the man quickly secured the door behind me, as if he expected me to try running away.

I sat, and the bright April sunlight suddenly flooded in from the large windows set above the witness bench, like some blinding celestial fingers reaching in towards me. They hurt my eyes.

I wanted to look back, if only to steal a glance over my shoulder at the gallery behind me, but I was afraid to go against my Counsel's advice. I knew that *they* were not here to take any useful part in my trial. They were only there on account of the sensational stories reported about me in the *Port Hope Guide*. They were there for the thrill of hearing the morbid details dragged out for their own perverse entertainment; and to gloat at my imminent downfall. I could feel their presence behind me – like a murder of black crows waiting to pick at each sordid morsel as soon as it passed out from the witnesses' lips. That, and given half the chance, for the opportunity to peck at my eyes. Ghouls! That was all that they were, and so I decided that I definitely would not look back. I wasn't going to give them the satisfaction of seeing my face and then imagining my sense of terror and despair. Instead, I was adamant that I would hold my head high and let them burn their eyes on my every movement.

Directly in front and below me, there stood a highly polished dark-wood table. Here the barrister for the Crown, Mr Thomas Hodgins was sitting with an open folder of papers perched upon his knee; papers through which he was furiously sifting. Hodgins must have heard the door of my box close, for he glanced straight at me, for all but a moment. Then he quickly looked away again. For all intents, I might just as well have been made of glass for the way he was able to look straight through me.

A few moments later, a somewhat dishevelled Mr Jex arrived, only to drop his papers upon the courtroom floor. Then, as he scurried about trying to retrieve them, everyone else suddenly rose to their feet for the entrance of Judge Burton. As they did so, I could not help but notice how tall Mr Hodgins was when juxtaposed against the profile of my own lawyer. They looked like David and Goliath.

Judge Burton took his seat and Mr Jex half-turned in my direction and smiled before quickly looking away to face the front of the room and His Lordship.

The trial opened and the charges of infanticide and *'abandoning a two-day-old baby'* were solemnly read out against me. I could not make out the words being spoken straight away, because I was too nervous to take it all in. Then I heard my name and I realised that I was being asked for my plea. Before I could gather my nerve to reply, the question was loudly repeated.

'Mary Ann Wetherup, how do you plead? Guilty or not guilty to the charges as stated.'

I saw Mr Jex half turn in my direction again as he then gestured for me to answer. I stood and I stated loudly that I pleaded 'not guilty' and then I sat again.

The first witness to be called, George Portugais, had the look of a man who had not slept well in a very long time. He was a muscular man, of swarthy appearance, and who I supposed to have been around thirty years of age. As I watched him from the isolation of the dock, I found myself admiring his strong outward appearance, which over the coming minutes would belie the rare gentleness of this man's true nature.

As Portugais stepped into the witness stand, I noticed a string of rosary beads spilling out from out from the clasp of his fist. With faltering words, he swore his oath upon the Holy Bible and then crossed himself as he said 'amen'. He was a carpenter by trade, and he had been out on Concession Eight on the morning of the last day of October, chopping cordwood with his labourer, a Mister Hubbard.

'We had been chopping wood up near Rice Lake all morning,' he recalled. 'By noon we had worked up a real appetite. So, as we set our axes aside, I said to Hubbard that I knew of an empty house nearby where we could get out of the cold for a while and eat our lunch. And maybe even boil up some hot coffee.'

'And this house?' Mr Hodgins, for the prosecution, asked. 'Was it was occupied?'

'No. It was not,' Portugais answered. 'But I already knew this before. Only the day before, I had heard the owner complain that the tenants had just upped and left without a word. Or even paying their debts!'

A rowdy mumble rippled through the room. Many amongst both the onlookers and jury alike, recognised that particular area in question and therefore also the family in question, though at that point in the proceedings they remained unidentified.

Judge Burton called for silence so that George Portugais might be allowed to continue with his account.

'We lit a small fire in the old stove and rested up at the house for an hour or so before going back out into the cold to work. As we reached the clearing once more, I noticed that Hubbard was eyeing a large dog that was sniffing about in the bushes. Then the dog suddenly came running out with something dangling from its mouth. Hubbard called over to me and said, 'Look! George! That dog has got a woodchuck. Help me get it, so I can make some oil for my rheumatics!'[13]'

---

[13]   This use for this rodent was an old Algonquin Indian remedy.

This remark raised a laugh from some people in the court but only a deep frown from Judge Burton. Then again, I could not imagine a fine gentleman like His Honour considering rubbing the oil of a dead critter on himself to ease the bone ache.

'I called the dog,' Portugais continued. 'And to my surprise, the beast obeyed me. But then, as Hubbard made his move towards it, the dog suddenly started snarling through its teeth at him. So quickly, I bent down and picked up a rock and threw it at the dog really hard. It hit him on the back and he lets out an almighty yelp. And then he ran off. But the dog had dropped what it was carrying and so Hubbard ran over to pick it up.'

Portugais fell silent for a few moments, perhaps having difficulty in finding the words to describe what happened next. Then his voice cracked and his face began to contort as he struggled to carry on with his testimony.

Judge Burton glanced up over of his silver-rimmed spectacles and offered Portugais the faintest glimmer of a smile, as if to reassure the poor man that all would be better for sharing his dreadful burden, and said calmly, 'In your own time, Mr Portugais...'

George Portugais raised his rosary beads to his mouth and pressed the gold-coloured crucifix attached to it firmly against his lips in a kiss. This action strengthened him enough to carry on.

'Hubbard reached the spot... then... then he suddenly let out a groan and started to wretch. I ran to him, quickly, to see what the problem was. Then I saw *it*. I saw it... and it made me feel sick, too.'

Then Portugais broke down. For several minutes it appeared that he might not be capable of continuing with his evidence. However, after a glass of water was fetched to revive him, and with tears still welling in his dark brown eyes, Portugais eventually managed to compose himself once more and to continue speaking again.

'It was not a woodchuck lying in the snow,' Portugais blurted. 'It was a... child! It was a tiny human child! Or at least it was part of a child. That wicked dog had chewed much of it away!'

After this dreadful revelation, a gasp of horror went up. I, too, felt sick at the awful scene now painted indelibly in my mind. But, heeding my lawyer's cautioning of the previous day, I fought the rising nausea and did my best not to show any feeling. Then the visibly shaking George Portugais was excused to resume his place back on the witness bench. My defence barrister, Mr Jex, had not asked to cross examine George Portugais' evidence. Instead he sat impassively at his desk with his arms folded and a far away look on his face. It is only when the Moores were brought to the stand and sworn in that Mr Jex sprang into action – objecting that their 'evidence' was comprised of little more than malicious gossip and hearsay and argued, vehemently, that it should not therefore be admissible. To the obvious dissatisfaction of Mr Hodgins, Judge Burton agreed, and so the witnesses were dismissed unheard.

Listening to the testimonies of witnesses as they came and went was like being forced to relive the most dreadful minutes of my life. Only this time they were being played out to a room full of strangers from the perspective of others: people who did not know me, and who therefore could not possibly have understood what I had been through, or even what I was going through then. I could see the look on the jurors' faces; faces that were already harbouring their own opinions about me – opinions based upon cold words and assumptions published in the newspapers, or gleaned from spiteful rumours and malicious gossip. None of then knew me, and I wondered, how I could ever expect justice from them? Who was going to take my side in all of this and be persuaded that I had not killed my own child?

After a recess for lunch, the court called upon, Dr Weston Leroy Herriman, to come forward and give his evidence. I remember Detective Murray previously commenting upon the fact that Herriman was a devout Methodist, and so I wondered why the good doctor's attitude towards me before had seemed to be less than Christian.

Herriman was much older than Portugais, nearer to Judge Burton's age, I think. He appeared to be the kind of physician in whom most people would find comfort, especially when seen beside a sickbed. I would not, though. I had already met him at the School House, where I had found him to be cold and indifferent. I could remember him touching my body, not saying anything to me, and not making any eye contact with me, not even once. I might just as well have been a corpse upon his table instead of a living breathing woman.

The doctor took his oath calmly and then stood for a moment, with his eyes half shut, as if in silent prayer. Then, as directed by Mr Hodgins, Herriman began to speak, giving his evidence to electric silence.

'Dr Herriman,' Hodgins began, 'am I right in stating that it was you who examined the defendant shortly after what remained of the child was found at Hope?'

'Yes sir, you are correct.'

'And would you be kind enough to tell the court what your findings were?'

I felt myself cringe as he then proceeded to talk about my body in the most intimate of details to this room full of strangers. It was excruciatingly embarrassing – knowing that as he did so, everyone's eyes were trained upon me. There was no hiding place for me in the dock.

'I made an examination of the prisoner's breasts and found them to be flabby. The cuticle of one was roughened as if some hot application had been applied. On pressing the

168

nipple between my fingertips, some drops of good-looking milk flowed and also a creamy, thickish, yellow fluid. From this, supported by a second opinion of a colleague, Dr Corbett, I determined that the defendant had recently given birth.'

A great muttering rippled along the gallery behind me, and ahead I saw two members of the jury passing comments behind their hands to one another and then grinning. It was then that I wished that the floor directly beneath me would somehow open so that I could slide down into the basement below and shelter in some dark, shadowy corner where no one would find me.

Dr Herriman was then drawn by Hodgins towards the subject of my baby and into outlining his findings in that respect. As he did so, I tried to do as Mr Jex had advised me; to let my mind fixate elsewhere. I tried to blot out his words – by instead concentrating on Dr Herriman's appearance. I forced myself to consider how, despite his receding snowy white hair, he still had black bushy eyebrows. And then I focused on the expressions passing across Herriman's densely bearded face – like waves in a tempest, with his eyes flashing like lightening. But I simply could not keep it up. The droning cleared of its own accord into words that filtered into my brain and then grabbed my immediate attention.

'I saw the remains of the deceased very shortly after they were discovered,' I suddenly heard Herriman say, 'and I examined them as well as one might, given the circumstances. Initially, they were wrapped in what I now understand to have been the plaid work shirt of George Portugais. They had been laid out in a small basket, which in turn had been placed inside a wooden chest. Straight away I recognised them as being a part of a new born infant and that they were in a good state of preservation. This was due partly, I think, to the fact that they had been frozen during the extremely cold weather preceding their discovery...'

I remembered waking at night to the bitter cold inside my parents' home as I lay on the floor by the old cast iron stove, long after the fire had burnt out. Of how I would shiver beneath my scant blankets with only the gentle kicks of my baby inside me for solace.

'...I noted no foetor,' the doctor continued, 'nor any bad smell about them which makes me think that death must have taken place very shortly before the body had been disposed of out of doors, and that thereafter it froze quickly...'

I remembered the scent of my newly born baby as she snuggled into my weary arms. When I had gently kissed her tiny head, she had smelt wonderful to me. So all the more revolting was it for me to have to then hear about, in wretched detail, the state of the copse of that very same child, found as it was only a few days after.

'...All the lower part of the body was gone,' Herriman added, glancing down briefly at his papers before continuing. 'What remained consisted of the head, neck, both arms, both hands, and a part of the wall of the chest. On the right side, all the true ribs and false ribs were present. On the left side, the first, second and anterior of three quarters of the three ribs, and the integument covering them on the back, the parts only extended as low as the fourth or fifth dorsal vertebrae and integument covering much of them. All the viscera of bowels and chest were gone...'

I could not bear to hear anymore. All I could see in my mind's eye was the image of Pa's mangy dog chewing on the body of my beautiful baby, as if she were a lump of dead meat. I wanted to scream out for Herriman to stop. I wanted to vomit. And even now, I do not know how I managed to contain my emotions as I sat in that wretched box – but I did. I did because I knew that my life depended on it.

'If I may be permitted,' Dr Herriman looked towards Judge Burton, 'at this point I would like to read aloud from my notes made at the post mortem to clarify the facts...'

'By all means,' Burton replied. 'Carry on Doctor.'

With that, Herriman picked up some more pages of notes that had accompanied him to the stand. He opened them to the second page and continued giving evidence by reading out his autopsy findings. As I watched the faces of the unlearned laymen amongst the jury, as the detailed analyses of the tiny corpse was spun out, I could see little doubt in the jurors' minds of the dreadful gravity of this matter. In the natural pauses of Herriman's slow and deliberate delivery, the room had fallen so silent that I could even hear my own heart beating.

If you had asked me then how my trial was going to end, I would have had no hesitation at all in telling you that they were going to find me guilty. I just knew it. I could sense it hanging in the air. I could see it etched upon the jurors' faces. If I am to be honest, I must admit that I could not blame them. Had I been sitting where they were sitting, I would have shared their thoughts.

'...occiput and forehead, thirteen-and-a-quarter inches... around the head from chin to occiput, fifteen-and-one-quarter inches. The arm from top of shoulder to tip of middle finger, eight-and-three-quarter inches. The hands are plump, and the finger nails extend beyond the tips of the fingers. The head is covered with a fair coating of auburn hair...'

I felt faint as I recalled, vividly, my baby's tiny hand clasping a hold of my finger: of me running my own fingers across the shock of hair upon her head and thinking how it was just the colour of mine. It was then that I could no longer hold back a lump that came to my throat, or the tears that began to trickle down my face. I tried to wipe them away without drawing any more attention to myself, but feared that I had been seen.

'... All of the parts appear to be well developed,' Herriman's words droned on in my head, '... and are firm and well nourished and have the appearance of a newborn infant at full time of maturity.'

'Then this infant was not the result of a miscarriage?' Hodgins interjected, not for his own learned benefit but for that of the jury.'

'No sir,' Dr Herriman replied. 'There can be no question at all. This was full-term, viable human being.'

'Thank you, Doctor Herriman. Please be so kind as to continue.'

'I observed several puncture wounds about the infant's neck and face, as if made by the teeth of a dog. The inside of the chest has the appearance of having had its contents recently removed. It is moist and bloody looking, contrasting strongly with the surrounding edges. The membrainis pupilaris is not present. There are some particles of sand around the finger nails and some dried blood over the back of one hand. The colour of the skin on the hands is pale and soft and not denuded. But that on the face and neck, chest and arms, particularly the front parts as far as near the wrists, is quite red. And in many places, denuded of the epidermis. The epidermis...' Herriman coughed, then coughed again before continuing with a distinct crackle now to his voice, 'when not off, in most places rubs off easily. Some spots are not so red. The back part is slightly blushed and not much denuded. The redness continues over the forehead to the top of the head. On the face the epidermis is very red indeed and much denuded. A microscopic examination of the hair from the head shows it to have been singed...'

Doctor Herriman paused for a moment to gratefully take a sip or two from a fresh glass tumbler of water which had been brought to the stand.

172

'I beg your pardon, your honour,' the Doctor said to the Judge, 'I had a slight tickle in my throat, but it is clear now, I think.'

'When you are quite ready, Doctor,' Hodgins politely urged Herriman on.

'The left eyelids, when open, do not have the red appearance. There is only a slight redness on the inner side of the upper lid while the inside of the lower lid is quite pale. The eyeball is not red. The eyelids of the right eye are not quite so red as the rest of the face, but redder than the left. The inside of both eyelids are quite red and highly congestive. The white of the eyeball is distinctly discoloured. The flesh on each cheek of the child's face is hardened and calloused, to the extent of a silver dollar. The inside of the lips are very red. Also the tongue. The gums are paler. Some clear mucus flows from the left nostril...'

'And how, Dr Herriman, in layman's terms if you please, do you suppose this infant met its death?'

'Death, while swift would not have been instant and would have inflicted considerable agony upon the poor creature...,' he said before adding damningly, 'I believe that while alive, this child was placed upon some exceedingly hot surface and was literally roasted alive...'

Suddenly fury broke out in the courtroom, as almost disbelieving jurors, witnesses and bystanders, chorused their collective outrage and sense of horror at Doctor Herriman's submission. And then, try as he might, Judge Burton could not restore order to the court. So, instead, he was forced to adjourn the proceedings until the following morning. I was led away back to the cells below – as bystanders jeered abusively at me and spat upon me. And one woman screamed, 'May God forgive you, Mary Ann, for we shan't!'

I remember suddenly thinking about a dog I once saw. It was somewhere along the Fourth Line, when we lived back in Dummer and I was visiting my Grandpa John. It was surrounded by three other stronger dogs that were snarling and snapping at it. The victimised dog was cowering and shaking with fear and had its tail slung between its hind legs. And even when it had rolled onto its back in submission, the other dogs were still attacking it. I couldn't bear the sight of those dogs being so cruel to one of their own, so I bent down and picked up a stone and threw it at the biggest dog's head. The stone found its mark and the dog yowled in pain as it streaked off with its two companions close behind.

In those moments when I was led away from the mob baying about me, I imagined myself being attacked by a pack of dogs. And it wasn't fair. I knew that I had not led a blameless life. I knew that I had done some bad things over the years. But I did not deserve what those people were putting me through. I did not. I really did not...

Chapter Five

I could not sleep at all that night. Instead, I lay upon my bunk with my head swimming with all that had been said in court that day. And I felt sickened. Before then, I had only been able to imagine the dreadful agonies felt by my baby in those final few moments of her life. For me to have to sit and listen as minute detail after detail of every mind-numbingly horrific injury inflicted upon her was read aloud, only deepened my distress as the most dreadful events leading up to them came raging back to me in indescribable torment. I had heard it said that the imagination can be a terrible faculty for making things unseen seem far worse than the actually are. However, I now know with certainty that a picture of the truth can be infinitely more terrible than anything the imagination can paint.

As I lay awake listening to the chimes of the clock outside marking the passing hours of the night, I kept wondering about what was going to happen the next day. What would it be like when eventually it would be my time to take the stand and testify before the court.

In my head I kept going over all that I had confided in Detective Murray that day in the cells when the *'great detective'* had broken my resilience – to the point where I revealed everything. I eventually told him what had really happened on that dreadful day my baby was murdered. For murder it surely had been – the most brutal cold blooded slaughter of an infant.

It is enough, Mary Ann!' Murray had shouted, slamming his note book down upon the table. 'It is enough to convince *any* jury in the land to convict you of murder. And when they do - you *will* hang, Mary Ann. You will hang by the neck until you are dead.'

At first I had just sat there, staring back at Murray and with my heart banging away so hard that I thought it would burst. Murray must surely have been able to see it for himself, leaping in my chest. Hanging? I didn't want to hang.

Still I had held my tongue until poker-faced Murray had thrown down his final card.

'Then again,' he added calmly, 'perhaps your mother thinks that you deserve to hang. And she will be glad to hear when you have. After all, you told me before how worthless even she can see that you are.'

That was enough to stir up the sting in me and let loose all the resentment I had long held for *her*.

Then I shrieked at him. 'It's my mother who should hang!'

'And why is that?' Murray demanded.

'She is the one!' I told him. 'She is the one who killed my baby...'

The truth was out. I could not take it back.

As I had said to Murray before, Ma had always been the most difficult of women. At best she could be abrupt and rude – even in her normal discourse with Pa, us children, and neighbours. At her worst she would snap and snarl at every turn like a mad dog – striking out viciously for no apparent reason, for absolutely no reason that any sane person could fathom. From time to time it seemed as if an incredibly dark and venomous demon had entered the core of her being and completely possessed her. Again I say that there never seemed to be any reason for such manifest evil. Something that you might think would vex her bad would wash over her like a soft breeze. Yet another time, the tiniest thing could set her off into a whirlwind of abuse and screeching that could stop your blood dead from flowing through your veins just out of the fear of what she might say or do next.

So I had explained to Murray, 'The number of times that my sister and I hid under the table when I was young, I cannot begin to count. We would be shaking in fear of our lives! But she would reach under, and pull me out, screaming, by my hair and then beat me until her muscles grew weary. Then, with age I suppose, Ma seemed to quieten down a great deal – that was until I had returned home to her for the last time. Then, she suddenly reverted to her old vile self. And yet for all this, as incredible as it may seem, she was still my mother, and so I loved her.'

I explained to Murray that when I had come home pregnant again in the previous summer, Ma seemed to take it well enough. Indeed, she had kept so calm during those last few days leading up to the birth of my baby, that I should have known that something was wrong.

When I went into labour it was as if something inside Ma snapped. As each new contraction grew increasingly stronger, the vile cursing that spewed from her mouth was ever more fearful. She kept swearing that she would have a Judgement Day on earth and do some reckoning herself. I paid her no heed. How could I do other? I was too far into the grip of my labour pains to do anything about it anyway.

Shortly after, my baby came. She was a beautiful baby girl and perfect in every way, with a mouth like a rose bud and a fine curls of hair. I looked at her and was suddenly filled with such a warm feeling. Looking into her tiny face was like looking into that of her father.

'Mary,' I remember saying to my mother. 'I think I shall call her Mary...'

I can recall sitting on my mattress the following day, propped up with my back against the wall with my baby slumbering peacefully in my arms. I remember feeling hot though: hellishly hot. For some reason known only to her, Ma had over stoked the stove and it was furnace hot.

Pa complained.

'Hey, woman!' he said. 'I'm feeling sick from the heat! What on earth do you think you are doing?'

'If you do nay like it, then you'd best get out!' she snapped at him. 'And take the children with you!'

So he did, leaving me alone in the house with Ma.

I must have dozed off to sleep myself. Ma must have been watching and waiting for that to happen, because the next thing I can remember is that she was suddenly jerking the baby up and away from me. The poor little mite must have been startled because she let out such a cry that it made me sit bolt upright like a spring.

By the time I had gathered my senses, Ma had got my baby by the arms and was dangling the poor thing over the stove.

'I'll teach you!' she screamed at me in a voice far above the baby's wailing. 'I'll teach you to try to crowd me out of my own house!'

I explained to Murray that before I'd had time to get up to stop her, Ma had laid my baby on the stove. I tried to describe my baby's sickening squeal and the awful stench of her flesh burning. I told him how I try frantically to pull Ma away from the stove so that I can get to my little Mary. But I was still weak from giving birth and Ma was so strong in her rage that she threw me across the room knocking me senseless. Then, I told him how all of a sudden the terrible squealing stopped. All was silent as I picked myself up from the floor. All was silent apart from a sickening hissing sound coming from the strove – like Ma was frying up bacon. I tried to scream. In my mind I was screaming, but no sound was coming out of my mouth. I was mute with shock.

'Then... then I think I fainted...' I had told Murray. 'Because when I opened my eyes I was slumped back on the floor. I frantically looked for the baby in my skirts, because for a moment I thought that I must have had a nightmare. Only it is not some terrible dream. Ma had truly murdered my baby. She was coming back inside the house and my baby was gone...'

Then Detective Murray said something that took me completely by surprise, because until that morning I had believed him to be a vain and self-serving man, only interested in furthering his own career and reputation. And yet what he said to me at that moment had seemed utterly heartfelt and sincere.

'Mary Ann,' he said, 'in the interests of justice, and for the sake of your poor innocent child, I shall make it my raison d'être to bring your murdering mother to trial. I will make it my personal mission to hunt her down and bring her back to face trial'. And despite the freezing depth of the wicked winter weather, true to his word, he lost no time in tracking her down so that she could be brought to justice.

But now it was all up to me. I had to tell the court the next day *exactly* what my mother had done, knowing that if she were to be found guilty, she would most likely hang. For a mother to commit infanticide, however horribly, might sometimes be excused on the grounds of diminished responsibility – the effects of terrible depression that sometimes follows giving birth – and therefore warrants some leniency in court. But for a woman to snatch her infant grandchild from the sleeping mother's arms and then murder her... Murray had said that Ma could expect to be shown no such mercy.

If Ma was hanged, then Pa would lose his wife and my brothers and sisters would lose their mother. But for her heinous crime she would need to face the full measure of the law. And if not, I would be found guilty instead, and then I would be condemned as the evil mother who had roasted her own baby to death.

'How can I hope for any justice?' I had asked Detective Murray during his last visit to me in prison, not long after he had returned to Cobourg with my ma and pa. 'So much has already been said about me in the newspaper that people are already saying that I am guilty? Why isn't the court bringing my ma to trial instead?'

'This is not like some schoolyard fight, Mary Ann,' he answered, 'when the teacher already has you by the ear, assuming that you are the primary miscreant. You may well point your finger at another child, trying to tell who the truly guilty party is but it is going to be hard to convince that teacher otherwise without solid proof. Believe me, now is not the time... The legal wheels have already been set in motion and a date for your trial set. And as you so rightly say, the press have not been kindly disposed towards you. But the time to make such an accusation is once all the evidence has been presented before the jury. Then you shall have the opportunity to tell the court what really happened. And when you do, you must tell them in exactly the same way as you told me. Do you understand?'

I nodded.

'If you tell the court, exactly as you told me, then I promise that you will be acquitted by the jury. Then they will arrest your mother, Mary Ann, but only if you can first convince them of the truth.'

I had lots of time after that to think. I often thought about my Pa and my brothers and sisters burying my dead mother; I though of the dreadful pain that would cause them- and me. My baby was gone. Nothing anyone did now was ever going to bring her back.

At first light I told the wardress that I urgently needed to send a message to Mr Jex. I told her that needed to ask him if there was a way in which I could spare Ma the hangman; some other way beside me refusing to testify against her. If she did indeed pass the message on, Mr Jex did not make reply...

Chapter Six

Come the next morning in court, with Mr Jex not wanting to cross examine Dr Herriman's evidence, it was my parents' turn to take the stand.

The statements that they had made to Detective Murray were read out and they were made to swear their oath before the grand jury that all they had said in those statements was true. Then they readily affirmed that they had told the truth.

'Is it true,' Mr Hodgins asked, 'that the accused, your daughter, Mary Ann Wetherup, did reside at your house on Grey's Farm in the Township of Hope between late July and October twenty-seventh, eighteen-hundred-and-seventy-nine?

'Yes,' my father replied for them both.

'And did the said Mary Ann Wetherup, on or about the twenty-fifth of October last, give birth to a female infant at your house.'

Again, my father replied, 'Yes sir.'

I looked at Pa hoping against hope that he might turn to look at me, but he did not. Suddenly, yet again, I felt overwhelmed by the most indescribably painful and infinitely deep sense of loss, emptiness, and loneliness, the combination of which tore me apart at the very core of my being.

I will never forget the look of sheer panic on Pa's face on that day my daughter died – when he had come home to find me shaking with hysteria and the baby missing. I will never forget how he had then looked towards Ma, and then realized... He knew immediately that she had done something unspeakable.

'What have you done, woman?' he yelled. 'What have you done?'

182

At first Ma wouldn't tell him. She just sat rocking in her chair, saying, 'I have taught her lesson... I have taught her a lesson... that is all.'

Pa tried to comfort me, but I couldn't stop sobbing.

'She killed my baby, Pa!' is all that I had been able to tell him.

The baby obviously wasn't in the house, and so he went outside. Pa was gone for what seemed an eternity... before he returned with his face ashen. He had then gone straight to his jar and poured out what little was left of his whiskey into a tin cup which, after taking a great gulp himself, he then gave to me.

'Drink this up,' he had said softly, 'it will help lessen the shock.'

He didn't look at Ma at all. I do not think that he could bring himself to do so, for I think that just then he despised her – he loathed the woman he had once adored and chosen to marry in his youth.

But later, as we stood together at the train stop, Pa looked at me with tears in his eyes and pleaded with me not to tell anyone about what had happened.

'She shouldn't have done it,' he admitted. 'She should never have done it, and she deserves to be punished. But if anyone finds out, they will hang her. They will hang her for sure, but she is my wife, Mary Ann. I could not bear to see your mother hang. That would kill me!'

And so, very foolishly, I promised Pa that I would not tell anyone about Ma's most cruel and evil deed. I had promised him and apart from my private confession to Detective Murray, I had stood by that promise. And because I had made that decision, I was now set to pay for it with my life...

Pa's nervous cough brought me back to the courtroom.

Hodgins was asking my father if I had taken my baby, alive, with me when I left their house, because this is what he had sworn in his original statement before Police Magistrate Irvine.

When Pa replied that I had, gasps reverberated about the room as, with renewed shock and despair. I slumped back in my seat. Pa was lying, and yet I felt crushed by guilt. I had left home without my baby – because my mother had murdered her! I had fled in panic, with any shred of reason battered and numbed by nauseating shock. I had desperately needed to get as far away far as I could from my mother, and the brutal and horrific truth of it all.

At the end of Pa's testimony, Thomas Hodgins could not help himself from glancing in my direction – as he returned to his seat with an air of triumph. He was hardly able to conceal a great, deep smirk of self-satisfaction revealed in the corners of his thin lips. There seemed little more for him to do now that my imminent conviction was assured.

I was innocent, but at that moment I could not see how I could even hope to be found as such. Meanwhile, such a commotion surged forth from the gallery that Judge Burton tersely called for order – so that, as all could plainly sense, the dregs of this case could be drained and my fate then swiftly sealed.

My defence, Mr Jex, rose slowly from his seat and then, almost apologetically, began his cross examination of Pa.

'Is it true,' Jex asked Pa, using exactly the same words that Hodgins had used, 'that the accused, your daughter, Mary Ann Wetherup, did reside at your house on Grey's Farm in the Township of Hope between late July and October twenty-seventh, eighteen-hundred-and-seventy-nine?

'No,' Pa replied loudly.

I could not believe my ears. And, as it appeared, neither could anyone else. As soon as Pa had uttered that one word, pandemonium broke out. So his Lordship, Judge Burton, banged his table with all his might in an effort to bring the proceedings to order. But only with the aid of constables and ushers, who rose as one to force those standing in uproar to settle down, did he eventually re-establish order.

Then, again, Mr Jex repeated the question. And when Pa, again, replied loudly that it was not true, again, order broke down – into a cacophony of chaos.

The proceedings were hastily adjourned as the Judge ordered a constable to take Pa and Ma out of the court and into a side room.

After a lengthy recess, the court proceedings resumed. Meanwhile, the constable who had charge of my parents, informed Judge Burton that Pa had agreed to 'tell the truth this time', if only Pa could be allowed back into court to do so. And Mr Hodgins, apparently desperately eager to carry on and wind up the proceedings to his advantage, requested that Pa be permitted to take the witness stand once more. Reluctantly, the Judge agreed.

'May I remind you Mr Wetherup,' Judge Burton warned, 'that you are still under oath?'

'Yes, your honour,' Pa answered meekly.

'And,' the Judge continued, 'that you are now prepared to tell the truth, the whole truth, and nothing but the truth?'

'Yes, your honour, I am.'

'Then Mr Jex,' Judge Burton said, 'you may resume your cross examination.'

Mr Jex rose slowly from his seat and approached the witness stand again.

'Is it true,' Jex asked Pa, 'that the accused, your daughter, Mary Ann Wetherup, did reside at your house on Grey's Farm in the Township of Hope between late July and October twenty-seventh, eighteen-hundred-and-seventy-nine?'

To utter silence, my pa replied loudly, 'Yes.'

His answer was loud enough to let Hodgins' smirk reappear.

'When I put this question to you earlier in front of this very court, you had replied to me that she had not. Can you please tell the jury why you have now changed your answer to 'yes'? Mr Jex asked calmly.

Pa took a great intake of air before replying.

'That would be because while I was taken out, the constable warned me that I had better come back inside here an stick by my original statement because if I did not, things were going to go very badly for me...'

This time, instead of pandemonium, a deathly hush fell upon the court – so that you could have heard a handkerchief drop.

I did not understand exactly at that moment the gravity of what Pa had just said, but one glance towards the horrified expression of both Hodgins and the Judge's faces told me that something monumental had just happened.

But before any verbal reaction could come from either the Queen's Council or his Lordship the Judge, Mr Jex quickly carried on.

'Did your daughter give birth to a child in your house, last October?'

'No sir,' Pa said. 'No sir, she never had any child at any time in my house. And she never took no child with her when she left either...'

'Then why did you say that that she had when you first gave your sworn statement last December?'

'It was because I was made to, sir,' my pa said firmly. 'My wife and me was intimidated by the detective bringing us back from Bruce County. And also by the Police Magistrate once we arrived here at Cobourg!'

The room erupted once more to cries 'shame' from the gallery.

With his face looking like it might explode, Judge Burton immediately called the constable before him and publicly rebuked him. And then, with the expression on his face little diminished, he turned towards the jury and directed then not to find me guilty on the evidence given either by my father or my mother. Furthermore, he told the jury that there was now no evidence at all to prove that the dead infant belonged to me.

'You are free to go, Miss Wetherup.' Judge Burton said, although, as I sensed, he spoke somewhat begrudgingly.

Yet from the gallery behind me, angry spectators jeered and screamed vile threats at me, because they suspected that I was literally getting away with murder.

Mr Jex came to the dock as the officer opened the door to set me free.

'I am sorry, Miss Wetherup,' he whispered as he leaned in, 'but it was the only way that I could be certain of obtaining a *satisfactory* outcome for both you and your parents. Now I fear that you shall have to run the gauntlet of that angry mob.'

I realised then that, somehow, Jex had managed to orchestrate the whole thing with the collusion of my parents. I realised then that must have been why Pa would not look me – in case he gave himself away. Yet where was I now free to go to? I may have gained my liberty but in the process I had been stripped of my reputation, and my name had not been cleared in people's minds.

Outside the court there was a mass of people waiting for me. All they could conceive from what had just transpired in court was that Mary Ann Wetherup the baby

187

murderer was getting away unpunished. I had denied myself the chance to speak, and therefore denied the world the opportunity of knowing that I had not committed that heinous crime for which I had already spent many months in jail. There was to be no real justice for either me or my murdered baby. Instead, I was lucky to escape with my life – which now hung in tatters. But, obviously, it was the sacrifice that had to be made to free myself and spare Ma from the hangman. I had to be grateful, I supposed, considering how close I had come to the alternative.

I knew straight off that it was now going to be impossible for me to even contemplate going back to Port Hope. I realised that I would never be able to pick up my previous life, or stay in the county, or even to return to Dummer, where I had grown up. My name was now so blackened that I would have to get as far away from Hope as I could. So I made for the backwoods of Bruce, where even the *Daily Guide* could not follow me.

***

I was at liberty, but Ma and Pa were not. Directly after my trial, Judge Burton had them both arrested. It would be more than five months before their case was bought to trial and for all that time they were kept in jail.

On the thirtieth of September, my parents faced an Indictment for Perjury before the Court of Oyer and Terminer. Both admitted giving false statements, but claimed that they had only done so as the result of intimidation by Detective Murray whilst he was bringing them to Cobourg.

What could the judge do, other than to let them walk free? If Ma were brought to trial for killing my child, then this sorry bag of worms would be spilled open to public scrutiny. With Ontario's only detective discredited, what then would be the outcome of his many other cases waiting to come to trial?

Pa had taken his term of imprisonment in his stride, but, surprisingly, Ma came out of prison as a changed woman. It broke her, for certain, of her bad temper. But it also ruined her health.

By the first week in October, Ma and Pa had also reached our relatives in Bruce, and so began my very uneasy truce with my estranged parents. It had been almost eleven months since Detective Murray had caught up with them and forced them to return to Hope. In the meantime, the younger children had been abandoned to the care of our mother's sisters, Margaret Esplin and Mary Mclean.

It was the following New Year that I first met William Norton at a neighbouring party. I remember that time well, because just a few days later, my widowed aunt Mary tragically slipped in the snow and was paralysed. She died two months later.

When the census enumerator called on my family that year, Ma and Pa gave their ages as forty-five, some ten years younger than their actual ages – so as not to attract curiosity over the fact that two of *their* children had born so unusually late in Ma's life. Nosey neighbours may have thought that Ma looked old and haggard beyond her age, but it was no secret that she was also becoming a very sick woman.

My own age was greatly underreported as being a mere twenty-three, again to help conceal my true identity. I looked very youthful still, and so the pretence was not as hard to keep up as one might have thought, especially as within the year Pa and most of the rest of my family had returned to living in Hope, taking my illegitimate children with them. Indeed, Margaret and Joseph were never told that I was in fact anything other than their loving *sister*.

At last I found anonymity. William Norton and I married, and after the birth of our first son, Robert, we moved to Keppel Township in Grey. William found work as a farm labourer and when the railway came into the district shortly thereafter; our fortunes seemed to further look up. I had begun to enjoy my simple life as a wife and mother and believed that at last I was beginning to heal from the emotional wounds I had suffered in Hope.

While William and I were expecting our third son, James, a dreadful thing occurred not far from where we were living. A man named John Bailey and his hired man were brutally murdered, and then the house in which they had been living was burned down in a bid to cover up the crime. Such was the outrage that a reward of eight-hundred dollars was offered in return for information that led to the murderers being brought to justice.

A short time later, William and I were in town. We had just been to the general store, and were walking past the hotel when a gentleman hurried out and almost knocked our oldest boy flying. This man then turned and began to proffer his profuse apology...that is until he and I came face to face. I could not help myself... I froze in utter shock. And so did the man, before he then rushed off down the street.

'Who was that?' William asked.

'I haven't a clue,' I said.

'Well he looked as though he knew you, Mary Ann,' William persisted.

'Well I am certain that he did not!' I snapped, continuing on my way with the children.

Some months passed by and then it came out in the newspapers. Two detectives had been sent from Toronto to try to trap Bailey's killers and had been inside that same hotel luring a female accomplice into making a confession. The suspects were duly arrested, but when the case came to trial there was not enough evidence to convict them. One of the detectives had been the much celebrated *'Old Never-let–go'* himself, the Inspector of the Department of Criminal Investigation of the Department of Justice – Detective John Wilson Murray. I knew then why Murray had pretended not to have known me. He had been working undercover.

For almost fifteen years I had enjoyed married life with my husband. Through those years I had at last experienced the joy of mothering my own brood of children, and my relationship with William had been an almost entirely happy one. However, by the time I was supposedly thirty-five, my hair had turned quite grey and my looks had faded rapidly. And in the following year, when our youngest child Frank was born at my true age of forty-six, William's feelings for me seemed to cool, and he had begun to suspect that I had maybe lied about my age when we married.

Then that fateful day dawned when the remnant of my happiness fell to pieces. That was the day when the *stranger* accosted me in that street and ousted my deepest shame.

'What did that man mean?' William demanded with an anger that I had never before seen in him. 'What did he mean when he called you a murderer?'

The wicked tongues of our neighbours had made short work of telling my husband.

I had to tell William. At last I had to tell him the truth about my past. I don't know if he believed me when I t swore to him that I had not killed my baby. But how could he even imagine me being capable of such a thing? Hadn't he shared in my joy at the birth of our own babies, and then watched me raise them with him, with all the love that a mother and wife could give? But it was as if he had wiped away all of those happy memories we

What I found most hurtful to me in this erroneous piece of sensational writing was that he could not even get the gender of my poor dead baby right. This 'great detective', who once claimed to be so moved by my innocent child's death, could not even recall that it was a daughter that I had lost, and not a 'male child' as he had stated in his book. Once I thought that he had genuinely cared, but at last I concluded that my first impression of him had been correct – that he was shallow, self-serving, publicity hungry, and low enough to have turned my tragedy into a flippant work of fiction.

Although Murray's sketched-out character of me was damning, and no doubt coloured up to appeal to his eager readers, at least the nub of truth about the whole tragic affair was now set down in black and white. The world now knew that my mother had murdered my baby- and not me. After so many years of my own self-imposed silence, the story was out. And to my surprise, all I could feel was relief. The past and I would just have to try to live together...

End

Edith May's Story

Edith May's story

Edith May Masters was born in Tooting, South London, England in 1899.

Chapter One

He was on leave; fourteen days' leave from the battlefront in France. He could have chosen to come anywhere in England. Anywhere at all. But he settled on coming to London to 'see the sights', I suppose just in case he would never get the chance to do so again. He could have stayed anywhere in London – but as luck would have it, the friend with whom he made the crossing from France had been asked by his family back home to look up relatives just a few streets away from where I lived in Wimbledon. And since Bill Weatherup had no definite plans of his own, he had simply tagged along. And so we met.

By then the War was in its fourth year. Four bloody years! I was only eighteen and to me it had seemed to be going on forever. And, as my friend Hattie and I considered things; 'we couldn't see no bleedin' end to it in sight.'

Hattie lived a couple of roads away from me and was my best mate. *Hattie* wasn't her real name though – it was Sylvia. No, she got the name *Hattie* at school on account of how she always wore a hat – whether she was indoors or out. Most people didn't know why she always wore a hat and must have assumed that she simply had a particular fancy for them. But I knew the truth. I knew that she wore hats to cover up a big bald patch she had on her head since contracting a bad case of ringworm. Her wispy ginger hair had never properly grown back over the affected area of her scalp. Her left eye wasn't quite right either and would sometimes seem to be wandering on its own in the opposite direction to the right one, which meant she never got a look in from the lads. A *'lazy eye'* is what they called it – but if it was lazy, then it was the only lazy thing about Hattie. I never met anyone who worked as hard as she did. And she was the nicest person I had ever met, and she didn't have a bad bone in her. But my mum didn't like Hattie or her family at all. *'Dirty Irish'*, she called them, and said how I shouldn't be having anything to do with the likes of them. But Hattie wasn't Irish, and nor was her mother. Her dad was though, but he had pushed off not long after Hattie's brother Teddy was born. Teddy wasn't born right; his legs were withered and one of his arms, too. It was very soon after Teddy was born when Hattie's dad just upped and went and never came back. Her mum always looked exhausted; she worked all hours at four or five different jobs just to make ends meet. So I never paid my mum any heed over Hattie. I liked Hattie and her whole blooming family, *dirty Irish* or not.

It was no barrel of laughs, I can tell you, being a young woman back then. As far as I could remember there had been shortages of just about everything, apart from shortages. And we had gone hungry, so hungry at times that I swear I could feel my belly button kissing my backbone. And we were terrified too; terrified of the Huns.

From the very start of the war we heard rumours about how the Huns could send their bloomin' great dirigibles across the sea to attack us, but it hadn't quite sunk in. Most of us hadn't a clue what a 'dirigible' was, or even heard the word before. Not many of us had even seen airplanes.

Soon the posters started going up at the underground stations and on the omnibuses. They depicted a the black silhouette of St Paul's Cathedral and the City against a midnight blue background with a great silver cigar-shaped airship hanging in the sky and picked out by the beam of a giant searchlight. Beneath this ominous picture and in large letters the sombre message was clear; *'It is far better to face the bullets than to be killed at home by a bomb. – Join the Army at once & help to stop an air raid. – God save the King.'*

Those dirigibles soon turned out to the stuff of nightmares. Then the very mention of the word *'Zeppelin'* was enough to frighten anyone living in London.

The first air raid on London came on the night of the last day of May in nineteen-fifteen. They were cunning sods, those Huns! They would wait for moonless nights and then sneak across to bomb us. Mainly the East End copped it, and the dockland area, or anywhere else connected with the War Effort.

There were reports in the newspapers about the raids, but my dad said that they only ever told half the truth so as not to cause panic. He would often hear stories down at the pub from dockers and the like – about the fires set by incendiaries dropping, and about all the mayhem they had caused. It didn't bother us much at first, not in our part of south London, because we were a long way from the East End, but that soon changed.

Between the twenty-third and twenty-forth of September the following year, nine *Zeppelin* airships reached London. I heard 'em. I heard explosions that night and had jumped out of my bed and across to the open bedroom window.

'What the heck was that bang, Edie?' My sister Nance exclaimed, almost elbowing me out of the window for trying to see what was going on.

In the distance we saw a red glow begin to tinge the moonless night sky, which was quickly brightened by the sweep of searchlight beams.

'Is that Mitcham?' Nance asked.

'I dunno,' I said. 'I think it's further towards the Vale. It sounded like a bombs.'

No sooner had the word 'bomb' left my mouth than there was another 'boom' in the distance. All Nance and I could do was stand watching in the darkness as the red glow in the distance was joined with another. Then we watched and prayed that whatever was out there did not come our way.

Those bastard *Zeppelins* dropped some three-hundred-and-seventy- one bombs in all, and we in the suburbs south of London bore the brunt of it all. One of the 'booms' Nance and I heard had come from a few miles away in Streatham Vale, where several houses were hit. The families inside had been killed when the buildings caught fire and collapsed on them. Some homes in Brixton were also bombed.

My dad's mate said how he had been walking home from working in Mitcham that night and had seen one of the bloomin' great things glide across the sky above Figgs Marsh. '*Awesome*', is how he said it was, and how, for such a massive and horrible thing, it had moved across the sky quite gracefully. He then described the gentle whirring sound it made. It was not noisy like an airplane.

The *Zeppelins* were so large and moved so slowly that our lot managed to shoot a lot of them down; so many that, after that raid, they seemed to stop coming altogether. Either that or else we just weren't being told about them anymore.

Then on the thirteenth of June, nineteen-seventeen, for the first time there was a daylight bombing raid on London, but this time by fourteen Gotha fixed-wing aircraft. Most of the bombs fell on the East End. The most horrible part of it all was that one bomb that fell on the upper North Street School in Poplar.

It had been a beautiful fine summer's day – with the sky clear and bright – as the planes started bombing just before noon. The school had been full of kids who were still in their classes when a bomb smashed into the roof. It came right through and into the girls' classrooms on the top floor, from where it sliced through to the boys' class on the middle floor, before crashing into the infants' area below, where it exploded.

Of the eighteen children who were killed, sixteen were little ones between the ages of four and six. The following week, a huge funeral of these poor children took place – when fifteen were buried in a mass grave in the East London Cemetery. Just looking at the pictures in the *Daily Sketch* was enough to break your heart.

It wasn't just the fear of the Huns coming to bomb us to bits that got to Hattie and me. It was hearing, day after day, from families all around us about how many of their soldier loved ones had been lost in the trenches, or about how many sailors had been torpedoed by U-Boats. It was always young blokes we heard about; blokes Hattie and I had grown up with, or gone to school with, or hung about the street corners with; the blokes who had 'copped it *over there* and wasn't comin' home no more...'

'At this rate there won't be no bleedin' blokes left at all,' Hattie exclaimed one afternoon, as we were dipping a batch of sheets at the laundry. 'Then who are we goin' to marry, wot wiv so many being dead, Edie? There's gonna be an awful lot of old maids in the years to come. It stands to reason, dunnit?'

Hattie was never what you would call *'bright'*, but that day what she said struck me as being very true. With so many blokes not coming home there was bound to be a shortage of eligible men. You only had to cop a look at the fellas who were left behind to see what a shoddy lot they were, and mostly only still here because they had come up short in some department or another. So even the Army didn't want them. Either they were defective in body somehow, or worse... in the 'ead! Whatever, I didn't fancy ending up with any of them as a husband.

'It's alright for you, Edie,' Hattie continued. 'The blokes swarm round you like you was honey... And you've got Will...'

Will Pankhurst. Yes, I'd had hands-like-plates-of-sausages Will Pankhurst, for all the good it had done me. Will had been my first real sweetheart, and anyone must surely know how that is.

Will lived around the corner not far from Holy Trinity. When we started getting sweet on each other the war had only just started, and everyone was saying how it was going to be all over by Christmas. But instead it went on... So when I was sixteen, he joined the Navy and I was broken-hearted at the thought of being parted from him. Everyone knew that I was Will's girl. We'd even had our picture taken together, with him in his uniform and me in my sister's pale blue two-piece, which came out looking like new in the photo. Will said how I was the only girl for him and so, before he went, we both had tattoos done. He had 'I love Edie' on his chest in a heart and I had 'I love William Pankhurst' done in dark blue lettering on the top of my arm. Aw, you should have heard how my mother kicked up a stink when she found out!

'You silly little cow!' she shouted. 'You better hope he comes back then... 'cos you're going to be stuck with that for the rest of your life!'

I didn't care. I loved Will, and nothing was going to change that. And if he didn't? Well, I had already made up my mind that I wasn't ever going to love anyone else anyway.

I was already working at the laundry with Hattie by then. It was terrible after Will left. All I could do was think about him and how much I missed him. I poured my heart out to Hattie, and then I wrote long letters pouring my heart out to him. Sometimes he would write long letters back to me, but they would be few and far apart. Between letters, my nerves would be all a jitter whenever we heard in the papers about a ship being torpedoed, and I could never rest easy until it had been confirmed that it was not his.

Will did come home though. He came back twice on leave, but of course I had to share him with his family, so we hardly got any time to be alone together. Then I came home one day, passed his house and knew... The door was open and a neighbour came out wiping her eyes with a handkerchief. She looked up and saw me and her face said it all – Will was gone. His ship had been sunk by the Germans and he was '*missing – presumed drowned*'. I was heart-broken.

After Will, I was never quite the same again. It was the day on day, week on week, month on month hearing about death that ground me right down. It was as if with every death that I heard about, a bit of me was withering up and dying with them. That was until, perhaps as some sort of act of self preservation, I began switching off from the bad news, trying to blot it out of my mind. So instead of engaging with what was happening, I tried to just live for the day – as if were a Mayfly. At eighteen or nineteen, keeping constant company with never ending news of death can do that to a young woman. So I no longer concentrated all my affections on one fellow. Instead, I spread mine about among the lot of them, determined to love them while they were with me, and then forget about them completely once they were gone. When I started going out on the town again with Hattie, I went with plenty of fellas, but I never let them 'get to my heart'. And if I thought that they were, I would drop them like a stone and move on to the next. I was young and I wanted to have a good time – but I never wanted to fall in love again. Love hurt too much. All I wanted was to go gadding about with a few soldiers and sailors home on leave. And then I would show them good a time before they had to go back *over there* to face that *what-I-didn't-want-to-know* place. Apart from my mother, who cared? As far as I could see, I wasn't doing any harm to anyone. I just wanted to make the most out of an awful situation – by seizing every opportunity to squeeze a bit of fun out of life, because none of us knew what lay ahead. If anything.

Chapter Two

Will Pankhurst's death had been *clean and sanitary*. One day he had been alive and on leave – laughing and joking. And then on another a letter arrived to inform us that he was suddenly gone. Although we all knew he was dead, we had been spared the dying part. It was the same eventuality for most of us left behind, because letters rarely went into the details of the death. We were spared that part, at least. We did not have to endure hearing the agonised screams of our loved ones, or their silence that followed as the last, rasping breath departed their bodies, or to see an unarticulated corpse in its final wretched repose. The closest we back home got to experiencing the dead of the battlefield was the wretched sight of the wounded, and even some of those poor men were compelled to go about in the public places wearing linen masks so as not to frighten or offend onlookers in the street.

One day a bundle of something, parcelled up in brown paper and string, arrived at the laundry for '*special attention*'. It had been delivered by a servant who had walked all the way from Wimbledon Ridgeway with it. The manager pulled me and Hattie off the line and into a small side room to deal with it.

'Me mum cleans up that way. There are a lot of posh houses there,' Hattie remarked, as I read out the return address on the label attached to the parcel.

'I wonder what's in it...' I said.

Apart from the usual intake, at the laundry we would sometimes receive items of a delicate or sensitive nature, to be washed, dried, and ironed, that for some reason or another could not or would not be dealt with by a household's own servants. For that reason alone we laundresses often dreaded being charged with such a job by the manager.

No sooner had we cut the string and the parcel began to unravel, Hattie and I shrunk away in disgust.

'Aw!' Hattie exclaimed, covering her face with her apron. 'Sumfin' mus' be dead in there!'

The smell was almost enough to make me wretch, but I knew that we had to get on with the job, no matter how rotten the stench. Gingerly, I pulled apart the brown paper – sending the contents spilling out across the surface of the work table. It was a dead army officer's kit.

The uniform, though neatly folded, was still damp and caked with mud; a foul smelling mud, not wholesome and earthy at all like the mud you find in a sack full of potatoes. Instead this mud was more like I would imagine dirt to be if just shovelled it out from an occupied grave.

When I was just a kid, my brothers had managed to open an old doorway leading down into a family crypt at a nearby church. They had not done so out of malice or for any sacrilegious reason, or even with much thought beforehand. They were just naughty little boys who had done it for a dare and then gone inside for a look about. I wouldn't go with them at first, for fear that a ghost might come and get me, but eventually they persuaded me to join them. There wasn't much down there to see, except for a great wall of compartments like a sealed honeycomb. But instead of being filled with sweet and aromatic honey, every cell held a rotted corpse. The stench of that place remained with me all those years since. It was an awful smell of decomposition – the smell that suddenly pervaded that washroom.

Working at arms' length with one hand, and shielding my mouth and nose with the other, I started to sort through the clothing. I teased out the muddy tunic to find that there was a great ragged rip in the front of it, just above the left-hand bottom pocket. The edges of it were caked solid with dark dried blood. I knew at once that this must have been the site of the poor bloke's fatal wound. He'd copped a gut full of shrapnel most likely. We checked the pockets, one by one, but they were empty, apart from the remains of unsmoked *Weights* cigarette and an empty box of *Swan Vestas*.

Then, I turned the tunic over, to discover a great dirty imprint of a boot, as if someone had walked over the soldier as he lay face down on the battlefield. After the tunic, we found blood caked onto every other item of clothing in the pile, including underwear. They conjured up such a shocking and pitiful picture of the end of a brave soldier's life.

'Why didn't they just burn them?' Hattie said.

'I know why?' I replied. 'It's probably the last *real* bit of 'im this family have left. When Dad's younger brother, Daniel, copped it at Wipers, 'is wife begged for somefin' of 'is to be sent back. Anyfin'. But she never got nuffin'.'

Only the wounded came back from the front. The fallen remained there; either buried by their comrades, as this officer had, or else left among the anonymous dead who rotted away where they had fallen.

Hattie sprinkled the clothes with soap flakes and then, as we set them to soak in a great tub of hot water, the blood began to be reanimated, as if the dead soldier's wounds had suddenly opened again. It leached out of the clothes and into the water in deep red ribbons, before forming a pinkish scum at the edges of the tub. There was so much blood that we had to empty the tub and then refill it three times before it stopped coming. When the blood at last stopped dissipating, we scrubbed at the clothing until we had got out almost every trace of mud and blood. Our hands had become red and sore from the process. Then, once we were done, Hattie and I took the items of clothing out into the yard to dry in the sunshine, only bringing them inside again once they were fresh and smelling of the summer breeze.

Then, before I went home for the day, I took a flat iron and solemnly ironed the officer's clothes. As I did, I folded each piece gently and wrapped it tenderly in white tissue paper. When I had finished, I parcelled the uniform in crisp brown paper, making it ready to go back to the customer. To some people the whole process might have seemed like an act of utter futility, but for me it left a deep feeling of satisfaction. I felt as though I had done something to at least ease someone else's grief.

It was not long afterwards that I met Bill Weatherup. After work, Hattie and I were walking arm in arm along Merton High Street one soggy evening in March, nineteen-eighteen. Just after an omnibus turned in at Merton Garage, two soldiers jumped off it and crossed the road in front of us. They were strolling along with their kit bags slung over their shoulders and chatting away nine to the dozen. Their accents were beautiful! All sort of soft and sweet – like golden syrup.

''Ere...' Hattie elbowed me in the ribs,' 'listen up, Edie. 'Them blokes in front are Yanks...'

'So, what?' I said.

'So,' she replied, in a hushed tone, 'I bet they've got a bob or two!' And then she giggled that squeaky little giggle of hers, like that of a small piglet being passed through a mangle. They heard. They heard and both took a glance back at us, so Hattie and I immediately looked down and carried on walking, as if we haven't noticed them. But they stopped. And then, before we had time to notice, we walked right into them. There they were, apologizing profusely to us, when I looked up and I caught Bill's piercing blue eyes staring right back at me.

The long and the short of it was that Bill and his mate invited us for a drink down at the *Nelson's Arm's*. Afterwards, they took us to the pictures. And then after that, Bill and I were together every day until his leave was up and he had to go back to rejoin his unit in France.

I got the impression that Bill, before he'd joined the Army, hadn't been away from his home much. He certainly didn't seem to know his way around a woman! He was sweet though, really sweet! And he seemed taken by me straight off. Bill said that the way I laughed was beautiful, like tinkling bells, and how he adored my English accent and the way that I always wore cotton gloves when we were out on a date. I didn't have the courage to tell him that the reason I did so was to hide my rough red hands after working all day at the laundry.

Just before he had to go back to France, Bill asked me if he could write to me, and asked me if I would be *his girl*. I had said 'yes', though I intended carrying on living in the way I had before we met.

Shortly after Bill's return across the channel, his letters began to arrive. They were chatty at first, and sweet, and rather naïve. Bill spoke about the time we had spent together as if it had meant something, as if he had spun the ten grotty days we'd had of drinking, along with the opportune 'how's yer father', into some great romance. Then I got to thinking that perhaps this was the only memory that he had allowed to be planted in his mind – to help him through *I-didn't-want-to-know-what* in that awful *I-didn't-want-to-know-where* place. So I found myself writing sweet letters back to him. Perhaps they were sweeter and headier than I should have written. But what did it matter? There was no harm in it, I told myself, because nothing would ever come of it. That is, nothing apart from perhaps giving a poor bloke *over there* some ammunition to help him get through it all.

Chapter Three

We were told it was coming, but even so, we didn't dare believe it until it was official. Then the whole of ruddy London went wild with delight! When we heard that the fighting on the Western Front was over! The Armistice, at the eleventh hour on the eleventh day of the eleventh month, in that year of eighteen-eighteen, was met with almost unbelievably ecstatic delight! Despite the freezing cold, spontaneous celebrations burst out everywhere. And so my mum, dad, brothers and sisters, and I, spilled out into the street together – to join the jubilant throngs in a great impromptu open air party.

The strange thing was, though, that the next day it was if nothing at all had changed. Nothing seemed different – it was like the day before had all been a dream. The sky was still grey and overcast, it was cold, and there were the same miserable shortages. The only notable difference was that we knew that the fighting *over there* was finished; that no more of our brave lads had to die, but also that those who were dead were still dead.

Our boys started coming home thick and fast after that. It was going to take some sorting out though, bringing so many blokes back to *Old Blighty*. Will Pankhurst's brother, John, came home really quickly, but he wasn't *right* any more. He looked alright on the outside, but if you got to talking to him down at the pub, it was as if he had somehow been hollowed out inside. He had become extraordinarily quiet, moody, and withdrawn, and not like his old self at all. Then again, a lot of the blokes were like that when they got home. They were also often filled with guilt – because they had survived when so many blokes they had known had not.

'It's the enemy you don't see that'll do for you.' John had been heard to say to Will, when he was last on leave.

John had been right. Below deck shovelling coal in the engine room, Will hadn't seen the U-boat that torpedoed him, just as John hadn't seen the big black depression that would swallow up his soul. Eventually, lost in the depths of his dark and impenetrable world, John had lodged a chair up against the scullery door and quietly cut his own throat with a razor. Imagine going through all that misery in the trenches, only to come home and top yourself!

***

It had already begun by that summer of nineteen-eighteen, only the newspapers had kept the news about it wrapped up and buried deep within their pages. Having wormed its way out from the decomposition and rat infested trenches of the battlefields of Europe, *it* crossed the Channel and invaded England unopposed. The General Medical Council had initially resisted the use of the word 'pandemic', but as the autumn wore on into winter, the growing number of deaths could no longer be ignored. The *Spanish Influenza* was stalking the streets of London.

Mum said that there had been a bad outbreak of flu some twenty years before, and that no doubt this one would go the same way – after getting in and causing a bad throat and a few uncomfortable days, it would soon work itself out again.

'Common sense and few mugs of hot *Oxo* should see us all through,' she said.

As time would bear out though, this flu was going to come and go again so easily. Instead it would prove itself deadly.

We started hearing about friends of friends who had caught it, and then about our friends themselves. Then we quickly grew alarmed when we heard about the high number

211

of deaths among those friends. These deaths weren't just among elderly and frail people, as might have been expected at first. Death even struck people who would otherwise have been expected to shake the flu off easily, including young people like Hattie and me.

Then there were more horrible stories going around about it. How some-one could wake one morning with nothing more than a slight shiver or two, and think no more about it. Then, by lunch time, their skin could have started turning a peculiar shade of purplish blue. Before the day was out, they could then be struggling for breath, as they coughed up something looking like redcurrant jelly that was suddenly clogging their lungs. Then they died.

What with the dreadful shortage of doctors and nurses, and with hospitals already crowded with people wounded in the war, most of those who caught the flu were left to cope as best they could in their own homes, and with no known remedy to cure it. Meanwhile, Dad assured Mum that he had heard a doctor recommend regular tots of whiskey and rum to keep it at bay, and so he was anxious to follow this advice.

Through it all, we who were well were expected to go off to work as usual and *run the gauntlet*, hoping and praying that we wouldn't catch the disease from anyone next to us. Dad warned us not to go on the omnibuses, even though the floors and seats were liberally sprayed each night with disinfectant. He said that, instead, we should walk to the laundry in the open air, but with our coats buttoned right up – so that a collar could be pulled up to cover the mouth and nose.

'You should be alright inside, once you are at the laundry,' he said, 'what with all that steam and carbolic soap in the air.'

But I wasn't as sure, and I told him so. Business at the laundry was brisk and Hattie and I increasingly came across bundle after bundle of soiled sheets that no doubt some poor soul had died in. When we complained to the governor, all he did was give us girls each a thin mask that had been rinsed in disinfectant and then left to dry.

Yet what else could we do? We couldn't stay at home until the flu went away. What would we have done for money? And how or where could we have fun without risking copping the flu? The cinemas were still open, but what with having to sit so close to other people, Hattie and I were too scared to go. And we were too afraid to mix with soldiers, because that is how they say this wretched Spanish Influenza got here in the first place. And so, instead, we spent dreary evenings at home with our respective families, where we were bored out of our minds and just hoping and praying for spring to come, when hopefully the flu would die out.

I hadn't seen Bill for almost a year, since the time when we had met. He was a nice enough bloke, but if I am honest I must mention that in my hearts of hearts I never expected our short time together to lead anywhere. He had been an Allied soldier far from home and serving his country in France. And, as I've already mentioned, I felt that if the long and sometimes over passionate letters I sent him helped him to get through his ordeal, what harm could I be doing?

In early February I got a letter postmarked '*Liverpool*'. Bill was back in England. Bill was back and already being prepared for 'demobilization', and then he would soon be sent home to Canada.

I don't know what I thought. Of course I had realised for some months now that his unit would be returning from France. All about us, soldiers were coming home to London from the war. I saw them everyday – on the streets, in the buses, everywhere. And it was frightening. It was frightening to be a young woman of nineteen seeing the battered husks of the lads I grew up with coming home with disabled bodies and disfigured faces, or with their nerves shattered. Many looked haggard, as they crept about in a manner more fitting for weary old men. And yet these were the *lucky ones* – because they were still alive to come home. Countless others, including those with smiling faces I had known from my youth, were never coming home again. And so the presence of the living only confounded the enormous realisation of just how many were dead. Some of those men who were returning already had wives and loved ones waiting for them, but what of the growing ranks of widows and grieving lovers who now had no-one to welcome? Not only did they have no-one, but with so many of our generation slaughtered on the battlefields of Europe, there was little hope of them ever finding a man of their own again.

In his letter, Bill informed me that the Army had just received word that the Canadian Government was about to pass an order offering free passage for all Canadian dependants from their homes in England to Canada. And then, to my great surprise, Bill asked me to marry him.

'What are you going to do?' Hattie asked when I showed her the letter.

'I don't know,' I replied. 'I really don't know.'

'Have you told your mum, yet?'

'Blimey! No! She'd have a blue fit. I wanted to ask you first, Hat. What would you do?'

Hattie didn't hesitate for a second. 'I'd marry him like a shot, Edie,' she said. 'What else is there here for us anyway?'

What indeed, except for more of the same. But Canada? Wasn't Canada almost the same as America? And America looked so wonderful in the movies. A new life, in a new country, and far away from my mother. The appeal of it all was just too much to resist. So I wrote a very long letter back to Bill, saying how much I loved him, and how I had been dreaming of him popping the question ever since we met, but that I hardly dared to hope that my dreams would come true. It was all a lie. But I didn't want him to go changing his mind in the cold light of day, or worse once he had leave and got the chance to sample any other English women. 'Yes,' I told him. Yes, I would marry him!

My mother and I had never got on. We were like chalk and cheese, and for as long as I can remember we had rubbed each other up the wrong way. But it was different with my sister Annie, or *Nance*, as we all called her. I don't know if it was because she was a little bit older than I was, and because she was the first born, she and Mum got on like a house on fire. But I just couldn't seem to get on with either of them. Nance could never do anything wrong, but I, as far as my mum was concerned, could never do anything right, which only stoked the sibling rivalry between my sister and me. And after Will died, and I started going out more casually with blokes... Well, Mum was always having a go at me then; saying how I was too flighty by half and would come a cropper if I didn't watch out. And she went on and on about how I had not better come home expecting a baby out of wedlock. I thought that was rich coming from her – considering how, as I was looking through the drawer for my birth certificate, I accidentally stumbled upon her marriage lines instead. I could hardly believe that she could be such a hypocrite! When I read what I found in the drawer I realised that I had been all of thirteen years of age before she and Dad sneaked off to get wed.

Dad never had much to say about anything when he was sober, unless he was prompted to by Mum. He seemed happy enough to come home after a day's painting and papering and sit by the fire reading his newspaper as he waited for his dinner. After that he'd be off down to the pub until closing time. And that was when we had to be wary of him. He was a different bloke altogether after a drink had got into him, and then he was

215

likely to knock anyone about if they spoke out of turn to him. Especially Mum. The only comments I got from Dad about Bill, before we got married, came if he happened to be about when the post was delivered. Then he'd eye up any letters for me from Bill saying, 'Ah! I see there's another one from that Yank of yours, Edie!' Everyone persisted in calling him a 'Yank', no matter how many times I reminded them that Bill was Canadian.

I had half expected Mum to be glad when I told her that I was getting married to Bill. But no, she couldn't be happy for me. Why was I marrying a foreigner, was all she wanted to know. Why on earth would I want to go off to Canada? I didn't give her the answer I had churning in my mind, though I was sorely tempted to say something!

Bill came to me on a three-day pass. And so, on the nineteenth of February, despite my mother's misgivings, we were married at Holy Trinity Church, just off Wimbledon Broadway. We celebrated with ham sandwiches and pale ale in the pub across the road. After that, we spent the night and all of the following day at a nearby hotel, before Bill and his best man had to head off back to camp at Knotty Ash.

I didn't see him again until he was posted briefly at Whitley in Surrey that May, but had soon been whisked away again to Rhyl, back to Knotty Ash, and then on to Buxton, to prepare for demobbing – which had been promised to the men as some time in the beginning of autumn.

It was going to be a long lonely summer, with only a gold wedding ring and Hattie to see me through it...

Chapter Four

Although the fighting on the Western Front had ceased with the Armistice, the war was not officially at an end until peace negotiations with the Hun were over and the Treaty of Versailles was signed on June the twenty-eighth of that year. Yet even as the negotiations were still going on, all across the country plans were being made about marking it properly, once Peace had officially come. And so, on July nineteenth, London was destined to become the focus of a nationwide Peace Day celebration, and Hattie and I weren't going to miss out on that. So we made a plan.

After work on the Friday evening, we both went home, had our suppers, and then went straight to bed. But before I went up, I made myself an enormous cheese sandwich with two doorsteps of bread, which I carefully wrapped in paper and set in the larder ready for me to grab the next morning.

'You behave now!' was Mum's warning, as I made my way past the open sitting room door.

'Of course I will,' I snapped. 'I'm a married woman, I'll 'ave you know!'

As I started up the bare wooden stairs, my mum shouted up, 'And no bleedin' waking yer dad up when you go in the morning! He'll have a head like a bear when he gets in from the pub.'

'And no bleedin' waking me up...' I couldn't resist mimicking.

'I 'eard that you cheeky little cow!' Mum shouted up behind me. So I scuttled up the remaining steps and into my shared, box- bedroom.

It was hard getting off to sleep, what with it still being so light outside and with my curtains being so thin and all. Local kids were still playing in the street below my window, and every playful squeal seemed to land like a trumpet call on my ears as I lay on my side trying to get to sleep. This, coupled with excitement about the following day, made me think that I never would drift off.

Then I got to thinking about Bill, and wondered if he would be among the parade. The last I had heard from him was in a letter that arrived only a couple of days before. In it he said that they'd all heard that there was some sort of row – all very hush-hush – at the Canadian Headquarters, due to an argument over the question of 'precedence' between two distinguished Generals. There were probably some knock-on effects, and so he didn't think any of his lot would be taking part at all.

'Shame that,' I had said to Hattie disappointedly. 'I was really lookin' forward to seein' him and his mates march by, and giving 'em a rousin' good cheer.'

Still, I lived in hope that in the end he might be there.

I must have nodded off soon after that, but my sleep didn't last long. When Nance came to bed she turned on the light and made as much noise as she pleased, before finally settling herself down for the night. I was very cross but didn't say anything. What was the point? She would only have gone squealing to Mum.

As luck would have it, I woke up again just a moment or two before the clock could go off, and so I was able to turn off the alarm. I had gone to bed half dressed and so I quickly grabbed the rest of my clothes and my shoes and tip-toed out the room and down the stairs to the kitchen. There I finished dressing, put on my shoes and made my way outside to use the lavvy.

Once indoors again, I brushed my hair and pinned on my hat as best I could in the dark. Then I went to the larder to fetch my sandwich. As I did, my hand brushed against one of my dad's bottles of brown ale, which made it wobble and attract my attention. I hesitated before deciding to pinch it and take it with me. I figured that because Dad had been so drunk the night before he probably wouldn't even notice if one was missing.

Lastly, I took out my gloves from my coat pocket, wriggled them on, and crept along the hallway. Lifting the front door latch as quietly as I could, I slipped out and then set off down the road like a greyhound.

It was funny being out so early. It was still night and yet it wasn't properly dark – not like it is in the winter. Usually I didn't like being out in the small hours on my own but that morning I wasn't bothered at all.

Hattie was sitting and waiting for me on a garden wall in Haydon's Road. When she spotted me coming she jumped down and loped towards me like an excited puppy.

'I never seen yer look so happy!' I said in a hushed voice.

Hayden's Road was dead quiet. There wasn't another living soul about as she and I locked arms and marched off down it towards the High Street. Here and there, and coming along both sides of the street, we were met with the sight of other people shuffling through the half- light and heading off towards London.

'Mmm! Smell that, Edie? Ain't that smashin'?'

Hattie was right. That wafting aroma of bread baking as it hit the early morning air smelt almost as good as heaven. Gosh! But didn't I suddenly come over all hungry? Just then a lad in his white apron slipped out from a side door of the bakers' to light up a fag.

'Goin' to the parade?' he called out to us.

'Yes, we are,' we replied in unison.

He must have read my mind, because he popped back inside sharpish and came out with something cradled in a cloth.

'Here, girls!' he announced cheerily, as he proffered the contents to us. 'Sumfin' for the journey!'

He gave us buns; two lovely, fat, hot currant buns! Luckily, we had our gloves, because they were still hot enough for us to have burnt our hands on them. We shoved them in our pockets and thanked him before quickly getting on our way. His generosity had been an act of uncommon kindness that would turn out to typify that day: it was as if everyone Hattie and I came across was drunk on happiness and goodwill.

We decided to save the buns until we had walked far enough to deserve them, so we pushed on along the main drag through Tooting, the Bec, and Balham, until nearly exhausted we reached Clapham. All the while we encountered more and more people up and milling about the street.

We got to Clapham Common and decided to rest for a bit and to eat our buns. Above the stretch of Common the sky was lightening, as dawn showed encouraging signs of breaking though the covering of cloud overhead.

'What time do you think it is, Edie?'

'I dunno, Hat,' I said. 'Half past four? Five maybe?'

We hadn't been to the Common for ages. Last time Hattie and I had, it was scarred up badly from where trenches had been dug across parts of it; something to do with the War most likely. Hattie and I had been there with a couple of blokes to listen to a concert at the bandstand. That seemed so long ago now.

When we had finished eating, we went to get a drink from the public fountain and to have a quick pee behind the bushes. Then, feeling much livelier than before, we made our way across the Common, towards Battersea and the Thames. Once we were on the other side of the river, Hattie and I were soon walking down Buckingham Palace Road and, cheered on by glimpses of famous London landmarks, were soon at our desired destination.

After arriving in the Mall, we sat down to nibble a bit off our sandwiches before saving the rest for later. It was still very early in the morning when had we arrived. Spectators along the Mall were only one or two deep, so we were able to pick out a really nice spot for ourselves close to the Victoria Monument, with a good view of Buckingham Palace beyond. However, within an hour or so, Hattie and I were hemmed in by excited sightseers, packed at least eight deep behind us. Soon even the tall gates in the distance leading to Constitution Hill were festooned with the outlines of human figures. All about us we could see sailors and Australian soldiers, easily marked out by their distinctive hats, who seemed to have picked out the most daring of roosts for themselves, places where none but the brave or foolhardy would dare to perch.

I had seen Buckingham Palace before, one Sunday when I was walking out with my Will. I remember feeling disappointed that our King and Queen could live in such dreary looking place. But on that day, oh my, didn't it look cheerful? What with flags and spectators at every window.

In front of where Hattie and I stood, the white marble Victoria Monument gleamed brightly like a blooming great iced wedding cake; studded about the upper terrace with some exotic looking potted palms, placed there I suppose as decoration.

'Wot a beautiful angel!' Hattie suddenly sighed, pointing up at the figure of Victory, who was standing with outstretched wings, perched high upon the pinnacle of the monument. 'Ain't she beautiful, Edie?'

Hattie had a thing about angels, you see. In fact, she liked all sorts of religious statues and things like that. I supposed it was on account of her being Catholic and really believing in them, and in God, and saints and all that. But angels were what Hattie really loved most.

Although I had only looked up to please her, even I had to admit that, picked out against the slate grey sky by a still defiant shaft of sunlight, Hattie's *'angel'* did indeed look breathtakingly beautiful.

Hattie soon broke the mood.

'Gonna hiss down, innit?' she said deflated.

'No,' I said. 'I don't think it is, Hat. I don't think that it can rain on this parade. Besides...' I added, taking a great intake of breath just to show her, 'you can always smell the rain on the breeze and I don't smell it yet, do you?'

Hattie beamed a great smile once more and agreed that she couldn't either. Besides, even if it did rain, I couldn't see it stopping the determination of all of us who had gathered to enjoying the day.

As people continued to pack in behind us, Hattie and I kept our eyes firmly trained towards the coming and goings at the monument opposite, as it too began to fill up quickly. Our wounded war heroes, in blue with white-aproned nurses in attendance, were among the first to arrive on the scene in a convoy of motor lorries.

Hattie and I along with the countless other people gave these broken but victorious soldiers a rousing cheer of appreciation, as orderlies wheeled them down makeshift ramps and parked them up in a line in a prime position by the roadside. Many had disguised their blue uniforms by draping themselves in bunting and flags, and all seemed to be equipped with some sort of instrument or hand bell which they would later play or ring out in exuberance.

'Good to see 'em happy at least,' I remember commenting to Hattie, 'despite all wot's happened to 'em.'

Then Hattie and I watched with growing excitement as a steady stream of smartly dressed women and top-hatted toffs, sporting red button-holes, were dropped off from their motor cars and then directed, by the smartest looking bobbies[14] I have ever seen, to their various positions of privilege upon the gleaming island monument. We had no idea who most of those people were though.

However, soon others arrived who even Hattie and I could identify immediately, having recognised them from photographs in the *Daily Sketch*. The first couple was Mr Winston Churchill and his wife, and the crowd gave them a rousing cheer! Following shortly behind them came Mr Asquith, whose wife was most strikingly dressed. Then the Prime Minister, Mr Lloyd George, arrived to such a great roar of approval from all sides that, on alighting from his sombre-looking vehicle, he immediately took off his top hat and then, smiling broadly, bowed to the crowd, a gesture that drew even more cheers. Mrs Asquith, dressed in a beautiful blue and grey gown topped off with a great feathered hat and looking equally delighted by the cheers of appreciation, stopped briefly to strike a pose beside her husband. Then they were both led off to take up their allotted place with the highest echelon of VIPs upon the monument.

By that time, on our side of the Mall, the street vendors were weaving in and out of the crowd and doing a roaring trade as they sold all sorts of souvenirs and flags.

'Buy an official programme!' was by far the loudest cry all around us.

Hattie leaned across to one vendor and managed to buy a large paper napkin for a penny.

---

[14] Policemen.

The napkin was prettily decorated with a ring of pink roses encircling the black-printed words; *'Souvenir in Commemoration of The Great Peace Celebrations in London-19th July 1919.'*

Directly underneath were five head and shoulder sketches of General Haig, His Majesty the King in military uniform, Her Majesty the Queen, the top-hatted Prime Minister and Sir David Beatty in his naval hat; under that, the programme for day's events was listed.

'I ain't ever gonna use this,' Hattie enthused. I'm gonna keep it for the rest of me life.'

Somehow I knew even then that Hattie would. For her, nothing ever faded or browned or tattered with age. She was always the eternal optimist and I guess that is why I loved her so. And she was always a real tonic to whatever ill I had.

What struck me most about the crowd was how good-tempered everyone was. For such an enormous gathering, it was very good humoured indeed. Everyone gave way to one another, disabled men and otherwise. Even the blooming bobbies were full of friendly words.

Although we had already spotted what we took to be royal guests being delivered into Buckingham Palace by a string of fancy carriages and such, none of us had reckoned on how Their Majesties would eventually arrive at their pavilion by the monument.

Almost exactly at noon the King, dressed in Service uniform, walked out from the great arched gateway of the palace, flanked by both Queens – his wife and his mother – followed by a grand train of princes and princess, and Court ladies. The King' mother, Queen Alexandra, looked especially elegant; wearing a sequined coat of moonlight blue and a small tight-fitting brimless hat of fine starched net swathed with sequins of a corresponding shade. Her Majesty, the Queen, also looking radiant, wore a gown of the palest lavender with an overdress of exquisitely embroidered chiffon, and matched with a similarly styled hat as that of Queen Alexandra's, but decorated with sprays of tiny flowers.

The entire party was smiling broadly as they walked, without herald or military attendance, to take their places on their dais at the front of the pavilion that overlooked the Mall. The very sight of them, coupled with the rapturous roar of loyalty and patriotism from the crowd, was enough to brig tears of pride even to the most war-hardened eyes.

Barely had the Royal family acknowledged their welcome than the strains of 'Over There' filled the air, as the parade began with ranks of young American troops and then their massed red, white and blue 'Old Glories', which were held in the American fashion, so that the fabric billowed out into such a vibrant show of colour as to solicit a multitude of 'oohs' and 'ahs' from the delighted onlookers. Then, smiling exuberantly came General 'Black' Jack Pershing, riding a horse that zigzagged as if it had come from a blooming circus. He kept on smiling, too, right up until he reached the King, when he gave His Majesty the finest of salutes. Hattie and I were almost jumping up and down with excitement as the Yanks marched by. Later, we agreed that their colourful display was the most picturesque of the entire parade, apart of course from that of our own beloved Guards, with their splendid uniforms and laurelled staffs. Oh my, but how my heart always fluttered to see a man in uniform!

Cheers continued to ricochet through the air as the Belgium, Chinese and Czechoslovakian contingents passed by and then peaked to an ear splitting crescendo as old, upright and grim-faced Marshal Foch rode out from the formality of the French line, with his baton held high in honour of King George high upon the dais. After Foch's theatrical salute, the Price of Wales went around to the back of the memorial to warmly greet the General as he dismounted, before then being led by the Prince to a place of honour beside the King, to watch the rest of the French forces pass by. The common soldiers bore bright posies of flowers upon their once bloodied bayonets while Foch's Generals presented outstretched swords which glinted like silver streaks in the brave but ever weakening rays of sunshine. Following swiftly on came the Greeks, Italians, Japanese, Polish, Portuguese, Rumanians, Serbians, and Siamese, before suddenly the rollicking strains of 'A Life On the Ocean Wave' struck up.

Cries of 'Look! Look! Our boys are coming!' went up from all around us with a great tide of excitement as Sir David Beatty, representing our sailors, came striding up the Mall with a Union Jack whipping in the breeze above his head. After saluting the King, Beatty too fell out to take up his place upon the dais; to watch with pride as the perfect lines of blue and white marched by to a surge of cheers. And what a rousing outpouring of appreciation and pride was given to the W.R.N.S. and naval nurses as they too marched daintily by.

'I wish someone was selling water,' Hattie said afterwards. 'My throat is getting so sore what wiv all this shouting.'

''Ere, I nicked a bottle of me dad's beer,' I said, getting it out of my bag and undoing the bung. 'Wanna swig?'

Hattie giggled as we took turns at sipping from the bottle until it was gone, but we soon had mouths as dry as pockets again.

'I wish I'd pinched two now,' I said.

'Just as well you didn't,' Hattie laughed, 'or we'd only be needing to spend a penny on somefin' else, and I can't see any where near 'ere to go for a pee. And even if there was, I bet we lose our place for sure!'

After a slight and welcome pause to rest our straining voices, Sir Douglas Haig came in sight leading his two-mile-long troop of our good khaki clad *'Foot Sloggers'*- our British infantry soldiers. Like those elite who had gone before, after giving his salute, Haig dismounted to join the King urged on by shouts of 'Duggie! Duggie!' from the masses.

I then suddenly became more conscious of other people around me in the crowd than at any other time during the parade. Intermittently, I observed how some people recognised and responded to certain regiments as they passed by. Quite clearly they were honouring either men they knew in a regiment or those who had once belonged to the regiment but had been killed. I saw many in tears too; tears shed for those loved ones missing from the ranks but not missing in the hearts and minds of their proud but heartbroken families and friends. Watching others dab at their eyes with handkerchiefs brought a lump to my throat and tears to my own.

A woman beside had also been crying as she turned to me and said;

'D'you know, luvvie, when my Alf was killed at Wipers, I vowed then how I would hide myself away should this day ever come... That I wouldn't take part in no celebrations. But now I 'ave, and I've seen all this; I know that *he* would have wanted me to be here.'

I expect she, like many others that day, went away with a little less bitterness in her heart than she had when she had arrived.

'Look!' Hattie exclaimed, breaking free to dig me hard in the ribs. 'Look, Edie. Ain't them Canadians? A smaller contingent of soldiers was just marching by but their flag had not quite unfurled... so it was hard to see what was on it.'

'I could be,' I said. But if it is, I can't make out my Bill among them.'

Then, as if to stop melancholy from creeping in to overtake the mood of celebration, suddenly four spruce tanks suddenly came trundling up the Mall. To cries of great delight, they rolled up to the King and then quite unexpectedly began to exude great plumes of blue smoke which almost completely hid His Majesty and company from view for several minutes. Above and on high, the massive effigy of our late Queen Victoria looked down on the proceedings below. It seemed then that, for once, her stony lips just might have been giving way for a crack of smile to grace her grim face. Had she been alive, perhaps in those brief minutes of joy she just might also have been amused by the unexpected goings on below.

Then we watched white pigeons loosed to fill the air – before flying off towards the palace gardens – just as the V.A.Ds[15] began to swing by with perfect precision, to the warm adoration of the onlookers. Last, but not least, after two and a half hours, came the kaki and blue of the air force.

As the tail of the parade moved on to disappear into the Park, in the distance I could see the low ragged edges of slate-coloured clouds break away into slender, dark ribbons that draped towards the earth. Soon the smudgy grey skies overhead began to cry down gentle sun-lit tears from the heavens, which fell almost unheeded by those gathered below.

Then, slowly, the crowd began to disperse. Perhaps, like Hattie and me, all those people weren't certain where to go next. There were lots of entertainments planned in the various parks in the capital, but Hattie and I didn't fancy any of them. We were footsore

---

[15]   Members of the Voluntary Aid Detachment serving as nursing assistants during World War 1.

and weary, and so we decided instead that we'd sit by the gardens and eat the remainder of our sandwiches before going home again.

When we had eaten, Hattie and I tried to get another drink, but all the pubs we came to had already run dry of everything. So instead, we found a public convenience and joined the long queue outside it. After sharing a cubicle with our last penny, we washed our hands and then cupped them under the washbasin tap for a long and much needed drink of water. Afterwards, we started the long slog back to Merton.

'You know,' Hattie said on the way, 'I feel like a part of 'istory now, Edie. Don't you?'

'Yes,' I answered. 'Yes Hat, I do.'

Chapter Five

It seemed surreal at times, you know, what with the War being over and all. Now, suddenly, it was as if the world was impatient to be hurrying on with the future. As if the living were now desperate to distance themselves from the dead and all of that fighting and killing. After four years of civilian stagnation, change was suddenly on us so quickly it was hard to keep up!

Only three years before the word 'airship' had immediately summoned up dreadful visions of Hun *Zeppelins* slipping into England on dark, moonless nights to drop bombs on us. But all of a sudden, that summer, the newspapers were all in praise of them, telling how a British airship, the R34, had crossed the Atlantic and reached Minneola, New York, in just one-hundred-and-eight-hours, and then returned again in only seventy-five. It was the first ever round-trip crossing of the Atlantic by air! And after that, there was talk about the possibility of regular passenger flights between Europe and America in the future.

Not only that, but two of our war pilots, Alcock and Brown, had also flown non-stop across the Atlantic from Newfoundland that June, in an adapted Vickers bomber. Although, of course, it is unthinkable that it will ever be possible to build aeroplanes big enough to carry a lot of passengers at once, there was nevertheless talk about them maybe being used to carry regular mail between the two continents.

Suddenly, the world seemed to be shrinking, and so for me Canada no longer seemed such a far off place, as it had when Bill first asked me to go there with him. So instead of thinking of it as a necessary evil, I began to find myself filling with the happy anticipation of going.

A few weeks after I had married Bill, something unexpected had come along to really cheer me up. A *'separation allowance'* was what the Canadian Army called it. I'd had no idea that I would be getting it once I married Bill. And it was a good sum coming in, so for the first time in my life I had money to spend, instead of being perpetually skint.

Hattie loved nothing better than to go down Wimbledon High Street with me: all the way from where we lived near Haydon's Road right down to the bottom of Wimbledon Hill and the Metropolitan District Railway station. We used to do it all the time. We would walk the entire length of the Broadway which was always, and I mean always, buzzing with life. In fact there was no holding back Hattie's enthusiasm once we had gone past the Public Baths and turned the corner of Latimer Road and headed towards Holy Trinity Church. She simply loved looking in all the shop windows. And so had I – even at all those countless times when we hardly had enough money between us to buy a stale bun to help see us on our way.

There was the cinema too, which in truth wasn't much to look at on the outside. Before I got married, Hattie and I used to haunt the place as often as we could. Well, as often as we could get some bloke or another to foot the tickets for four pennies' worth 'o dark, and a quick fumble in the back row. Hattie loved going to the pictures, especially to see *Charlie Chaplin*. It had been our escape: it lifted our spirits and freed our imaginations to help us rise above the grim reality of living in war-time London. We could make believe that we were as beautiful as Mary Pickford, being saved from a fate worse than death by some handsome looking bloke. Or when the Keystone Cops or our Charlie came flickering his away across the silver screen, we could laugh out loud till we cried and let go of all our misery, if only for a while. We could escape to the only place we had. So when I at last had some money of my own, I could afford to take Hattie to the pictures myself. So I did.

On the corner of *Russell Road* stood the great red brick '*New Wimbledon Theatre*'. Way up high above its colonnade entrance, jutting out from the main building, was a three-sided, three-story tower. On the first story were three great double doors with fancy carved stone surrounds. These opened on to a small balcony edged with an ornate ironwork railing that overlooked the grand entrance to the theatre below. If we were out on an evening, we sometimes saw the toffs in all there finery standing out there as they took air during the intermission of a performance, and we imagined what it would be like to be rich like they were.

The tower was topped off with a great green dome. Up at the very top of this, resting on top off a great globe stood what Hattie cheerily dubbed '*The Golden Angel of the Horseshoe*'.

'It's an angel alright,' I would tease her, 'but I don't fink that's no horse shoe that she's 'olding!'

But after I got my allowance it was different. Then I had money to spend and Hattie and I weren't just window shopping any more. Then I could go into some of those fancy stores that, before, we had only dared to peep in through the windows.

'It will be just like a floating honeymoon,' I remember Hattie sighing, as we stood at the lingerie counter of *Ely's* department store, looking at all the lacy bits and pieces they had on show.

I saw the assistant giving us the eye, and then go sloping off to get the departmental supervisor, because she thought we were up to no good. So then I took great delight in pretending to check inside my purse before taking out a ten-bob note – just to show that I had got money

'Yes,' I said very loudly, 'cruising across the Atlantic on a bloomin' great ocean liner...'

After that, the assistant came over all smiles and helpful.

'Is that new clothes?' asked my mother, eyeing my bags when I got home.

'Yes, it is.'

'Is that all you can find to waste your money on?'

'It's not a waste. I want to look good for my Bill when he sees me. Besides, I can't be going on the ship to Canada dressed in rags.'

'Well my girl, I hope that husband of yours can still afford to keep you once his army pay ends.'

''e will be. Don't you worry. 'is family owns a great big farm,' I bragged.

'Even so, don't you think you should be saving some of that money just in case?'

'What I do is my affair,' I said, as I stormed up to my room. I was angry with her. Even after I'd had almost nothing all my life, she seemed to begrudge me any bit of happiness I had coming my way.

***

It was hard, that last day at the laundry. After work, having picked up my wages from the manager's office, I was the first into the cloakroom to put on my hat and coat, ready to go home. But then, as I walked out again, I found the rest of the girls gathered to give me rousing cheer. All of them hugged me and wished me the best of luck for my new life in Canada. I had always moaned about working at the laundry, but leaving that place for the very last time brought such a lump to my throat that it had me in tears.

Hattie and I walked home together as usual, and I was only too aware of how little she had to say for a change. Her head was hanging so far down that I couldn't see her face at all. It was only when we had reached the corner of my road that I suddenly realised that she had been crying.

'Chin up, Hat!' I said. 'I ain't bleedin' dead, you know.'

'I know,' she sniffed, 'but you might as well be after today.'

'Why would you say that?'

'Well, I ain't ever going to see you again, after this, am I?'

'Oh Hat, of course you will!' I told her. 'It might not be for some time, but you *will* see me again, I promise. I'm sure that I'll come back again to visit, like, in a few years' time. And until I do, you and me can write letters to each other. We'll always be friend's Hat. There ain't nuffin' ever going to change that!'

We stopped and I wiped away her tears with my glove. Then I threw my arms around her and gave her a big, big hug. Hattie squeezed me back so hard that I thought that my spine might crack. Then we parted; she to go her way and me to go mine. I stood for a few moments watching her walk away from me and I swear my heart was trembling. Then Hattie stopped, turned and gave me a solemn wave. I waved back and then turned the corner. I didn't see her after that.

I had packed and repacked my belongings several times over into the new carpet bag that I had bought at Tooting Market. And yet there I was, late the night before I was due to go, and still frantically checking that I had included everything I was going to need. I was leaving that house for good and I knew that I wasn't coming back – and I was glad.

Next morning, as I got ready to catch the six-thirty train, Nance handed me her best hat pin to use on my new hat.

"ere, Edie,' she smiled. 'Sumfing to remember me by.' It was the first time my sister had ever given me anything of hers *willingly*. Then she hugged me, and I reassured her that *everything* was going to turn out alright.

Dad had already said goodbye earlier, as he had gone off to work, but Mum? Mum didn't utter so much as a word all the time I was getting ready to leave. When I was ready, I gave her a hug and asked if she would like to walk me to the station. But as I gave her a peck on the cheek, Mum just stood there rigid and replied coolly that she was 'too busy' to do that.

'I'll write.' I said cheerily.

'You do that,' she said. 'But remember this, my girl, you have made your bed and now I expect you to lie in it. Don't go thinking that you can turn round and come back here once you get fed up with your fancy new life!'

'I won't Mum,' I said, 'I am going to be happy with Bill.'

With that, I picked up my bag from the hall floor and walked off towards the railway station to catch the string of trains that would eventually take me to Liverpool Riverside Station. As I waited on Wimbledon platform, I was thinking how lucky I was: lucky that I was getting away from there and lucky that I wasn't going to be around when the time came that Mum's precious Nance would be forced to tell her that she was up the stick[16]. It was bound to happen sometime since I knew that she had fallen in with a bloke herself.

The train I had caught from Kings Cross soon became crowded. Then I found myself crammed up against the window and looking out at the city flashing by in a haze of movement – for a while that seemed to last an eternity – until suddenly we were out of the suburbs and into an open landscape and speeding towards the North. I hadn't realised

---

[16]   Pregnant.

before just how much countryside there was outside of London, or how green and lovely England really was.

When, after several changes of train, I finally got to Liverpool Riverside Station, I found it swarming with soldiers carrying kit bags. There were so many that I was frightened that I might get hurt in the crush. I had got my papers out ready, but I couldn't see Bill anywhere amongst the surge of Khaki. So I made my way to the west side of the station where I followed other women who had soldier escorts, walking with their baggage along *Princess Parade* – the covered roadway that had been built before the war so that posh passengers heading for the great Ocean Liners would not be exposed to inclement weather.

As the throng edged nearer to *Princess Landing*, our ship, *RMS Adriatic,* suddenly loomed to fill my field of vision. She was an enormous twenty-thousand-ton *Olympic Class* ship, one of the *White Star Line's Great Four*.

When I saw her, with her two great red and black funnels, I immediately thought of that other *White Star Line ship* – the *Titanic*. Thoughts of the ill-fated *Titanic* had been with me ever since Bill had asked me to marry him and sail to Canada. It wasn't the sea that had filled me with such feelings of trepidation at making this monumental journey into the unknown, but the thought of hitting an iceberg. I remember being a child and hearing the terrible stories about the sinking of the *Titanic,* of how an iceberg had torn a hole in this 'unsinkable' ship, sending one-thousand-five-hundred-and-seventeen people to a watery grave.

At school, as we had skipped with our ropes in the playground singing *'The big ship sails on the Ally-Ally–Oh'*, the words had suddenly taken on a dark and sinister meaning. Recently, I'd had nightmares about 'that' happening to us too. But what I had not realised

236

was that the *Adriatic* had brought many of the survivors of that previous tragedy back to England from America, so when I heard about this I took it to be a good omen.

When *Adriatic* was launched some fourteen years before, her passengers and crew could boast about her being the first ocean liner to have an indoor swimming pool and a Turkish bath. Not that I would get to see these. As usual, the best parts of the ship were reserved for the officers and their wives, while the likes of a mere private's bride were confined to third class. Still, all in all, everything turned out to be much better than I could have imagined.

When I reached the ship, my papers were scrutinised and my name duly checked off a great printed list before I was allowed to embark. Then, as I was half way up the gang-plank I heard a familiar voice cry out; 'Edie! Edie! Here I am!'

It was Bill. He was still down below on the quayside, and although it was impossible for us to reach each other, I suddenly felt a wave of relief wash over me as I blew him a kiss before I continued to struggle on board with my bag.

I was assigned to a neat little cabin which I was to share with three other women – all nice sorts and, like me, newly married to Canadian soldiers. Inside, I was met by a quartet of wooden bunks, all with matching red and white woven covers bearing the design of a life-ring with the words '*White Star Line*' in bold lettering against a trellis-style background. Folded over crisply at the head end of this lay a white sheet over a single but plump-looking pillow. Between the two sets of bunks was a single drop-down, dark-wood shelf and above that, a small brass-edged mirror was screwed securely into the wall. There was a large communal wash-room at the end of the corridor, where we women could make our ablutions in relative comfort each morning and night. There were also three baths with piping-hot running water for which we had to sign up to in pairs to obtain just one twenty-minute slot during our crossing. It was luxury!

I introduced myself to my room-mates before taking off my hat and quickly stowing my bag, as directed, under the lower bunk. Then, after much encouragement by these others, I made my first brave and not very lady-like attempt to get onto my bunk at the top. In the process I split the seams of my new pink bloomers, much to the raucous squeals of laughter of my new companions. Once I had mastered that manoeuvre though, I was quite glad that I had been given an upper bunk. It felt safe and secure sleeping up high–and fun.

As I settled myself in, I listened to the others' bright and hopeful talk about what the future was going to hold for us. I got so swept along by their exited chatter that I soon found myself hardly able to contain my own excitement at finally being on my way to start my new life in Canada with Bill. One week; one week at sea and we would be there!

When I had looked at a map in the old battered atlas that my young brother had pilfered from school, I had somehow got it into my mind that we would be sailing down the coast of England and then heading off across the Atlantic from there. So I was surprised to learn instead that we would be passing out by the northern coast of Ireland.

Another thing I had not expected was to be feeling so sick once we had headed out from the shelter of Liverpool. The worst part of the voyage came upon us pretty quickly after we had. We reached a place with a great swell which I heard being referred by some of the sailors as 'Devil's Hole'. Not only did many of us passengers feel terribly queasy, but some of the crew were sea sick too. Once we were clear of that though, we all soon found our sea legs and had no more problems with sickness at all, even though the sea turned quite rough on our fourth day out, when we women settled for staying put in our cabin.

There were many wives on board with children, most of whom were very young babies. In the night I often heard the sound of their wails drifting along the corridors – making me feel very thankful that I was not bunked in with their mothers. When the cries had stilled, if I was still wakeful, I could lie and take comfort listening to the gentle thump, thump, thump which during the busy days seemed to disappear into our collective sub-consciousness. It was the sound of the Adriatic's massive engines pounding away like a great beating heart.

Although we wives were housed in a different part of the ship from the men, we were delighted to find that our soldier husbands would be permitted to spend a lot of time in our company. I would meet with Bill every morning for breakfast, after dinner and then for tea at around five, which we were always ready for because the sea air made us ravenous.

'Imagine waking up to bacon and eggs *every* morning!' I wrote in tiny handwriting on the back of a postcard to Hattie. There was so much that I wanted to tell her, but there was too little space in which to write about it. So I did my best at cramming as many words in as possible by turning the card sideways and then, writing from edge to edge, filling the open space completely.

In the long intervals between meals, when I was able to spend much of the day with Bill, our favourite pursuit became cuddling up together on deck and then talking for hours, as we looked out across the endless sea.

Before that voyage, I hadn't seen the ocean before, though of course I had heard about it in rhymes and poems at school, of how beautifully blue it was. However, I was very disappointed when I saw it for the first time myself at Liverpool Docks. It looked so grey and dingy and not a bit as I had imagined. Yet whenever I sat out with Bill, the sea always seemed as blue as his eyes and peaked to perfection by foaming white horses.

Sometimes, if we got chilly, Bill would disappear off to the canteen and come back with two steaming mugs of hot Bovril. We got to know each other so well during those times on board the *Adriatic*. The best time of all was the evenings. While most of the others stayed below enjoying impromptu concerts or jolly sing-songs around the piano on *'C Deck'*, Bill and I would stay up top snuggled down together under a warm rug. We liked watching the crimson sun dying upon the water, before slipping silently beneath the limitless expanse of glittering water, and then spooning together as the moon rose and the stars came out like sparkling sequins on a great velvety black blanket. It was then that I truly began to fall in love with my husband.

One curious thing that I had not expected to happen was for the hands of the ship's clocks to be put back every day: sometimes by the best part of an hour. Passengers who owned watches were regularly reminded to alter their time in line with the ship's. As a result, our daily routine would suddenly shift in real time, leaving our bodies and minds unable to keep up. As a result, every morning I found myself wide awake earlier and earlier.

As we drew closer to the still invisible Canada, I noticed the mornings growing colder and mistier. And as we neared Newfoundland, I noticed a distinct change in my Bill as well. It was if he could somehow *sense* the land of his birth upon the salty breeze.

We were alone on deck together when suddenly, with excitement in his eyes, he exclaimed, 'Smell that, Edie? That's the smell of God's own country...'

It was just after this that I saw my first iceberg; a menacing great towering island of ice lying some way astern of the *Adriatic*. And then, shortly afterwards, Bill and I spotted a second and a third iceberg. My heart quickened, especially as night closed in, when I thought of the likelihood of more being out there.

'Don't worry, Edie,' Bill reassured me. 'I heard that the Captain has already been radioed ahead to warn him of the location of these icebergs, and that no more have been spotted by the ships that have already gone on ahead of us.'

So later I slept a little better than I might have, but still thoughts of the demise of the *Titanic* lingered in the back of my mind. But I needn't have worried at all, because the next afternoon we docked in Halifax, and then sped onwards towards Ontario and Bill's home county of Northumberland.

Chapter Six

At first, I was led to believe that I would be allowed to stay with Bill for a few days at Warkworth, before he was demobbed. But as things turned out, I was sent on ahead – alone – to his family home. I had also been expecting to go to a town called '*Cramahe*, only to be told that Bill's widowed mother had recently relocated to a village called Norham in the *Township of Percy*. There, I soon discovered that I could have easily walked back to Warkworth from his mother's new home, but Bill might as well have been based a thousand miles away.

Meanwhile, I did not feel in the least bit perturbed at going on ahead of my husband. Bill had assured me that his family would be thrilled to see me – with or without him. So I went on with visions of my arrival and falling into the open arms of my new *mother*. I could hardly wait!

When the *Township of Percy* turned out to be nothing like I had imagined I was more than somewhat disappointed. *'Township'* is a curious word that the Canadian's use. I naturally assumed *'township'* to mean an actual town like we have in England- a bustling built up area crammed full of houses and shops and the like. After having been born and brought up in the crowded suburbs of London, as I journeyed along the Percy Road, it looked to me as if I had wandered into back end of nowhere. This 'town' that I had imagined was no more than a straggle of mostly small settlements.

The Weatherup 'farm' that I had imagined coming to in my mind did not live up to my expectation either. In fact, when I first saw the shabby timber-framed house that I was unceremoniously dumped outside of by the surly driver of my horse drawn vehicle, I almost cried with disappointment. The only timber-framed houses I could recall from where I had lived in England where along the Merton High Street and the older parts of Wimbledon. As far as I was concerned, tired, old-fashioned, clap-board cottages were for poor people to live in. Almost all of the houses where I lived in Wimbledon were built of London clay bricks; strong, modern houses with all of the modern conveniences like running water, piped in gas and a flushing outside *lavvy* connected up to a main sewer.

This Weatherup *'farm'* consisted of the two story house, which stood the corner of the aptly named 'Gravel Road' with a largish parcel of partially cultivated land betwixt it and the blacksmith's just a step further on. As I picked up my luggage from the dirt and summoned up my courage to walk to the front door of the house, I had no idea what lay ahead.

My welcome at Mrs Weatherup's home had not matched the one that I had dreamed of and naively *expected* as I had lain locked in my husband's warm embrace crossing the ocean. I thought that there would be smiles and happiness at my arrival, when in reality what I received was the same welcome one might have expected at bad news. In fact as I stood on the door step nervously introducing myself to leathery-faced Sarah Weatherup, I was not certain if she was even going to let me across the threshold.

'So you're Edith May, then?' Mrs Weatherup said, eyeing me like my mother would eye a dubious-looking gypsy who pitched up at her door selling *lucky* heather.

'Yes,' I replied in my best English accent. 'Charmed to meet you, Mrs Weatherup, I'm sure.'

But Mrs Weatherup did not look in the least bit charmed to meet me.

Looking back, I realise now that my new mother-in-law had been unprepared for me; not just in practical terms, but mentally, too. The differences between our two backgrounds were worlds apart.

After what seemed to be an age-long impasse, with me standing there holding my bag and her coldly looking me up and down, at last Mrs Weatherup said begrudgingly,

'I suppose you had better come in then.'

Even with a bright sunny day outside, the inside of the house looked drab and dreary, but immaculately clean. The parlour, into which I was initially shown, was scantily furnished with a sturdy but unstylish table and chairs. Above the fire place was a large dark wood over-mantle affair inlaid with a mirror where the silver backing had long since started to come away, leaving behind brownish marks like the foxing that can be found on old books. Upon the shelf stood a solitary framed wedding photograph of a surprisingly beautiful, serene young woman, dressed in a white with a large bow at her neck. Standing beside the bride was her dewy-eyed groom, suited and with a centre parting in his barely slicked-down hair. Both bore sombre looks as if frightened by the prospect of married life that lay before them. I could hardly believe it when I was later told that the couple were Bill's mother and father. Beside the photograph stood a curious, china ornament which I took was for holding matches, although it was empty.

I almost tripped on the large, faded rag rug that only partly covered the bare wooden floor as I put down my luggage and made towards the chair that Mrs Weatherup had grimly gestured me to. I sat down while she then sat herself down at the far side of the table, from which position she continued to closely scrutinise me.

'We are short on space,' she said after almost a minute or so of uncomfortable silence, 'so I am afraid that you and Bill cannot have a room to yourselves. You will have to make do with sleeping in with my daughter, Angeline, and when he gets here Bill can bunk in with one of his brothers.'

I just smiled and nodded with willing resignation while trying desperately not to let the disappointment show on my face; I had been married for more than six months and yet I still was not able to share a bed with my own husband.

After that, an uneasy silence set in between her and me which I hadn't got the courage to break. It was the most uncomfortable experience I can ever recall. Then, like sunshine breaking through on a grey London day, Angeline Weatherup burst in through the kitchen door.

'Hello,' she beamed warmly, 'you must be Edie? I'm your new sister. You can call me Annie.'

Angeline and I took to each other at once.

Although Sarah Weatherup had ten children, only Angeline, and her younger brothers, Charlie and Fred, still lived at home. The older daughters, Ida, Mary, and Ella, were all grown up and married, as was her eldest son, John. There had been another son, George, but he had died from Tuberculosis at the age of just twenty, not long before Bill had gone off to war. And another brother, James, had died in infancy.

Bill had already told me that his father, Robert, had passed away when he had only been a boy of seven and that he had no memory of him. As for any extended Weatherup family, strangely, Bill had made no mention of there being any at all. In fact, no-one in his family mentioned any, which I found somewhat odd.

'I love your clothes,' Angeline enthused. 'And your shoes,' she added, looking down at my feet. 'They're really pretty.'

Before I could thank her for her welcome compliment, Mrs Weatherup cut me dead.

'They may be fine for London, Annie, I am sure. But they are totally impractical for here!'

'Well I like them!' Angeline continued, unafraid about sticking to her opinions and despite her mother's obvious disapproval. 'Would you like me to show you our room?' she chirped on, like a songbird. 'I can help you unpack your things while Mom makes us all some tea.'

I was so grateful to take up her lead.

Upstairs, in our bedroom, the décor was even simpler than downstairs, though it was cosy and clean. Angeline showed me the bed; a great double bed that looked all the bigger in the tiny room she and I would have to share – just like I had done with my sister Nance back home.

Selfishly, at first, I wondered why Bill and I could not have been given this room and the double bed. His two brothers could then have bunked in together; leaving the remaining small, single-bedded room for Angeline. Was it simply to snub me? I wondered. However, I quickly came to realise why it was that Angeline needed the extra 'bed space' – she was prone to epileptic seizures from birth, many of which came in her sleep.

'Do you like it?' Angeline asked, with a trace of apprehension in her voice.

'Yes,' I replied. 'I do like it – a lot!'

To me, Bill's sister was like an angel. Although the family had chosen to shorten her name to 'Annie', I will always remember her fondly as Angeline. I would find her always gentle, loving, and patient, despite the burdens of her lot in life. She was such a pretty girl, too. But even though she was only a few months older than I was, she was forced to dress in the dowdy castoffs from her much older and somewhat unstylish female relatives. Fashion, I would soon discover, had not reached Percy for at least a decade. Even so, Angeline was so beautiful that she could have worn a flour sack without it diminishing her beauty one little bit. And how she loved to hear me talk about England! In fact, she adored everything English – especially the way I spoke.

'When you and Bill go back to visit England,' she asked, on that first exciting night as we snuggled under the bedcovers together, 'can I come with you?'

'Of course, you can,' I replied. And with that her face lit up like a London gas lamp at dusk.

Angeline admired the way my hair was styled and hankered after having her waist-length hair cut shorter, like mine was, but she knew for certain that her mother would forbid her to do so. Mrs Weatherup would never allow any such thing – not since commenting that mine looked unnaturally like a boy's hairstyle. That was such a shame, because whatever my mother-in-law's opinion, that style would have suited Angeline so well, and I know it would have made her so very happy.

'I overslept that first night, because when I woke up next morning, Angeline was already up and off to see to the cow and the chickens. As I groggily rubbed my culture-shocked and travel-weary eyes, I could hear heated voices wafting up from downstairs. I grabbed my gown and tip-toed out onto the landing to see if I could make out what was going on below. Then I heard him... it was Bill. One of the voices arguing belonged to my husband. He was home!

'But I did not stop to think...' I heard him say firmly.

'That's always been the trouble with you, William! You never stop to think, do you? I was relying on that fifteen dollars coming in...'

'I did not know,' he stressed, 'that they would stop the money from coming to you...'

'And going to that... that trinket of yours!'

'Edie is my wife!' Bill snapped.

'She's more ornament than use, son!' his mother came back. 'You only have to give her a glance to see where *my* allowance went. On fancy clothes and fancy shoes, that's where. And *that* is what I lost *my farm* for?'

'It's not *her* fault, Mom – it's mine. So don't you go taking it out on her! And what about John?' Bill argued. 'I was stupid enough to think that with me gone, my own brother might have done a bit more to help you out!'

Then, with Sarah Weatherup damning words still ringing in my ears, I crept back into the bedroom and slunk under the bedcovers, where I began to cry my heart out. I'd had no idea: no idea that Bill's mother had lost the farm at Cramahe because of me.

That previous winter of nineteen-eighteen had been incredibly difficult. The Spanish Flu had vested its evil spite on Canada, too, just as viciously as it had done in Europe. So Mrs Weatherup had also run up a few unexpected extra bills, but knew that she would be able to clear them come spring, once the next instalment of *her* Separation Allowance had arrived from the Army at the Post Office. The only problem was that, unknown to her, Bill had got married and the allowance had then been automatically transferred to his new next of kin – me. And she was right. To my utter shame, it was true that I had wantonly squandered a great deal of that money.

When Bill came up to my room a few minutes later, I had pretended to be asleep. When he *'woke'* me, I acted as if I was oblivious to the row that I had just heard him have with his mother. He hugged and kissed me, and then urged me to get dressed, because he was eager to take me out and show me my way around the place.

When I ventured downstairs, Mrs Weatherup was cooking breakfast, which we all sat down to in utter silence. As I tried to eat, I felt my stomach tightening in knots, so that I hardly had any appetite at all. From those moments, I was painfully aware of being caught in the midst of an uneasy truce between mother and son. And I was only too mindful that I was the cause of much bitterness at a time when they should have been celebrating Bill's survival and their reunion after being apart for so long. There was nothing I could say to try to make amends or to ease the unhappiness, because neither Bill nor his mother would readily admit that they had argued. And I dared not let them know that I had overheard them from the top of the stairs. However, it was at that table that I made the conscious decision to try to fit in, and eventually to somehow make amends in some way so that perhaps this rift could be mended as soon as possible. Since understanding exactly why Sarah Weatherup was so set against me, I was desperate to prove that her *Simple Jack* had not traded in the family cow for a bag of useless beans after all. I was determined to set about proving to her that I could be an asset to both my husband and her family, no matter how much future circumstance and events might contrive to thwart my mission.

The following day was a perfect 'drying day', and so I got up early, fetched some water from the well, rolled up my sleeves, and set about washing my dirty underwear from the journey across from England. Mrs Weatherup watched me keenly from the door of the pantry as I wrung out my pink frilly bloomers. She then told me, in no uncertain terms, that I was not to hang *those things* out on the line in plain sight of Bill's brothers. Instead, I was to secret them amongst the folds of the freshly washed bed linen that she herself was about to peg out. I said nothing. Instead I smiled sweetly and I obediently set about doing as she had asked, without realising that at that very same moment I was about to provoke her full wrath.

'Cover yourself up!' Mrs Weatherup snapped, fixing her steely blue-grey eyes firmly upon the tattoo on my arm. 'I do not want the neighbours seeing *that* abhorrence!'

I immediately did as she ordered. After all, I had told myself beneath pursed lips, I wouldn't have wanted some old biddy in this Victorian-minded backwater seeing it and fainting! If only I could have blanked-out the '*Pankhurst*' part of the tattoo leaving just the 'William' intact... but I had tried to do that before, back home in Tooting. I had taken my mother's scouring pad from the scullery and rubbed it all over the tattoo until it bled. Then it had oozed up and scabbed over into a big red crust, but after that had fallen away, there underneath, and as clear as day, the bold blue lettering was still visible. After that, I never bothered to try removing it again.

Bill didn't mind though. He had seen my tattoo often enough and it didn't bother him a bit. He understood that I had known this other *William* long before I met him and knew that he had been killed. After all, my husband had known a lot blokes in the trenches who'd had girlfriends waiting for them back home; blokes who had also been killed.

My own Mum hadn't liked my tattoo either, but at least she had understood. There wasn't one person that she knew who hadn't lost someone in the war. Mrs Weatherup and the others living out of the way in Percy Township had no idea what being at war had really been like for *us*. Sure, some of the people around about had lost sons to it, but it was a long distance war to them. I *knew* intimately what war was like. After all, this war had been on *our* own bloody doorstep! Unlike us, the inhabitants of Percy hadn't had to cower under their staircases in raw terror – at the prospect of bombs dropping on them.

Norham and its inhabitants were so very old fashioned. They were as staid as my grandmother's old whalebone corset, and just as musty. To my quiet amusement, no sooner had I first stepped outside the homestead with Bill, than I found myself the stuff of gossip. If I walked out to the general store, all eyes were trained on me. I could guess what the village cronies were saying behind my back; 'There she goes. That's the fancy woman who stole Sarah Weatherup's son and her farm from under her...'

I saw them, looking me over from head to foot; my hair, my tightly cut clothes, and my bow-fronted shoes – nothing of which could meet with *their* approval. I bit my lip and made as if I did not care. But I did care. I cared deeply. I knew that I wasn't wanted in Norham, but there seemed little that I could do about it. Even if I had wanted to leave altogether, there was no way back home for me now. And I had no intention of leaving my Bill.

Chapter Seven

I made myself useful. Wherever and whenever I could, I gave a helping hand about the Weatherup home, though I was too frightened at first to go near the family cow, and I dreaded the mind-numbing monotony of churning butter. However, in time, I even mastered both tasks. Mostly, I helped share Angeline's daily chores, which served to draw us even closer. Truly, if it had not been for her moral support, I would have bundled up my belongings within the first week and moved into the local boarding house.

Don't get me wrong, my Bill stood up for me right enough – to begin with. But over those first months, it seemed that the longer we stayed in that house with his mother, the less inclined he seemed to support me. Sarah Weatherup, it appeared, was winning this particular war of attrition. I felt trapped, but Angeline saw to it that I did not feel completely alone. Had it not been for her and regular letters from Hattie, I think I would have curled up and given in completely.

That first winter went by slowly. It was slower than any I can recall in England. In the suburbs of London, what with so many people living in houses packed close together, it was like having an army of worker ants on hand: all primed and ready to swing into action. When snow fell it was soon shovelled away from the pavements and into neat little ridges at the side of the roads. Householders would then dash outside and tip out the contents of their ash pans onto the walkways to aid pedestrians in getting a grip in the icy weather.

In Norham, clearing snow seemed a thankless task. And usually, when it fell there, it came down in cartloads! Then, unlike in London, so much came at once that clearing it away seemed like a futile task. As a result, only the snow which impeded necessary passage was tackled, or a body could be shovelling snow from dawn until dusk and then not have much to show for all the effort.

In Canada winter was also the season for eating *'wild food'* – the proceeds of hunting – something we never did back home in English cities, where the only *'wildlife'* I saw was rats and pigeons. Things would suddenly turn up on the Weatherup kitchen table – complete with fur and in need of gutting – that I did not even recognise, let alone want to eat.

Then Bill would scold me, saying that I ate less than a bird. Mrs Weatherup would simply glare at me across the dinner table as if every scrap that did not make it past my lips was a direct insult to her and the whole of Canada. To me it seemed that no matter what I did, she took umbrage at, meeting my eyes with that same taciturn stare of hers.

During the worst weather we stayed put in the house, which only heightened the tension I felt between Bill's mother and me. Worse for me was the fact that my husband and I had no time alone together – to strengthen our withering bond as man and wife. And I knew that the longer that situation went on, the more easily I could find myself undermined in his affections. Despite the disappointment of discovering that my new life in Canada was not as rosy a picture as my husband had painted in my mind during our all too brief courtship, I loved Bill, and I so wanted to make this marriage work!

My letters home to my family belied the true state of my situation. I avoided disclosing what weighed heavily on my mind by instead cheerily writing colourful descriptions of all the positive things I had seen in the country. I wrote about how beautiful the trees were as they turned to autumn colours that year, and how fresh and clean the air was. It was not a bit like all the muck we had to inhale back home, when on some winter days was so thick that you'd swear that you could slice it up and butter it for tea. And there were times when there was so much sulphur in the air that it cut the back of your throat just trying to breathe. With hindsight, I think that perhaps my descriptions of my life in Canada were too cheery and far too positive.

Anyway, in comparison with what I wrote, news from home was grim and black. Dad's younger brother, my lovely Uncle Tom, did not return from the Great War as expected. It was all the more of a shame because he was such a diamond bloke. Uncle Tom had been *Acting Sergeant* in some far off place called Mesopotamia and had only just written home to my dad not long before I had left for Canada. Mum's letter arrived at Norham not long after the New Year, informing me that they had heard that he was killed at the end of September. Poor bloke. Just like my Uncle Daniel, he had ended up buried who knows where, and with none of his family able to pay their final respects to him. Then, at the very end of Mum's letter and almost as a by line, she dropped a real bombshell: adding that she and Dad had another baby in December, but that it had died shortly afterwards.

Come spring, Bill got an offer of work not far away in Orland Village in Brighton Township. It was some general farm labouring and sheep shearing – which Bill was good at. And, joy of joys, I could go with him! At last we could be together in the same bed, like every other husband and wife, for the first time since our honeymoon back in Wimbledon more than a year before. Then of course the inevitable happened: that June I fell pregnant.

My Bill seemed genuinely pleased at the thought of us having a child – as was dear Angeline. Oh, she was ecstatic beyond description at the thought of a baby coming into the house... a baby she could also love and help care for. And once the baby had quickened, she loved nothing more than to be allowed to place her hand upon my belly and feel the baby moving beneath my skin.

Sarah Weatherup already had other grandchildren, and Bill's brother John and his wife Bessie had presented her with another grandson just earlier that year. But this time something would be different; my baby would be the first to be born in that house and it would be the first baby Angeline would be directly involved with caring for. She was so excited that it was all that she could talk about.

Bill's mother took the news with her usual stern exterior, as if conceding to the sealing of her poor son's fate. With a baby on the way, any faint hopes she may have held of an annulment of our marriage must surely have been dashed.

At the end of September, Bill and I moved back into the Weatherup family home for the winter, and this time into a room of our own. Without any discussion, Mrs Weatherup had given up her own double bed and taken to sleeping in the parlour instead. There was no work for Bill in Brighton at that time of year, but there was still plenty that needed doing at his mother's home before the really bad weather came, and so he busied himself with that.

All seemed to be going fairly well between us at the Weatherup household... until one morning about a fortnight after Bill and I had returned. Angeline had already gone outside much earlier to see to the cow and the chickens. But when she didn't return after some considerable time had passed, I decided to go out after her to see if she needed my help.

At first I could not see her, but then I noticed a patch of tall grass behind the cow shed quivering wildly. As I made towards it, I saw Angeline writhing on the ground – in the grip of a violent epileptic seizure. So I rushed over to her and got down beside her and did as I had seen her mother do during a previous fit. Although wary of being hit in the stomach, I quickly laid one of my legs over hers, grasped her flailing arms, and then drew them in gently to her side, to reduce the risk of her harming herself. All the while watching carefully to ensure that Angeline did not swallow her tongue and choke on it. Meanwhile, I shouted out for help. But no-one in the house heard me. So I lay there beside her in a body hold until the seizure passed and Angeline lay quiet and still, as if in a deep sleep. Then I got up and ran into the house to ask for help.

Bill was away at his brother John's, so it was left to young Fred and Charlie to carry Angeline into the house and up to her room. She lay there sleeping peacefully and deeply on her bed until some time past noon, when she managed to get up and make her way downstairs unaided. Although still visibly groggy, she nonetheless managed a cheery smile.

Over the following hour or so, Angeline's condition improved rapidly, until she was back to her usual self by supper time. Afterwards, no more was thought of this latest seizure. After all, Angeline had encountered countless such episodes before and she always recovered well.

But the following morning Angeline failed to appear downstairs at her usual time, and so thinking that her daughter must have needed extra rest, Bill's mother left her to sleep in. However, as it neared eleven, Mrs Weatherup made her way up to Angeline's bedroom to wake her. She found her daughter lying cold, still, and face-down on the bed, with her head buried deep in her pillows. Angeline was dead. Alone in her room, she had suffered a second seizure during the night and had smothered to death.

All that followed Angeline's sudden death was heartbreak for us all, but especially so for Bill's mother. Mrs Weatherup would talk about it to her neighbours and the endless stream of callers who came to the house. But then when they had gone, she said very little to Bill or the rest of us in the house. And she would not weep in sight of us – not even on the day of Angeline's funeral. I heard her crying, though. In the small hours of the empty nights that followed, I heard her crying in her room below, as I lay awake with my own child kicking inside me. I could only imagine the pain that she was going through at losing her beloved daughter. I felt anger, too. I was angry about such a sweet and lovely person, my very dear sister-in-law, being snatched away so cruelly.

I had not known before, but Sarah Weatherup's own brother had suffered from epilepsy from infancy. He died at the tender age of ten. So I began to understand all the more keenly just how hard it must have been for Sarah – having spent all those years raising Angeline – anxiously watching and waiting for every seizure to pass. She probably lived in dread of a terrible day that might come, when Angeline might lose her life in exactly the same manner in which her own brother had lost his.

***

It was in the small hours of a freezing cold morning in early February when I woke with the most dreadful cramps in my abdomen. My moans woke Bill, who then ran downstairs to fetch his mother. She confirmed what I already dreaded; I had gone into labour.

Outside it was snowing heavily, as it had been for several days. As a result, we already knew that the road from Norham was blocked and therefore we were cut off from Warkworth and the nearest doctor. Like it or not, it would be up to my mother-in-law to deliver my baby, and despite reassurances from Bill about the numerous babies she had delivered before, I was naturally nervous about having to let her deliver mine.

Mrs Weatherup made me get up and, against my own determination to stay put in my bed, had me grope my way down to the kitchen, where she quickly lit the range.

'I'll make us a nice cup of tea, Edie,' she said cheerily. 'And while I do so, why don't you try walking about a bit. It will help with the pain and to bring the baby along.'

At first I thought that she was joking. The last thing I wanted was a cup of tea, and to shuffle about the kitchen while periodically doubling over as the pain came and went in waves.

Bill did not seem to know what to do to help me, other than to hold my hand, but even that stopped after a short while. Then I was dumbfounded when his mother piped up, 'Best you go back to your bed, son. There's no point in you losing sleep when Edie and I can deal with this well enough'.

And I was even more dumbfounded, if that's possible, when he went.

Over the coming hours the contractions grew steadily stronger and closer together, and yet still Mrs Weatherup kept making me get up from the chair and move about. At one point I even thought that she was trying to punish me – by not letting me go back to my bed. Eventually, I could barely manage to walk around the kitchen table without holding on to the chairs for support, while Bill's mother rubbed my back.

Dawn was beginning to break as my mother-in-law decided that it was time for us to make a move. And so, with her support, I slowly made my way towards the stairs. I was surprised when, instead of leading me back up to my room, she led me into her own, where the bed had already been stripped and overlaid with thick draw sheets.

Mrs Weatherup helped me onto her bed and then propped my back up with four very lumpy pillows. As she did so, I suddenly felt the most dreadful sensation – as if I were about to pass a cannon ball out through my bowels. I screamed out in panic.

'I need to look under your nightgown, Edie,' Mrs Weatherup said calmly, 'so that I can see if the baby is coming.'

Although I was terribly embarrassed to be showing my private bits and pieces to her, I was in no fit state to do anything other than that which she asked. So, gingerly, I took a deep breath and hoisted my nighty up to my waist.

'I can see the top of its head. It won't be long now, Edie. Just do as I say and it will soon be all over.'

With the next contraction Sarah Weatherup delivered my child.

'What are you going to call him,' Ma asked, wiping his little face clean. 'John, after your father?'

'No...' I said weakly. 'Bill and me thought... we might call him *Frederick Charles*... after his uncles. What do you think... Mrs Weatherup?'

'I think that's a fine name for my grandson,' she smiled.

As if by some miracle, from that moment onwards she and I suddenly shared an unbreakable bond. No longer was *'Ma'*, as she now insisted I call her, my greatest critic. Instead, she suddenly became my greatest and most welcome ally. I still do not understand exactly how that came to be. How this hard-headed woman from stern Canadian pioneer stock could suddenly take to her brazen and streetwise London daughter-in-law, who had unwittingly caused her so much grief, is unfathomable for me. Anyway, it happened! And I was just so very grateful and happy that it had. I put much of this amazing turn-around down to the love we shared for my beautiful newborn son.

I had not given much thought as to what kind of mother I would be. With my own mother, babies had just happened to come along during my childhood, and I had not noticed much change in her at all. And so I naively hadn't expected having a baby to change me much either. But it did. In fact, I suddenly found myself changing so much that I no longer recognised myself! And, to be honest, I must admit that it had been a selfish self. But suddenly I found that I was no longer living in the centre of my own universe. Instead, my baby Freddie was. And I had given up my place of honour willingly. I adored him! And Freddie had helped heal the gaping rift between me and his Grandma Sarah.

From that time onwards, I always went to Ma if I had anything at all on my mind, and she was always there to help and comfort me. This was just as well, because my relationship with my husband began to slide towards a rocky patch.

Spring came and Bill planned to return to Orland to work. As Freddie was still so tiny, Bill insisted that our baby and I stay on at Norham with his mother. I did not relish the thought of being parted from him, but understood why it was for the best.

I had long ago noticed an overgrown and neglected patch at the far end of the Weatherup plot. And there, hidden under the tangle of weeds and briar I had noticed what looked to be the remains of an old animal shelter. Knowing that Bill had set some money aside from what we had earned the previous year, I decided to ask him for my share of it.

'What do you want money for?' he asked abruptly, as if I had no right to be asking.

'I thought that as I was staying on here with Ma, I could invest that money in rearing a few pigs.'

'Pigs? You Edie? Rearing pigs?' He scoffed, 'What do you know about rearing pigs?'

Before I could answer, Ma chipped in to back me up.

'If Edie can care for a baby, Bill, I am certain she is more than capable of rearing a few pigs! Besides, I will be here to help her out *if* she needs me.'

And so with that open support from Ma the matter was settled, and within a few days of Charlie and Fred helping me to clean up the sty and clear the brambles, I was the proud owner of three of the cutest looking piglets ever seen on God's earth.

Sows often birth more pigs than they can suckle and so the littlest or weakest one, the *runt* as it is often called, often gets pushed out of the way by its stronger siblings in the rush to find a teat. Piglets are shrewd creatures: the strongest one seems to know by instinct how to seek out the best teat closest to its mother's head, where once having staked its claim, will refuse to be moved from it on subsequent feeds. Indeed, once this feeding order upon the teats has been established, the weakest piglet is resigned to the least productive teat – or worse still, no teat at all – as was the case with the particular runts we were to get. As a result, for survival, these 'surplus' offspring needed putting to another sow with teats to spare, or else reared by hand, which can be as intensive as raising a human baby. Apart from this, if a runt is a runt by reason of being born weaker than the other piglets, rather than being deprived of a teat, it will most likely to die in any case. And so to a pig farmer these runts are usually considered more trouble than they are worth, which opened an easy way for Ma and me to pick out and buy some newly born piglets for a mere pittance. And contrary to expectations, all three thrived in our care.

The only pigs I had ever seen back in England had been cut in half and then hung from hooks at the butchers in the High Street. I had never seen a live one before I came to Canada. So the first time Ma and I went to a nearby farm to buy some of our own pigs, the big 'uns looked ferocious to me.

'These sows won't hurt you, Edie!' Ma had laughed, as with considerable trepidation I peered over a sty wall. 'They might nudge you a bit at first, just to see who the boss is. But if they do, you just nudge them back real hard so they know that it's you!'

261

Though I wasn't so sure, Ma proved me right. I got to know our own pigs from little 'uns, and so by the time they were adults I had no fear of them at all. In fact, I was utterly captivated by them. They seemed so intelligent! And I was amazed to find that if left to their own devices, my pigs were actually capable of 'harvesting' odd branches sprung up from an old stump in their run and then *'building'* themselves a sort of shelter in which they then took great delight in sleeping. My pigs *knew* me, too, and not just my voice: they seemed to recognise me by sight. Whenever I went outside, whether to fetch some wood or to hang up the washing, my pigs would snort and squeal after me in their own greeting.

Buying special pig food was expensive – too expensive for me to contemplate. And unlike the local pig farmers, we hadn't the ground to plant a special crop to help feed them. So Charlie and Fred were wonderful in helping me out by setting up a run to collect swill in a hand cart each day from around Norham.

When Bill came home that fall, Ma and I could proudly show off two reasonably good sows and a passable boar pig as reward for our efforts. And as a bonus, since the three runts had come from three different farms, we would be able to mate both sows with our own boar. I was a bit sad to see the pigs go off to slaughter, but I must admit that they made for some exceedingly good eating!

Those next few years, while raising Freddie and my pigs with Ma, were the happiest of my life. I really loved sharing those summers in Norham with Ma. If only my life could have stayed like that, I would have been the most contented woman on earth. But everything didn't stay as it was. Life changed. And although I did not know this at the time, I would never find such happiness again.

My little Freddie wasn't the only new arrival that year to Norham. In the April, my sister Nance and her husband, Harry Field, arrived in Canada aboard the *Melitia*.

Although Nance and Harry had only been married six months, they brought an eleven-month-old baby with them who they proudly introduced as *their* daughter – Gladys May. I was shocked, because I had not been told about her birth. And I was perplexed, because Nance refused to be drawn further.

Ma had said how *nice* it would for me to have family close by. I remember telling her bluntly that as far as I was concerned they were not wanted and that I had not encouraged them to come. However, as it transpired, their decision to come was very much down to me. It had been my glowing reports of Canada in my letters back home that had put the idea into my sister's mind for her and her husband to emigrate. The problem was that once Nance and Harry had seen Norham for themselves, they did not like it one little bit. It was just *too* different from what they were used to back home. Nance missed her home comforts too much, and she and Harry did not take well to going without them. Also, Harry had been expecting to find work as a packer, as he had back home. But there were no jobs for packers where we lived, and he knew nothing about farming.

On his papers, Harry had even had the brass neck to put down my Bill's name as his prospective employer! To Bill's credit, he put about a good word for him, which soon fixed Harry up with both a steady job and a place to stay. But out of 'gratitude', Harry repaid him by gaining a fine reputation as an untrustworthy, work-shy blighter, and so he soon got fired. After that, my Bill swore that he would never help him out again. It was a sheer relief all round when Nance and Harry eventually cleared off and settled in Campbellford – just far enough away to give us some peace. That was about the time that the stock markets in America slowly began to rise once more after their dramatic post war decline. Bill's and my future started to look rosy.

263

In the spring of nineteen-twenty-three, as Bill was getting ready to go off to work in Brighton once more, he asked if I would go with him this time. Ma said that the change of air would be good for me, and that now Freddie was older, he could stay behind with her. But the thought of being parted from my precious little Freddie held me back. That and the fact that I was pregnant again.

'Brighton is hardly a world away, Edie,' Ma said reassuringly. 'You can easily get back to visit Freddie.

'See, Edie,' Bill coaxed.

'But what about the baby? ' I reminded them, as if I needed to.

'You'll be home again before its due in October,' Bill argued.

Reluctantly, I gave in. But, oh, how I wish now that I had stayed with Ma!

I found it so hot that August! Hot and so overwhelmingly draining! And matters weren't helped when I unexpectedly went into labour. I was only seven months pregnant.

When my waters broke, on August the second, we realised that it was far too early for the baby to come and so Bill sent for the family doctor to come out to us immediately. When he arrived, some three hours later, I was all but ready to push.

Dr Armstrong quickly rolled up his sleeves and examined me down below. As he did, I saw the expectant look on his face change. He then he explained that he suspected that the cord was wrapped about my baby's neck and that, unless he could free it quickly, then the child would strangle as it was born.

'On no account push, Mrs Weatherup,' Dr Armstrong warned. 'Do you understand? You must not push. When the next contraction comes, pant hard through your open mouth instead until I tell you otherwise.'

I was terrified. How on earth was I going to resist the urge to push?

The next contraction quickly came and I panted for all my might, but the pain of Dr Armstrong's frenetic intervention in trying to save my child was almost unbearable. At the height of my agony I screamed so hard between pants that I almost snapped Bill's arm off as I grabbed it. All I could think about was my desperate desire to push as my body was urging me. Again, a contraction came and went, but still Dr Armstrong could not free the umbilical cord. Then, on the third contraction, just as he succeeded, my daughter Bessie was born.

Even as Dr Armstrong laid her tiny bloodied body on my belly, I could see immediately that something wasn't quite right with her. Bessie seemed to stay very blue for a long time after her first breaths and it seemed like ages before she began to pink up. She was floppier and much smaller than Freddie had been at birth, and she had a covering of downy fine hair over much of her body. But it was the shape of her head that caught my attention the most. It seemed very misshapen and bruised all over.

The doctor quickly cleaned Bessie up before wrapping her snugly in a piece of linen. And then, just as he was about to place her in my arms, it happened... my baby went rigid and her eyes rolled back into her head. She had begun to convulse.

Dr Armstrong quickly took Bessie from me and laid her on the foot of the bed, where he examined her thoroughly. After a few moments the seizure eased and then he gently handed her back to me. He did not say what was wrong with her, but I could tell from his face that all was far from going well.

I cradled Bessie in my arms, afraid of letting her go. I did not want to let her go, despite my state of near exhaustion, and I did not want to try going to sleep. I just wanted my little baby girl to be alright. Then, thankfully, she rallied enough to suckle, which we took to be a good sign. But it was not. It was to be no more than a sucker's gap before the storm.

Bessie soon began to convulse again, and again. After this happened several more times within the space of barely an hour, Dr Armstrong told Bill and me that there was nothing else that he could do for our baby. Bessie had apparently sustained some sort of injury to her head during her delayed passage into the world, and so her chances of survival rested in God's hands. 'If only the seizures would ease,' the doctor explained, 'she just *might* survive.' But Bessie died the following day. Suddenly I fully understood Ma Weatherup's pain.

Unknown to me at the time, Dr Armstrong had spoken to Bill after becoming concerned at my utter desolation at the loss of my baby.

'The best thing would be to try for another a baby as quickly as possible,' Dr Armstrong advised my husband. 'The expectation of another child would be the quickest way for your wife to get over the loss of this one.'

The fool! The callous fool! I wasn't a child crying over the loss of a broken dolly! I wasn't a child whose heart could easily be mended by being given a replacement toy. My body had made that child I had just lost, and my mind had lived in the joyful expectation of her arrival for many months. She had come and then died so quickly that neither my mind nor my body could be persuaded of it. Milk flowed from my engorged breasts, but there was no baby to suckle. My arms yearned to cradle Bessie, but they dangled empty and bereft at my side. Yet, above all else, it was my mind that remained firmly in denial of my daughter's death. If I slept, I dreamed of her, convinced that she still lay curled up safely within my belly. But then I would awake and my misery would quickly be realised

266

again and I would break down into a flood of tears. That fool of a doctor! I did not want *another* baby. With every fibre of my being I yearned for the baby I had just lost.

I took Bill's gentle sexual advances to be his way of trying to console me and so I did not turn him away. To be held softly in my husband's arms felt comforting, though to be truthful, I barely knew what I was doing those first few weeks. Then, when the terrible truth dawned on me that I might again be pregnant, barely four weeks after Bessie's death, I felt as though Bill had tricked me.

Bill had met the news as if it was the solution to everything, as if he expected that somehow I would magically be cured of my grief and that everything would 'return to normal' once more. Instead, all that I could feel was the deep, deep, midnight-black depression within me intensifying, as was my growing resentment towards this new 'interloper' that would soon demand the love and attention that I had reserved for my Bessie. I did not want this *other* baby.

When my baby daughter arrived the following June, while we were again living at Brighton, I felt nothing towards her. Her big blue eyes would search out my face as she mewed like a kitten for my attention, but I would look away. She would cry to be changed or fed, and I would ignore her. Then when she howled, Bill would fly into one of his increasingly frequent rages and shout, 'What's the matter with you Edie? Why won't you see to our baby?'

The baby, the baby – I could not even bear to call her by her name – Doris. In my mind, it seemed that if I were to so much as utter her name I would somehow be betraying my dead Bessie. On the brink of desperation himself, a few days after Doris' birth, Bill took me back to Norham and Ma.

It was as if I were lost; that somehow I had lost myself somewhere during that past awful year. And because Doris had arrived, it felt as if I no longer had a bit of my life left that I could call my own. She got in the way of everything. Everything revolved around that baby and *her* demands.

And all I got from Bill was rowing and accusations – that I cared more for Freddie and the pigs than I did for Doris. Ma? Ma was altogether different. She did not scold me or criticise me. It was as if she understood exactly how I was feeling, and so she would gently coax me into caring for Doris, and when I was floundering, she took over completely until I could. I tried so hard to climb out from under my deep dark cloud, but it seemed that every time I managed to do so, something else bad came along to drag me back down again. It was like I was drowning in misery and I just could help myself swim anymore.

'I want to go home,' I confided in Ma. ' If only I could go home for a while, for a visit, then maybe I could shake this all off and get back to how I used to be.'

But Bill wouldn't hear a word of it and flew into a terrible temper when I asked him. 'You are not going Edie!' he raged. 'I won't bloody allow it!'

Ma didn't say anything at first. Instead she went off to Warkworth instead to see Dr Armstrong to ask his opinion. Then she returned and confronted Bill herself, informing him in no uncertain terms of how the doctor had agreed that a visit home to England might be just what I needed. And so with great reluctance, Bill eventually agreed.

Come the last week in May, nineteen-twenty-five, four-year-old Freddie, baby Doris, and I, were aboard the White Star Line's *'Doric',* heading out of Quebec and on our way to England.

Chapter Eight

It was strange being back in Wimbledon. It seemed almost as if I had never been away. My old home in Cowper Road looked just the same, apart from the front door being repainted; that and the fact that my parents no longer lived there anymore. They had moved just across the road to number twenty-five where, instead of living in a whole house, they had settled into a purpose-built ground floor 'maisonette' comprising just two rooms, and a kitchen and scullery.

I was genuinely glad to see my mum, and I hoped that our time apart and her meeting her grandchildren would serve to ease our strained relationship. At first, as I sat in the kitchen feeding Doris, with Mum taking young Freddie up on her lap for a cuddle, I thought that it had.

'We was so sorry, Bill and me, when we heard that your baby died,' I said.

'It wasn't right,' Mum said, pouring out a cup of milky tea for Freddie. 'I knew it wasn't right the moment I clapped eyes on it. It had one of those strange, oriental faces and a great big tongue. Yer dad and me never wanted another baby anyway. Not at our time of life. It was a relief, really. A relief and a blessing all round when she went.'

I felt so sad for that baby Florence. After all, she would have been my little sister. And yet what really got to me was how easily my mother had 'dismissed' her. I suppose that was the difference between us. There I was, almost two years on, and still grieving for my Bessie. But then I was soon thinking about how at least that poor little mite had been spared all I had been put through. And as pleasant as those first minutes of my return had been, it didn't take Mum long to have a real go at me.

269

'I hear our Nance is having a dreadful time in Canada,' she said accusingly. 'And I heard all about how your Bill wouldn't help Harry get settled.'

'That's not true, Mum,' I replied. 'Bill did all he could. He fixed Harry up with a good job. It's not his fault if the lazy sod wouldn't work to keep it!'

'Harry's not lazy!' Mum snapped back. 'Nance says that it's really hard getting used to that type of work, that's all. But those bloody farmers wouldn't give him a chance. Nance says that they never wanted to give him a job in the first place, because they would much rather give a job to one of their own.'

I knew all about Harry and the other Fields. They were a bad lot. I had even tried to warn Nance off Harry when she first started stepping out with him. Yet as Mum continued talking she was making him out to be some sort of saint, now that he was married to her precious Nance.

'Nance says... If Nance says so, then it must be bleeding true?' I wanted to scream. But I bit my tongue.

I knew from bitter experience that it would be pointless trying to convince Mum that she was wrong. My mother would not hear one bad word said against either Nance or her precious Harry Field, so I gave up on the subject. And I needed to keep in with Mum, because I had so very little money for living expenses that I was reliant on staying with her.

'How long are here for?' Mum asked.

I replied that I didn't know exactly. I didn't dare tell her that things had not been so good between me and Bill lately. All I said was that I had been feeling terribly homesick lately and that I was missing her and my family real bad.

270

My dad seemed really pleased to see me when he got in from work, but then again he was generally alright for as long as he was sober.

'My Edie!' he exclaimed, before giving me a big hug and a kiss. ''Ow are you girl?'

'Alright, Dad,' I said giving him a great hug back. 'I'm alright and all the better for seeing you!'

'And who's this?' he said, grinning at little Freddie. ''Ave yer come to see yer old granddad boy?'

He seemed genuinely please to meet my children, and more so than my mum I would say. And Dad was good with young Freddie, even though the poor lad was terribly shy of his granddad to begin with, and at first hid his face in my skirt and clung to my leg. However, he eventually came out of his shell, and by the time Dad had eaten his dinner, Freddie was seated happily on his knee.

With Freddie now settled and Doris curled up fast asleep in the laundry basket, I said to Mum and Dad; 'I think I'll pop out for a bit. You'll be alight with the kids for five minutes, won't you?'

'Pop out? Dad asked. Why? Where are you off to?'

'Just down the road to call in and see how Hattie is? I've not had a letter from her in ages.'

'That scruffy little mate of yours? Hasn't yer mother told you, girl?'

'Told me what?' I asked.

'She's dead,' Mum said.

As Mum said those awful words, she sat there carrying on with her knitting as if she was talking about next door's cat instead of the person she had known damned well was my dearest friend.

271

'Hattie? Dead?' It was like someone had just kicked me in the stomach. I suddenly felt sick and queasy.

'Yes,' Dad continued. 'Her, her ma and that crippled brother of hers. All dead. Terrible it was. Must be all of six months now since it 'appened. I thought that Mum had written to you...'

'No, I hadn't. I've been busy,' Mum said, excusing herself.

'How? How did she...' I couldn't bring myself to say the word *'die'*.

'Fire,' my mother sighed, as if it was a real inconvenience for her to have to tell me. 'They was all burned to death. They think a candle set light to the 'ouse when they was sleeping. Serves 'em right. They should have paid for the gas.'

My Hattie – dead? I couldn't take it in. I really couldn't. And really I couldn't take anymore of my mother. I put on my hat and coat.

'You still going out, girl?' Dad asked gently, as Freddie began to drift off to sleep in his arms.

'Yes, Dad,' I said, choking back my tears. 'I think I need some fresh air.'

I walked slowly down Cowper Road, turned the corner and made my way towards Hattie's.

'That evil cow!' I kept telling myself. 'That evil cow talking about Hattie like that!' I hated my mother for what she had just said, for gloating when she knew how I felt about Hattie.

It was only when I got to Hattie's house and looked at it that the extent of the damage that it all really sunk in. Although the shattered windows were all boarded up, I could see great licks of black soot on the brickwork around them that the fire had left. The door, wedged ajar and barely hanging on one hinge, looked like it was made out of coal

272

and brittle-looking, blackened debris spilled out of the house and onto the garden path. The sight of the burnt doorstep really upset me. I remembered how often I had seen Hattie's mum, down on her hands and knees, scrubbing and polishing it on a Saturday morning when I called round to go out with Hattie.

Then something caught my eye. Amongst the debris I spotted a battered tin; an old Oxo tin. It was Hattie's memory tin; all blackened and bashed in, battered and discarded. With great difficulty I managed to prise it open with my finger nails. Among the pitiful contents inside were countless stubs of old cinema tickets to films that we had watched together. There was also the carefully folded paper napkin she had bought at the Peace Day Parade along with a couple of letters that I had written to her from Canada. I just stood there for a long time, holding the tin and sobbing my bleeding heart out.

It was then that a rough-looking woman came from across the street. She must have seen me from her window because she came straight out from her house and over to have a word with me.

'Bloody shame!' she exclaimed, standing beside me with her arms crossed. 'It was a rotten way to go, too. We could 'ear them all screaming like. But none of us could get inside to help 'em. An' by the time the fire engine got 'ere, it was too bloody late. It 'ad all gone quiet. 'Orrible it was. Ruddy 'orrible!'

I asked the woman if she knew where Hattie and her family had been buried and she told me that she did.

It wasn't hard to find it in the graveyard- the small bare mound of earth in the pauper's plot where Hattie's family had been buried together.

'One day, Hat,' I said softly, as I knelt to pay my respects, 'I'm going to sell all my pigs in Canada and buy you a blooming great angel for a headstone. One day, Hat...'

***

I hadn't realised how grim things were becoming economically back home since I'd been away. The rich seemed to be doing alright, as usual, and if anything else they seemed to be getting richer. We working class, we were the ones who were feeling the pinch. It was alright for my dad because he was a skilled painter and decorator, though at times even he had trouble lining up enough work to keep him going. For my younger brothers it was worse: no one was taking on lads when there were married men with families looking for work. Although my brothers often went out on jobs with Dad, there was no money in it for them. Instead they simply hoped that by doing so, they could earn the right for a good word to be put in for them with the boss when things eventually picked up. Jobs were in short supply after the war, and yet everyone was hopeful that things would soon perk up.

I had been staying at my parents' home for almost a month or more when Mum asked me when *exactly* I was going home. I said that I wasn't quite ready to do so yet, but that I was willing to look for a job to help pay my way until I did. But Dad wouldn't have a word of it, despite my mum's continual whingeing about how my kids and I were eating her out of house and home. But then the shoe dropped. Nance wrote a letter to Mum telling her how Bill had gone '*crazy*' because I had '*walked out*' on him.

'Well, my girl, is this true?' Mum screeched at me, waving the letter in the air like a victory flag. 'Have you left him?'

'No!' I said emphatically. 'I have not left Bill.'

'Well, Nance says 'ere that you 'ave...'

I don't know what she is going on about!'

'Then tell me exactly when you plan on going back?' she demanded.

'Soon,' I said. 'As soon as Bill sends me the tickets 'ome.'

'Well that had better be soon, my girl, because I'm not putting up with you and your brats much longer if you have left him.'

I can swear that Mum stood over me at that kitchen table that day – watching every word I wrote to Bill as I asked him to hurry up and sell some of my pigs to buy me and the kids our passage home. Then when I had, she marched me down to the Post Office to mail it. After that, there followed an uneasy truce as I waited for his reply.

It would be a lie if I were to say that the idea of leaving Bill altogether had never crossed my mind, because it had. On the way to the ship, getting away from him was all I could think about, because things had become so very bad between us during those last few weeks before I left. And I don't think he really believed me when I told him that I would be coming back. Yet he had given in and agreed to let me bring the children with me. But then it would have been hard for him to have said otherwise with his mother backing me up.

Ma had believed me. Ma had spoken about the future and how things would be when the kids and I came home, and even about how Freddie would be going to school. Ma Weatherup had been so good to me that I felt guilty about even thinking of taking her precious grandchildren away from her. Being back in England, staying with my mother, I knew that I must have been out of my mind to have thought of leaving Bill. At last I had come to my senses. I really could not wait to get home to Ontario, so that I could try to patch things up with my husband.

Things at home in England weren't as I had remembered them. Without Hattie striding down the Broadway beside me, Wimbledon had lost its appeal. The shops looked shabby and so did the people I passed in the streets. They looked even glummer than they had been at the height of the Great War. And even *the Angel of the horse shoe* on top of

275

the theatre had lost her sparkle. After living in Norham, everything seemed so very overcrowded. I felt hemmed in and lost among the endless stands of brick buildings, while the sky above suddenly seemed so small and watery and pale when compared with the bright and endless expanse of blue back in Canada.

At times I felt like I was suffocating in the dirty London air. My lungs gasped for a great breath full of clean Norham freshness, while my mouth thirsted to taste the sweet water from Ma Weatherup's well once more. I wanted to go home. I wanted to go home to Canada as soon as I could. I wanted to go back to my Bill. I was missing him so much!

I waited and waited. But no word came back from Canada. I wrote again, but this time I addressed my letter directly to Ma, thinking that the reason I had not received any reply or money might have been because Bill was still working away and that my letter had not yet reached him.

While I waited again, I got myself a part-time job back at my old laundry in Wandsworth, so that I could at least pay my way with Mum while she begrudgingly looked after the kids.

Eventually a letter did come, but it was from neither Bill nor his mother. It was from Nance. On the day it arrived, I found my mother waiting on the doorstep, waiting for me to come home from work. I knew then, as soon as I saw her with her arms folded and with *that* look on her face that something was up.

'Hello Mum.'

'Don't you Mum me,' she said. 'Get yerself indoors. I've got a bone to pick with you!'

As soon as I was inside, she snatched the letter off the mantle and thrust it in front of me, as if I already knew what was in it.

'What have you got to say about this then?' she hissed.

I could see the haste in my sister's handwriting, and as I read on I could imagine how frantic Nance must have been to be the first person to unload all the bad news it contained. And I think, just to be doubly sure that I got the message, she had made certain that I would get it via my mother.

'So that's it,' Mum gloated. 'That precious husband of yours has taken up with a sixteen-year-old floozy!'

'I don't believe it.'

'What? You think your sister would lie about a thing like this?'

'No I didn't say that. I am just saying that just because Nance says so it doesn't make it true!'

'Nance don't lie!' she shouted.

'I'm not saying she's lying. I am just saying that I think she is wrong. Bill wouldn't do a thing like that.'

'Bill wouldn't do a thing like that,' she mimicked cruelly. 'Well,' she continued, 'Nance says he has, and I believe her. So don't you go expecting me to keep on taking you and his brats in after all this!'

I didn't expect this of her. But what I *had* expected was a little bit more compassion from my own mother, as I broke down and cried and cried. But all Mum could do was to taunt me over my downfall.

In the wake of this shocking news, my mother had made it crystal clear that I had outstayed my welcome in her house. And so, I desperately, tried to find somewhere else to go. But what could I do? To be able to afford a place of my own, even one room in a house, meant that I would have to find a full-time job that paid much more than I got at the laundry. To do that, I would need to have someone with whom I could leave baby Doris. It wouldn't be as difficult with Freddie, because he could go to school most of the day. But Doris would definitely need looking after. When I broached the problem with my mother, she told me quite bluntly, 'No.' She would not help me. As far as she was concerned I had made my own bed and now I could lie on it.

So I kept searching. But there weren't any jobs for women that would pay anything like a living wage. When our boys had come back from the war, they had taken back many of the jobs that women had been filling. Then there was the economic slump that threw many more out of work.

Despite my best efforts, I kept failing to secure either a job or a home for my children and myself, and so I was forced to tell my father that Mum's ultimatum had left me with no other choice than to contemplate placing Freddie and Doris in a children's home. When I said that, Dad flew into a rage. There was such a stigma attached to that option that Dad refused to hear even another word about it.

'I will not have any grandchild of mine going into a children's home!' he shouted, as he banged the kitchen table with his fist.

So my mother had to grudgingly agree to a compromise. She and Dad would take in Doris, but that was as far as Mum said they could go. They could not afford to carry on supporting me and Freddie, too. And so somehow we would have to fend for ourselves.

Not long after I left my parents' home, a letter arrived from Ma Weatherup. In it she apologised profusely that she had been unable to talk her '*wayward son*' around into sending for me and the children. Ma said that she was truly devastated by the turn of events, and that she felt ashamed about her own son choosing to ignore her pleas for him to pay the fares for our children and me to return to Canada. I could understand Bill's

278

anger at me for going away in the first place, but I couldn't believe that he would be so callous and spiteful as to turn his back on his own children.

I knew who the girl cited in both letters was. Her name was Pearl. Bill and I had a blazing row over her once. Pearl's family had lived at Orland, where both Bill and I had worked away. I remembered how, even way back then, at barely fourteen years of age, Pearl had been the most brazen of little creatures. She used to sidle up to my Bill at the slightest opportunity and openly flirted with him. Oh, he had tried to have me laugh it off – but I hated it! Pearl had a certain way about her – *that way* – which I had often seen about young London girls during the war. They were young girls who were far too keen for their own good to be getting on with the business of becoming a woman. I recognised what they looked like because I had been that way too.

Oh God forgive me, but what was I thinking when I left Canada? I realise now that I had been depressed for a long time after the death of our baby. But I must have been completely out of my mind to have left everything there, and to have left my marriage wide open to invasion by that little wanton. What had I done to my children? We might not have been rich in Canada, but now Freddie and I were surely destitute in England.

It was Freddie I felt most sorry for. Doris was too young to have any memories of Canada, but Freddie wasn't. He adored his father and his grandmother, and his aunts and uncles, and he asked after them constantly. Because of my stupidity he had lost them all. I know I was partly to blame for the breakdown of my marriage, but I also know that it could have been saved had it not been for Pearl. I might even have found it in my heart to forgive that girl for stealing my husband, but I could never forgive her for stealing my little boy's father away from him, and for stealing the family life he had known in Canada.

And worst of all, Freddie was innocent in all this. He hadn't done anything to deserve this cruel punishment from his own father.

Once the shock of hearing about my husband's affair with that girl had sunk in, I tried telling myself that I didn't care about Bill anymore and that he and that girl were welcome to each other. But in reality I could not stop myself from wanting him and hoping that I might somehow get him back.

That next eighteen months or so were living hell – as Freddie and I shifted from place to place while I tried to make a living for the two of us as best I could. I lied about Freddie's age and got him into school early so that I could at least go to work for the day. I got a job in service and a room for Freddie and me for a while by passing myself off as a war widow. But as the slump really took a hold, even those in the big houses started feeling the pinch and letting their staff go. Then I worked in a hotel, but the manager started coming on to me... so Freddie and I were compelled to move on again. But I was determined – to some how I would get the money together for a passage back to Canada and that I would make Bill take me and his children back again.

Ma Weatherup continued to write to me and kept saying that if only I could get to Norham, she would make him take me back. Yet I could hardly make enough money to feed us, let alone enough for tickets to Canada.

All I could scrape together was enough money to have a photograph of the children taken. Freddie barely smiled. Sporting a severely short hair cut after suffering a bad case of head lice and with the cuffs of his outgrown knitted jumper – a good two or three inches short of his stick-thin wrists – he towered above curly-haired Doris. She, clothed in an older child's cut-down dress, stood with arms behind her back smiling angelically, while her big brother's hand rested lovingly upon her shoulder. I sent it to their grandmother Sarah, knowing that she would show it to their father. Surely, I reasoned, when Bill saw that photo it was bound to melt his heart.

Then, after I had posted the photo, when it seemed that I had hit rock bottom and that I could sink no deeper into depression, on one of my visits to see Doris my mother showed me another damning letter from Nance. My sister said that, according to the latest gossip, Pearl had given birth to a baby girl. And although no one was saying out loud who the father of the baby was, rumour whispered that it was Bill's. As I received that news, I realised that all hope of reconciliation with my husband was dead.

That was also the year of the Wall Street Crash in America, which resulted in life in England quickly going from bad to worse. And so Freddie and I found ourselves regularly moving from place to place like gypsies. As soon as I found a place where we could live, something would happen to stop me from being able to pay the rent. So then we would pack our few belongings into a ragged old bag and slink away in the middle of the night.

Eventually, out of sheer desperation, I fell in with a bad crowd. This included a few male friends. But these men never stayed around for long. After all, what man would want to take in a woman with children when there were so many unmarried women available without added 'complications'?

Then I felt my determination to struggle on gradually trickling out of me. I began to lose my will to cope. While I still had the hope of reconciliation with Bill, I had always somehow managed to summon up the courage and fortitude to carry on living in that hope. But even the shreds of that hope had gone... and so I gave up trying.

Meanwhile, Doris was growing up fast. And she no longer seemed like my little girl, because my mother had moulded her into *hers*. Dorothy and Freddie had become so different, because they had been growing up apart from each other. Doris was quiet and ever compliant, while Freddie was much more like I used to be at his age – spirited and strong willed. While Doris was growing up at Cowper Road with my parents and my younger siblings, Freddie was growing up alone with me. I shared my every tear and heartache with him, and so he had become more than my son. He had become my best friend and confidant. He cared for me, too, becoming as protective as a man should, though he was still a child. And because Freddie loved me, he had always given me more reason to struggle on. But even that strength I had gleaned from him no longer seemed sustaining enough.

I woke really early on a morning that remains burned into my mind forever. So early that the birds outside were only just beginning to sing, as the first streaks of dawn paled the sullen sky. A short while later, in the cold light of day, from my side of our dingy room I lay in my bed watching Freddie. He was curled up asleep on his worn old mattress. On the battered chair next to his bed lay his pile of raggedy school clothes he had folded so neatly the night before. And beneath the chair stood his scuffed, unpolished, tired old boots – full of holes that he had tried to patch umpteen times with pieces of newspaper, with the hope that it would keep out the wet. But those efforts proved to be miserably fruitless. He would be awake soon, and I knew that all I had to give him for breakfast was a stale nobby[17] of bread and a cup of hot water. And I also knew that he would not complain. Suddenly, I felt overwhelmed by sorrow for him. It was entirely my fault that we had been forced to live like this.

As Freddie eventually began to rouse, I called across to him quietly.

---

[17]   The end slice of a loaf.

'Go back to sleep,' I told him. 'There's no need for you to get up yet. You can stay home from school today and spend it with me instead. We could walk in the park and then go see Gran and Granddad later...'

He sighed and slept on.

Doris had recently started school, so Freddie and I gave her a lovely surprise that afternoon by turning up at the playground gate to collect her. She was so happy to see us that her little face beamed from ear to ear. Then I walked hand in hand with my children, chatting, all the way to my parents' home.

Mum didn't look pleased to see Freddie and me when she opened the front door, but Dad was home so she didn't say anything.

'Watch yer young Freddie!' Dad exclaimed, rubbing him hard on the head like he always did. 'You look hungry lad. What d'you say to a bit of yer Gran's bread and dripping[18]'

'Yes please, Granddad,' Freddie said politely.

While the kids ate, Mum and Dad and I sat around the kitchen table drinking a cup of tea together. And all at once I felt a peaceful calm wash over me like a warm wave.

'Are you alright girl?' my father asked.

'Yes.' I replied. 'Why?'

'You just had a far away look in yer eyes, that's all.'

'I'm alright,' I reassured him. 'I was just thinking.'

Then a moment or two later, I put my empty cup down on the saucer and said to my father: 'D'you know, Dad, I just need to pop down to the shops for something? Will it be alright to leave Freddie here for a while?'

---

[18]   The fat exuded from roasting meat, separated from the other juices and solidified.

'Lumme! Of course it will!' he exclaimed with a chuckle. 'Take as long as you need, girl.'

I got up, kissed Dad on the cheek, and then made to leave. But as I got to the kitchen door I felt compelled to stop and take one last look at the children. They seemed so content together; sitting on the floor leafing through the pages of Doris' picture book. I could not bring myself to disturb their happiness by saying goodbye. So instead, I slowly turned about and slipped out.

After Edith May Weatherup left her parents' house that day, she was never seen or heard of again. To date, no trace or record of her subsequent whereabouts has ever been found.

The End

Author's notes

Although I was born the fourth of five siblings, I perceived my childhood, nonetheless, to be quite a lonely one. One of the few memories I have from that time of playing happily is of me crouching beside my dad's open wardrobe and covertly playing with his war medals, which he kept wrapped in an old orange dust cloth.

I loved to run my fingers across the three bronze coloured-stars and the two big silver coloured 'coins' depicting the late King George's head. I was particularly taken by the feel of the brightly-coloured ribbons between my fingers from which each one dangled so temptingly. I knew that I shouldn't be touching them. I knew that I shouldn't even be looking inside the wardrobe, let alone going through my father's things. But I could not help myself. I knew that the medals were there and they fascinated me so. And besides, I never got caught!

If there were two things that Dad rarely talked about when I was a child, one was his service during the Second World War. At the time I found it hard to understand why he would not want to talk about something as *exciting* as the War, especially so because whenever a documentary was shown on television about it, he would surely be sat in his armchair watching it, often with me curled up on the floor beside him.

The same applied to the ubiquitous British war films, of which dozens were made in the forties and fifties and which then always seemed to on the television during the sixties. It was only much later that I truly came to realise what a terrible thing war was. Then I also came to understand the dreadful things that my father must have experienced through it.

The second thing Dad never mentioned was his side of the family. Strangely, as a child I had not found that in the least bit odd, especially as my mother rarely talked about hers either. I grew up having Nan and Granddad who I think we saw quite regularly, as well as two aunts that we did not. Both my father and mother, as I now know, had only one sibling each- a younger sister. There were also two other shadowy 'aunties', Ivy and Annie, who I cannot recall ever visiting us, although both appear in a rare family photograph in which I am a mere baby in my maternal Nan's arms. I later discovered that these aunts were my grandmother's sisters.

In my innocence I had assumed that the reason I had only one set of grandparents must have been because Dad's parents had died, and that the reason why no-one talked about them was because it was obviously just too sad to so. Likewise, I took it for granted that my mother had only one sibling, Ann, and that my father had only one too – the rarely seen or talked about '*Auntie Dot*'. It did not occur to me that in an era of traditionally 'big' families that maybe there could be more.

The other thing that I took for granted was that I possessed an exceptionally unusual gift for memorising family photographs and snatches of conversation from my childhood, which could have meant little or nothing to me at the time, and yet which in recent times has served me well when sifting these through my mind as I began trying to set about tracing out my family tree.

I had also grown up with this strange notion in the back of my mind that my father was Canadian, which again was something no-one at home ever seemed to talk about. I recall asking about it once when a Canadian girl joined my class in junior school, but was cut abruptly short by my mother. Later, though when I asked Dad he told me yes- it was true that he had been born in Canada but no more. In fact, it wasn't until my parents had been divorced for more than twenty-years and I was a middle-aged mother that I began slowly trying to fit the pieces of my family history together.

I should have gone to Canada in two-thousand-and-five after the publication of my first novel, *'Mayflower Maid'*, when I had been invited to give a presentation in Plymouth, Massachusetts, just a relatively short hop from the Canadian boarder. My by then eighty-four-year old dad, Fred, had just been told that his cancer was terminal and for the first time I can ever recall, he began to talk a little to me about his childhood.

'You should try to get up to Ontario,' he had urged me, 'and see if you can't find out where the Town of Percy is.'

I had known that he had been born in Canada and simply assumed that he had come over to fight in the War, married my mother and then settled here. I had also never questioned why his only other relative seemed to be his sister Doris- my 'Auntie Dot'. The truth, as it turned out was of course much more intriguing.

Dad handed me a piece of paper on which he had written down the name of his grandmother, *Annie Middleton,* and that of her husband, *John Masters*. Then Dad told me that his mother, Edith May, had married a Canadian WW1 soldier and that she had immigrated to Ontario. And all that my father knew about his own origins was that his birth certificate was issued for *the 'Township of Percy'* in Ontario'.

For some unknown reason, a few years after emigrating Edith May had returned to Wimbledon, South London to visit her family (when Dad was about four-years old and his sister still only a baby) but had never returned to Canada. Dad explained that when the time came for Edith May to leave for Ontario, her husband had refused to send the money for the tickets home because he had taken up with another woman.

Then my father casually dropped what for me was a bombshell; that his mother, Edith May, had then one day simply walked out of his life and *disappeared*. Although he remembered his mother well (after all he had lived with her as a boy until he was about eleven years old) he had no recollection of his father or Canada at all. He did, however, speak fondly of having had a grandmother who he did remember vaguely and who he knew had written letters to his mother, Edith, when she was in England. And the one fact that he was adamant about was that his father had 'taken up' with a sixteen-year-old girl back in Canada-information that could only have come directly from Edith May herself or her family.

Due to intense hurricane activity that year, I never did make it across to Canada having been holed up in storm-lashed Plymouth for longer than expected. And although I had started to try to research our *Weatherup* family genealogy I had not gotten very far. I could not even find a town called *Percy* on the Canadian road map I had bought.

When I got back to England and had to tell my expectant Dad that I had not gone to Ontario after all, I felt that I had failed him dismally. I knew that Dad also held hopes that I might find out what had become of his mother before he died: although he never actually said that in so many words, I could tell. After all, why else had he suddenly been so willing to pass on such information as he had to me after all those years of silence upon the matter. I struggled to do that for him but I really didn't know how to and sadly by the time I had learned, Fred had passed away. After that I felt so unhappy over not being able to fulfil this wish for him that for a time I decided to give up on family history altogether.

Then, after my grief at losing him and my sense of utter failure began to ease, the BBC's 'Who Do You Think You Are' series slipped unexpectedly into my regular TV viewing and I found myself suddenly spurred on to start '*hunting*' again.

All I had to go on at first was Edith May's and William marriage certificate and had no idea at all about how to access Canadian records. As far as William's identity went, all I knew was his age at marriage and that his father, 'Robert Weatherup' was listed as deceased. By that time I had also taken a CLAIT course in using computers and so suddenly had gained the necessary skills to become quite competent at surfing the internet.

Then the biggest break of all came when I registered as a member of the on line genealogy site – *Ancestry*. Suddenly I found that I now had access to all kinds of records- both in England and in Canada- and more importantly, access to other researcher's family trees and direct contact with other members who might be willing to help me with information for mine. It was an absolute godsend!

On *Ancestry* I failed to find a birth certificate for a 'William Weatherup'. So for a while I was stumped. Then I followed one of the Ancestry on-line suggestions that I use their extensive data base of military records. I subsequently found five William '*Wetherups*' of about the right age in Ontario of whom all had enlisted to serve in WW1 and who had subsequently survived. However I failed to find any whose next of kin was listed as 'Robert Weatherup' or who had lived in a township named Percy.

Then, thanks once more to *Ancestry* and the invaluable hints that the site offers to its members on how to go about searching out their '*lost*' ancestors, I was then encouraged to trawl through the census records for 1901 in search of a living Robert Weatherup. There I found a Robert *Wetherup* with a son William of about the right age as my missing grandfather living in place called Cramahe (which it turns out is close by to a collection of several places in Northumberland County of Ontario which was once more commonly known as the Township of Percy – a name which no longer appears on modern maps). After that, there was no stopping me!

After Edith May had disappeared from my late father's life, Dad had been nearing his teens. He then joined Doris in being brought up in the care of his maternal grandparents, John and Annie Masters. It was during the Great Depression of the nineteen-thirties and his grandparents were getting on in years, and so as a result, began to slide into poverty. My father often intimated to me that life was desperately hard. Only recently did I learn that Dad had to sleep at night on a make-shift bed in the freezing kitchen until he left home. And Fred's personal relationship with his grandparents was not a happy one either and I later learned that his grandfather had not been all adverse to taking off his thick leather belt and using it to beat the lad.

My father Fred's grievances with his grandparents do not seem to have been shared by his sister, Doris – my Aunt *Dot*. From all she has said, she seems to have fond memories of her grandmother and her numerous aunts and uncles. I think it such a shame that, while growing up, I never got the opportunity to know any of this Masters side of my family for myself, or to meet any of my Grandmother Edith May's siblings. Sadly Doris also readily admitted that her grandfather also used to hit his wife from time to time- especially after to much to drink.

By all accounts, Dad had been a bright schoolboy and had earned himself a scholarship to a prestigious local college. But he had been unable to take it up because his grandparents were too poor to buy him either shoes or a uniform.

Desperately unhappy with his lot in life under his grandparent's guardianship, my father ran off and, after lying about his age, enlisted in the British Army. He trained at Woolwich – to become a Gunner in the Royal Artillery.

Having traced Robert Wetherup's family back in time using *Ancestry's* Canadian Census collection, I again hit a brick wall. I had found Robert as a boy living in Dummer with his family and father - James. Robert was listed as having been born in Canada and his father as being Irish. I also found a Thomas Wetherup living in Hope who was just the right age to be a sibling of James- but who I then surmised could be so as he was born in England.

Without an Irish birth certificate for James (practically as rare as hen's teeth for the time of his birth) I thought that I could go no further back with the family line. Then, again using one of *Ancestry's* useful features which meant that I could actually *'turn the pages'* of the virtual census book holding James' details, I discovered that I could then look at *every* inhabitant of the township in order to work out if there were any other family members listed as living nearby. Then I suddenly noticed a John *Witherup* was also living in Dummer who- despite the different spelling- I was certain was James' father.

Through *Ancestry,* I also learned that John Witherup was an ex-British soldier and so armed with that valuable information I was then able to search out his records from the *National Archives* in the UK.

When I first discovered the Army discharge records from 1826 for my great, great, great grandfather John Witherup, I was flooded with a mixture of emotions. I was absolutely delighted to have been able to trace this man at all, but then to have his entire Army career mapped out and fully documented before me was utterly amazing! Who, when tracing their family genealogy, would not be delighted to have that? And yet, at times, I was also brought close to tears, because I had found this all out just too late to be able to have shared it with my father before he passed away. I knew that he would have marvelled at the strange coincidences I had unearthed – not least because he had been an ardent fan of the *'Sharpe'* series of television dramas based on the Bernard Cornwell novels. My Dad had loved the Napoleonic era, and would have been thrilled to have discovered that his own great, great, grandfather had served in many of the very same conflicts as that of the hero of that series. And that, like Dad, his ancestor had also trained at Woolwich to become a Gunner in the Royal Artillery!

With further research, I was also pleased to be able to discover the identity of my great, great, great Grandmother Mary (Hendren/Hendron) Witherup, and then, again on *Ancestry,* all of the Woolwich baptismal records for their English-born children- including the Thomas Wetherup I had found listed in Hope.

 Mary ~I later deduced had died in Dummer some time before 1847. How, I do not know, but in a Township which still did not have its own doctor back then, it could have been as a result of the simplest infection or of the gravest affliction. Nor did I find any record of where she was buried as records for that time are far from complete and formal churches and graveyards barely yet established. However, whilst writing her story I came to the overwhelming feeling that Mary had been interred on the land where they had lived at Dummer and so wrote it as such in her story.

One record that does exist is a marriage for the second of November, eighteen-forty-nine. It reads *'John Witherup, yeoman of Dummer to Ann Victoria Carroll, widow of Hamilton'.* Therefore Mary must have died prior to that date. John's second wife presumably died sometime before the eighteen-seventy-one census from which her name is missing, but I have been unable to find either a record of her death or a burial.

The date of John Witherup's death also remains unknown at the date of writing, as does his last resting place. The last official date recording him as being alive is that of the Dummer Census of eighteen-seventy-one, which again I found thanks to *Ancestry.* In that

John is described as being a 'widower' and living out his old age in the company of a Thomas Hendren junior on the Third Line. Was he buried with Mary I wondered?

Before my research into John and Mary Witherup's life, I had never heard of the year without a summer due to the high amount of volcanic ash in the atmosphere. It was the lack of animal foodstuff, such as oats for horses, at this time that may have inspired German inventor Karl Davis to experiment to find ways of 'horseless transport'. Shortly afterwards he invented the 'Draisine' or velocipede – the forerunner of the modern bicycle.

In that year of eighteen-sixteen, with July's 'incessant rainfall' and that 'wet, uncongenial summer', a certain Mary Shelly found herself and her friends forced to spend much of their summer holiday in Switzerland indoors. So, to while away some time, and to keep themselves amused no doubt, they hit upon the idea of holding a competition to see who could pen the scariest story. Mary Shelly wrote *'Frankenstein, or The Modern Prometheus'* and her friend, William Polidori, wrote *'the Vampyre'.*

The dreadful crop failures at that time experienced both in Europe and in North America proved a major factor in the family of one Joseph Smith moving from Sharon, Vermont to Palmyra, New York, precipitating a chain of events that would culminate in the writing of the *Book of Mormon* and the founding of the *Church of Jesus Christ of the Latter-day Saints.*

During my research I read *'Roughing it in The Bush'*, the account of a contemporary English settler, Susanna Moodie, who had lived near Douro in Ontario. In her book, the celebrated Moodie describes her husband's and her own struggles and periods of depravation whilst trying to tame their grant of land not that far from Dummer.

In a chapter entitled *'The Walk To Dummer'* Moodie describes a contemporary of her husband, Captain N , who had been *'allured by the bait that had been the ruin of so many of his class, the offer of a large grant of land... a large extent of stony barren land.'* Having turned to drink, in eighteen-thirty-eight or thereabouts Captain N had eventually absconded leaving his poor wife and young children to their fate in their shanty at Dummer. Moodie writes about embarking upon a *'mission of mercy'* in order to take food aid to the wife of Captain N whom she eventually finds in a state of near starvation. Although Moody writes movingly and at length about this Captain's wife, she makes no mention at all about the sorry condition of many of those ordinary soldiers, like John Witherup, who had severed under men like her own husband and whose misery she must also have encountered along the way. Men who had not enjoyed the advantages of life accorded to her officer husband. It was a fascinating chapter to read and as I did I almost half expected Mrs Moody to introduce me to my own ancestors by name- as she does other inhabitants of that area whom John must have surely known.

Moving forward once more from John and on to the next generation and the story of Mary Ann Wetherup... I believe that her mother, Ellen Wetherup, was almost certainly a daughter of Dummer settler Robert Haighle and his wife, Janet McRoberts- which I again discovered using *Ancestry*. I suspect that neither Robert nor Janet were able to read or write very well (if at all), as it was so for many settlers of that time. As a result the name became corrupted through subsequent census records to become 'Hatchel'. This may well reflect Robert's own broad Scot's pronunciation of his name as either close to sounding like *'Hackle'* or even perhaps as with the use of a 'soft G', which would sound like 'Hajle'. Both are tantalising close to Hatchel for a Canadian / English enumerator to make that out as he struggled to write down the family name. And I would suggest other family researchers hold that thought in mind when looking for records.

I have also independently found a marriage recorded for a couple named Robert Haighle and Janet McRoberts dated February 16th 1827, in Urr in Scotland – exactly where one would expect to find one for this couple.

In the book, *'Origins~The History of Dummer Township' by Jean Murray Cole'*, two letters are reproduced (both or either of which may have been dictated). The first is from Robert Haighle, dated January seventeenth, eighteen-thirty-five, to his Father and brother and sent to *'Mr John Haighle, Newark, Milton of Urr, Dumfries in Scotland'*. In it, Robert outlines the family voyage across to Canada and reports the death of their youngest unnamed child. He also tells how his (unnamed) mother-in-law died at Goss Island, and how a daughter, *Margret aged seven*, caught cholera – but survived.

The second letter, dated January twenty-eight, eighteen-forty-four at Dummer, is from Janet to her *'brother'* – Mr. John *Haigil*, farmer, of *'Milton of Orr, By Dumfrish'*, Scotland.' *Kirkcudbrightshire'*, where the remaining members of the Haighle family are found in the eighteen-forty-one Census, is also sometimes referred to *'Gallowayshire'*. Later, the Hatchels' daughter Elizabeth's marriage lines name the bride's mother as *'Tepi McRoberts'*, which seems to support my assumption that *McRoberts* is indeed Janet Hatchel's maiden name.

In this equally long and unpunctuated letter, as it was with the first (which an illiterate Janet may have been dictated to a barely literate third party to set down), she relates the hardships arising from the death of her husband Robert. (In the book, *'Origins~The History of Dummer Township'*, it is stated that it is believed that he was killed in eighteen-forty-two by a falling tree). This letter ends '*your loving sister in law jeanet highil*' which again highlights the fluidity of spelling at this time.

Interestingly, Janet writes in this letter; 'and as for my children they have thrashed all our thrashing since their father dide...' The youngest recorded Hatchel children, Elizabeth and Mary were born around eighteen-thirty-eight and eighteen-forty respectively. To my knowledge, no baptismal records for any of the children have so far been found.

The census of the population of the Township of Dummer, taken on the first Monday in January, eighteen-forty, shows the Hatchel family as consisting of one male over sixteen years of age (Robert), one female over sixteen (Janet) and three females under sixteen. Dating the birth of people using only such records as the Census is well known for not being very reliable. In many instances the records for the same person can be followed through on three of four or even more censuses with the age varying from that which might be expected to be recorded with each one. One only has to take the example of James and Ellen Wetherup's own family unit, where their ages in eighteen-eighty-one vary wildly from the eighteen-seventy-one census; albeit that in this instance it may have been quite a deliberate deception on the Wetherup's part.

However, in a population that was often illiterate and perhaps wanting also in numeracy, many may not have even possessed a written record of their own birth to refer to, and so had to 'guestimate' their ages-sometimes wrongly. In later censuses, we at least start to get the day and month of birth recorded which is most helpful as that fact is not so easily forgotten.

The Hatchel family lived just a short distance away from John Witherup and his family in the eighteen-thirties and into the forties. On *Ancestry* in the eighteen-fifty-one census of Dummer, James Wetherup, his wife Ellen and youngest children are listed as living in a shanty and are entered immediately after 'Jannette Hatchel' and her family, likely suggesting that James had married one of Janet's daughters and was perhaps living on her plot- as was usual.

Shortly after this census, Janet and her remaining two daughters moved to Bruce County, after the marriage of Margaret Hatchel and Henry Esplin of Dummer. In Bruce, Janet's daughter, Mary, subsequently married Malcolm Mclean, and her sister Elizabeth married Joseph Schrader.

I have been unable to find a death registration for Janet Hatchel. But, intriguingly, on *Ancestry* I found one for a *Janet McRoberts* in the Bruce area for a woman of the correct age, and who's birth place is given as '*Gallowayshire*' in Scotland, which correlates closely to the Dumfries district, where Robert and Janet's marriage was recorded. Janet Hatchel is buried in Burgoyne Cemetery, Saugeen Township, Bruce County, Ontario. Daughters Mary (w/o Malcolm Mclean), Margaret (w/o Henry Esplen) are also interred at Burgoyne.

There is also the naming pattern of related children on both sides of the families to consider. Back in Scotland, in Robert *Haighle's* remaining family there are children named both Janet and Ellen – a very common name of the time which in itself means very little. However, on looking at the names of James and Ellen Wetherup's children, it is possible to see a typical naming pattern taking place, as if Ellen was in fact a Haighle. The first born son, *John*, is named after James' Father, John Witherup. The second child, the infamous Mary Ann, was named in honour of James' mother, Mary Ann Hendren. The next eldest son should have been named in honour of his maternal grandfather, which if I am correct, should have been '*Robert*' in honour of Robert Haighle. That Wetherup son was indeed named Robert. The next child, a son, was named '*James*', obviously in honour of his father. The next daughter, however, breaks with this pattern, because she is named '*Ellen*'.

However, these were still *early days* as far as regulations for registering the births of children went, and even when this later becomes a compulsory obligation, the Wetherups prove rather lax about following it. I have discovered that many later descendants of this extended family did not always comply either.

Also we only have the census records taken at ten year intervals to confirm the number and identities of James and Ellen's children, it is very possible that there could have been a child named 'Janet' – who may have lived and died between censuses. James and Ellen Wetherup's son, James, married Elizabeth Jane King and had a daughter they named '*Jannett*', but whom often went by the name '*Jessie*'. Was she named for her grandmother Haighle?

Marriage records, again found on *Ancestry,* are an invaluable source of information – especially as they often carry the name of witnesses who usually turn out to be relatives. A usually foolproof way of identifying the maiden name of a mother is to look at the marriage lines of any of her offspring- where it is often given. In the case of Ellen Wetherup, this appears at first to have only served to further muddy the waters. Son John cites his mother as being '*Ellen Hacken*', brother James as 'Hatchell', brother Robert as '*Helen Maclean*', while daughter Elizabeth names her mother as '*Ellen Esplin*'. The other children at marriage name their mother simply as '*Ellen Wetherup*' or as John cites at his second marriage – '*Ellenor Wetherop*'. On son James Wetherup's death certificate his mother's name is entered at first as '*unknown*', but is then crossed out with '*Ellen Esplin*' inserted instead.

As I have already said, my Dad grew up knowing almost next to nothing about his own Canadian family history - as did many of his contemporary family members back in Ontario. And yet the recurrent nightmare that haunted my sleep during the first day or so after the birth of all of my own children is uncannily close to what I now know certainly happened to Mary Ann Wetherup's own child. And which I could not possibly have had prior knowledge

In my dreams, I would awake in my bed in a state of absolute exhaustion, and then smell the aroma of roasting meat wafting up from downstairs. Then, because I could not recall putting a meal on to cook, I would go to the kitchen and investigate. There, when I opened the door of the hot oven, I would be stunned by the sickening sight of my newly born baby roasting in a baking tray!

Naturally, this recurring nightmare used to upset me very deeply – always filling me with utter horror – particularly because I could never understand how or why I could dream about something so mind-numbingly dreadful. But now I firmly believe that, somehow, I was *'tuning in'* to past events that truly happened. And as readers of the 'author notes' in my previous novels may recall, this appears not to be the first time that such a thing has happened to me during the course of my writing my historical novels. I do not understand how or why these 'insights' into past lives have happened, nor do I believe in the suggestion put to me by some people that I *'have lived before'*, or that I am psychic. I do, however, find it utterly fascinating, if not also a somewhat disturbing. Then again I have often wondered what hidden information might be being handed down along with our genes. After all, how does a migrating young bird *know* to fly south and to return to nesting sites used by its parents?

299

Those terrible events of the Halloween of eighteen-seventy-nine have passed into realms of urban myth, and yet the truth behind them – the story of Mary Ann Wetherup's infanticide case, seem to have been long forgotten by the people of Hope. Yet at the time, it must have caused great heartache for her – and *other* members of the Wetherup family.

One of those affected may well have been Mary Ann's uncle, Thomas Wetherup, the son of Mary and John Witherup. Being such an uncommon surname, and living in close proximity, it would have been hard for Thomas and Wealthy Wetherup to have distanced themselves from the fallout of the notoriety heaped over Mary Ann in the press. Everyone living in Hope must have surely known that they were related.

It was not so bad for Ellen and James; because directly after they were released from jail they must have returned to Bruce County, because it is there that they appear in the January census of eighteen-eighty-one, reunited with Mary Ann and the other Wetherup children.

Wealthy Wetherup was already at the time of the trial suffering from congestive heart failure and would eventually die within a year or two, on September thirtieth, eighteen-eighty-three. This must have been a severe blow to Thomas after almost forty years of marriage, and although it may not have been directly responsible for what happened to him next, Mary Ann's trial probably did not help matters.

On June thirteenth, eighteen-eighty-four, the *Port Hope Guide* reported the attempted suicide of Thomas Wetherup (of Zion);

'It appears that his mind has been wandering for some time past, he having tried to shoot himself some time ago, but his sons hid the gun thus preventing that act. On the evening of Thursday last, he returned home and after telling his sons what he was going to do, entered a bedroom and took a dose of strychnine and shortly after fell off the bed,

by this time an entrance was forced and upon seeing the true state of affairs. Dr Adair, of Newtonville, was summoned and only arrived in time to save his life. He is lingering yet in a low state, symptoms of poisoning by strychnine manufacturing themselves occasionally.'

A report in the 'Port Hope Guide' from June twentieth of that year reads;

'Mr Thomas Wetherup has recovered from the effects of the strychnine which he took some time ago, and we understand he has sold some of his farm stock and implements and is going to sell his crops and remove from Zion.'

Attempted suicide in itself would have been regarded as a dreadful scandal, and yet scandal for the Wetherup family was not yet at an end.

An article from 'The New York Times' published on the twentieth of March, eighteen-eighty-seven tells of a sorry episode in which Thomas' son, John, was charged with felonious assault.

'Toronto, Ontario, March 19. - John Wetherup was arrested a short distance from Port Hope on a charge of committing an assault on Eliza Straitan, an orphan girl of 15 years of age. The girl, who had in the first place laid the information against Wetherup, cannot be found by the Crown officers. A detective has ascertained that she had been spirited away to Pennsylvania by parties interested in Wetherup. George Staples was arrested on a charge of spiriting away the girl, and has been committed for trial. Wetherup is still held by the authorities pending the search for the girl, who is now supposed to be in Philadelphia, where it is alleged, she is consigned by parties interested in securing Wetherup's discharge.'

My enquiries have failed to find a corresponding newspaper article existing in any Canadian archive. At the time John Wetherup was married. His wife, Dorcas Staples, had been almost half John's age when they wed.

The following year, it appears that John Wetherup may have had his comeuppance. On August tenth, eighteen-eighty-eight, according to the *'Lindsay Post'* John Wetherup appears to have met with an unfortunate accident:

'Port Hope – Terrible Threshing Machine Accident – On Friday morning while assisting his neighbour, William Oglow, to thresh barley at lot 12, 2nd concession, Hope, John Wetherup, while passing over the feed-board of the machine struck his head on a beam and fell into the feeder, both his feet being torn to pieces.'

A similar article in the *'Port Hope Guide'* of that day, expands the facts by saying that the incident took place on the farm of William Walker (a little west of Zion) and that *'some person'* had the presence of mind to cast the belt off, or doubtless he would have lost his life.

Thomas Wetherup Senior lived until the age of seventy-eight. He died on the twenty-sixth of April, nineteen-hundred and four at the home of his son, John, *'Sunny Hollow',* south of Omemee.

Life for Mary Ann's younger sister, Ellen, must also have been affected too, because she appears to have been already living with the very same Moore family that had given evidence against Mary Ann at her trial. Ellen and husband John Job Moore had their first child together early in eighteen-eighty-one. It died very shortly afterwards.

Mary Ann's older brother, John, had already married (in eighteen-seventy) and settled not too far from Hope. Curiously, a James Wetherup, born eighteen-sixty-seven, is listed with the newlyweds on the eighteen-seventy-one Hope census. Was he really a child of John's? And if not, then whose was he? John later settled in Alnwick.

My own great grandfather, Robert Wetherup (and brother to Mary Ann) had married shortly after the trial at Cobourg. He and his wife, Sarah Jane (McCracken), also settled in Alnwick, before later being listed as living in Cramahe. Again, bearing the tainted Wetherup name could not have been easy for Robert and his bride. Indeed, on later speaking with a newly- discovered, living Weatherup relative, she had testified to the fact that when she was young and living in Northumberland County in the nineteen-forties, she remembers being warned by an elderly female relative to never, on any account, admit to being related to the *'Garden Hill Wetherups'*. Indeed, none of my living Weatherup family in Canada had any knowledge whatsoever about the Mary Ann Wetherup trial, and so were as surprised as I had been when first I had made the connection. Some, though naturally shocked, were also intrigued and eager to find out more. For interest, I am including a brief biography of Detective John Wilson Murray at the end of this book. Due to copyright restrictions, I cannot include his chapter on Mary Ann.

It was not simply because the trial of Mary Ann Wetherup had been sensational at the time that I wanted to write about her. It was the fact that neither she nor her murdered child had received proper justice that urged me on. After all, the real culprit was never brought to trail and sentenced for this little baby's cruel murder. At least by retelling this story, I have felt that I am able to give some sort justice to that baby at last and perhaps for Mary Ann, too.

303

Incidentally, Mary Ann (Norton) died at Lot 24 Concession 21, Keppel Township in Grey County on May eighth, nineteen-eleven, from the results of a severe cold. *The Wiarton Echo* from that week reports;

'Died on Monday morning, Mary Ann Norton, age 59. Funeral was from home of her daughter Mrs. J. Gault then to Oxenden Cemetery.'

Mary Ann's daughter, Lily, would marry her Moore cousin, the son of Mary Ann's sister Ellen.

***

In writing this book, I had begun to truly feel that I was making a real journey of discovery. In researching and finding out about my long lost ancestors, I began to feel that in a way I was also discovering an unknown side of myself. Playing alone in the London garden of my childhood home, unlike my street-wise contemporaries, I used to relish in pretending that I was a farmer clearing a great patch of virgin land. Later in my forties I revelled in owning my own pig, something incomprehensible to the rest of my family. And I also found so many similarities between my life and that of some of my predecessors that are too numerous to go into here. Yet I had still failed to make that ultimate voyage of discovery – to go to see Canada for myself.

Then, in the September of two-thousand and ten, after completing *'Living In Hope'* and sending it to edit, I was suddenly presented with the opportunity to do just that. During a break in a visit to the United States, a very close girl friend of mine offered to drive me up to Ontario- and so I seized it.

After leaving Niagara early on the second morning, we had driven directly to the town of Cobourg. I could hardly contain my excitement as we passed through places I had only come across before on *Ancestry* research documents.

My first stop in Cobourg was to visit the courtroom at Victoria Hall where both Mary Ann Wetherup and her father had stood trial. It was so strange to enter that now defunct but intact courtroom that I had written about so intently in my novel. Walking up the steps and into the dock felt eerily familiar – almost as if I had lived that out before some half-remembered past life. It is more than a mere sense of déjà-vu I am certain for an author to suddenly be confronted by the reality of their fiction. For a moment or two I actually felt as if I *was* Mary Ann: that somehow fleetingly she and I had 'melded' into one somewhere between the present and the past. It is an experience that I know I shall never, ever forget.

That evening we drove from Cobourg to Peterborough where we stayed overnight before heading out to find Warsaw and Dummer the next morning. I had already been able to identify the location of that grant of land that John Witherup had received from old records. And with the aid of modern on-line satellite maps, I was also able to identify its modern neighbours - the Coopers who now farm the adjacent property. I had made contact with Ruth Cooper and her husband earlier that year and so contacted her again to tell of my impending visit. When I arrived, I found her husband waiting for me and he graciously agreed to show me around.

Mr Cooper turned out to be such a lovely character. Mounting a well-used looking quad bike, he a led our sturdy SUV to the site of John Witherup's original shanty. It marked out by a great pile of collapsed rocks which Mr Cooper then explained that until recently had clearly formed the cellar beneath it.

I cannot explain in words the sorrow that had suddenly then welled up inside me as I stood there. I was moved almost to tears as I surveyed what had been my ancestors' grant of land and I could so easily imagine the misery and heartache they must have suffered over it. The land in reality was far worse than even I had supposed from my careful study of the contemporary records from *Ancestry* from which I had gleaned how little land John had managed to clear in his time there and what crops he was able to grow compared to other more favourable plots. It did not escape my notice that even as I had neared the Cooper's home at Dummer that there were much better looking plots of land close by than was given to poor John Witherup.

My previous research had led me to believe that my ancestor John Witherup's wife, and perhaps even he, were buried somewhere on that plot of land he had received from Crown. So you can imagine how my heart was then tugged when we came across several man-made, oval mounds of stones not far from the shanty- ovals that Mr Cooper informed me were undoubtedly graves. I stood beside them for few moments to say a silent prayer and then picked up a few stones as keepsakes. Whether or not Mary Witherop occupies one I have no way of knowing for certain and probably never will. But in my heart I believe that she does.

After leaving the Coopers behind at Dummer, we headed off for nearby Warsaw and to see the caves at Indian River. I had written an imaginary scene where John and Mary go for a walk there and so wanted to see it for myself. The reality lived up to the image in my mind's eye; I really did feel that John and Mary had been there. I found it an enchanting place to walk and was sad to have had only such a brief a time there before having to head off to an appointment at the Dorothy House Museum at Garden Hill which had arranged to especially open up for me late that afternoon.

Garden Hill is where the Wetherups lived at the time of the murder. I was delighted to find that the original General Store dating from eighteen-fifty-six, and which the family would have used, still existed. Just a little further along on the opposite side of the road, the Dorothy House Museum is a quaint example of the type of houses from that time. Outside the museum is a plaque dedicated to the work of a local Dr. Beatty, whom I immediately recognised as the name of the physician who signed James Wetherup's death certificate I had found on *Ancestry*. The Haskell family also once lived in this area.

That night we stayed in Campbellford – the last known address for Edith May's sister 'Nancy' Fields. Then on my third day in Canada, came the most emotional and gratifying part of my trip to Ontario- going to Norham, near Warkworth in Ontario and meeting living cousins of my late father- cousins who had grown up knowing about his existence but nothing about where he had 'disappeared' off to. Not only was it a thrill to meet them, but just across the road from the Weatherup house we initially gathered in was the house in which I believe my father was born and Edith May briefly lived. It had belonged to Sarah Weatherup up until her death.

To then be taken to nearby Stone's Cemetery and to be able to stand beside my grandfather Bill's grave gave me an immense feeling of closure on my father's behalf - and an overwhelming sense of reconciliation. After that, I visited Red Cloud cemetery where Robert Weatherup was buried and just across the road from it, where my great grandmother Sarah and her husband Robert had farmed at Cramahe.

The next morning, my party agreed to meet up again with my new Weatherup family for breakfast in Campbellford before beginning our long drive back to the USA. Sitting and happily chatting away over our simple meal was one of the highlights of not only my trip – but my life. I felt so happy and as if I truly belonged there in Canada. In all

307

for me it had really been a journey of a lifetime. And as my late father's cousin Earl so graciously pointed out- I had come to Canada as a stranger but I was now leaving as family.'

Through my writing and search I feel much closer now to my Dad, Fred, than ever before, and my sincerest hope in writing both this and my previous books is that my children, and hopefully their children, will also come to *know* me better – even after I am gone. With this book, I would like them to know my father, my grandfather and all of our ancestors over the past two hundred years or more, and how all of the other families I have also mentioned tie in to us. Also that maybe countless others tied into those lines will then learn a little more about their ancestors, too – and in turn how I tie into their family genealogy.

During my research into my own Weatherup family, I have also research, and worked up all of the other Weatherup (and variant) family trees of those living in Ontario prior to nineteen-hundred and am almost certain that all are related to one another. I am happy to help other descendants tie their own lines into these.

As for those who read this book and who have no connection at all to my family or those mentioned in it, well I live in hope that they will be intrigued enough to go off in search of their own family trees and to learn about the lives and struggles of their forbearers, far beyond just the paper record of their births, marriages and deaths. And to plead with them not to stop there, as to do so does the dead no justice at all. A collection of facts and figures, noted neatly down on a family tree, in my opinion is far from enough. To my mind, too many people involved in researching their family history seem to fall into the trap of adding the names of past family members as if they were merely fitting pieces into a jigsaw. Completing an entire jigsaw may be very satisfying, but how much thought do we really give to say all those individual bits of blue that make up the sky? Or likewise to those names that we find and then enter up on our family data sheets who go beyond the memory of our current generation? How can we truly know where we have come from without trying to spend a bit of time trying to find out what sort of lives these people led. Because that is the trap that so many family history researchers unwittingly fall into – of treating these past folk as mere collection of entries and not as once living, breathing individuals from the past. People who once had hopes and fears just as we do: people who have physically handed on a part of themselves to us via their DNA to make us the individuals that we are today.

Finally I am a great believer that no one ever ceases to *be* until their names are forgotten completely by those who come after. And I for one would like to think that when I am gone again to dust, I shall not cease to exist entirely. And with that I would urge all of my readers to at least attempt to leave some written record of their lives behind for future generations.

Sue Allan

Detective John Wilson Murray.

John Wilson Murray, provincial detective for Ontario; was born twenty-fifth of June, eighteen-forty in Edinburgh. His parents were Daniel Duncan Murray, a sea captain, and Jeanette Wilson.

The only source for John Wilson Murray's early life and *career* are his memoirs. However they appear to contain many *inaccuracies'*, shall we say, about later events and so I would respectfully suggest that no great reliance should be placed on them.

Murray's family moved to North America when he was a young boy. He was educated partly in both countries before enlisting in the United States Navy on June fifth, eighteen-fifty-seven. He joined the *Michigan* at Chicago. Murray later claimed to have been commissioned in eighteen-sixty-two and to have served under Rear-Admiral David Glasgow Farragut in the Gulf of Mexico and on the Mississippi River – though at the time of writing I can find no evidence to collaborate that, and if he had served in the region, he did not see the action he claimed to have been involved in.

By March eighteen-sixty-four, Murray was an acting gunner on the *Michigan* – a lightly armed steamer based at Erie, Pennsylvania. This vessel was mainly assigned to patrolling the Great Lakes, recruiting, and supervision of the prison camp for Confederate officers on Johnson's Island, opposite Sandusky, Ohio.

It was during this period when Murray served on the *Michigan* that two attempts were made by Confederate agents to capture the ship in a bid to release the officers. In his memoires, Murray alludes to having taken a leading role in thwarting the second of these attempts – again a claim that cannot be substantiated.

Murray was honourably discharged from the U S Navy on the thirty-first of January, eighteen-sixty-six. He later claimed that at the end of that year he joined the Treasury Department as an agent investigating counterfeiting. Again, this claim is dubious. What is certain is that in eighteen-sixty-eight he joined the Erie police force as a detective.

In the summer of eighteen-seventy-three, as a result of his acquaintance with an Erie businessman named William Lawrence Scott, Murray became the detective of the newly completed Canada Southern Railway after Scott had become its President. On more than one occasion, Murray successfully foiled attempts to derail and rob CSR trains.

Murray's quickly earned a reputation in Ontario Government circles for being "well up in his business", and within a short time he had been seconded to the Government to track down a counterfeiting operation. It was a case in which he was successful.

In May eighteen-seventy-five, Murray was offered a full-time, but temporary, appointment, as *'Government Detective Officer'* at the grand salary of fifteen-hundred dollars per annum. The position was soon made permanent, and Murray was hence-forth deemed to be a constable of 'every county and district in Ontario', with the authority to act in any part of the province.

Murray's job, in his own words, was to *'follow criminals to any place and run them down'*. However, Murray does not seem to have generally intervened in a case until his help was *directly* requested by the local authorities. According to Murray's memoires[19], these requests were evidently numerous. Contemporary newspaper articles and Government correspondence, confirm his involvement in numerous cases including those

---

[19]   *Memoirs of a great detective: incidents in the life of John Wilson Murray* - first published in London in 1904.

in such a variety of places such as Caledonia, Cornwall, Manitoulin Island, Ottawa, Pickering, Toronto and Welland.

Murray quickly became well-known among those in the criminal justice system and also a celebrity of sorts due to his constant appearance in newspaper articles covering his cases. By the time of Murray's death, he was the *'most famous police official in Canada'* and according to the front-page story in the Toronto *Globe*, 'thousands of people knew him by sight'. In his obituary in the Toronto *Daily Mail and Empire* his name was said to have been "intimately associated with the prosecution of nearly every criminal case of importance in the province outside of the larger cities," and, at last, this claim was probably not an exaggeration.

John Wilson Murray died while still employed as a detective, on the twelfth of June, nineteen-hundred-and-six, at his home in Toronto as the result of a stroke he suffered three days before.

Acknowledgments.

I would really like to thank the following for the invaluable help they have given in researching this book. Without them, the stories told in this book would not be nearly so complete nor interesting.

Jodie Aokie (Trent University, Peterborough)

Val Arsenault

Fern Batdorf

Dan Buchanan

Dorothy House Museum.

John Draper (cobourginternet.com)

Michal Laliberte

Barbara Lindsey

Lyn Lowry

Annette McCandless

Brian Mills

Kath Nemaric (KJN Genealogy)

Mary Beth Robinson

Bernie Roche

Lilyan Silver

Michael Stephenson (ontariogenealogy.com)

'The Digger' (glenavyhistory.com)

Ruth Thompson

Susan Toms

Craig and Earl Weatherup

Greg Weatherup

Laurie Whatley

George Weatherup

Ella Weatherup

Also by Sue Allan

The Mayflower Maid -

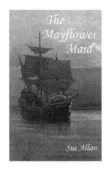

The first part of the New World Trilogy

400 years ago a group of like minded men and women fled England and religious persecution to start a new life on a new continent - America. One woman's story begins here....

In the infant colony of Plymouth in 1623 a woman lies consumed with fever. In her delirium she insists her name is not the one everyone has come to know and love her by.

The story of Dorothy's tragic journey amongst the Pilgrim Fathers is a vivid and moving account of a pivotal moment in history. The story of how she became the Mayflower Maid is an unforgettable tale of love and loss set amidst the strife and religious bigotry of Seventeenth Century England.

Jamestown Woman -

The second part of the New World Trilogy

Having weathered the perils of the Mayflower's voyage and the early days of the Plymouth colony; Dorothy neé Bessie and her husband Thomas are now cast adrift into even more stormy and dangerous waters. Seventeenth century politics are a violent and deadly business, as they are about to find out.

Sue Allan continues her spellbinding chronicles of the Mayflower Maid in 'Jamestown Woman', and once again fate casts her and Thomas into the paths of the great and not so good. The giant firgures of King James I, Captain John Smith and Oliver Cromwell cast their shadows over the lives of the Puritans as England is about to be engulfed by the horrors of The Civil war.

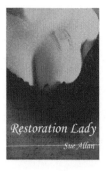

Restoration Lady -

The third and final part of New World Trilogy

The much anticipated finale to this wonderful story following events in post civil war England.

Stripped of her title and wealth Bessie faces revenge from past enemies, accusations of witchcraft and the catastrophes of the plague and Great Fire of London.

This concluding part of the New World Trilogy is gripping reading for all followers of Bessie - the Mayflower Maid.

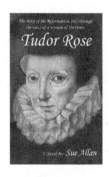

Tudor Rose -

The story of the Reformation, told through the voice of a woman of the times.

Based upon her original writings, 'Tudor Rose' is the remarkable true-life story of Lady Rose Hickman of London and Gainsborough Hall.

Witness, through Rose's eyes, the coronation of Anne Boleyn, the funeral of Jane Seymour and all of the intrigues of the court of King Henry VIII.

Feel with Rose the painful unfolding of the English Reformation and the personal suffering endured by her family and loved ones.

Celebrate with Rose a life that spans the reign of two Tudor Kings and nine Tudor Queens into that of King James I.

for more info visit www.domtom.co.uk